THE
RESEMBLANCE

THE
RESEMBLANCE

Lauren Nossett

FLATIRON
BOOKS
NEW YORK

THE RESEMBLANCE. Copyright © 2022 by Lauren Nossett. All rights reserved. Printed in the United States of America. For information, address Flatiron Books, 120 Broadway, New York, NY 10271.

www.flatironbooks.com

Designed by Susan Walsh

Library of Congress Cataloging-in-Publication Data

Names: Nossett, Lauren, 1986– author.
Title: The resemblance / Lauren Nossett.
Description: First edition. | New York : Flatiron Books, 2022.
Identifiers: LCCN 2022009365 | ISBN 9781250843241 (hardcover) |
   ISBN 9781250843258 (ebook)
Subjects: LCGFT: Campus fiction. | Thrillers (Fiction). | Novels.
Classification: LCC PS3614.O7838 R47 2022 | DDC 813/.6—dc23/eng/20220318
LC record available at https://lccn.loc.gov/2022009365

Our books may be purchased in bulk for promotional, educational, or business use. Please contact your local bookseller or the Macmillan Corporate and Premium Sales Department at 1-800-221-7945, extension 5442, or by email at MacmillanSpecialMarkets@macmillan.com.

First Edition: 2022

10 9 8 7 6 5 4 3 2 1

For Gray, forever and always

Give me to the wild beasts: their jaws will devour me.
—**The Epic of the Narte**

THE
RESEMBLANCE

| Prologue |

I am too late.

I know this before my fingers grasp the handle. Before the heavy oak door melts under my palm, and I see bodies reduced to flashing eyes and teeth under a black light.

Unknown hands press against my skin. Music pulses through the floor. The air tastes like spilled beer, cheap cologne, and vomit. I fight against the urge to be sick.

My eyes scan the foyer.

There's a commotion on the stairs. A man throws a glass bottle and it explodes against the wall. Raised voices. A woman holds her drink aloft. She turns as I barrel past her, as if she knows I do not belong.

I take the steps two at a time. A couple writhes on the landing, grasping and pawing at me as I struggle to break free.

"Have you seen—" I ask.

But they only point upward, so I keep going.

The air grows brittle in my lungs as I climb. Higher and higher. The music tumbles away, and I hear laughter. His laughter. Coming from the other end of the hall.

Light streams through the door as I stumble through it.

There's a flash of recognition in his eyes, but he's already tilting backward, hand outstretched, mouth wide with surprise.

A half dozen men stand, laughter frozen on their lips. No one moves as I tear through them, propelling myself forward by pushing my hands against their shoulders.

But I'm not fast enough.

I'm never fast enough.

By the time I reach the window ledge, the night air has swallowed him, and he's falling, still falling, with his fingers reaching out for me.

The vision disappears in mist, but the pain remains in my chest.

No matter how many times I race through those halls, the ending is the same.

Even in my dreams, I cannot save him.

PART I

| One |

In my mind's eye, it's always autumn in Athens. Those sweltering days of summer are immediately forgotten when the first red leaf twists off its branch. On North Campus, a gold winged elm and scarlet oak stand like sacred guardians, ancient harbingers of wisdom and secrets. Just before the unadorned face of New College, a sugar maple shudders in the wind. But despite the breeze stirring the leaves on the pavement, the day is heating up. There's a trickle of sweat between my shoulder blades. And there's something else, something I can't quite define, a tingling under my skin, a shadow at the corner of my eye. A feeling that the world's askew and waiting to right itself.

I climb the concrete steps to the iron light poles of the university's arches and stride through despite the local lore that says I have no right to do so. The buildings strangling the long stretch of browning grass are what's left of the original campus. If you take a tour, overeager sophomores will tell you about Greek Revival architecture and the Old Chapel, with its famous painting of St. Peter's Cathedral, once upon a time the largest framed oil painting in the world. They'll tell you the meaning of the words inscribed in Latin above the massive columns of the library entrance: to teach and to inquire into the nature of things. They'll tell you that there are other libraries on campus and between them all, there are more than 4.5 million books, 6.5 million microforms, and thousands of newspapers, photographs, and other documents. They might tell you about the double-barreled cannon three blocks away in front of city hall and the tree that owns itself at the corner of South Finley and Dearing Streets. What they won't tell you are the less quaint, more shameful symbols of the university's long history—the ghosts of the hushed-up murder-suicide in Waddel, the skull under Baldwin Hall, the sorority girls in blackface in an old yearbook—all the barely concealed secrets that rear their heads at the wrong moments, like some Barnesian grotesque animal, reminding you that cruelty's predictable.

The building that houses my mother's office is no exception. Named after a Georgia governor who was a firm believer in public education for free whites and slavery for all Blacks, he advocated secession during the Civil War, then resisted the Confederate draft, was briefly imprisoned, and got a shout-out in Margaret Mitchell's *Gone with the Wind*. After the war he found a new, state-sanctioned way to keep slavery alive and leased Black convicts from the Georgia government for his coal mining operations. Now there's a statue of him and his wife at the state capitol and a U-shaped building named in his honor on the university's campus.

Joe Brown Hall was built in 1932 to serve as a boys' dormitory. One Thanksgiving holiday in the '70s, all the young men left except one. No one found him until after the break, and well—you can imagine. The smell was awful; the other boys complained. There were rumors the janitors couldn't clean the blood off the floor—never mind that the boy hung himself. So they sealed it up, including the stairwell that led to the boy's room. A dozen or so steps are now called "The Staircase to Nowhere" with a charming door-sized painting that makes it look like the stairs keep going. As a girl, I'd run up the steps to knock and then run away and hide on the opposite end, waiting for this invisible boy, this long-forgotten brother, to appear. No one ever came looking for me, but it didn't escape my attention that for all my banging, the sounds reverberating behind the wall were hollow.

My mother's office is lined with books, interspersed with student projects, framed snapshots of Germany, and quotes by Goethe—she's been a professor at the university for thirty years, and one look at her walls lets you know what she teaches.

You might think that with all the photos of Bavarian hillsides and German newspapers strewn about, she misses her homeland. But as far as I know, she's never been back—not after she graduated summa cum laude from Berkeley, not during the summers for research, not even to bury her parents. Outside the classroom, she refuses to speak German. Maybe she feels guilty for not visiting her parents before they died. Maybe speaking in German would blur the lines she tries so hard to define between work and home, or maybe after hours and hours of teaching eighteen-year-olds, she didn't have the energy or patience to teach me. Whatever it was, despite all the years I spent in her office, I never learned to speak German.

Now she's behind her desk, a book in one hand, pen and paper in the other. Her whole person is neat and tidy, every inch buttoned, straightened, and tucked into place, but she looks deflated. In the summer, she'll regain some of her buoyancy, the years will drop from her shoulders, and whatever internal demon it is that drives her will soften its grip. But in the middle of fall semester, everything about her seems squeezed tight.

She doesn't look surprised to see me. The late-morning sun casts a hazy glow through her office window. It's peaceful in the way it always is between classes, full of the easy chatter of other professors in the hall, students sitting cross-legged in front of classrooms, heads bent over books. It's easy—when you're in the middle of it—to forget all the stuff going on under the surface: the vicious departmental meetings, infighting and backstabbing, petty gossip. Not to mention the adjuncts living in poverty, the underage drinking, sexual assault, hazing, cheating, and lying of the students. As one of my mother's English colleagues is fond of saying: Hell is empty, all the devils are here.

I sit on the edge of one of the maroon chairs meant for students, and my mother leans over to flip the switch on her electric kettle. The smell of coffee, books, and old carpet is familiar. As a child I used to sit here while my mother worked, my feet hanging above the ground kicking an uneven rhythm against her desk until she looked up and told me to stop. Sometimes, I would kick for hours. It was a kind of game I played to see how long it took her to notice. And often, she wouldn't. When students knocked timidly on her door, I would dive under her desk to hide, and she would pretend I wasn't there. I always thought I had the students fooled, until inevitably they would stand, thank my mother, and yell "Bye, Marlitt" on their way out.

"Truman passed you over again," my mother says, her critical gray eyes flicking between me and her computer screen.

I nod.

"And now you don't know what to do with yourself." Her look is sympathetic, and I'm so grateful she doesn't trivialize my disappointment that my breath catches in my chest.

I sigh. This—the desire to work—at least, she can understand.

My mother's waiting for me to say something, peering at me through her black-framed glasses. She does the same thing to her students. I guess she thinks that if she's patient enough, one of them will come up with something brilliant. We stare at each other—me with the resolute stubbornness of an only child; her with the professorial certainty that I'll talk eventually, and whatever I say later will be better than if she pushes me now.

But then, somewhere, beyond the warm, paned glass and her potted plants, there it is. The aberration in the otherwise normal day.

It's the screams that get me running. Primal and full of terror, these aren't the kind of shrieks that dissolve into giddy laughter, but the kind that set your teeth on edge, the kind you might hear in the woods or down a dark alley, the kind that send adrenaline coursing through your limbs in an instinctive motion of fight or flight.

Before my mother can flinch, I am out of the chair and in the carpeted hallway, through the side door, and throwing myself down the concrete steps. I think she calls after me, but her voice is miles away. And as I dodge students with their backpacks, heads down, lost in their phones, I remember I've always been good at this. And that whatever Truman says, this, the instinct that drives me toward the center of the action, not away from it, is what makes me good at my job.

Students are congregating at the Lumpkin Street crosswalk. They're rigid, suspended in motion. Hands raised to mouths, feet still outstretched, forward momentum thwarted like they've hit an invisible wall. I skid to a stop, and there's a swell silent and still, all sounds of traffic, the gasps and murmurs of the crowd obliterated for one long moment, cresting at the precipice, before the wave crashes down. And everything else rushes in, the endless scream, students clutching each other, voices—*Call 911, is he breathing? What happened? The other guy—he just drove off. Didn't stop.* And then my own voice, yelling for them to get out of the way, holding my badge in the air. They scatter the way young people always do when they hear "police." And there's a clear path from me to the street.

He's on his side, a bloody arm stretched out above his head, one leg bent under the other, and his hip twisting at an impossible angle. Medium height, dressed in khaki shorts and a blue polo shirt, a pair of Ray-Bans askew on his face, so I can see one eye open, unblinking at the asphalt. With his mouth agape and brown curls falling over his flushed cheek, he looks young; but based on the tuft of hair curling out from the top button of his shirt, the way the fabric stretches across his shoulders, the bruise-colored shadows under his eyes, and slight pouch of a beer belly, I guess he's around twenty, likes to party, and should be sitting in the back of a lecture hall instead of lying dead on the street.

I squat in front of him, phone at my ear.

I read once that death isn't instant. Our brains are still ticking for ten minutes or so, even after our hearts stop, meaning that in some way, we may be conscious of our own death. As I wait to be put through, I rock back on my heels, still close enough to see the chipped tooth and blood dripping from his lips. I'm wondering whether he bit his tongue, whether some part of him knows this, knows that he's dead, that I'm here, and he's not alone, when the operator says, "What's your emergency?"

"I'm at the Lumpkin and Baxter Street intersection, there's been a—"

"Pedestrian accident, yes." A few clicks of a keyboard. "There's an ambulance en route now. The police are on their way."

I hang up and dial Teddy.

He answers on the first ring.

"Hey," he says, "sorry about Truman. I told him you could handle it, but he thought Oliver—"

"There's been a hit-and-run on campus."

"Yeah—we heard, but—"

"You should meet me here."

"Hit-and-run's not our—"

"Trust me, Teddy. Get here as fast as you can. Take the car, not your bike."

I'm ashamed to say, but as soon as I realized the polo-and-khaki-clad boy in the street was dead and the driver had left him to bleed out on the asphalt, I knew I wanted this case.

Behind me I can feel the students on their cell phones, swarming, taking video footage and remonstrating. The light changes from red to green. Cars back up on Lumpkin and Baxter, honking and doing U-turns in the street.

"He's not breathing!" a student screams.

No shit, I think. He also has no pulse, no pupillary constriction when I shine my phone flashlight in his eye. And he's released his bowels.

"Is he dead?"

Wails from all sides.

And then the howling ambulance and police sirens. A woman in blue circles me with yellow tape, and Teddy's voice purrs, low and calm at my elbow.

"I called the techs, but they were already on their way." I look up at him to find he's gazing over my shoulder, his mouth a hard line. "Aisha will want to take a closer look at the body." Another beat. "What happened?"

I tell him about the screams, my dash down Lumpkin, the students, and the condition of the body when I arrived.

"I got here two minutes, three max, after he was hit."

"And he was—" Teddy's crouched low. He's wearing bright orange sneakers and one side of his dress pants is rolled up.

I lower my voice. "Dead, yeah. On impact's my guess, but we'll see what Aisha says."

We look back at the boy. His skin's already beginning to lose its pink flush, a result of the blood draining away from his veins. His muscles have relaxed, and even the tension is gone from his eyelids. This is why some people think the dead look like they're sleeping; but up close, it's what's not there that gives it away: the absence of breath, reflex, all the tiny movements that disappear when our hearts stop beating.

"Get back," the female officer barks at a boy leaning over the crime tape with his phone.

"We should do something about these students," Teddy says. We've angled our shoulders to block the body from view. Behind us, the crowd sways and heaves. Someone is swearing.

I sigh. "Let's separate the gawkers from the witnesses. When I arrived, there were ten or so at the crosswalk." We both glance over our shoulders. The crowd has swollen to fifty. Cars are no longer turning around, but people have parked, left doors open, and run down the hills on either side to see what happened.

"I was first on the scene," I hiss as I stand and brush off my jeans. There's a smear of blood on the cuff of my blouse.

He smiles, but his brown eyes are wary. "I told Oliver I was meeting you for coffee and a snack, which—"

I dig through my bag and hand him a granola bar.

"Right." He takes a bite. "We'll figure something out."

I roll my eyes. Teddy is a wonderful, annoyingly kind and patient person, who people always are surprised to learn is a homicide detective. And Teddy hates lying, so whenever he does, he has to caveat it with some kernel of truth. But he's also insatiable. If his stomach grumbles, if he looks over with a pained grin and says he's hungry, you better feed that man before his jawline tightens and his eyes turn red. I'm serious, "hangry" is an understatement—it's more like hang-furious, hang up the phone and buy that man a bag of pretzels. I've learned to pack snacks—in the car, in my bag. I've even found smushed Snickers bars at the bottom of the washing machine because I've stuck them in my pockets and forgotten about them. Once you feed him, all is right in the world and he goes back to normal like a reverse gremlin.

Appetite and moral conscience appeased, Teddy surveys the throng of people. I do, too. Looking for anyone too eager and out of place or too nonchalant, hanging back but watching us under hooded eyes. My mother stands at the edge of the crowd. She nods, her shoulders straight, head erect, and then, with a look that suggests she thinks I've found what I was looking for, turns back toward Joe Brown Hall. A gray-haired man in a brown suit and overlarge tote bag pushes his way through the students.

"Get to class," he shouts without any acknowledgment of the body in the street.

A handful scatter but only one or two start to walk away.

Teddy detaches himself from me.

"Before any of you leave," he shouts, and holds his badge in the air—a few students duck. "We want to speak with those of you who witnessed the accident." He doesn't say "hit-and-run" or identify us as homicide detectives, and the students hover, unsure.

"The rest of you can go"—and when they don't move—"this won't count as an excused absence."

That sends a few scrambling. One, a white girl with her head down and notebook clutched to her chest, makes a beeline for the student learning center.

"You," I yell, and half a dozen students look up, startled. They stare as I march toward the sidewalk. I'm five nine, dark haired and green eyed, with a round face and angular body—not ridiculously tall or pretty, but tall enough and pretty enough to draw attention. The height plus the badge stops a few students in their tracks. "You were a witness. You need to stay."

"But I—" The girl blinks helplessly.

"If you witnessed anything, I'd like you to wait—" I repeat, looking past her and all the others for a space out of the way but close enough that we can keep an eye on them "—on the learning center steps." I gesture to the long concrete stairs behind her. "The rest of you can go."

The techs are here in full force now. Police usher people back to their cars, set up roadblocks, and direct everyone away from the scene.

I see Aisha's head above the crowd with a flood of relief. She's the best forensic examiner we've got, the kind that handles everything from single vehicle crashes to multiple homicides with a determination and grace that makes the rest of us look somewhat philistine.

"What can you tell me?"

"Student. White male. Late teens, early twenties. Hit-and-run. Died on impact or very shortly thereafter."

She nods and sweeps her long black hair into a tight bun. At first, she walks the perimeter, scanning the roads in both directions. Then she paces the length of the crosswalk, times the change of the light from green to yellow, yellow to red. Notes the split second between the red light and white walking man.

I know better than to break her concentration. She takes photographs of everything—the body, the asphalt, the dozen or so students pressed against the orange barricade. Then her sketchbook appears, and a video camera. Someone will construct 360-degree images of the scene, so once the body's gone, the road cleaned up, and the students dispersed, we can return to this moment again and again. She still hasn't touched anything, and I know she's going to murder me when she sees the blood on my sleeve and learns how close I was to the body.

It doesn't matter that it's a hit-and-run, Aisha's still going to look for fingermarks, hairs, and fibers. Her movements are slow and intentional as she makes her way around the body, collects and tags potential evidence, packaging it in plastic bags and vials so nothing's disturbed on its way to the lab. Every gesture is methodical. No exhale of sympathy, no headshake at the wasted youth. I could watch her all day, but the students on the steps in front of the learning center are getting anxious.

There are twenty or so of them, and two in the front watch me pace back and forth like puppies following the trajectory of a ball. The rest hunker down against backpacks and stare at their phones. An odd group; some are still wearing pajamas although the day is creeping toward noon, hair disheveled on purpose—freshmen relishing the sudden lack of dress code and parental input. The girls wear a collection of high-waisted jeans and T-shirts; the guys shuffle back and forth in their shorts and different shades of the same polos or university tees. One of them, a boy with a hoodie pulled low over his face, keeps muttering to himself and making me uneasy.

I sigh. The more times they repeat this story to friends in class and the dining halls, the more they're going to start embellishing, filling in blanks, and believing their own half-truths. It's the same reason it's going to take a lot more than me being first on the scene for Truman to let me have this case.

In my peripheral, an orange stretcher appears with a white cover. He's been dead for twenty minutes now, but there's no way Aisha will move him in a body bag. Students circle the barricade hyena-like, snapping photos with their cell phones. I can almost feel Aisha wishing the guy had been stabbed in an apartment or moved to the basement of a building so she could conduct her investigation in private.

"Hello," I yell to get their attention. "I'm Detective Kaplan, and this is Detective White. You were all witnesses to a hit-and-run this morning. We need to talk to each of you."

There are instant grumbles.

"I have a test at one," a girl with wide eyes yelps.

"We've got practice this afternoon," two uncommonly tall boys say in sync.

I take a deep breath and resist the urge to smack them. Behind me, a body's being loaded unnecessarily into an ambulance, and they're worried about class and their sports team.

"I'm sure you all have places to be," Teddy says diplomatically before I can tell them just how fucked up their perspectives are. "But this takes priority." He looks at me, an upward turn at the corner of his lips. "Detective Kaplan will write each of you notes, stating you were needed for a police investigation."

Asshole, I think, but it's half-hearted, and I give a reassuring nod to the students.

Most are appeased by this, but the wide-eyed girl presses a notebook to her chest and mutters peevishly, "But I've been studying all night."

I take the boy in the hoodie. His energy is making me nervous, and I can't tell if that's because he knows something or is just a weird kid. Either way, I want him out of my sight.

Teddy will talk to the girls. With his chiseled jaw and wide smile, he has the extra talent of making people squirm under his attention, but his calm, easy going attitude wins him their confidence. This doesn't always work. There's a type—usually forty- to eighty-year-old white males and sixtyish white females—who regard him with suspicion, the former with racially charged, sometimes homophobic slurs (Teddy's Black, not gay, but racists and homophobes seem to share hate in common) and purse-clutching by the latter.

College women, though, love Teddy.

Generously, he picks the notebook-clutching girl. "We'll see if we can't get you to your test on time." He smiles, and some of the stiffness goes out of her shoulders.

I, on the other hand, have to keep a straight face, or no one will take me seriously.

"Name?" I ask, positioning myself squarely in front of hoodie-boy.

"Tom Jones."

"Seriously?"

He gives me a blank, petulant stare, and I see his pale skin is pockmarked, like the dotted and scratched surface of a student desk. I think of my mother with her generational complaints—he probably doesn't know who Indiana Jones is, I think, never mind Tom Jones.

"All right, Tom, tell me what you saw—and start from the beginning. What direction were you walking? Who was next to you? What did the car look like?"

"What about what I had for breakfast?"

"Sure," I say magnanimously. "Let's start there."

He rolls his eyes and mutters something about not eating breakfast.

The interview is a complete waste of time. He didn't see anything. Not the car. Not the driver. Looked up just when our victim collided with the ground.

For a split second, a wave of panic washes over his face—like he's just realized what happened.

"I think he was—is he—dead?"

I click my pen. "Thank you, Tom Jones. You've been very helpful."

He wasn't, but I don't have the same issue with lying as Teddy.

As he trudges away, I sense a change in the air. I turn to see Aisha closing the rear doors to the ambulance. She's still wearing latex gloves as she taps the side of the vehicle. It speeds off, sirens roaring, although the guy's no longer in a hurry to get anywhere.

I feel a rush of relief. Not because of the gawkers—they'll linger as long as the crime scene tape's in place—but because now I can finally concentrate. This whole time I've had one eye on the body, mindful of its presence as I ask questions and take notes, aware of the gradual cooling of its internal temperature, gravity pulling blood to the skin closest to the ground as I scan the crowd for outliers, but it's not my problem anymore.

I stuff my hands in my pockets and turn toward the street.

I spent my whole life on this campus, straining against my mother's grasp to watch tall cranes and men in hard hats build the Ramsey Center, later getting drunk outside her building and glaring as another group expanded the student learning center, bulldozed a parking lot, built a garage; the landscape ever changing, the skyline interrupted by new buildings, but always people shuffling to and from classes, a kaleidoscope of sounds and colors, the streets full of energy and life. Now, students trudge up Baxter Hill casting curious looks backward, faces peer down from the redbrick dining hall on the corner, and an outline of a dead boy glints in the middle of the gray asphalt.

I turn back to the students on the steps and withdraw a weepy, curly haired girl from under the sheltering wing of a boy, who looks embarrassed and uncomfortable. It's clear he doesn't know what to do with her blubbering, but two decades of training in southern-style chivalry have left him with no other option than putting his arm around her shoulder. He blinks at me when I call her over, and his relief is so palpable I almost laugh.

"Name?"

"Morgan Walker," she says between sniffs.

"All right, Morgan," I say kindly. "This is important. I need you to tell me everything that happened. Did you go to class this morning?"

She nods tearfully. "I have a nine A.M. biology class with Dr. Cho." She adds the last bit hopefully like I might know the professor.

When I don't say anything, she takes a deep breath and wipes under her eyelashes with her fingertips, smudging mascara across her cheeks like inky feathers.

"And . . . I was really tired and kept falling asleep in class . . . so I went to the student learning center to grab a coffee." She gestures to the building behind her. "But when I got there, I just felt so heavy, and, I don't know, I didn't think coffee would help, and even though I have another class at eleven forty-five, I thought it would be better to take a nap."

"So you were walking back to your dorm?"

She bobs her head like I've just thrown her a lifeline.

"I live in Brumby. Up the hill?"

It's suddenly dawned on her that I'm not a student or a professor and that I might not know everything about campus life. And I don't. But I know Brumby's the all-women's dorm that's a calf-strengthening walk from the bottom of Baxter, past the shiny new Gameday Center and dilapidated rows of public housing. Nothing useful yet, but I make a note.

"And so I was tired, but I was trying to hurry so I could get at least thirty minutes of sleep. And there were a bunch of people waiting— probably to go to Bolton for breakfast. And I saw Jay—he was standing right in front of me."

My head snaps up. "Jay?"

"The boy . . . who . . . who was hit."

"You knew him?"

She nods, and her cheeks, still wet with tears, redden.

"I didn't know him, know him. I just—I've seen him around at parties and stuff. He's a Kap-O and his frat does things with my sorority . . ." She points to the blue letters on her T-shirt.

I'm scribbling as fast as I can.

"Jay . . . ," I say, scratching my mouth with the side of my pen. "Do you know his last name?"

She hesitates but then shakes her head.

"And what was Jay doing before he was hit?"

She scrunches her nose like she's trying to remember, but I have the feeling she was watching him carefully.

"He was looking at his phone and, I don't know, kind of laughing, I think. But I was behind him," she says quickly. "So I could only see his back. But it was shaking like he was laughing."

She's right about the phone. I saw it a few feet away from the body, screen shattered, with glass that looked like ice crystals.

"And then?"

"And then there was a gap in the cars. The light was still green, but not everyone waits for the crossing sign—and he looked up . . . and I guess he figured that the black car was still pretty far away . . . I almost followed him, but then . . . I saw—" She takes a deep breath. "Instead of slowing down—the light had turned yellow—it looked like the car was speeding up . . . and so I hesitated . . . and I almost called out to him . . . but I—" She buries her face in her hands and her voice is muffled by her palms. "I didn't. And the car—" Her shoulders shake, and when she opens her mouth, spit clings to the corners. "He flew up in the air, and the driver . . . the driver looked . . . he looked happy. And then he sped off. And Jay was . . . all twisted and—"

"Looked happy?" I repeat, interrupting her.

She uncovers her face and blinks at me like she just remembered I was there. A breeze lifts her curls. Behind her, students filter in and out of the double glass doors, shouldering backpacks and laughing. A cluster of guys in sweatpants yell to the one who broke away from the group.

She furrows her brow. "Yeah," she says. "He was smiling."

"Smiling." I hesitate. I've seen traffic camera footage from hit-and-run incidents. Often the driver looks surprised, horrified, or in shock, caught in a motion of trying to turn or slam on the brakes, shoulders tensed, eyes wide, mouth formed into a large O. But smiling—that's a new one. "You're sure?"

She nods. "Like it was the best day of his life."

I frown. Tap my notebook.

"You said 'he.' So the driver was male. Did you get a good look at his face?"

The line between her eyes deepens.

"Yeah, but—"

"But what?"

She takes a tight little breath and tugs on her backpack, hands balled into tiny fists.

"It doesn't make any sense."

| Two |

The station's a small, nondescript gray building less than a five-minute drive from downtown and six from the university. The parking lot's relatively empty, but Lieutenant Barry Truman's silver Charger is parked at the far end, prohibitively hugging the white line in case anyone would be so bold as to get near his beloved vehicle. Oliver's VW Golf is parked three spaces away. Teddy's road bike's locked to the staff entrance steps. You'd have to be pretty ballsy to steal a bike from a police lot, but Truman won't let him bring it inside, and Teddy loves the thing too much to take his chances.

Inside, the task room is a hodgepodge of tables and small desks and gray chairs that squeak every time you move. Wooden bookshelves overflow with mildewed folders and a handful of yellowed paperbacks someone left ages ago, presumably when we weren't understaffed, and people sat around waiting for the phones to ring. I'm convinced they're all donations from the university, like the metal filing cabinets and framed map of old Athens. But whenever I suggest it, Truman grumbles about the administration, and I have the sense that one of us must answer to the other but am never sure who holds the keys to the city—the university opened its doors first, and here that counts for something.

Like an overeager student, I'm the earliest to arrive, but I've also got the most to prove. It's a long story, but the gist of it is that Truman has a daughter a few years younger than me and they're close in a cheesy,

TV family kind of way. He has two younger children—boys—but Alice is his favorite. She's always stopping by the station, bringing coffee and the clichéd doughnuts, and cracking jokes about how her friends think she's a narc. And Truman's decided, despite all my subtle and not so subtle efforts to show him otherwise, that he's a father figure to me. He has gender-specific ideas of what this entails, which results in Teddy and Oliver getting the gang-related double homicides, the sadistic, random-victim hack jobs, and I'm assigned the easy-to-solve murder-suicides and domestics where the murder weapon is discovered before I even show up. The kind of cases that involve lots of paperwork, long statutory periods for discovery, and postponed trial dates, but the most danger I face is from banging my own head against the wall.

Just this morning, he handed one of my cases to Oliver. I was the investigating officer, the first on the scene, the one to notice the extra wineglass on the table when the victim was found alone. But the suspect got out on bail, and Truman was suddenly concerned about my preparedness for a trial on an open-and-shut case that had been dragging on since last December—essentially an HR-approved way for him to act on his irrational fears for my safety.

It might be my imagination, but I think he grimaces when he sees me. Truman's stocky and bald with a thick neck and wide-set eyes. Of Irish-German descent, he blames behavioral quirks like his quick temper and fastidiousness on his grandmothers, who, though long dead, seem to have made lasting marks. When he's out of earshot, we call him "the bull" or "bull Truman," as much for the head-down stare he gives you when he's angry as for his stubborn nature, but it's mostly affectionate. Oliver Graves—medium height, slim, with straight dark hair swooped over his forehead, all prim and proper in a suit and tie—trudges alongside him, raises an eyebrow at the board, and takes a seat at one of the old desks. Teddy jogs in with a handful of papers. He's changed his shirt and looks crisp and fresh, while I've sweated through my bloodstained blouse.

I've been busy—typed up my witness notes; taped the photos of our victim on the rolling whiteboard, one with his bruised face, another of his nail-bitten fingers, the smashed phone, and the larger scene of the incident; and written everything we know about him so far. Name: Jay Harper Kemp. Sex: male. Race: white. Age: twenty. Affiliations: University of Georgia student, political science major, Kappa Phi Omicron member.

"It's not the first time a student has been hit crossing this intersection," I begin before anyone can stop me. "In fact, Lumpkin Street is the second-most dangerous crosswalk for pedestrian crashes, with the most on Broad. A professor called this afternoon to report that he hit a female student last year. The light was green, but the student was talking on her phone and, he says, oblivious to the world around her. She rolled up on the hood and staggered off, seemingly uninjured. He yelled after her, but she just waved and kept walking up Baxter—he assumed to one of the dorms. She never filed a police report, and he couldn't remember anything about her except that she was wearing a white dress. It's clear the guy feels guilty, but it's just further proof the crosswalk's dangerous."

"And the students are idiots," Oliver mutters.

"Everyone under thirty is an idiot," Truman thunders good-naturedly.

He pats Oliver, who just celebrated his twenty-seventh birthday, on the shoulder. We're a young squad—for Homicide anyway. I'm twenty-nine and Teddy's thirty-two.

"They all think they're invincible, which," Truman continues with a gesture to the whiteboard and our victim's photo, "clearly they're not. I can't tell you how many times I've almost hit a student jaywalking and they just laugh and skip away—'I almost died,'" he mimics, throwing his hands above his head. "Hilarious." He shakes his head. "What else?"

"Our victim was the first off the sidewalk. Witnesses confirm the light was still green when he stepped into the street but are inconsistent on whether it had changed to red by the time he was hit. Dara's pulling the traffic camera footage now. We're still waiting on the lab, but based on witness testimony, there's no evidence our victim was drunk, on stimulants, synthetic cannabinoids, or other illegal drugs that may have impaired his judgment. No evidence that he was pushed either. The medical examiner thinks the victim was looking down when hit—witnesses say at his phone—and that he was hit by a car going at least forty miles an hour. This is also consistent with the witness reports—they all agreed the car didn't brake, and almost half reported that the car sped up. Of course, we're still waiting on the official conclusion, but the car was accelerating down the hill, and the light was changing. It's possible the suspect didn't see the victim and simply wanted to make the light, but—" I hesitate.

"What?" Truman looks up. He has no patience for dramatics, and I know I need to tread carefully here.

"The one thing all the witnesses agree on is the driver didn't slow," I say cautiously, "and that he was smiling."

Truman frowns, and Oliver stirs in his seat.

"We believe the suspect is driving a 2015 to 2017 black BMW 3 or 5 series with front-end damage, and possibly a broken windshield and deployed airbags. There was no passenger. There are helicopters out now. When we catch this guy, Forensics says we should look for linear abrasions on his chest caused by seat belt compression."

"Does this hold if he didn't brake?" Oliver asks.

Truman interrupts before I can answer. "Did anyone get a good look at the driver?"

Teddy and I exchange glances before I clear my throat and continue: "There were two students standing at the crosswalk who report looking at the vehicle instead of the traffic light or our victim. Both gave the same description." I pause. "They described the suspect as a white male around twenty years old, broad nose, high cheekbones, wearing a blue or gray polo."

Oliver swings his head around to look at the Polaroid taped to the whiteboard.

"And both say," I gesture to the photo, "that he looked identical to the victim."

Truman's still stretched good-naturedly out in his chair, hands folded across his lap, but his eyes have grown watchful. His mouth twists as he examines Teddy and then me. Like we might be joking for some unimaginable reason. I keep my body language neutral, but my heart is hammering. *Mine, mine, mine,* I think.

When Oliver realizes Truman won't respond, he chokes back a laugh. "What—like an evil twin?"

Teddy smirks. We've worked together long enough that he knows what I'm thinking—all these frat boys with their short chino shorts and fishing shirts, Beatles-swooped hair, and Croakies sunglasses look alike. And although we haven't confirmed, I put money on him living at one of those gutted plantation houses on Milledge with beer cans smothering the front yard.

"Have we got an ID of the victim?"

"A witness identified him as Jay Kemp," I say, even though the name is printed clearly on the whiteboard. "And this matches the student ID we found in his wallet."

"Driver's license?"

I look at Teddy, and he picks up the thread. "The driver's license didn't match his student ID. We think it's fake, or more likely stolen or passed on from an older fraternity brother. It says he's twenty-four." A good age to get into the bars downtown and buy a keg from a package store without question.

Truman frowns, makes a note. "Check up on it. Siblings?" he asks grudgingly.

"No," I say. "No brother, sister, certainly no twin. No cousins either. His mother's an only child and his father has one sister, married but child-free."

Oliver lets out a disappointed sigh.

"Criminal history?"

"No. But one citation for disorderly conduct, two years ago, public intoxication. Nothing since."

Truman rubs his chin and stares at the board.

"Kappa Phi Omicron, huh?"

I nod.

Oliver gives me a look I can't read. He's heard me spout my opinions about fraternities and Greek life at large. If it were up to me, the university would do away with the whole thing. They're cesspools of underage drinking and sexual assault. And I've already run through my favorite possible scenarios—our victim's a junior, so revenge for hazing fits neatly at the top of my list, followed by stealing someone's girlfriend, and your run-of-the-mill brotherhood rivalry. Oliver insists that not all fraternities are bad—one of his brothers was a fraternity president—and that charity work and networking form valuable opportunities for young men. Inevitably he'll cite higher retention and graduation rates, a strong affinity with the college, and volunteer work as all the amazing benefits of Greek life. I feel like he's drunk the Kool-Aid, and whenever we have this argument—basically every other fall weekend when a girl comes into the front lobby requesting a rape kit—I chant "No means yes, yes means anal" under my breath, so I can watch his face blanch and get him to shut up. None of them share my aversion, and I have a sudden longing for my mother's mind for statistics and her confident voice daring anyone to interrupt: one in five, she'd say, that's how many college women will be assaulted before they graduate; 74 percent, that's how much more likely women in sororities are to be raped, and 300 percent—men in fraternities are three times more likely to commit rape. And at least one—at least one student will die this year in a hazing-related incident.

It's no wonder I grew up slightly biased against Greek life; but if you're from a college town, you have to choose sides early: give me weird, slightly self-righteous indie kids and gray-haired townies any day over Vineyard Vines–wearing douchebags who talk about hangovers like they're gold medals and girls like they owe them something.

But as it is, I'm holding this all close to my chest, lest Truman put Oliver on the case with Teddy instead of me, citing female access to frat bathrooms or something.

"Has the family been notified?"

"We're working on it. They're out of the country. His dad's some insurance bigwig. They own a place in Five Points, but the neighbors say they're rarely home."

Truman stirs in his chair, and Oliver glances at the whiteboard again.

If you're not from Athens, you wouldn't know it, but all the well-to-do families are connected. Big money often—but not always—means old money. And old-money Athens is its own beast: an ancient gorilla making shady deals and brewing up regional monopoly schemes, from local sewage companies to contract bids with the state.

"What did you say his last name was?"

"Kemp. His father is," I thumb through my yellow notepad, "Robert—goes by Bob—Kemp."

Truman rubs a hand over his head. "All right, then. I want you talking to everyone who knew this kid—friends, teachers, classmates, girlfriends," he hesitates, "boyfriends. I'll get in contact with the parents."

I nudge the side of Teddy's chair. Oliver jots something on his notepad.

"What are you waiting for?" Truman growls.

And we scramble to pick up our things and get back to our desks.

Truman heaves himself out of his chair and follows us. Before he disappears into the lamplit abyss that is his personal office, I hear his voice behind me. "Yeah, hey, it's me—" and then the door falls shut, absorbing his words like the foam pyramids in an anechoic chamber.

Teddy and I spend the next hour comparing notes and waiting for more data to come in from the medical examiner and forensics. It's almost eight o'clock when it becomes clear we're not going to get anything good until tomorrow and decide to call it a night.

He hooks his helmet strap with two fingers and slings it over his shoulder like another man might with his suit jacket.

"Normal Bar?"

"You read my mind."

Outside, I wait for him to unlock his bike, and then I follow him in my car to the bar. He keeps waving for me to pass, but I stay resolutely behind him. After seeing the way people drive in this town, I'm less than optimistic about Teddy biking in the dark, bike light and reflectors or not.

Ten minutes later we're sitting in our usual corner booth, shelling peanuts and sipping our respective drinks—beer for him, wine for me—when I hear a familiar voice echo across the bar.

"Marley!"

I turn to see that Cindy, Teddy's girlfriend, has spotted us from the front door and is running toward our booth with her arms outstretched. She's Korean American, about a head shorter than me, with her hair pulled back into a messy ponytail, and full of a radiant warmth that seems to draw the eye of everyone in the room.

"Did you get the cookies?" she asks merrily.

I think of the lilac box I shoved off my desk to make room for my interview notes. At the time, a part of me assumed it was for Truman, which, of course, in hindsight doesn't make any sense.

"Teddy was supposed to tell you they were from me. And the muffins?"

My jaw drops open, and I stare daggers at Teddy across the table.

"Those were for her?" he says through a mouthful of boiled peanuts.

Cindy smacks his arm. "They were for both of you!"

For a woman who works ten-to-twelve-hour shifts as a nurse practitioner, Cindy is a beacon of energy and an excellent baker, whom I once tried very hard not to like, but whose bright chatter and quick wit made it impossible. She's also the only person I let call me a nickname.

"All right, you two, I'm grabbing a drink. And then I want to hear all about this new case."

I glare at Teddy.

We're not supposed to talk about our cases. Obviously, we do sometimes, but it's been less than ten hours, which means he must have been so eager to tell Cindy what happened that he snuck out to call her while I was finishing paperwork.

The bartender helps Cindy instantly, swinging his hair out of his eyes and leaning forward to hand her a drink. I'm pretty sure he's still talking when she grabs it and saunters back to our table, sliding into the booth next to me.

"But seriously," she says, looking from me to Teddy. "What's going on?"

"What makes you think something's going on?" I ask, although her skills of deduction are even better than Teddy's, and she has on more than one occasion taken us through our behavior and body language Sherlock-style to prove her point.

"Well first, because you're at the bar you always go to after something interesting happens at work. And second, because you both have that gleam in your eyes like you're up to something. Probably stealing a case away from poor Ollie."

Teddy shakes his head, and I laugh.

I've got nothing against Oliver. But early on he was such an over-achiever that Teddy and I found it quite satisfying to put him in his place.

"Right," she says. "Well, since you won't tell me, maybe I can guess." She leans forward so her head's almost in the middle of the table, stretched equally between us. "Does this have something to do with the student hit-and-run on campus?"

"How did you—?"

She taps her nose.

"We were told to be ready, but they never came. I figured—dead at the scene." She grins.

I grimace. Nurses and doctors have a frankness about death that can make even homicide detectives seem like emotional nutjobs.

"So . . ."

"So," Teddy repeats.

She beams at us like a proud gymnast who's just landed a layout back-flip with a twist.

"Have you heard from Aisha?"

"Not other than the time of death—which Marlitt already knew."

I think she'll bite—wanting to guess how I came by this precious bit of information—but she's pulsing on the edge of her seat, eager to tell us everything she knows about pedestrian injuries.

"All right, this is what you should look for. Basically, the severity of the damage is going to depend on the shape and speed of the vehicle. So if your victim was hit by a four-door sedan, he'll have what we call a bumper injury—on his legs, same height as the bumper. If, say, the victim was hit by one of the university buses with the flat faces, he'd have injuries on his chest."

"It was a BMW."

"Really? Huh. Those techs," she shakes her head, "they were all saying it was a bus and speculating about how the university would handle it. There's a rumor that if you get hit by a bus, you get free tuition. Not that it would matter in this case"—she crosses her eyes and draws her finger across her neck—"but anyway, speed matters here, too. If it's a low-speed collision, say around fifteen miles per hour, the victim will land in front or to the side of the vehicle—this can still be bad because the victim could get run over or even dragged . . ." Her eyes light on Teddy, and for a twisted moment I think she's hoping for this out of medical curiosity. But neither of us move.

"Okay," she continues with just a hint of disappointment, "if it's medium speed—anywhere from twenty to forty miles per hour—the victim might get thrown up onto the hood or against the front windshield of the vehicle, but if it's high speed—anywhere from forty-five to, I don't know, seventy-five miles an hour—the victim would be flung into the air and then crash onto the ground. They may be found thirty or forty feet from the site of impact. And often it's hitting the ground that does the worst damage—severe head trauma, brain meeting road—even if the skull doesn't break, the brain bouncing from side to side can cause tearing of the internal lining, tissues, and blood vessels and then you've got internal bleeding, bruising, and swelling. It's the same kind of trauma you might see if they'd fallen off a building."

I close my eyes a moment and will the image to disappear.

"Say the driver was going forty-five to fifty," Teddy asks, "would the victim still be thrown that far?"

"Maybe." Cindy grabs a boiled peanut. "But not necessarily. Definitely would be tossed up on the window though."

I think of the blood pooling on the asphalt, crimson stains leaking from our victim's nose and mouth, and kick Teddy's foot under the table.

This also confirms what our witnesses said—the driver didn't slow. If anything—considering the thirty-five-mile-an-hour speed limit—he sped up. Teddy and I are mouthing words across the table, but Cindy's too giddy with medical knowledge to notice.

"Most pedestrian-related accidents—at least those I've seen—happen when a person steps off a curb, so they're hit from the side. Usually, the driver sees the pedestrian too late and slams on their brakes. This makes the bumper nosedive so the first point of contact is with the lower leg— it's so common that there's a name for pedestrian-car injuries—they're called the Waddell's triad: basically, leg fracture, organ injury, head injury." She taps her leg, stomach, and head, like the children's song in reverse, and then, reading my thoughts, hums "Head, Shoulders, Knees, and Toes," while repeating leg, organ, head, and head.

"Too soon?"

I roll my eyes. "Have some couth." But I'm humming, too. No Waddell's triad for our victim, at least not that involves the bumper down.

I'm convinced our driver didn't brake.

By the time I slip the key into my front door, the world outside has transitioned into that inky darkness that's particular to late autumn. The street's unusually quiet, but then it's a weeknight and all the kiddos who had been zooming around on their bikes earlier are tucked in bed for school tomorrow morning. The neighborhood's still dressed in orange and black. Yard stakes and grim reapers and engorged spiders left over from Halloween festivities cast strange shadows under streetlamps. I smell wood from a fire burning, although it doesn't seem cold enough yet, and hear the uncanny laugh track from a television through an open window.

I flip on the lights. My house is a small bungalow on a semiquiet street. It's one story, with an attic that's been turned into the primary bedroom. The inside smells of birch and lemon and damp autumn leaves. There's no foyer, and the house is built shotgun-style—you open the front door and can see straight to the back. Not the kind of place you could walk out of the bathroom at night with lights on and towel off, at least not without giving your neighbors an eyeful. The house received a quick renovation before I bought it, so it's got the whole open-concept thing going for it. When you walk in, there's a couch and a couple of chairs facing the fireplace on your left. A wall with a hand-me-down armoire on the right. If you keep walking, you'll find the long dining room table I inherited from an aunt, and then a kitchen that feigns openness with half a wall blown out and a small square of appliances in a room with yellow laminate flooring. My guess is the money ran out before they could make upgrades to the wooden cabinets and bronze-colored hardware. But I'm proud of this house where everything has its place and is ordered in a way that's all mine. With the chaos and mess outside, its birch floors and thick white paint, battered records, and unwashed wineglasses are my refuge. Buying it was my first real adult decision, and sometimes when I hear the house groan as it settles, I think we're growing older together.

An owl hoots lazily outside. I put on a record and head for the kitchen, thinking about Jay Kemp. By now, his death will be all over the news. Nothing fascinates the good people of Athens more than a life snuffed out at its prime. I hope Truman's been able to notify the parents. Try not to picture their faces as I pour myself a glass of wine and scrounge around the cabinets for something that looks edible. I settle on a can of tomato soup and heat it on the stove instead of in the microwave, telling myself this makes it healthier somehow.

As I stand spooning soup out of the pot and listening to Dylan sing about another lifetime, I close my eyes and replay the scene from this morning. The smell of coffee, the brightening sun, and then the sound of screaming.

What was missing? I think.

But I know—the squeal of the brakes. You always hear the grating shriek of metal against metal first—and then, driven by some perverse instinct, listen for the crash. I heard it in reverse. I'm certain. A thud—somewhere under students talking in the hall and my mother's evaluating gaze—and then the scream, but of the witnesses, not the brakes.

The Lumpkin-Baxter crosswalk sits in the valley of three hills. Lumpkin Street ascends north and south, and Baxter rises west. We've been operating under the assumption that someone going down the hill would have naturally accelerated. And perhaps, if they weren't paying attention, they may not have braked in time to save Jay's life. But I've driven down that hill a million times. And I think it would be just as unnatural to take your foot off the brake pedal as it would be to take your hand off the wheel.

I leave the soup cooling on the stove and grab my keys.

I need to know.

Ten minutes later I'm sitting in the parking lot behind Saint Mary's Episcopal Chapel. From here, my plan is to take a left onto Lumpkin and get up to forty—five miles over the speed limit. And then—barring pedestrians and other vehicles—I'm not going to touch my brakes until the car crosses the crime scene.

I would have called Teddy, but he's probably with Cindy. And anyway, I'm not entirely sure he'd approve of my plan. I'm always a little too impulsive for his liking.

No one's sure where I get it from—the reckless, don't-think-twice, constant need for motion. My mother's a rule follower to a fault—you can't become a professor without always double-checking your *i*'s and crossing your *t*'s. My father's a different story. These days he might be called a helicopter parent, but "overprotective" is the word that comes to mind. In this, he and Truman have something in common. Imagine me, six years old, begging for a trampoline. Roller skates. One of those battery-powered cars. Every children's toy was a death trap according to my father. Picture me deciding to make my own fun: climbing the tree in our backyard, throwing peaches at squirrels while my friend Craig watched, wide-eyed. Pedaling my bike down Prince Avenue to get us candy from the corner store. My father, red-faced and fuming like I had taken off for Atlanta: "You have to be careful, Marlitt." Those were the words that marked my childhood. The same words I hear now as I ease onto Lumpkin and take my foot off the brake.

I've always thought my father's legendary protectiveness was about control more than anything else. You see it a lot in abuse cases—not that I was abused; my father would have circled me in Bubble Wrap and sent me to school wearing a helmet and shoulder pads if he could have. But the desire to keep tabs on me, the wariness of my more rambunctious friends, and the insistence I be home by a ridiculously early hour scream of controlling tendencies. He's been around my feminist mother long enough to know better than to show it in obvious ways, but the biggest fights they ever had were over me—curfew, the length of my shorts, whether I could spend the night at Craig's, what to do when they realized I'd been sneaking out to do just that. My mother's policy forever governed by "If a boy can do it, so can she." My father not so much, but he knew better than to argue this line of reasoning with my mother. Craig's theory was different. The oldest in a family of four, he attributed my father's protectiveness to an only-kid syndrome, an all-his-progeny-in-one-basket kind of thing.

I'm not a child anymore. Whatever his faults, I know that my father's overprotectiveness stems from love. Both his parents died when he was in his early twenties. It makes sense he'd want to hold me close. But all those helmets were strapped too tight, the heavy woolen turtlenecks itched, the rain boots chafed. What kind of child worries about wet socks when there are puddles glinting in the sun? How do you learn to swim with a life vest perennially strapped to your chest? The desire for risk was pushed deeper every time my father reminded me to wear my seat belt, watch out for deer, be home by nine, so that when my world finally broke apart, I chose the most dangerous job I could find.

On Lumpkin, a few students trudge up the hill to the honors dormitory, but I'm not going fast enough yet to pique their interest. The student learning center comes into view—a beacon of light in the dark—and I'm still accelerating. Forty-five miles an hour.

You might think with all the coddling and babying that I'd be a sniffling, trembling mess, incapable of leaving the house, and too scared to look down to tie my shoes for fear of a tree falling on my head. But here's the thing about my father—he always worried enough for the both of us. For all of us—Athenians, Americans, atheists, Adventists, and agnostics alike. He worried so much that I was never afraid of anything. There wasn't enough room for all that fear, the what-ifs, second-guessing, and thinking ten steps ahead. I was never afraid of getting hurt, getting caught, or even getting killed. It's childish, I know, especially given all I've seen that proves otherwise, but—and I wouldn't even tell this to Teddy—secretly, I've always felt invincible.

I'm up to fifty, and the light has switched from red to green—a good sign. If it turned red, I'd have to do this experiment all over again. Our hit-and-run driver might be willing to blaze through a changing light, but I'm not. My feet plant firmly on the floorboard. And I'm right. Already this feels unnatural. Intentional.

I'm not saying I don't experience fear—I've seen enough to worry about every female coed walking home alone at night, my mother teaching testosterone-filled young men one bad grade away from marching onto campus with a machine gun. Hell, half her colleagues look one frazzled tenure review away from burning the whole place down. Just read a day's news section of the *Athens Banner Herald*—some asshole strangles a dog and hangs it on a pole, schoolmates attack an eight-year-old boy, a man admits to raping a woman and a child, a woman pistol-whips a teen, a brawl at an auto repair shop. It's reverse evolution and frightening in its randomness and ridiculousness. But that's why I chose this job. My fearlessness is a gift. I owe it to people like my father, all those coeds, and professors to put it to good use.

The base of the hill shallows beneath the light, so that the car slows before I reach the intersection and the hill creeps subtly upward as I skirt the crosswalk. A lone student lingers there, jacket pulled tight against the wind so I can only see a pale face, feet tapping side to side as they wait for me. Forty miles per hour. Thirty-five. Thirty.

It hits me as I cross the intersection: The witnesses were right. Not only did our driver not slam on the brakes, he pressed the gas.

In my rearview mirror, the student in the rain jacket runs across the street under the swaying green light.

| Three |

There are fraternity houses scattered all over Athens, plunked down on Cloverhurst and Pulaski, looming over Carriage and River Road like rectangular hotels on a Monopoly board, but most are on Milledge—a sidewalk-lined, well-trafficked street less than a mile from the university. Some are grand, white-brick plantation homes with Corinthian columns, wraparound front porches, and rocking chairs. Others are new builds or old Craftsmen repurposed for housing dozens of hotheaded young men with a penchant for drinking, fighting, and sex. And living at the house doesn't come cheap. If you're there with a meal plan, you're looking at an extra five grand a semester—that's on top of tuition, books, and everything else.

This one's red brick with Doric columns supporting a triangular roof, like an oversized bank. I recognize it because it's been in the news twice this year—once in the spring for organizing an Old South parade, in which members traipsed around wearing Confederate uniforms, carrying battle flags, and escorting women in hoop skirts past a historically Black sorority celebrating its fiftieth anniversary, and another two weeks ago for dunking pledges in trash cans full of ice water.

They're not the only fraternity making headlines, of course. It seems that every day, somewhere in the country, someone falls off a balcony or a sleeping porch at a fraternity party, resulting in everything from sprained ankles to broken pelvises, permanent brain damage, and death. The endless fascination of fraternity boys with shoving things up their asses, from exploding bottle rockets to the near-fatal wine enemas is click-bait fodder—the sheer ridiculousness masking the bigger problem that these young men risk killing themselves for a few laughs. And it's not just at the big research universities. An Ivy League grad published an article about his experience swimming in fecal matter and semen. There was that charming email guide from a Georgia Tech fraternity called "Luring Your Rapebait." Cindy saw two Sigma chapter pledges in the ER after they were forced to drink whiskey until they puked into a Little Mermaid kiddie pool. They had bruises everywhere, she told us, on their legs, arms, even buttocks.

Teddy thinks my frequent recitation of Greek misdeeds borders on obsession. Oliver rolls his eyes anytime I forward a news article. And it's true. I collect them, these horrendously sad and never-ending accounts all across the nation, pile them up in my memory, so I can bury the thing at its core. But compared to other stories, those guys with the bruises were lucky. There was the nineteen-year-old who inhaled eighteen drinks in ninety minutes and died after he fell down the stairs; his brothers, who waited twelve hours before they called 911. The "Bible studies" in which pledges have to drink if they answer fraternity questions incorrectly. Young men dying alone in rooms full of people, dying because of underage drinking and negligence, dying because no one will take responsibility. Because after the crowds are gone, the vomit cleaned off the floors, the tears wept at the funeral, everyone will point their fingers in opposite directions. The universities, the chapter officers, the police.

As we pull up the drive, I check Teddy's face. He's calm, but oddly quiet. In the morning light, the bags under his eyes have taken a deeper hue. And I realize that I was so worried about being sidelined, I didn't ask him if he wanted this case. We talked about bringing Oliver with us— he's one polo shirt away from a frat boy anyhow—but decided against it. No reason to make me superfluous when Truman's already unsure about my presence. But I took it for granted that Teddy wanted this one as badly as I did.

It's only Wednesday, but it's also 8:00 A.M. and I'm expecting a yard full of beer cans, a stale after-party smell, and hungover, half-dressed men with obscene images drawn on their foreheads. In the dozen or so times I ran through our visit to the house this morning, it didn't once occur to me that the place would be quiet and somber.

The chapter president is waiting for us at the front door. From a distance, he's all golden-blond hair, tall and lanky, compensating for his height by ducking his head like a bashful giraffe. But up close, he looks awful—clothes a mess, eyes swollen and red rimmed. *Hungover*, I think, before he takes a long, watery breath and I realize he's been crying.

"Thank you for coming," he says, shaking my hand and then Teddy's. He looks us both in the eyes, and I can feel Teddy's mood shift. We've been preparing for resistance—come-back-with-a-warrant kind of nonsense— and this welcome, although preferable, relaxes Teddy but puts me on edge.

"I'm Tripp Holmes," the golden boy says. "We're all pretty shaken up. Jay was a real—" but his voice wobbles and he seems incapable of finishing. Instead, he waves us toward the massive wooden double doors, one of which he holds open so we can step inside. I take a deep breath, squash down a flood of memories, and follow him.

We're greeted by a sweeping foyer with wide arches. The floors are tiled, protecting, I suspect, glorious old hardwoods from dirty shoes and spilled beer. To the right is a light-filled room with a long table, window seat, and built-in bookshelves. There's a student curled in an armchair with an open book on his lap, and it's unclear whether he's studying or sleeping. But all the same, the mornings here seem peaceful. It's the way my shoes stick to the floor and the smell—musty, with faint whiffs of lemon Pine-Sol, frying bacon, and Axe body spray masking something earthier, feral, like a wet animal mixed with weed—that remind me we're at a fraternity house and not some quaint boarding school.

Tripp shifts next to us and runs his hand through his hair. He clears his throat. "How does this work?" he asks.

"Why don't you start by giving us a tour of the house," I suggest.

"A tour—?" His pale brows crumple in confusion.

"So we can get an idea of Jay's day-to-day life here."

Something loosens in his shoulders. "Okay, sure."

He ushers us farther into the foyer. "We have eighty-nine active brothers. Thirty-five live in the house. Two brothers per room. Except for the president—he gets his own. The chapter at UGA was founded in 1910, making it one of the oldest on campus." He gestures to a glass case at the opposite end. "Those are our trophies, awarded to the top chapters in the country. The photos are of famous former members—starters on the football team, UGA coaches, CEOs . . ." I walk toward the case for a closer look and see the athletes Tripp indicated, one or two B-list celebrities, and also former governors, a US senator, and the current UGA president, Ed Williams.

"That," he points to the sunlit room on the right, "is our study room. At Kap-O, we value academic success. Most people don't know this," he tucks a wayward strand of hair behind his ear, "but the average fraternity member's scholastic GPA is higher than the average non-Greek university student's GPA. In fact, more than seventy-five percent of our members have at least a three point oh."

Teddy catches my eye, but I beam encouragingly at Tripp. He smiles back.

"Over here," he says with a renewed bounce to his step as he leads us through a pair of closed doors on the right, "is our chapter room."

We stand at the entrance of a sprawling space that must extend beyond the length of the foyer. A half dozen fans whirl over our heads despite the room being empty. There's something oddly sterile about the place—rows of folding chairs in the front and a collection of leather couches and a flat-screen television in the back, a flag with bold-faced fraternity letters, and, for some reason, an ATM, but that's it—nothing personal, nothing to indicate the thirty-five different personalities of the house's current residents. But maybe it's not supposed to. This is a space that will see a rotation of faces. Every year, men who have considered themselves a part of the house's very foundation will be replaced by new ones who will grow to view themselves as just as indispensable, and so on, and so on. The room's a reminder of a shared vision and shared identity, molding its residents, not the other way around.

"This is where we conduct fraternity business and hold social gatherings," Tripp tells us. "Now it's set up for a meeting. But we clear out the chairs if there's a party."

I pull out my notepad and begin writing—mostly flower doodles and nonsense, but I want him to get used to me scribbling while he talks.

"That," he points to a ten-foot portrait of an auburn-haired man with an oiled beard and mustache, "is our founder, J. E. B. Stuart. Jeb for short."

I let my eyes linger on the painting. Jeb's knee-high boots are crossed demurely; one gloved hand clutches a sword, the other a feathered hat. Gold stitching and buttons give his jacket, with a red flower in his lapel and matching red-lined cape, an elegant, if effeminate flair.

Next to the portrait is a body of text written in a fine calligraphic hand.

"What's this?"

"It's Kap-O's creed. We recite it before every meeting."

"Do you know it by heart?"

Tripp smiles shyly and then clears his throat. I take a step back so I can see his face and read along as he speaks.

"'The Honorable Man is the man who promotes brotherhood and friendship, whose self-control is refined and practiced, who is confident in his accomplishments and yet boasts of neither riches nor achievements, who is a leader in his community and shepherd of his family, who guards the virtue of himself and others, who respects the humanity of all, especially those lesser than himself; and who is a model of strength for the weak, a beacon of wisdom for the ignorant, and a symbol of courage for the coward.'"

A shiver sneaks up my neck. There's something uncanny in his repetition. The pauses are all there, not a word too many or too few, but there's no room for error or individual emphasis. He looks straight ahead. And he doesn't blink.

At the base of the text it reads: *Kappa Phi Omicron Creed, James Ewell Brown "Jeb" Stuart, 1852.*

"Right," Teddy says, and I wonder if he's noticed the way Tripp's eyes have glazed over or the nearly sixty-year gap between Jeb's death and the fraternity's founding. "Did Jay have issues with any of the other brothers? Any fights or girl problems?"

"Jay?" Tripp seems genuinely perplexed by his question. "Everybody loved Jay. They wanted to be his friend. Hell," he glances back at the portrait, "they wanted to be him. The girls loved him, too, but he wasn't really the girlfriend type, if you know what I mean."

"Gotcha," Teddy says with a grin.

I resist the urge to roll my eyes. Teddy can do bro-y if he has to, but it always seems forced to me. Tripp doesn't notice.

"Did he ever," Teddy gives him a sly look, "you know, with someone else's girlfriend?"

"No way." Tripp shakes his head. "We have rules. And that's like rule number four—no messing with someone else's girl."

I raise my eyebrow. The girl as boy's property doesn't surprise me, nor does the assumption of heteronormativity, but the fact that there's a list of numbered rules somewhere is so quaint it's almost amusing. I wonder what's number ten—no drawing dicks on foreheads?

"What's rule number one?" Teddy asks.

"Never betray the brotherhood," Tripp says promptly in the manner of a well-trained military cadet.

Then he turns on his heels and leads us through a door on the opposite side of the chapter room.

As I watch him recede, that shiver is back and with it a feeling like I've just missed something important.

Teddy and I follow him into a windowless hallway.

"What are these?" I ask, pointing to the framed images on the side wall.

"Oh." Tripp stops and runs a hand through his hair. "That's our annual magazine. It's supposed to be like *Sports Illustrated* but for Kap-O. You know—highlights of the year, awards and stuff."

Bless his heart, he blushes when I step forward to examine a cover. A girl front and center sits on the hood of a Porsche with her legs spread, and six or so fraternity brothers spray her with hoses so her small nipples gleam through her tank top.

"And who's this?"

The flush deepens. "That's our Kap-O dream girl. We used to have a calendar with twelve, but it got too much, you know, choosing twelve girls. So now we just have one for the year."

"And what's her name?"

"Her?" He scratches his head. "I'm not sure. She's from a few years ago.

"This," he points to a framed headshot of a girl with a toothy smile and auburn hair to the right of the magazine covers, "is our current dream girl. Her name's Katie Coleman. She's a Gamma Delta."

I step back. If you blur your eyes together, they all look the same, with only slight variations of hair color: white, fit, with sweet smiles and tasteful amounts of makeup. But there's something wistful in Tripp's voice, and I think he might be a little in love with Katie Coleman.

"And what does it mean—to be the Kap-O dream girl?"

He's still staring at the photograph. "Well, it's an honor to be chosen," he says slowly. "You know, out of hundreds—thousands even—of other girls. And the dream girl helps promote our events, makes sure all her sisters come to our parties. Sometimes she even brings Chick-fil-A to our meetings."

"She brings you lunch?" I taste something like vomit at the back of my throat.

"Yeah—breakfast, too."

"Why would she—" but Teddy pinches my arm before I can finish.

"Why don't you show us Jay's room," he suggests, and starts walking as if he knows the way.

Tripp jogs to catch up with him, and, I think, so he doesn't have to talk to me.

I'm left staring at the grooves on the black frames and the bright eyes in the photographs—boys on boats, on the fifty-yard line at Sanford Stadium, stretched between columns of the house, all with their choice girl of the year in less-than-respectable positions. I look hard at the girls' smiling faces for any flicker of doubt or resentment—*No*, I think, *I don't see it.* But what about the other girls Tripp mentioned? It's hard for me to imagine anyone biting at the bit to hand-deliver breakfast to a bunch of boys with swooped hair and polo shirts, but who knows? I also can't imagine wanting to perform secret rituals, commit to some vague set of rules just for the hell of it, or share a house with thirty or so other less-than-hygienic people—male or female.

I think of the new brothers filling out college applications. Opening acceptance letters. The excitement on their faces. Their first day here, dragging suitcases through unfamiliar halls, pulsing with anticipation and a sense of belonging. Learning new skills—how to work the laundry machines and pull an all-nighter for a morning test—jostling to make an impression—who can do the most push-ups, tap a keg, build an ice luge. *They're just boys*, a voice whispers. But that's not entirely right either.

"Jay's room is on the third floor," Tripp yells from the door at the end of the hall.

"I'm right behind you," I call back, hoping he'll get the hint and not stand there waiting for me.

We all have our own ways of approaching a case—I try to picture every detail I can about the victim's life so I can build a world with him in it and look for inconsistencies. Teddy asks as many questions as possible—finding out information but also gauging reactions and hesitations, looking for lies and omissions. I listen to his voice and their footsteps echo in the stairwell as I try to imagine Jay walking through the hall. I draw a mental picture of his face, blow life back into his features, color into his cheeks, bounce into his fluffy brown hair. His stride would have all the false confidence of youth and inherited wealth; of that, I'm certain. But would he be boisterous, yelling to the other brothers? Laughing? Showing off? Would he have looked at the wall of dream girls? Maybe with a longing glance for this year's girl? Or glower at one particular brother? Was he looking over his shoulder? Did he have any idea that this place would be a poor receptacle for his memory, the sound of his laughter, the smell of his skin already erased in a house of so many? None of the Jays I imagine—loud, funny, anxious—seem to fit, and when Tripp yells again, I feel Jay slip through my fingers.

I continue down the hall, listening for the sound of Jay's voice. Again I think, confident, with perhaps a southern lilt. He would jog up the stairs—*Not a patient one*, I think, *considering his manner of death*—so I do the same when I reach them.

On the third floor, past a precarious line of cables stretching across the carpet, Tripp's standing outside a room two doors down. He ducks his head and waves to me. And I think, not unkindly, of a blond ostrich.

He moves aside so I can enter but remains in the hall, unwilling or unable to set foot in Jay's room.

There are two beds—one on each side of a striped floor rug—and a white porcelain sink.

"Which bed's Jay's?" Teddy asks, mercifully contracting the verb so the past tense is unnecessary.

"That one." Tripp points to the mattress on the left.

I clench my jaw.

A twin, it looks like a child's bed with a half-askew navy-blue comforter and a pile of dirty clothes kicked to the bottom.

I indicate the neatly made bed on the opposite side. "We'll need to talk to his roommate."

"Cade Abernathy," Tripp says from the hallway.

"Where is he?"

Tripp squirms. "I haven't seen him in a few days. He spends most nights at his girlfriend's apartment. She lives on the south side."

"And does he know about Jay?"

"I sent a message as soon as we found out. We're having a special meeting this afternoon."

"Why?" I shove my notebook in my back pocket and flick through the dirty clothes on Jay's bed with the end of my pen.

Tripp blinks at me.

I stare back.

"You know," he says, shifting from side to side, "to talk about what happened, make a statement, funeral arrangements."

"Won't his parents do that?" Even though I haven't touched anything, I rub my hands on the side of my pants.

Tripp's eyes flick from me to Teddy. He's worried I've caught him in a lie or that he's given something away; what, I'm not sure.

"Well, the service and stuff—sure. But we want to make sure he's remembered properly."

Or get your stories straight, I think.

It occurs to me there might be another reason Tripp greeted us on the stairs today instead of one of the other brothers. With his sheepish grin and mop of yellow hair, he's about as threatening as a golden retriever. I give him a hard look but he's staring dejectedly at the floor—a small slump to his shoulders. I don't think it's an act but know better than to assume his pitiable state reflects his sorrow at Jay's death. It could also be guilt.

I turn to the room. Empty bottles of Gatorade and cans of Mountain Dew give off a sugar-sweet odor mixed with the unwashed gym clothes in a pile on the floor. I look around for beer cans or handles of vodka and see none, which means someone has been here already. When I glance back at Tripp, he's still blinking at his shoes. A towel hangs off the closet door, a handwritten quote taped next to it: *When you can't make them see the light, make them feel the heat.* There's a large wall calendar with a photo of a mountain range at the top, full of events at the bottom. Home games, away games, tailgates, a big party for Halloween, prices for a fog machine rental, cover bands. Facing this level of organization, some of my earlier images of Jay dissolve. It's strange, though, with all this detail, that the calendar is still tacked to October.

I flip up the page. There are a few dates penciled in for November: a weekend in Jacksonville, a Georgia–Auburn tailgate, the Georgia Tech game Thanksgiving weekend, *Hell* written in large letters across the first full week, but that's it.

I pull out my phone and snatch a few photos.

Next, I tug a three-ring binder off a narrow bookshelf and flip through colorful save-the-date invitations, math problems, and what looks like biology notes, all dated two years earlier.

There are matching desks under the windows. Jay's holds a spider's web of cords.

"Where's his laptop?"

Tripp's head jerks, and he tries to mask his reaction by stretching his arm.

He pretends he didn't hear me.

"His . . . ?"

"Laptop."

"He probably had it with him."

"No," I say firmly. Jay wasn't even wearing a backpack—not a notebook, pen, or piece of paper on him, and certainly no laptop. "He didn't. Any idea where it might be?"

Tripp shrugs, but there's something stiff and unnatural about the gesture.

"He might have let one of the brothers borrow it," he says slowly. "I can ask at the meeting."

My mouth tightens. "You can ask now. Or I will open every door until we find it."

His eyes widen. "That's not necessary," he says carefully, and I see him think, *You need a warrant*, but he's playing cooperative, at least for the moment. "I'll message everyone."

He pulls out his phone and I look at my watch. It's 8:19. If we need his phone records, I'll know exactly what time he texted whoever has Jay's laptop.

Minutes pass. Teddy withdraws a pair of gloves, and Tripp's eyes grow large, but he says nothing as Teddy lifts Jay's mattress, goes through the pockets of his dirty jeans, and opens his desk drawers.

I keep an ear out for our laptop borrower and stoop to examine the books stacked under the coffee table. I'm surprised to see they're mostly biographies—Thomas Jefferson, Ronald Reagan, and Antonin Scalia.

I hear hurried footsteps, and Tripp disappears from the door. I stand, but Teddy's already in the hall, depositing the laptop into an evidence bag. Next to him stands a young man in slacks and a crisp button-down. With dark hair, a broad nose, and eyes slightly too close together, he looks like a well-put-together Fred Flintstone. A little too put-together for his age and the hour.

"This is Michael Williams, our treasurer."

"Detectives White and Kaplan."

Michael's lip curls at my name. My father's Jewish, nonpracticing, and I rarely think about my heritage, but Michael's look reminds me that other people do.

"We'll need your fingerprints," I growl.

His eyes pass over me to appraise Teddy. "Sure."

"Williams," Teddy says. "Any relation to Ed Williams?"

Michael's lip curl turns into a smirk.

Right, so we're dealing with the university president's son here. He may think that gives him a free pass, but I don't.

"Why did you borrow Jay's laptop?"

"I didn't." Michael arches his eyebrow. "I found it."

I turn to Tripp, but his face has gone blank.

"You found it where?"

"In the study room. On a chair." He looks bored. Apparently, this conversation is a massive waste of his time.

"So you're telling me that when our techs open this," I tap the metal top with my pen, "they'll find only Jay's fingerprints on the keys and the last log-in will be before his time of death?"

Tripp flinches.

"No," Michael says slowly. "I'm not telling you anything other than that I found it on a chair in the study room. Anyone might have used it between then and now."

"So other people had Jay's password?"

He shrugs.

"And where were you yesterday morning?"

"Here," Michael says, gesturing upward. "With about fifteen other brothers, eating breakfast."

I glance at Teddy. It should be easy enough to verify.

"You can ask them," Michael adds, unnecessarily.

I take a deep breath and walk back into Jay's room.

From his window, there's a view of Milledge: cars with their windows open, hands in the breeze, students swinging backpacks, laughing on the sidewalk. They're all so buoyant, these young people. Not a thought of age or time, except when they'll be twenty-one and whether or not they'll be late for class. I sigh and spin around the room. But that's not quite right either. There's more going on than drinking and parties and the occasional schoolwork. I want to paint them with the same brush, all these shiny young faces, but the details are important. The dream girls and missing laptop. The dirty mattress encroaching on the tidy one. The stress of being in a new place with new people and new rules. The fraternity code. And between all these fine lines, unspoken expectations, and wires running between bedrooms, there's one that lights the fuse. We just have to follow it backward to find the right one: the reason someone wanted Jay Kemp dead.

Twenty minutes later, we're back at the station, checking messages and sorting through documents that have piled up in our absence.

My desk is just how I like it, jotted notes on Post-its pasted to the wall, my lamp, and the top of my keyboard like a serial killer in the movies. Candy wrappers litter the floor—I would say they're all Teddy's, but the Starbursts are definitely mine. There's a rotting apple crammed in the bottom drawer—last week's failed attempt to eat healthy. Truman is a firm believer that cleanliness is near godliness, so I chuck the apple, half of it brown and soft, toward the bin and hit the wall instead.

"Haven't lost your basketball skills, I see," Teddy says behind me as I get up grudgingly to put the thing in the trash.

It takes immense effort, but I resist the urge to imitate him. I don't have siblings, and something about Teddy brings out the little-sister response in me. Perhaps it's because I never got it out as a kid. And Teddy has the sure confidence of the oldest of three—which naturally makes me want to take him down a peg. As an only child, I was never quite sure what my role was. I would say I prefer being the leader, but I can also disappear into the wallpaper like a middle child or tiptoe around the margins learning from everyone else's mistakes like the youngest. I try to see this as an advantage, but whenever Teddy talks about his sisters, I feel an acute sense of longing that verges on loss. It's not true that you can't miss what you never had. You can; and worse, it's all rose-colored and golden because it lives in your imagination, unspoiled by the reality of hurt feelings and petty rivalries and whatever else might happen in bigger families with everyone vying for attention or control.

"What do you got?" I ask instead. I've been reading over Jay's school records—Cs and Ds all his freshman and half his sophomore year, and then, oddly, As and Bs ever since—and have been trying to figure out what inspired the change. Cheating's my first guess. Fraternities are known to keep files of tests and final exams, prompting professors to write new questions every semester, but, of course, not all of them do. And there's also a complete change in coursework. His first year and a half, he took a lot of gen ed classes—math and science mostly—then spring of his sophomore year, he changes to more humanities courses, does great, and now he's taking—or was taking—classes for a political science major: Intro to Political Theory, Political Psychology, Criminal Procedure, and two outliers: Introduction to Ethics and Stellar and Galactic Astronomy.

"Dara sent over traffic camera footage of the vehicle turning left onto Broad Street after the accident," Teddy says.

That's it, I think, *we got him.*

"And?"

He looks for a sticky note–free spot on my desk, finds none, and lays three blown-up photos of a car on top of a note that reads: *white van, male, nineteen to twenty-four, waits for the last one.*

The first is the overlarge front license plate; thank god it's a BMW with its pretentious insistence on sticking to the European way—Georgia only requires license plates in the back—so here we've got a smudged face and numbers all in one.

Teddy grabs a Snickers bar out of my desk drawer, while I bend over the photos.

"The car belongs to our victim. Or rather, it's registered to his father, Robert Kemp. But Jay's listed on the insurance."

"What the fuck?" I exhale. "It's his car?"

"Could be a car robbery gone wrong," Teddy offers. "Some guy steals Jay's car and then runs him over with it."

I shake my head. "That might make sense in a parking lot. But Jay was coming from a pedestrian-only area on campus. The BMW was flying down Lumpkin."

I think of our witness who insisted the driver looked identical to Jay. "Any better photos of the driver?"

"Here." Teddy moves the top photo to reveal a grainy image of a man behind the wheel.

My stomach does a flip.

"Seriously, what the fuck?" I look at Teddy. The image is of a white male, young, early twenties, with a broad nose and high cheekbones. "Is someone messing with us?"

He smiles and pulls the Snickers bar apart into bite-size pieces. He offers me one, and I shake my head.

"Are you messing with me?"

"Me?" Teddy asks with a fake affronted look. "I would never."

"Then why are you smiling?"

"Come on, Marlitt. For months, you've had nothing but that white van case, and it's going nowhere and it's depressing, making me worry about Cassandra and Josie—"

I think of Teddy's sisters rolling their eyes in unison every time he tells them to be careful. It's not entirely true. I've had other cases: drug-related, domestics, but lately I've been assisting Sex Crimes with a case that involves a white van–owning asshole who offers college girls rides home and then rapes them.

"—and now you've got something interesting. And you're asking why I'm smiling? You wanted this case, remember? You could be buried in paperwork, proofreading a report for the third time—"

"All right, yeah, it's fucking stellar," I say. And then I do smile.

"Language," Truman yells out his office door.

| Four |

It's a beautiful afternoon; a soft orange light casts hazy gray shadows through the oak trees. Students lie on their backs in the brittle grass, sweatshirts tucked under their heads. A pair throws a Frisbee; a shirtless guy in blue jeans strums his guitar. All fresh and lovely, they're studying statistics and quoting their professors, enamored by their own thoughts, the mere thought of thinking, and all the radical, subversive ideas out there just waiting to be grasped. Old age is a distant, incomprehensible thing for other people to worry about. Young, they will live forever. They tremble with this new awareness, the connections they're forming with the world around them; their classmates vibrate with an energy that's so new and exciting that no one notices they're tripping over power lines, one rogue spark away from disaster.

I clutch a paper coffee cup in my hand, and Teddy jokes about caffeine as a necessary evil that supports our partnership.

"Initial impressions?" I ask.

Teddy does a half skip down the sidewalk like he's been waiting for this moment all morning; a few coeds stretched in front of an oak tree laugh.

"Who first?"

I think for a moment and then decide to save the best for last.

"Tripp," I say.

"Easy. I'd guess family's upper-middle-class. Not rich-rich, not like our boy Jay or Michael. But rich enough that he's never had to worry about money. Still, he's a hard-working kid. A–B student. Gets a little boost because teachers like him. He's not oblivious. He's learned the value of his good looks and easy smile. I imagine a grandmother once told him that old 'you catch more flies with honey' adage and he took it to heart. He looks you in the eye, inclines his head when you're speaking, wants to be liked but isn't sycophantic."

"Word of the day," I break in, "'sycophantic.'" I take a sip of coffee. Teddy's stated more or less what I've been thinking, but as he was talking I realized that Tripp's desire to be liked might come in handy and I slide that little trick into my pocket for later.

"So not our guy?"

"No, but that doesn't mean he's not hiding something. Did you notice his face when Michael gave us the laptop?"

I screw up my nose, thinking back. "Nothing stands out."

"Exactly." Teddy nods. "He'd been all smiles. Let me tell you about our trophies. Looks of concern. How can I help? Volunteers the roommate's name. And then Michael shows up with the laptop and his face goes blank."

"All right," I say, tapping the lid of my coffee cup thoughtfully with my fingernail. "Michael, then."

Teddy blows out a long breath. We skirt a fountain splattered with bloodred leaves. I badly want him to echo what I'm thinking, something along the lines of "pretentious, dickwad asshole," but Teddy's a bit of a Boy Scout when it comes to swearing—he only slips when he's truly angry—so I'll settle for stuck-up, douchebag, jerk.

"Smug," he says instead. "Everything about him—his clothes, his posture, his facial expressions, even his haircut—says: *I'm better than you.* And it's intentional. Just like Tripp with his puppy-dog smile, Michael's learned that these initial impressions get him what he wants. His whole demeanor says his daddy has a lawyer on retainer, so you better not piss him off. But," Teddy pauses, "Michael looks nothing like the driver. And

I checked his alibi. The dozen or so guys Michael ate breakfast with confirmed he was there, thereby also serving as one another's alibis, but a group like that—I don't care how much they might have practiced, if it wasn't true, it would be difficult for them to keep their stories straight. And they all tell relatively the same timeline of events: Monday-night football, small party, handful of girls came over, and then Michael trots down around ten A.M. the next morning. They remember because he kissed some blond bombshell right in front of the dining room, slapped her rear, and sent her on her way, to cheers, apparently."

I snort. If I wanted a memorable story from this group that's how I'd do it, too, but if he came down at ten, it leaves little time for him to climb behind the wheel of Jay's car, drive down Milledge—a street full of crosswalks and pedestrians—and take a left at Five Points, so he could be barreling down Lumpkin by the time Jay's ready to cross.

"And by all accounts, Michael stayed at breakfast for quite a while regaling the brothers with his conquests—the blonde was girl number two, if you believe him."

We spend the early part of the afternoon afternoon talking to Jay's professors. After a few cursory glances through attendance sheets or a quick phone call to teaching assistants, we learn he had almost perfect attendance. He was a good student. His philosophy professor, Dr. Watanabe, tells us he worked all weekend on a paper due Monday and got an A. No one reports any erratic behavior or mentions cheating or the change in grades. But I also get the impression that none of them really remember Jay. He's a name signed on a sheet, a seat in a chair, a letter grade in an online database. Just a face in a sea of faces, one they know better now from seeing it plastered all over the news than they did when he was present less than twenty feet away in a lecture hall. A couple faculty recognize me, but when I don't acknowledge my mother neither do they.

You might expect a somber mood to preside over campus in the aftermath of a student death, but the university is simply too large. There would have been an email announcement: "The university is greatly saddened by the loss of one of our own" kind of thing, but I wouldn't be surprised if half the students and a handful of faculty haven't heard what happened yet. My mother refuses to watch the local news, preferring international sources like the BBC or ZDF. And these days, most students prefer streaming sites to cable.

Leaving Baldwin Hall, I see a girl in the corner sniveling into her phone. I catch every other word but none of them sound like "Jay Kemp."

Teddy and I grab sandwiches from the student learning center and sit on a bench outside, watching the intersection where Jay was hit.

Most of the time if a student gets dragged into the station, they're belligerent—smudged mascara, puffy faced, hair like they've slept in it, swearing or crying or both—but tracing down the sidewalk are clear-eyed, freshly laundered students, clutching books, leaning against iron railings, and chatting about test grades and what they did over the weekend. It's the statistics that remind you everything's not rose doodles in the margins of notebooks, club meetings, intramural sports, and football games: substance abuse, depression, suicide, and sexual assault top the list, but there's also homesickness, eating disorders, and debilitating anxiety, students who don't leave their rooms for weeks, doctors prescribing cocktails of prescriptions independent of one another, and predators scoping out college bars.

The glass doors open behind us, followed by shuffling feet, a high-pitched squeal, and the laughter that marks the break between classes.

"We're wasting our time," I say, closing my notebook. I cross my arms and stare at the red traffic light against the blue-gray sky. "We should go at his brothers. Hard."

"With what?" Teddy turns to me. "Why are you so certain they're involved?" His voice is curious, not accusatory, but I feel a stab of defensiveness anyway.

The light changes again, and Teddy makes a note of the number of students on the sidewalk. He marks the two who dart across after the light turns green.

I squint at the sun. He's right—there's very little to go on. But everything inside me is screaming that Kap-O has something to do with it. That I've been given a chance to put things right.

"I had a friend in a fraternity," I say finally.

Teddy raises his eyebrow.

"A good friend," I add, feeling my face flush.

I went to Georgia State for a bit—mainly I wanted to get out of Athens, and Atlanta had that big-city appeal. Being a professor's kid is a lot like being a preacher's kid—you either drink the Kool-Aid or you rebel. You can try to impress your parents, their friends, and everyone else who decides that just because your mother's brilliant, you must be, too, or you can disappoint early and often. I was precocious, of course; but by high school, I had turned inward. I had one friend who understood—Craig—the son of one of my mother's colleagues. We met at a faculty holiday party, the only two children whose parents hadn't bothered with babysitters and instead marched us from fundraising event to university function to student art gallery show. Together, we bore the brunt of the endless pressure to perform, the tut-tuts of teachers, who shook their heads at us with assertions about wasted potential. It was Craig who convinced me to go to college. *We'll go together*, he said, brushing the hair out of my eyes so he could see me better. *We need degrees*, he insisted. *We need experience*, I argued, *not a piece of paper*. But I filled out the application anyway because that's what Craig was doing. We celebrated our acceptance letters with wine snuck from my parents' cabinet. *To our future*, he said. *To our escape*, I muttered. And I believed it.

My reasons for trying to talk Craig out of spring rush were entirely self-motivated. I worried about whom I'd eat lunch with and talk to after class. In the evenings, we had made a habit of watching Adult Swim on the futon in my apartment, cramming ourselves full of Dr Pepper and

Doritos, laughing late into the evenings. The thought of doing that by myself was enormously depressing.

"He wanted to join," I tell Teddy, "and no matter what I said—no matter how many sarcastic remarks I made about dress-alike Ken dolls and sharing a brain, I couldn't convince him otherwise. So he pledged." I close my eyes. "Fast-forward six weeks later after seeing him maybe twice when we used to see each other every day, sometimes multiple times a day, and I'm woken up by a banging on my bedroom door." Craig still had a key to my apartment, let himself in, and wanted to sleep on the floor in my room. "He was shaking, smelled awful, and wouldn't tell me what was going on. The next morning, he was up before dawn, mumbled something about not getting caught, and I didn't see him again for another month." I chew my bottom lip. "When I did see him—across the street, laughing with a pair of Ken dolls—he acted like he didn't recognize me. And when I marched over to him, he pretended like that night had never happened and, oh right, he had to go—sorry, chapter meeting. His friends must have thought he broke up with me or something, because I could hear them consoling him, telling him not to worry, that there'd be way hotter bitches at their party that night." I shake my head. Even now, the betrayal stings. "After that," I sigh, "I never spoke to him again. So yeah," I say, not meeting Teddy's eyes, "I've seen fraternities change nice guys into assholes, and I think this time, they might have changed one into a murderer."

We're both silent for a while, and I wonder if Teddy—who grew up surrounded by sisters who adored him and a mom who insisted on nightly family dinners—could ever understand what it means to lose a friend like that. The silences and loneliness of an only child, the way they stretched and cocooned around you. Craig was the only person who made me feel like I wasn't alone. And a fraternity took him from me. And so I know for all their promises of brotherhood and loyalty they're thieves and liars—stealing other people's brothers and abandoning them when it counts.

"And there's the fact they had Jay's laptop," I add, grasping onto a more professional reason for my suspicions. "There's a good possibility whatever was on there has been erased."

His look says there could be any number of things the brothers didn't want us to find. And none may be related to Jay's death.

"Dara's on it now. She'll let us know." He pauses. I think he'll ask more about Craig or tell me to keep my personal biases in check, but he doesn't. "Tripp said there's a memorial this afternoon. If we leave now, we might make it."

I cast a longing look at my sandwich before I toss it in the trash and groan as we begin trucking our way back up the tree-lined corridor. Teddy finishes his in one large bite.

"You're the one who wanted to park on Clayton," he murmurs as he sidesteps a student in headphones.

It's three o'clock and the service—or whatever it is—has already started, so we stand in the back of the chapter room. In the front is a table draped with a black cloth and a large portrait of Jay—not unlike what you might find at a real memorial. He's a few years younger, and the marbled gray background makes me think of high school senior photos. There's a pseudo monopoly here—one family runs Athens school photography— so they all have the same head tilt, smile, catch-the-gleam-in-your-eye kind of thing going on. I find myself wondering how the brothers managed to pull this together so quickly. Jay's been dead just over twenty-four hours, and they already have a blown-up portrait. Or maybe they all have overlarge photos hanging on a wall somewhere and there's a wide gap where Jay's used to be.

Spread across the table is a collection of items: a bubblehead bulldog, a red UGA jersey, a can of Mountain Dew, a Burger King crown, and a handful of smaller things I'd need to get closer to to identify. Sixty or so young men and less than half that number of women hunch in small groups along the side walls or slouch in folding chairs. Most are dressed in black, but a handful didn't get the memo. There's a girl in a jean skirt and an oversized sweatshirt that says PART BEAR in bold letters and a boy in sky-blue shorts and flip-flops, but he's blinking back tears, and I don't think it's for anyone's benefit other than his own. I'm still waiting on photographs of all the fraternity members. But I scan the crowd, looking for faces that resemble Jay's. For twitchy behavior. Guilty expressions. It's likely that whoever did this got the hell out of town, but if he didn't, there's a good chance he's in this room.

Michael stands at the front in a crisp black button-down, hair swooped back with some kind of pomade, and is talking about how last weekend he and Jay went fishing—just the two of them at a lake house, so peaceful—"And you know what he said to me?"—sniff—"he said, 'If this was it, man, if this was all there is—I think I'd die happy.'"

Tight sobs around the room.

I imagine the two of them, sitting on a wooden dock, backs silhouetted against the sunset in the distance, the sky pink and yellow mirrored on the lake. Fireflies flickering between blades of grass, bullfrogs croaking, cicadas drowning out the sound of the water lapping the shore, and black moccasins slithering just under the surface. But last weekend was cold, the fireflies dead, snakes already in brumation. Michael's voice is choked with emotion, but I'm not buying it.

Tripp jogs to the front and places a hand on Michael's shoulder. "Thanks for sharing that story with us, Mike. We all remember how much Jay-bird loved to fish, and it's nice to know he got to the weekend before he—he left us."

A weepy gasp from one of the girls in front of me.

"Does anyone else want to share?"

Bodies shift and chairs scrape the floor, but no one moves to the front. An awkward silence. For someone who was well liked by so many, there are few with anything to say. I scan the room. Those in the back have already marked our presence, and the knowledge seems to ripple until it reaches the front. There's a hiss of a whisper, gone before I know what's been said, but I feel Teddy tense at my side.

"Okay, well, then, I thought, I could read a poem?" Tripp's voice arches into a question.

There's a snicker and someone mutters "pussy" under his breath, but the others shush him.

Tripp reddens and clears his throat. It's the long neck and Adam's apple that make me think: *sad giraffe.*

He unfolds a paper from his pocket and begins to read.

> *Joyously his days of youth so glad*
> *Danced along, in rosy garb beclad,*
> *And the world, the world was then so sweet.*
> *And how kindly, how enchantingly*
> *Smiled the future, with what golden eye*
> *Did life's paradise his moments greet.*
> *While the tear his mother's eye escaped,*
> *Under him the realm of shadows gaped,*
> *And the fates his thread began to sever,*
> *Earth and Heaven then vanished from his sight.*
> *From the grave-thought shrunk he in affright,*
> *Sweet the world is to the dying ever.*

There are real sobs from the crowd now. A girl crumples over her knees and a boy rubs her back absently. I scan all those lithe and youthful bodies decked in black, and think of dangerous undercurrents of misdirected, short-circuiting energy. I think of lost brothers and Ken dolls, large fingers reaching down to organize them in rows, bending the crooks of their elbows so their heads touch their palms in contrition, but their faces remain the same. My hands begin to shake.

"Air," I mumble to Teddy. And then I'm stumbling out the double doors and down the concrete steps onto Milledge Avenue, staring into a browning lawn as if the answer for this sudden burst of panic might be written in the pine straw. A car flies by, and all I see is an arm stretched out the window, trying to grasp the wind.

Inside, there's a choir of low voices. I strain to listen—a chant, a psalm, I can't be sure. And then the words fall silent.

A moment later, the doors open, and men in dark suits file onto the porch. They huddle together in tight units—all knees and elbows leaning on one another for support. This confrontation with death has wounded them, a tiny bruise on their souls—maybe life isn't a fact, but rather something that can be snatched away at any moment—but then laughter erupts from one of the groups, and I wonder if I'm only projecting these thoughts of mortality onto their line-free faces.

Teddy will linger. He'll shoulder up to Tripp, make friends with the others, ask questions, and observe responses.

I walk away from the grass-lined brick house, my sights set on Five Points in the distance. Happy memories slip through my fingers—twenty-five-cent ice cream at Hodgson's, later, coffee in a retrofitted garage, a fancy dinner on graduation night at a restaurant with sinking foundations, sandbags in front whenever it rained—all those places no longer exist. The buildings stand, but their insides have been ripped out. *Time is fleeting*, a voice whispers, *our hearts are beating funeral marches to the grave.* Whitman? Longfellow?

Tripp quoted Schiller. How many students know their classical Weimar poets offhand? I see my mother's fingers trailing books on her office shelves, withdrawing a worn copy, and passing it to Tripp like a lifeline.

The sidewalk dips and narrows, and I sidestep a portion broken by tree roots. Power lines emerge from the pines, and a fire truck disappears behind a brick building. But there are no more boys in dark suits tearing at their hair.

"Detective Kaplan," Teddy's tense, professional voice calls from somewhere far away.

I turn and realize that I've walked so far the house is almost out of view and that, despite myself, I was thinking about Craig. About the party, the one with the hunch punch, and drugs, and girls passed out on couches, everyone too drunk, too young. About the blue lights that broke the dawn early the next morning, the girl who sobbed uncontrollably, and the brothers who looked passively on. The strange turn of events that brought me to where I am now, running away from another group of Ken dolls like I'm nineteen all over again, wondering whether, if Craig hadn't convinced me to go to school and then abandoned me for his stupid fraternity, I might have done something entirely different with my life.

A part of me broke that year. It wasn't so much the thought of being alone—I was used to that—but of being left behind. And I couldn't stand the thought of seeing Craig accidentally—of turning a corner and finding myself face-to-face with him, his brothers, and everything that happened. So I moved back to Athens, completely unmoored.

It's one of those things that only becomes clear when you trace all the colors and incongruous shapes backward and see how they fit together—a through line from your present to the past. But I know for certain that had I stayed in Atlanta, had I been abroad, had I been anywhere else besides my hometown trying to pull myself together, I wouldn't have been working at a bar downtown when it happened: the triple murder on a spring afternoon.

When I close my eyes, I still see them. The crowds of people waiting for a bike race. The theater troupe attending a picnic. At first, everyone assumed it was a theatrical stunt, a prop gun, because no one could grasp that what they witnessed—the mathematics professor gunning down his wife and two community theater actors—was real. But then people from the street rushed into the bar, word spread that the city was in lockdown, and police officers in combat gear went door-to-door.

To this day, I still remember the flash of blue lights, squeezing my eyes tight, thinking, *Not again, not ever.* Forcing them open, my body to move. Hands shaking as I pulled the door shut and fumbled with the lock. I remember the smell of rubber as we hunkered down on the floor behind the long bar and listened to the shouts outside the windows. The silent tears of the mother pressed into the floor next to me, the way she buried her face in her daughter's hair, shushing her, when she was the one crying. The look in the girl's dry eyes, the smear of blood on her cheek, and the knowledge that she'd forever avoid open spaces, jump at the sound of a balloon pop, fireworks, the high shriek of laughter. That from now on the smell of Saran-wrapped sandwiches and dirty bar mats would make her sick. That there'd be a hundred people just like her, who witnessed everything, would never stop witnessing, and would never be the same. I remember phones buzzing, the way their screens lit up, the mixture of relief and fear in voices as separated people tried to connect with loved ones.

But I remember something else, too. I remember the way the detectives skirted buildings, kicked in alley doors, and asked questions—the surge of adrenaline, of purpose, in protecting the community from people who pretend they're one thing, when really, they're something entirely different. Of course, it didn't occur to me then that most days weren't occupied by murders and manhunts, but by paperwork and politics, and that those two-faced villains might be the ones holding the badge. All I knew was the way the detectives worked in tandem, communicating with signs and symbols and quick glances, the kind of nonverbal indications that told you they worked every day side by side, understood each other, all their quirks and habits—I wanted that.

Ever since Craig left me standing alone on that street corner, I felt like I'd been holding my breath. I wanted consistency, I wanted purpose. But most of all, I wanted a partner. I wanted one person in this crazy, unpredictable world whom I could trust. A partner who whistled when he was happy, who knew the rhythm of my thoughts, who stole snacks from my desk, and bought me coffee in return, and no one kept track because there would always be another day, another candy bar, another caffeine run. But I've never been good at boundaries, drawing lines in the sand, and demarcating professional from personal, partner from friend, and friend from something else, so that now, as Teddy jogs to catch up with me, I look away from him, afraid he'll see it all—every conflicted thought and needy feeling—if I meet his gaze.

Together, we turn back in the direction of the car.

Teddy was there, too, the day of the triple homicide. He saw the community band together, lift each other up, hold on to one another for support. We hadn't met yet, but that tragedy shaped both our futures. Him, throwing down his bike, forgetting the race, and helping people indoors. Me, doling out shots and free beer, trying to calm everyone's nerves. It took five days before cadaver dogs found the professor's body. Five days shuttered behind windows and locked doors, five days questioning everything we knew about professors and picnics, innocent afternoons that turn into murder and bloodshed. And by the end, both of us had signed up for training.

The hum of traffic amplifies the silence between us as we walk. In one of the smaller houses, someone is practicing a violin. A Rottweiler barks behind a fence.

"What did they seem like to you?" he asks finally. "As a group?"

I think of the way their bodies heaved and swayed—a school of fish anticipating one another's movement. One doesn't mimic the other, but they're aware of the smallest vibrations, synchronizing together. "Close," I say, and pause, listening to the violin. "It's a bit like summer camp, isn't it? Tightly formed bonds, late-night talks, all those warm feelings of being accepted, but it's impermanent. Instead of a week, it's four years, maybe five, and then you go your separate ways."

The visual trappings were there—the matching shirts and handshakes—but something in the air felt fractured, frazzled.

I think of the plain walls and plastic chairs, rigid shoulders and bared teeth behind open palms, something hungry in their faces, eyes darting back and forth. The younger ones fidgeting, unsure how to behave, taking clues from older brothers.

But then again we were there. Teddy and I, investigating the death of one of their own. It was only natural, wasn't it, for tensions to be heightened?

I stop. Something else is bothering me. A wounded animal clawing at the back of my throat, scratching the tip of my tongue.

"The lake," I say.

He lifts an eyebrow.

"At the service, Michael said he and Jay went fishing last weekend—"

"Yeah, and the stars aligned, and their friendship will last forever."

I ignore this rare bit of sarcasm and push away the thought that something about this case is getting under his skin. "But when we talked to Dr. Watanabe, she said Jay spent all weekend writing his paper. That his work showed the time he put in."

Teddy sighs. "He cheated. Had someone else write it for him so he could get drunk and go fishing."

He rolls his neck and shoulders as the sprawling brick house comes back into view. I consider him from the corner of my eye.

"She seemed pretty sure," I say.

"So he's a good fake. Fraternity houses have files of all kinds of stuff—old tests, math assignments, and there are websites where you can pay someone to write an essay for you."

I shake my head. "My mother says she can always tell when students cheat, even if she doesn't report them. The style, language, content— she's read enough student papers over the years to know the difference."

"So what? You think Jay stayed in his room writing a paper all weekend and Michael went fishing with someone else? Or he just made the whole story up?"

"I don't know. But we have two conflicting accounts of what Jay did last weekend and I want to know why."

Teddy massages the side of his jaw. "Yeah, all right," he says finally. "But Marlitt . . ."

I hunch my shoulders instinctively. "I'm fine," I say, hearing the knife-edge of defensiveness in my voice. "Really, I just needed air. All that cologne and—" I feel the whirr of the breeze, accelerating cars speeding by, snippets of voices through open windows. "Let's just figure this one out quick," I grumble. "I'm sick of Greek life already."

"But it's only the first day of rush," Teddy jokes.

"Right," I say, as I get in the car. "I won't be holding my breath for any invitations."

It's five o'clock and the light's sliding down the station windows. Truman's gone. He left a sticky note on Teddy's computer to call him with updates.

"Coffee?"

"Thank god," I say, pushing a handful of photos off my desk. "If I have to look at one more white guy with a swoop haircut in fucking Sperrys I'm going to gouge my eyes out."

Teddy ignores this, but I feel his gaze on the back of my neck. "Any identical twins?"

"They're all fucking identical," I grumble. It's not true. Not entirely, anyway, but all that conformity makes my skin crawl. "There's one or two who look close. Same build, hair color. Eyes are different, but if our witnesses just had a split second to catch his face, I could see how they could be mistaken for Jay."

"Right. Let's talk to them after dinner."

I swear Teddy orients his day around meals, even if all he has time to eat is a protein bar.

"Why not now?"

"I have a security guard coming in. Says he's got something about the frat we should know."

I must look impressed.

"What?" He raises an eyebrow. "You think you're the only one with connections around here?"

"A lot of good that did us," I say moodily. Poking around the university, talking to Jay's professors and classmates, got us nowhere. I flip over another photo—red hair, freckles, sloppy smile—not our guy.

A few minutes later, the phone rings. Amy, our seventy-year-old, will-never-retire administrative assistant with a twangy southern accent and a fondness for blue eyeliner, huffs, loudly organizing papers at the front desk and breathing wheezily into the phone pressed between her ear and shoulder. I can hear her gathering her keys, wire glasses falling down her nose as she digs through her purse on the table. And I know that every minute extra we keep her here she'll be filing for overtime. "Someone's here to see you," she accuses from the other end of the line.

"Your guy's in the lobby," I tell Teddy.

He jumps up, and I flip over the next photo. Floppy blond hair, a splattering of acne across his unlined face. Pale green polo shirt. I'm not even sure what I'm looking for anymore.

The security guard is a Black man in his late fifties, hairline receding into a widow's peak, stomach thickening a little at the middle. He's in plain clothes—slacks and a faded blue golf shirt tucked neatly in the front—and looks around the task room, unsure.

"Take a seat," Teddy says. He's playing it casual, but he's tapping his pen against the side of his leg. Whatever the guy said on the phone has piqued his interest.

"Ray Harris," the man says to me as he sits awkwardly in the school desk Teddy indicated.

Teddy pulls around his chair so they're facing each other.

"You work security for the university?"

"I did." Ray nods. "Fifteen years." His voice is rich and low, but a deep-seated weariness stretches his vowels.

"You did?" Teddy emphasizes the past tense.

"Was let go last spring."

Teddy waits, but Ray doesn't offer an explanation. A fly buzzes above our heads, trapped in the plastic casing around the fluorescent lights.

"And when you were employed by the university, what were your responsibilities?"

Ray settles a little in his chair. "As security guards, we worked together with campus police to secure buildings and residences. Some of that is just making sure windows are shut, doors are locked. But it also involves patrolling, looking for suspicious activity, and then reporting it to campus police."

"And what was your experience with the Kappa Phi Omicron fraternity? Did you ever come across Jay Kemp during your rounds?"

Ray stares at his shoes.

"Jay—no, there were never any incidents concerning Jay, although I recognized him immediately in the photo on the news. He was always at their parties."

Teddy nods and makes a note. "He was the fraternity's social chair."

"Right." Ray gazes at his thumbs.

"So you didn't come here to talk about Jay." Teddy can't hide the disappointment in his voice.

"No. Not directly. It's more—something I thought you should know about Kappa Phi Omicron, the culture of the fraternity, I guess."

"All right." Teddy sits back and folds his hands on his stomach. "What should we know?"

"Twice I witnessed physical"—Ray shifts in his chair—"altercations involving Michael Williams. One was outside the house while I was on duty. There were several young men beating up another young man in the parking lot. I intervened, but the young man, the one being beaten, said it was fine—he was laughing, hysterically almost. The whole time the others were kicking him—in the ribs, the face—they were yelling at me to get back in my car, and the boy was laughing." He shakes his head. "Michael asked for my name and department, like he was going to report me or something. I don't know if he did, but I thought, the balls on that kid, you know? Here he was beating the living daylights out of some poor guy and he wanted my information."

"So what did you do?"

Ray flexes his hands. "What could I do? I informed my supervisors and Student Life, but I don't think they did anything."

"What happened the other time?" Teddy asks.

"The other time?"

The fly's still buzzing, and I glance up irritably.

"You said you witnessed two physical altercations involving Michael Williams."

"Right, yeah, there was a second . . . occurrence." Ray takes a long breath and stirs in his seat. "You have to understand . . . after the first incident—not immediately after, some weeks had passed since I reported it, but—I was told to stay away from Greek life. To keep checking university buildings, do my rounds, but to avoid frat row. Apparently, there'd been reports that I was"—his lips knit, and he looks away from me—"leering at the sorority girls. Driving by in my car. Sitting outside during parties. Making them uncomfortable. One report even said I was—"

I turn my body away as if to give him privacy, but he stares at a point above our heads.

"—masturbating in my car while the girls were sunbathing outside their house."

"Were you?" I ask in a neutral tone.

A flicker of anger, but then, a sigh. Resigned, a little sad even.

"Of course not. I tried to talk to some of the brothers during the days after the first fight—the ones who were standing around, not participating or jeering the others on—about intervening when it got too violent. Framed it like if I knew they could be counted on, I wouldn't have to drop by as much. Seemed like a win-win to me." Bewildered shake of the head. "Then two girls called—different sororities—with more or less the same complaint. And I was told to stay away."

I bite the underside of my lip. I imagine Michael's winning smile as he convinces the girls to call, getting them to think they're doing the world a favor, reporting a sexual predator. Using the small social progress in people believing victims for a change for his own agenda, and the girls blindly going along.

"But you didn't." Teddy nods in approval.

Ray looks at his hands.

"I did mostly, but—I knew there were things going on. How could I not? If something happened—" He sighs. "So I still drove by, later, on the weekends—you know, when they'd have their big blow-outs—and in my own vehicle, so they wouldn't know it was campus security. I never got out of the car. Even when it was clear there was underage drinking— girls stumbling, guys vomiting on the sidewalk—I stayed in my car."

"And Michael?"

"He was there—always—in the center of everything. I swear, some-times, I could hear his voice—it's really distinct, you know?—yelling to drink, dance, fuck—later at home, in my dreams."

I could hear him, too—his slow, purposeful drawl, amused by every-one else's inferiority. Shouting firm, not-to-be-disobeyed instructions.

"And then one night, I saw him run out of the house with a woman on his shoulders. He was laughing—she wasn't. And he dropped her—like she was a sack of potatoes—down the front stairs. And I," he swallows, "I stayed in the car. I waited, and she was just lying there—" His voice cracks and he takes a second to collect himself. "I thought—this is it. He's finally killed someone. And I did nothing to stop it. There was a small crowd around her—I don't think the others even noticed. They were still drinking and yelling in the yard. But I could see her through the gap in the group. Af-ter a while, she rolled onto her side and vomited. And they all . . . cheered." He shakes his head. "I called nine-one-one—pretended I was an annoyed neighbor, noise complaint, but then said I had seen a girl lying unconscious in front of the house. I hope that got her some medical attention, but I don't know. When I drove away another guy was carrying her back inside."

He doesn't say it, but he doesn't need to. Unconscious and semicon-scious girls don't get tucked neatly into bed in some vacant room. There are Facebook accounts and Snapchats full of naked, barely breathing girls with crude comments of what vile frat bro X did to barely breathing girl Y and asking who else wants a turn.

Ray looks like he's aged a decade since Teddy started the interview. "Do you think you could check on the girl? See if any reports came in that night? Or that morning?"

"We can do that," Teddy says. "Do you remember the date?"

"Yeah," Ray winces. "I do."

Teddy writes it down. The chances she wound up getting medical care or filing a report are about zero to none, and I think deep down Ray must know this, but he allows himself to be reassured.

He shifts in his chair, glances between me and Teddy. "You're proba-bly aware of this already, but—they're all well connected. And they think they're above the law. I'm not saying they killed Jay Kemp, or anything. Honestly, most of what I've seen was at night and involved a good bit of alcohol. But they don't like their autonomy questioned. If you start digging around," he looks at Teddy meaningfully, "I would be prepared for some hassle."

I glance at Teddy's head bent over his notes. That line around his mouth is back. The fly's stopped buzzing, and all I can hear is the steady murmur of the heating system and that electric current humming some-where deep beneath our feet.

| Five |

The look-alike fraternity brothers don't resemble Jay nearly as much in person. They came in late last night—our desks were still littered with folded, waxed boxes of Chinese takeout—and they both had alibis: 9:00 A.M. classes, which they swear they attended. One was in a biology lecture. The building's south of Sanford Stadium; and in theory, if he drove and parked his car in one of the neighboring lots, he could have snuck out of class early and zipped down Lumpkin with enough speed to murder our victim. But he swears the professor always lets out class late, and he met his girlfriend right after to walk her to her next class. All easy enough to check, and he's so moonfaced and intrigued by our questions that the level of strategy involved in this theory seems much too complex. The other was in a chemistry lab. The buildings are more or less side by side, but neither one saw the other. Jay-look-alike number two had a midterm and said he was one of the last to finish. The TA let him stay ten minutes after. I give her a call, and she confirms, so he's out, too, officially eliminating our only lead.

"I think the witnesses just saw Jay's reflection on the windshield as he somersaulted over the car," I say to Teddy as he passes me a cup of coffee.

He gives a warning look.

"Too soon?"

"We still need to talk with Jay's roommate. He hasn't returned any of my calls. I get the impression from Tripp that he and his girlfriend have set up a little love nest on the south side. He didn't bother to go to the memorial service, and they're not answering the door to anyone, but," he flashes a grin, "I think we should drop by to see if they're in."

"Great," I say. "Address?"

He pulls out his phone. "Tripp just texted it to me."

"He's texting you?"

"Ah, yes, Tripp's been very helpful. I did some digging. I was wrong about the money. He's on scholarship. Mom's an elementary school teacher. His sister has cerebral palsy. Did you know that?"

I shake my head. "Is this relevant?"

"Probably not, just thought it explained his helpfulness."

"Right," I say, not sure it explains anything at all.

From the outside, the love nest doesn't look like much. It's an older condominium. Nothing like the glossy new builds north of campus. This one's near the bowling alley and the nature preserve, past a collection of flat-faced two-story brick buildings with striped awnings—a cream structure in a cul-de-sac that faces a marsh.

"Which one is it?" I ask as we get out of the car.

"Top left." Teddy indicates the building nearest us, connected by a staircase and breezeway.

"Right, let's see if we can't get them out of bed."

We knock long enough that the downstairs neighbor—white guy, shaved head, wearing basketball shorts and nothing else—comes out to yell at us. At the sight of our badges, he disappears back into his apartment real quick, and I resist the urge to follow him.

He must have given them a heads-up that we're outside and not going anywhere, because a minute later there's movement behind the wall.

"Can I help you?"

The door's a sliver ajar. Behind it, the woman's flushed faced but glaring at us defiantly from an overlarge T-shirt that barely covers her thighs. Teddy looks away, but I'm unfazed. If she wants to talk to us in her underwear, that's fine by me.

"We need to speak with Cade Abernathy."

"He lives at Kap-O."

"Yes, but he hasn't slept there in two weeks," I say patiently. "We were there yesterday afternoon."

She blinks, and we both take out our badges.

"Samantha Barron?"

She flinches, just a quick twinge of her mouth, but I see it.

"Is this about Jay?"

"Yes."

She waits for me to say more, but I don't.

A glance over her shoulder down a dark hallway. "Just, um, give me a minute, okay?" And she shuts the door in our faces.

"One minute," I say to Teddy. "That's all she gets."

I turn to the iron railing and look over the manicured bushes that line the sidewalk. From there, the asphalt slopes into a pale curb overgrown with weeds and long grass and then a sunken pond. It's peaceful, and for a moment, I think I understand why—beyond the pants-less Samantha—Cade would prefer this place to the fraternity house. A heron stands in the marsh, so still that I almost miss him. But I let my eyes sharpen and bring him into focus against the green-gray backdrop.

"Hey."

I whip around.

Cade is tall with dark tousled hair and large, black-rimmed glasses above a band T-shirt and dark jeans. He's broad shouldered and handsome in a Clark Kent kind of way, like at any moment he might rip his shirt off and run somewhere to save the day. Behind him, Samantha smirks as if she's read my thoughts.

"Mr. Abernathy," Teddy says. "We'd like to talk to you about your roommate Jay Kemp."

"Right." Cade runs his hand over his face and looks down at Samantha, who's curled herself beneath his arm. "Okay if they come in?"

"Great," I say, before Samantha can answer, and they shuffle backward out of the doorway.

Inside, it's cozy and clean. To the left is a living area with two couches and a television, to the right a small dining table and a galley kitchen. Straight ahead is a long hallway. The door at the end is open, and a soft light reveals a bed in a state of disarray—sheets flung to one side, pillow shoved against the wall, a gold comforter thrown across the edge.

My stomach does a small flip, and a yearning, deep and unsettling, passes through my skin. Teddy seems to sense it—although I hope not what I'm actually feeling—and clears his throat.

"Shall we sit?" he asks, and turns to the couches rather than the table. His tone suggests this is just a nice comfortable chat. Nothing serious. They follow him and choose the smaller of the two sofas, Samantha still glued under Cade's shoulder.

Teddy sits in the middle of the longer couch with his legs spread, leaning toward them over his knees. I perch on the edge, farther away. Everything about Teddy's body language is telling me he thinks he should handle this one.

"Right, so you know why we're here."

Slight nods from both.

"On Tuesday morning at five past ten, Jay Kemp was hit by a vehicle while crossing the Lumpkin-Baxter Street crosswalk. The vehicle fled the scene, and Jay died shortly after impact."

A small intake of breath from Samantha, and she looks up worriedly into Cade's face. I think, meanly, that she would love it if he started crying.

"We're talking with everyone who knew Jay and have spoken to many of your brothers already, as well as Jay's professors and classmates"—this receives a small snort from Cade—"and we need to ask you some general questions about Jay, but first, can you tell us where you were Tuesday morning?"

"What—he's not a suspect?" A glare of wounded outrage from Samantha that reminds me strangely of my childhood cat whenever we shut her in the laundry room at night.

"I was here," Cade says, gesturing down the hall toward the bedroom, and, god help him, he blushes.

"From what time?"

Cade scratches his head. "Five or six the night before, until," he looks at Samantha, "now, I guess."

Oh lord, I think. This means the love birds haven't left their nest in three days.

"And can anyone confirm?" Teddy asks.

"I can." Samantha laughs, a little giddily.

"Anyone else?"

"What," Samantha smirks, "like, a threesome or something?"

"Do you have roommates?"

Her mouth forms an O, but she doesn't look embarrassed.

"Yes, two. Chloë and Alex."

"Were either of them home Tuesday morning?"

She shakes her head slowly. "I don't think so." A glance at Cade for confirmation. And then, "Actually, I remember hearing the door, maybe around nine thirty? I remember because I thought, well, if everyone was gone we could—" Another look at Cade and his flush deepens. "I'm kind of loud." It bursts from her, and Cade's clearly mortified, but she's gauging Teddy's and my reaction. We don't give her one.

"Okay, we can confirm with your roommate. Which one do you think that was?"

She looks disappointed by our lack of response. "I don't know." Her eyes flicker to the door. "Probably Alex. She's always forgetting shit, getting to the car, and having to run back in. I'm pretty sure I heard the door slam a couple times."

"Great. Thanks. That will help a lot." Teddy smiles, and Cade shifts, drawing her closer.

"Okay." Teddy sits back. "What can you tell us about Jay?"

A tightening, bracing movement from Samantha.

"You didn't like him?" I ask. Teddy's eyes flicker to me.

"He was an asshole."

Was. She's already relegated him to the past.

"Really?" I say, letting surprise inflect my voice although this doesn't surprise me at all. "All the guys say he was great, a really wonderful guy."

Her whole face has hardened while I'm speaking, but then it freezes, and I see in her eyes that she's realized if she's the only one who thinks he's an asshole, she might have just moved herself onto our suspect list.

I decide to back off. Teddy waits, and when I don't push it, he turns to Cade. "Is that why you don't sleep at the house anymore? Jay was an asshole?"

"No, I mean"—a slight twisting of Samantha under his arm—"he was a slob. You saw our room, right? Clothes, beer cans, and hash everywhere." I look at Teddy; so someone had cleaned up before we got there. "He would leave dip cups all over the place and they would start to mold. I have"—Cade pushes up his glasses—"allergies, and it was making me sick living there." I think somewhere back home, there's a mother who rushed to grab his inhaler and put her palm to his forehead whenever he so much as sniffled.

"So not an asshole?"

Another twist from Samantha.

"No. I mean he had some strange ideas about our rituals and brotherhood rights—"

"Strange ideas?" Samantha has completely untangled herself and almost jumped to the opposite side of the couch. She pulls her leg away, so no parts of their bodies are touching anymore. "He thought you should *share* me. Like I was your property—Kap-O property. And not just with him but with all the brothers. What kind of sick bullshit is that?"

She's looking at me now, furious, but also for validation.

"What the hell?" I say, matching her anger and directing it at Cade.

"Right? I mean . . ." Samantha wraps her arm around her leg, hugging it tightly to her chest. "I don't get the whole fraternity 'we share a code and a brain and have lame secret handshakes like six-year-olds with a no-girls-allowed clubhouse,' but that's whatever, you know?" She rolls her eyes. "Sharing girlfriends so they can be Eskimo brothers or something, and we have no say in the matter? Fuck that." She's on the edge of the couch now, body turned completely away from Cade, and talking directly to us. I think I'm starting to like her after all.

Cade has drawn into himself, eyes on the ground, warding off her words like blows, but not defending himself—or Jay, for that matter—either.

"Is that true?" I ask with a hint of accusation.

"It was mostly"—he squirms, pressing himself into the corner of the couch for support—"just talk, you know? We're brothers, we should share everything. It would make us closer."

"Yeah—every-*thing*." She spits at him. "Because he thinks girls are *objects*."

"Well, he changed his mind anyway."

I raise my eyebrow. "About sleeping with Samantha?"

She purses her lips, but her eyes are fire. *Don't talk about me like I'm not here*, her face reads.

"No—well, kind of." He pauses. "But he didn't think it was such a good idea once he had his own girlfriend."

"Jay had a girlfriend?" Teddy asks. "We heard he was more of a ladies' man."

An exaggerated eye roll from Samantha.

"He is—was, I mean—all last year—yeah. That was before I met Sam," a small glance her way, but she glares resolutely at the opposite wall, "and every other night almost, I had to find somewhere else to sleep. Eventually I just kept my pillow and a blanket in one of the cabinets in the rec room, so I could crash on the sofa, which sucked, because

ACOP

GEN

52848xxxxxxx

xxxxxxxx

Exb: 5171/5115

52080102380425

Item: 00101023804...

MYSTERY NOSSET

Printed: Saturday, February 10, 2024

some of the brothers would be up all night watching sports or playing darts," he pushes up his glasses, "and I had an eight A.M. on Monday, Wednesday, Friday." He shakes his head. "But then he met Katie."

A flash of something. "Katie Coleman?"

"Yeah," Cade breathes, not at all surprised, like everyone should know her name.

"The Kap-O dream girl," I remind Teddy.

Another eye roll from Samantha, and a nod from Cade.

"Then, he wasn't so big on sharing. So he kept it a secret."

"A secret? Why?" I'm rearranging my opinion of Jay again—from everything we've heard, I would have expected him to shout it from the rooftops.

"Probably for the same reason. The sharing thing—that was his rule, you know? So he couldn't exactly say, 'just kidding, changed my mind, and now Katie's with me—and only me.' He'd been adamant, you know? Like, if you didn't share, you were betraying the brotherhood."

Betraying brothers, I think, *where have I heard that before?*

"And Katie, she was"—he gets a dreamy look, but then notices Samantha glaring at him from the corner of his eye—"a lot of guys were into her."

"So that's why you stay here?" Teddy asks. But before Cade can answer, he turns to Samantha. "I imagine," he says softly, "you don't feel too safe at that house."

Samantha nods. The fury is gone, and something a little hurt has crept into her face. Cade, I think, must have never put two and two together. What being at the house would have been like for Samantha. All the brothers just waiting for their chance, feeling entitled even. I bet she never accepted a drink from any of them and locked Cade's door at night. But if Jay was in the room?

"What about Michael?" Teddy asks.

Something shifts in Cade's face.

"What about him?"

"We've had reports that he could be violent."

For a moment, Cade closes his eyes, and I wonder what he sees, but then he shakes his head. "I don't remember anything like that."

Liar, I think. And then, *Why?*

"Did any of the other brothers know that Jay was with Katie?"

Cade sighs and rubs a hand over his face. "I don't know. I haven't been there much this year. After—" Another look at Samantha, but she's still not meeting his gaze. "Anyway, I pretty much only go to mandatory stuff so I don't get kicked out, but I think, I don't know," a small shrug, "I think I might not renew my dues next year."

"Really?" A hopeful, almost loving glance from Samantha.

Cade smiles. "I think I've outgrown them." A flicker of something in Cade's voice. Defiance? Sadness? Love? I can't tell, but Samantha's back in his arms in a flash. I can almost hear her—*You'd do that for me?*—but she doesn't say it. She just beams at him.

Teddy clears his throat. "Thanks, you've both been really helpful. I'll just—"

They're kissing now, short little bursts, but only increasing in intensity.

"Right, I'll leave my card here." He puts his card on the coffee table. "Give me a call if you think of anything else."

And we're out the door as quickly as can be. From the corner of my eye, I see a streak of a T-shirt thrown in our direction.

We're both giggling as we race down the stairs and back to the parking lot.

"I mean—" Teddy laughs, casting a furtive glance back at the condo, "they could barely wait 'til we—" He catches my eye. Looks down.

Something tightens in my chest, but I grin. "Right?"

He's still chuckling as he starts the car, but it's forced. The glee gone out of it.

"Next up," I say when he throws it in reverse, "Katie Coleman."

As we pull out of the cul-de-sac, I look to the marsh and then to the upstairs window: the heron's gone, but the curtain flaps in the breeze.

W hat do you think?" Teddy asks as we drive past clusters of red-brick buildings. It's still early, and the wind sends brown and yellow leaves swirling ahead of us.

"About Cade?" I stretch my fingers and stare out the passenger window. Pine trees slice through blue and green Craftsman cottages. A group of shirtless young men in matching shorts jog in a cluster up the sidewalk, arms punching, yelling to be heard above their own breaths, the cars, and the tap-tap-tap of 808s.

I lean my head back. "Not our guy." I sigh. "Too preoccupied—I'd say right now he only has one thing on his mind, and it's not running over his roommate."

"Maybe." Teddy drums his fingers on the steering wheel. "Or maybe the whole girlfriend-sharing thing pissed him off. Or maybe Jay actually tried something with Sam."

"They could both be in on it," I offer, "provide each other alibis. Even if the roommate was there—she wouldn't know for sure Cade was in the bedroom . . ." I imagine Samantha faking sex noises and laugh.

Teddy grins, too. "Seems like a lot of effort though for two people who'd rather be—you know . . ."

I meet his gaze and look away.

"Did you catch his face when he talked about the dream girl?" I ask, keeping my eyes on the side window.

Teddy nods and signals, veering left onto to Milledge. "Could be pissed—especially if the brothers had been hassling Samantha, and then Jay's all about changing the rules."

I hadn't thought of that. "Yeah, Samantha, too. Could she talk Cade into murder, you think?"

"Could have—especially if Katie was getting special treatment all of a sudden."

"Yeah, and I've seen that look before—the dreamy dream girl look—on Tripp." I sigh. "But this is all assuming the hit-and-run was premeditated. First the person would have to steal Jay's car—which I suppose Cade could do pretty easily since they were roommates. He would just have to swipe his keys. But if that's the case, so could most of the brothers. But still—they'd have to know Jay would be by the student learning center around ten A.M., that he would step out into the intersection at just that moment. If anything—if it was intentional—it was a crime of passion. The guy wasn't planning it, but saw Jay, and then, bam—thought, *Here's an opportunity*. So maybe Samantha planted the seed, and Cade saw him, and remembered Jay and the whole thing with Sam and Katie Coleman, but, yeah," I shift in my seat, "I'm not convinced."

Every year, there are around two thousand hit-and-run fatalities in the US, and most perpetrators—if they're caught—get soft sentences or plea bargains. *It wasn't my fault. I didn't mean to. I wasn't paying attention*—never mind that there's a dad lying dead in the street who'll never see his kids again. A girl who'll never hug her parents. But if we can prove intent? Then maybe, just maybe, there'll be justice.

I chew on my fingernail, thinking of Samantha and Cade, Jay and Katie. "What do you think of all this secret girlfriend business? I mean fall semester started, when? Two months ago?"

"Two and a half."

"Right, so Jay meets Katie and what? He's in love? Suddenly talking about changing his own rules, and then willing to *betray the brotherhood*, if he buys into his own nonsense."

Teddy rubs his face. "I don't know. When you're that age—two months can seem like a lifetime."

"They're in college," I say, "not middle school."

He frowns. "Remember when Josie was dating that idiot skateboarder?

What was the kid's name? Chad or Chaz, something only a half-baked moron would call himself."

I roll my eyes at my reflection in the car window. His name was Charlie, but Teddy always insisted on getting it wrong. Behind the glare, a handful of students wait at the bus stop, earbuds in, staring at their phones. Teddy's overprotectiveness of his sisters is mostly endearing but occasionally insufferable. I hear Josie's voice: *I can take care of myself, thank you.*

"I remember." We caught them making out behind his mother's back porch once.

"Yeah, well," he says, and then slams on the brakes. He lays on the horn as a guy in red-and-black basketball shorts shoulders his bag and shuffles across the street. "I should arrest him for jaywalking," Teddy murmurs, glaring at the kid through the windshield. "You know what irritates me?" he asks, forgetting about Josie for a moment. "These kids think they're invincible."

"You sound like Truman."

"Wait—hear me out. So they think they're the only ones who can screw up, you know? Like, take basketball shorts over there"—he points to the kid now disappearing in the rearview mirror—"he knows he shouldn't do that, right, walk out in front of a moving vehicle? But he thinks he's the only one doing something wrong. He doesn't realize that I could be drunk, texting, yelling at my kids in the back seat. A whole number of things might distract me so that I'm not paying attention. I might be a crazy lunatic who decides that today's the day I end a life. He takes for granted that everyone around him is doing the right thing, and so it's no big deal if he messes up."

"Uh-huh," I say, watching another group of young people dart across the street ahead of us. "And what does this have to do with Katie and true love?"

"Nothing." He rubs his jaw. "It's just irritating, you know? Their complete lack of awareness. Josie was devastated after she and Chad-Chaz broke up. Cried for weeks. Said she had imagined a whole future with him. Buying a house, kids, even sitting on their front porch as old people in rocking chairs, for god's sake. Guess how long they'd been together?"

I look at him.

"No really, guess."

"Two months?"

"Five weeks. Five. But she'd already had enough time to imagine a whole lifetime with the guy."

"Dodged a bullet there," I say, stretching my arms above my head. Josie went to Emory and now works for Doctors Without Borders. Charlie works at a vape store or something. "And she was in high school," I remind him.

"She was seventeen. You really think that much changes in a year or two if you're in college, living with a dozen other kids just like you, Mommy and Daddy paying for everything, and all you have to do is show up for class?" A hint of bitterness there, but I don't push it. Teddy's dad died when he was nine; his mother would move mountains for him and his sisters, but money was always tight.

"Murder for love—poetic, I guess."

Teddy pulls the car alongside a beautiful white stucco house elevated a dozen or so feet above Milledge Avenue.

"Gamma Delta Alpha Delta, right?"

"Jesus—say that ten times fast."

| Six |

L ike Jay, Katie lives at her sorority house. Cast-iron railings and columns weave slender black webs up and down the double porches. It's a historic landmark—built for one of Georgia's first millionaires, and lived in by several others, before it was sold to Gamma Delta in the '80s. With its white paint and black shutters, the building reminds me of a plump zebra. As a child, I always wanted to live in that house—whenever we drove by, I pressed my face to the passenger window and imagined it was full of secret rooms hidden behind bookshelves and large fireplaces you could walk into. I didn't know about the handfuls of women who rotated in and out of the house every few years, the socials, and statistics. I just knew I loved the idea of it. The easy way my imagination could fill it with magic wardrobes and hidden passageways.

Teddy looks impressed in a way it's clear he hasn't given the house a second thought until now. But standing in front of the small fountain and double front staircase, the sounds of traffic ebbing behind him, he blinks at the white building towering over Milledge.

We pass two girls lying in the sloping yard, sharing a pair of headphones. Golden chrysanthemums and pale purple asters bloom in flower beds on either side of them. They're wrapped in a plaid blanket and don't look up when we near. I'm alarmed by their vulnerability, their implicit trust that we—two strangers approaching a few feet away—won't do them harm.

At the edge of the grass, a wooden stage is set up for some kind of
event. There's an empty popcorn machine, and painted road signs with
songs about destinations—LA WOMAN, VIVA LAS VEGAS, SWEET HOME ALA-
BAMA, DEVIL WENT DOWN TO GEORGIA—pointing in various directions, not
linked to the places on the signs at all. ALABAMA points north. LAS VEGAS
points east.

At the door, I catch Teddy's eye. Most of the time, he's better with
witnesses, but if something happened to Katie—if Jay couldn't control
his brothers, or hadn't, in fact, changed his mind about sharing like Cade
said, then Teddy needs to disappear into the wallpaper or behind some
long curtains quick so I can hear what she has to say.

There's a lull in the noisy stream of cars. He nods, and I take a deep
breath.

Inside, a chandelier shimmers and drips from the ceiling like a Dickens
wedding cake. A black spiral staircase snakes upward and disappears in
the shadows behind it. There's mail and cardboard packages on an entry
table, surrounding a vase overflowing with flowers. Double doors open
into a sitting room full of pillows, extra blankets folded in a basket, gold-
framed mirrors, and blue-and-white vases. Everything is pale—pale pink,
pale blue, pale yellow—but there are heavy, mahogany-stained antique
cabinets and side tables, giving the room the impression of a nineteenth-
century salon. Our footsteps echo loudly on the hardwoods, and I have
the feeling we're sneaking around uninvited and someone might call the
police before I remember—we are the police. I almost smile, but then I
hear heavy footsteps and a forceful southern drawl.

"Can I help you?"

The woman in the doorway is in her early sixties, platinum-dyed hair,
wearing white capris and a pink blouse that floats around her thickening
midsection. She stares at Teddy, pulls a phone from her pocket, and then
she turns to me. I can tell she's not reassured by my presence. But before
she can say whatever thinly veiled racist or condescending thought is
forming on her lips, I withdraw my badge.

"I'm Detective Kaplan and this is Detective White. We need to speak with Katie Coleman," I say as we walk back to the foyer.

She takes a deep breath and steps forward to inspect my badge like it might be fake. I wonder if she knows what she's looking for. I doubt it. But she raises an eyebrow at Teddy, so he pulls his out, too, and she nods to herself like she's satisfied.

"I'm Trudy Walton, the house mom here at Gamma Delta Alpha Delta."

Up close, she smells of tea leaves and lavender. She examines the vase on the center table and rubs a flower petal between her thumb and forefinger. "Katie's in her room. Says she has a migraine. She hasn't left since we heard about that poor boy at Kappa Phi Omicron. She's not talking to anyone."

She eyes the pair of us like if her sisters can't get her to talk, then we won't either.

I nod sympathetically. *We've all had our hearts broken*, my look says, *I remember what it was like to be eighteen, nineteen, however old Katie is.*

"I understand," I say. "We wouldn't be here if it wasn't important."

Trudy purses her lips, and a wry smile appears. If there's a house mom gossip train, she'll have the best seat of the year.

We follow her up the stairs, and I notice she takes them gingerly—one hand on the railing at all times.

At the top is a full-length mirror. I imagine a handful of girls reflected back at me—checking their outfits one last time before breakfast, their chapter meetings, or maybe even a date with Jay Kemp.

There are two hallways with doors down either side of the landing. I hear humming and the whirring of a hair dryer, a one-sided phone conversation, and canned sitcom laughter.

"Most of the girls are in class, but Katie's this way." Trudy gestures to the hallway on the right.

We pass an open door. Inside are two twin beds. The drawers underneath brim with cotton underwear and stiff, colorful T-shirts. There's a dream catcher above one bed, a poster of Audrey Hepburn above the other—*Breakfast at Tiffany*'s attire, blowing blue bubble gum. But Trudy continues walking.

She stops in front of a closed door. Soft gray light shines through the crack above the floorboard, but there's no indication anyone's inside.

"Katie, honey." Trudy knocks stiffly. "There are some people here to see you." A muffled sound between a sigh and a hiccup. Trudy knocks again, and when there's no answer, she arches an eyebrow at us.

"We can escort her down to the station or we can talk to her here," I say.

Trudy takes a long moment, getting the shape of me, whether or not I'm serious and whether or not she should insist I come back with a warrant.

I can see every true crime TV show she's watched and cozy mystery she's read flash under her eyelids, while she tries to remember if there's a protocol for this. What happens if she refuses? Aiding and abetting, she thinks, but then—that can't be right. Obstruction, but she doesn't even know why we're here.

She withdraws a key ring from her pocket.

"I don't like to open the doors without the girls' permission, but since this is an emergency . . ." She lets the word dangle. We say nothing.

Knocks again. "All right Katie, I'm coming in." A pause. No movement inside. She slips the key in the lock.

Katie's room is bright. The lights are off, but the drawn white curtains at the far end do little to prevent the day from streaming through. String bulbs drape from the ceiling. There's a white-lattice bedside table with matching cream lamps, fresh hydrangeas in a Mason jar, everything soft and delicate, more pillows and blankets than any one person could ever need, a purple rug on top of thin cream-colored carpet. It's dream-chic, like something out of an Anthropologie catalog. The desks on opposite sides of the wall are littered with photographs and sheets of notepaper, a book held open by a stuffed owl, a porcelain bowl overflowing with loose change, lacy bras hanging off the knobs.

There's a lump under the pale covers of the twin bed on the left side of the wall. It stirs at the sound of our footsteps.

"Katie," I say softly. "We need to ask you a few questions," I pause, "about Jay Kemp."

A gasping sound from beneath the covers, and then something that sounds suspiciously like "Who?"

"We need to talk to you about Jay."

A muffled "I don't know anyone named . . . Jay."

I look back at Teddy in the doorway, and then at Trudy, who's hovering just behind him in the hall.

"Katie," I say patiently, "you're this year's dream girl. Don't you know all the brothers at Kap-O?"

A movement that could be a nod or a head shake, I can't tell.

"I know this is hard," I say in my best bedside voice, "but I need you to sit up and talk to us."

There's a sigh as something unfurls beneath the blankets.

Katie doesn't look anything like the bright-eyed, smiling girl framed in the Kap-O hallway. Her hair's matted and pulled back into what yesterday might have been a ponytail but today is plastered in all directions around her neck. Her face is blotchy, the tip of her nose raw, and I suddenly understand the phrase "to cry your heart out." She's crumpled over on her bed like she's got nothing left.

Teddy and I exchange glances.

Sometimes we're cruel on purpose, slamming down photos of a man's dead wife, gray skin, face bruised, lip split open, just to see his reaction, and especially if he has a history. But this, trying to talk to Katie, is going to require a delicate hand.

"Now let's start again. Did you know Jay Kemp?"

A tiny, hoarse whisper. "Yes."

"Where did you meet?"

Her eyes float around the room. "I don't remember. Maybe at a party." Voice scraped, low and raw.

Not love at first sight then.

"And when was this?"

A stir, thinking. "Around the beginning of the semester. There were a lot of socials . . ."

I wait, but she doesn't say more.

"Okay, when did you start dating?"

A startled glance at me and then a small head shake. "We weren't dat-ing," she says flatly. Her green eyes are glassy, and she draws her arms up around her knees and pulls them to her chest.

"Katie"—the nurse act is wearing on me, but I try to keep it out of my voice—"you're not in trouble. We just need to know if Jay told you any-thing. If he was acting strange the last few weeks. Or if he said something to you about his brothers—maybe being mad at him."

A twitch of her eyelid but then she resumes the empty stare, and when I wait, holding her gaze, she shakes her head.

"I didn't know him that well," she murmurs. "He wouldn't have told me anything like that." Her eyes are going glassy again, and she's return-ing to some internal place, fingers fidgeting with her blanket.

"It's okay," I say quickly, trying to draw her back. "We know about the girlfriend-sharing thing. If you're worried about the other brothers finding out—"

"What girlfriend-sharing thing?" Her voice is dull, but her eyes flicker to me and then the hallway. Behind her head, the glass shudders against the fall wind.

"Miss Trudy," I call without looking away from Katie's face. "Would you mind giving us a moment alone?"

Katie flinches, and Trudy mumbles something about a man in a girl's room, but I hear her footsteps recede toward the stairs. I have a prickly feeling, one that tells me she's marching off to make phone calls, so I stand and shove the curtains away, glance at the street below, and then turn to get a good look at Katie and to figure out what we're dealing with.

"No," Katie murmurs. "Migraine."

Backlit by the midday light, she's pale. Her lips are purplish and chapped, and I think maybe she's telling the truth. Maybe not a migraine, but she's so upset she's made herself ill.

Teddy steps closer.

"We just need you to answer a few questions," he says softly. "And then we'll let you go back to sleep."

A faint smile. "Sleep," she repeats. Her eyelids begin to flutter.

I want to tell her that sleep's only a Band-Aid. That eventually, she'll have to open her eyes and deal with the fact that Jay's gone. No matter how far her dreams take her, she'll always have to return—to this room, to this campus, to a world without Jay.

"Katie." I lean in. "How well do you know the other brothers at Kap-O?"

She shrugs.

"Do you know Tripp Holmes?"

A small, confused nod.

"Were he and Jay friends?"

She squeezes her eyes tight. "I think so." A small, hoarse whisper.

"What about Michael Williams?"

If I hadn't been scrutinizing her face, I would have missed it. But she flinches.

"I don't know."

"Do you have any reason to think that maybe someone was mad at Jay? That anyone might want to hurt him?"

My back's to Teddy, but I can feel him moving around—unobtrusively flipping through pages of the book on her desk, staring at the posters on her wall, like he's bored and wants to get this over with. Finding a love note from Jay would be helpful, but too obvious. He must know this but is looking anyway.

Her eyes fix on the book in his hands.

"*The Life of Calvin Coolidge*," she says.

"What?" I ask, annoyed at Teddy for the distraction.

"It's for my final paper," she tells us, and then something like panic flashes across her face. "The rough draft's due tomorrow." She presses her hands to her stomach and doubles over.

"Katie?"

Her whole body begins to tremble, and she takes short, shallow breaths.

"I can't do it," she says, eyes round. "It's too much. I can't—can't breathe."

Her hands shake.

"Katie," I repeat, trying to be as calm as possible, "I think you're having a panic attack."

Her eyes widen. Her breaths turn into gasps.

"There's nothing to be afraid of. Have you had these before?"

A weak nod between inhales.

"Do you take any medication—"

Frantic head shake.

"It's okay. You're absolutely fine. You're safe. I'm right here. I'll help you through this. Just breathe. Can you take a deep breath? A little longer? Okay, now let it out, slowly."

I sit next to her on the bed. Teddy's at her desk. He's looking at me curiously—surprised, I think, by my patience. But my dad has panic attacks sometimes, and I know irritation only makes them worse. Katie's breaths are still shallow, but they're lengthening.

"I barely knew him," she says finally, with her eyes on the wall. And then in a small voice, "I swear."

My phone buzzes, and I look down to silence it when I see it's Truman. Shit.

I gesture to Teddy, *Sit with her*. He looks from me to the bed and frantically shakes his head.

"I'll be right outside," I tell Katie. *Truman*, I mouth.

"Kaplan," I say loudly as I head out the door.

"I don't know what the two of you are thinking," Truman growls in my ear, "but I want you both back here—now."

"But we just—"

"Fifteen minutes, in my office." The phone clicks.

I roll my head from side to side. On the opposite wall there's a bulletin board for announcements. Colorful papers advertise upcoming lecture series and tutor opportunities. A psychology study. A party for Kap-O the week after Thanksgiving.

"Thanks, Katie," I say, peeking my head in from the hall. "That's all for now." I don't tell her she's been a great help, because as far as I'm concerned this has been a colossal waste of time.

"If you remember anything that might be useful, here's my card." Teddy steps forward, but keeps his distance, hand outstretched.

In the hall, there's the sound of footsteps.

"Time to go," I murmur to Teddy, not wanting to give Trudy the pleasure of escorting us out.

As we leave, something flickers in the corner of my eye. I turn quickly to catch it, but nothing's there. The feeling stays even as we run down the steps to the car. The sky's darkening and the girls on the lawn are gone, but something creeps up the back of my neck. I gaze back at the house, trying to determine which room is Katie's, and see a wisp of auburn hair in the third window of the second floor. In spite of myself, I calculate the distance from the frame to the ground. I think of Katie's migraine, her gasps for breath, the panic attack—was that real? Or was she trying to get rid of us?

"I don't suppose we have time for lunch," Teddy says when we reach the car.

"Not unless you want Truman to feed it to us."

He grunts as he starts the engine.

Teddy hates when I drive, says I'm too distracted. I prefer observant, but he has a point. He's better at following traffic rules; I'm better at choosing the music and watching the coeds on the sidewalk. When I was in training, a guy boasted he could spot everything from your run-of-the-mill tweaker to your wife beater and psychopath with less than a glance out the passenger window. "It's the way a guy walks," he said. "Just one look tells you he's up to no good." I'd only been there two weeks, but I already knew his type—the way his breath quickened when he talked about patrol, keeping his neighborhood safe. He was itching to put hand-cuffs on the first guy who looked at him sideways. "Really?" I asked, all curious. "I heard you were supposed to measure the bumps on his skull." He avoided me from then on. But that's the problem. Too many cops drive around looking for people to arrest, acting on biases, and false assumptions like a limp means someone's holding and a hoodie means they're hiding something. But it's the clean-cut boys with bruises on their knuckles and drugs in their pockets that worry me. The men who know no one's looking for them and think they won't get caught.

Teddy sighs.

"What?" I ask.

"I just keep thinking—Katie's room felt so different than Jay's."

I nod. I felt it, too, all the cutsey decorations, the pillows, blankets, soft lamplight—everything designed to mimic the comforts of home.

"It felt . . . permanent somehow. Where Jay's felt—"

"Yeah, I know," I say. "Temporary." But I can't imagine Jay, or any of the guys for that matter, trotting out fancy pillows and alpaca wool throws.

"It's not just that. I was thinking—" He pauses, staring at the tree branches sweeping over the power lines. "There's something about living in a house. It shapes you." He must feel my eyes on him but keeps his on the road. "If you have all the room in the world, if you can run down the halls and not touch the walls with your hands outstretched, have your own bedroom, bathroom, you walk through life that way. But if you're sharing a one-bedroom apartment with your mom and siblings, you learn to tiptoe, to shrink in on yourself, and stay out of the way."

"So what about these guys sharing rooms and common spaces?"

Teddy rubs his face.

"That's what I mean. It would depend on how they grew up. Their personalities. Maybe they grew up in a small house and decided this was a chance for a fresh start—no more tiptoeing, they'd take up as much room as possible; or they're used to having the run of things and continue that way, no self-reflection, unless they come face-to-face with someone just like them."

"And then what?"

"They figure out who the alpha is."

I chew my lip and think of Tripp. He's the fraternity president, but did that make him an alpha? He was certainly a natural leader, but in that magnetic, likable way. Michael seemed more the type to bully his way around. And Jay? He's the unknown element, housed together with all those other volatile young men like a bad science experiment.

"Do you think it ever works in reverse?"

"What?"

"Do you think a guy used to taking up a lot of space would decide to take up a little?"

He raises an eyebrow. "No."

The asphalt is darkening in splotches, and I eye the gray sky warily. When Truman says thirty, he means twenty; fifteen means ten. So we're almost running to reach the building, both because of the first etches of lightning slashing the sky and because we know better than to push him.

My blouse is wet and sticking to places I'd rather the others not know the details of, but Oliver's bent over his computer and Truman's talking reassuringly to someone on the phone in his office, so neither sees Teddy and me as we head to our desks.

One of the lights is blinking on my phone. It's a cable-connected gray beast that's managed to survive the '70s with more buttons than I know what to do with and takes up the entire corner of my desk. I never did figure out how to set up my voicemail. So anyone who calls my office phone gets to hear the gruff voice of Don Polaski, the guy here before me, on the other end.

It takes four tries before I can access my voicemail.

"Hey Marlitt—are you ever going to change that message? You've had this number years now and your cell mailbox is full . . . anyway, got those phone records you asked for and am emailing them to you now. No transcripts yet. They're giving me a bit of hassle over there, but don't worry, I'm on it. So far we've got nothing on Jay's laptop. Looks like it's been wiped clean. Must have some tech wizards down at the Kap-O house." A wry laugh. "We'll keep at it but give me a ring if you need anything else. And change that message."

"Dara says they've got nothing on the laptop," I whisper to Teddy and give him an I-told-you-so look. "But we've got Jay's phone records."

"Let's see them."

"Waiting for my computer." It takes forever to boot up and the internet is slow as hell.

Teddy reaches into my desk drawer and fumbles around until he finds a granola bar.

"Almond?" He wrinkles his nose.

I grin. "We have to start eating like adults sometime."

Truman slams down his phone and we both jump.

"Two complaints in the last hour," he yells without bothering to get up from his desk. "My office. Now."

I glance at the computer. Still loading.

Getting called to Truman's office is a bit like being called to the principal. You have a sneaking suspicion of what you did wrong, but since it could be any number of things, you keep your mouth shut. Fortunately, Truman rarely makes us wait.

His face is blotchy, like smashed tomatoes, and the heat rises up his neck.

"A sorority house?" he shouts. "Why, in god's name, are you bothering the young women at Gamma Delta Alpha Delta?"

I open my mouth.

"I'm not finished. I had a phone call earlier from a very nice but rather upset southern lady, who told me you've been harassing her girls. That—Katie Coleman, is it?—was literally"—he shuffles the papers on his desk—"ill, too sick to go to class, and in—her—bed. And—" He gestures at me to zip it. His face has turned a deeper shade of red, almost purple. *Aubergine*, I think. "She called back just now to tell me you gave the poor girl a panic attack. Didn't I tell you to tread carefully? Jesus, I've already fielded calls from the fraternity—nice touch, by the way, showing up at their memorial service." He rolls his eyes, so we know just what he thinks about that. "But since it's one of their own, they're a bit more accommodating. But I shouldn't have to tell you that we don't interview young women—or anyone for that matter—unannounced and in their bedrooms, especially when they're in their jammies. Do I make myself clear?"

This is not in the least bit true. I've interviewed people at gravesites, basketball games, even hospital rooms. But we nod, both of us, eyes humbly on our shoes.

He waits, seems satisfied with our contrition, and then continues. "I've spoken with Jay's parents." His voice deflates a bit. Informing the parents is never easy. Doesn't matter how young, old, close, estranged, or otherwise. That's the part you hand off if you can. I feel Teddy shift. We're both wondering why Truman took this upon himself. "They arrive the day after tomorrow."

The phone starts to ring.

"God damn it," he swears. "And close that door behind you," he yells at me.

Oliver's got his cell cradled beneath his ear. *What's up?* he mouths to Teddy.

Teddy, bless him, just shrugs.

Back at my desk, a large spreadsheet illuminates my computer screen.

I cast an accusatory glance at Oliver, but he's oblivious, now deep in conversation with whomever's on the other line.

I hit Print and march over to the gray hulking machine that probably outdates Amy for the oldest piece of work in the building.

"All right, got the call logs," I tell Teddy, and begin scanning the list. "Wow."

"What?"

"I mean, look at this. Good thing most cell plans are unlimited these days." I shake my head in amazement. "Jay was on the phone all the time. When did he eat?"

Teddy scans the list with the tip of his finger. "I recognize this number."

"Katie?"

"Tripp." He frowns. "There are a bunch of seven-oh-six and four-oh-four numbers though."

I sigh. Athens and Atlanta area codes. "Could be anyone."

"But if you had to guess?"

"Fraternity brothers for sure."

He leans over my shoulder as I keep reading. "All right, now we're in the middle of August, huge uptick; I swear between texts and calls, there are almost a hundred a day." I breathe through my nose. "Got it," I say, and double-check the number written on Teddy's card. "August thirty-first. It's a Saturday."

"Who calls whom?"

"He texts her."

Teddy drums his fingers on my desk. "So he got her number at a party. Texts her the next day."

"Maybe. He could have got it earlier though and waited to text her. Either way, there goes her 'we barely knew each other' bullshit."

"Be good to know what they're saying. Otherwise she'll insist it's 'dream girl' fraternity business."

"Dara says she'll send the transcripts as soon as she has them." I stare at the list. "That's strange."

"What?"

I flip pages back and forth. "So in September, Jay's calling people all day long, and then starting the middle of October—" I draw arrows with my pen.

"What?"

"No calls or texts between three and four P.M."

"Maybe he had class."

"That didn't start until October?"

Teddy shrugs. "Maybe he got caught texting and the professor threatened to take his phone away."

A flash of my mother's face. It's an impossible battle, she always says. Asking them to not look at their phones for an hour is like asking them to remove a limb.

"Maybe."

Somewhere under my pile of notes is Jay's course schedule, and I don't remember him having any classes that late.

I turn back to the sheet.

"There's also no more calls to Katie Coleman." I shake my head. *Maybe she was telling the truth*, I think, as I scan down the list. "Look at all these messages the day before he died though, and then at ten-oh-three Tuesday morning—the last text is to—"

Teddy leans over my shoulder.

"Tripp, huh?"

He turns from the computer and gives Jay's photo on the board a long look.

"Strange he didn't mention that."

| Seven |

We have two interview rooms. One's for hard suspects—bare walls, water stains on ceiling tiles that nobody's bothered to replace, table in the middle, us on one side, suspect on the other. The kind you see on television where the guy's in handcuffs, slamming his fists on the table and demanding his lawyer. We let them sit for an hour or two, get squirmy, stare at that brown ceiling stain and think about how they're just like it—worthless, wastes of space, a blemish on their otherwise halfway decent communities—and then we'll come in and offer coffee or whatever, let them think the boredom and suspense is almost over, and leave them for another hour, periodically checking in through the two-way mirror.

This isn't where Teddy brings Tripp. Instead, he ushers him into the second interview room. It's smaller, with a sofa, two chairs, and a coffee table in the middle to keep us out of arm's reach. It's supposed to be cozy, but there's a camera blinking from the top right corner and a tape recorder in the middle of the table.

"Thanks so much for coming in," Teddy says as they walk by my desk. Tripp nods at me but looks relieved when I don't follow. I grumble and sift paperwork as if I'm not interested in what he's doing here. *It's no big deal*, my body language says, *just a matter of routine.*

"How was class today? Only a few more weeks, right?" Teddy's asking one mundane question after the next, so Tripp's guard drops and he gets used to answering.

Tripp says something I can't hear under all my paper shuffling.

But Teddy chuckles: "English, huh? Man, I was awful at English. Give me numbers all day, but ask me to analyze a poem, no thanks."

Tripp laughs along with him.

"I liked Whitman, though," I hear Teddy say before he steps through the door. "Have you read Whitman?"

I roll my eyes.

Teddy loves poetry. One look at his desk would have told Tripp that, and Teddy can't help himself; adding the truth about Whitman is like a nervous tic.

I count to twenty, let them get settled, and then head to the observation room—a dark, narrow space with two chairs set just behind the two-way mirror.

Tripp and Teddy are already seated. Tripp is trying to imitate Teddy's casual slump—one leg crossed widely over the opposite knee—but he's barely on the edge of the sofa and his top foot pulses furiously.

"Right," Teddy says, his voice hollow and tinny over the speakers. "Thanks again for coming in. I know the guys just want to get back to normal and having me and Detective Kaplan around makes that difficult."

Tripp nods, choosing to believe this rationale for asking him to the station.

"Am I," he asks with a weak laugh, "I'm not like a suspect or anything?"

"What?" Teddy guffaws. "Nah, man. It's just quieter in here than in the bullpen, you know? Phones ringing, papers piling up. It's hard to talk in there. I just have a few questions and think you might be able to help."

"I'll try." Tripp's head bobs up and down. *Helpful giraffe*, I think.

"Great. I appreciate that. And just so you know, you don't have to say anything you don't want to. You have the right to remain silent. And anything you say can and will be used against you in a court of law. You have the right to an attorney. If you can't afford an attorney, one will be provided for you. Okay, so we pulled Jay's phone records." Teddy's read Tripp his Miranda rights so quickly and casually, I'm not sure he's caught it, but there's a jerk of Tripp's shoulders at the mention of Jay's phone. "And we see that you and him were in pretty close contact—nothing unusual there, I'm sure all you guys message each other a lot."

Tripp's starting to look unsure, wondering whether conceding this fact is in his best interest, but since Teddy's put the printed call logs in front of him, he must decide there's not much use denying it.

"It's mostly fraternity business," he says slowly. "What band to invite for the next party. Who's in charge of getting the keg. And random stuff, too, like if we're watching a football game we'll text each other predictions."

Betting, I think. Not a big surprise. Something like 80 percent of all college students say they gamble, but it can become a huge problem if they're not careful. I knew a guy who started online gambling, dropped out of school, moved to Vegas, got addicted to coke, and ended up gunning down his father in his garage when he wouldn't give him money to support his addiction.

I scribble on my notepad: *Gambling? Did Jay owe money?*

He certainly had money, but maybe they played big. Or maybe they bet things that weren't theirs to give. I draw a line from "gambling" to "Katie Coleman" and flip back a few pages. *The car*, I think suddenly. Our hit-and-run driver was in Jay's car. Could someone have won Jay's keys in a bet?

"Of course." Teddy's nodding along. "I text my guys all the time—mostly shit-talk, you know, like who's gonna win our next pickup game, and, I dunno, funny pics from online."

"Yeah, and like who's kicking ass in Fortnite."

I see *What's Fortnite* in the slant of Teddy's eyebrows, but Tripp misses it.

"So like I said. No big deal. I just need you to look over these numbers and tell me if you recognize any of them. I figure they're mostly your brothers—talking about fraternity business and"—just a miniscule pause—"Fortnite."

We don't need Tripp to do this. Dara has already traced the numbers and sent us a list of who's who. But Teddy's watching Tripp's face as he reads down the lines.

"I, um, I don't really know anyone's number off the top of my head."

"Oh, sure." Teddy leans back in his chair. "Of course not. I think I've got my mom's number and Detective Kaplan's memorized, but that's it. I don't even know my girlfriend's."

Curious glance from Tripp like he's only just realized Teddy has a life outside of detective work. And I feel a tiny flutter I shouldn't with the realization he knows my number but not Cindy's.

"You probably have them all saved in your phone, right? That's why you don't need to remember them."

Head nod.

"Do you have your phone with you?"

Another nod.

"Right, so if you wouldn't mind, look at your contacts and let me know who Jay was calling."

Again Tripp must figure we're going to find out anyway, because after a beat, he leans forward, phone in one hand, list in the other.

"This is me." Tripp scans the list, his phone, list, then phone. "And this is Michael, more Michael, me, Cade," back to phone, "Tucker, Dirk, Brent, and Thad."

I snort. What kind of names are those?

"Garrett, Jonathan, and—" His face flushes, and I know he's reached our girl. "I, uh, I'm not sure who this is."

Teddy glances at the two-way mirror—the lie, I caught it, too.

"Really?" Teddy asks. "Yeah, there are a few to and from that number, so we were curious about that one." He leans in, trying to meet Tripp's eyes. "I'm surprised you don't recognize it."

Tripp rearranges his face, but his foot is pulsing frantically now, and he's staring at me—or rather, his own reflection in the mirror.

"Why?" he asks. And then slowly, "Who is it?"

Teddy waits. One second. Two. Until Tripp turns his gaze back to him.

"Katie Coleman. The Kap-O dream girl? I would have thought you'd have her number—with you being fraternity president, and her bringing you guys . . . breakfast . . . and such."

"Oh, yeah, I have it. I just . . . I didn't think to look for hers—I thought they were all brothers' numbers."

His eyes are on the call log.

He didn't know.

"There's something else, too," Teddy says. His voice has dropped, low and soft, and his finger has found the final page, the number at the bottom.

"You were the last person Jay messaged. Did you know that?"

Tripp shakes his head.

"Do you remember what he said? It might be important."

"Oh." Tripp's eyebrows draw together. "I think it was about the Auburn game. Jay was social chair, so he was always messaging about events—tailgates, cookouts, movie nights. He was really hands-on. Always giving the brothers something to look forward to." Tripp smiles sadly.

"Do you remember exactly what he said?" Teddy leans forward, his voice almost a whisper. "If he had any idea at all that something bad might happen, or someone might be after him, it could be written in a way to let us know."

"I don't—" Tripp's eyes are wide. "I think it was just 'talk to Mike.' That's it."

"Michael Williams?"

"Yeah . . ."

"Talk to him about what?"

"It was probably about the party budget. I don't know how that could be—"

"You mind if I take a look?"

"Oh, I—" Tripp pulls his phone back fast. "I, um, deleted it, sorry."

Teddy's brows come together. "Really? Why?" His voice stays neutral, only curious, but Tripp senses danger anyway.

"Just, storage, you know. I have a lot of photos and needed to make room . . ."

He may be one of the worst liars ever, but it doesn't matter. Because like an answered prayer, my phone buzzes. Text from Dara. "Check your inbox. Full transcripts. Happy reading." Followed by a kissy-face emoji.

Right, I think. *Go time.*

Outside the observation room, the station's quiet. Truman's office door is shut. Who knows whether that means he's gone for lunch or is still in there making secret phone calls. Oliver's chair is tucked neatly under his desk, his papers stacked and organized; even his wastebasket is empty. I make sure to give the table edge a good bump on my way past and watch his folders shift and pens roll out of place.

My computer glows serenely, giving no indication that it may hold the key to this whole mess. At the top of my inbox is Dara's email, "faster than expected—you're welcome" in the subject line and no note, just a very large attachment.

"Jesus fucking Christ," I say when I open it. And then turn to make sure Truman's door really is shut. I hit Print and march over to the break-in-case-of-emergency coffee machine in the corner. There's half a pot left, and it's cold and overcooked, but I'm too twitchy with excitement to brew a new one. *This is it*, I think. *Whatever they're hiding. Tripp. Michael. Katie. It has to be here.*

I think of Jay's laptop and Michael's bullshit "I found it" line and shake my head. If there was nothing to hide, why would they take Jay's computer?

But now we have Jay's phone records and the last three months' worth of texts. As an entire tree prints off the old gray printer, I imagine a sprawling concrete building somewhere in the Nevada desert with a whole blue-lit server devoted to Jay's cloud history. Whatever we need, let's hope it happened recently and not last year. Otherwise this is going to be a very long day.

Coffee and pages of text history in hand, I return to my desk. We should have interns for this, but budget cuts mean we do the grunt work, too. I rub my eyes and grab a ruler to force myself to go through the messages methodically and not skim ahead.

Like Teddy said, there's an uptick in texts beginning the middle of August, which must correspond to the start of classes.

Jay: Spring beach party was killer. Def do again.

Tripp: Def. Let's talk at chap meeting. Mike being weird about $$.

Jay: big surprise.

More texts back and forth between Jay and Tripp. All the amazing events Jay's developing. Scheduling concerns. Detailed lists of things he wants to improve for the next party. A group message about some girl all the brothers thought was hot. A few crude comments from a number I don't recognize concerning what he'd do to said girl. I star the number for Teddy. Jay's silent on the girl though. I make a note of the date and wonder if he might already be crushing on Katie. Texts back and forth between him and Cade about the state of their room.

Cade: made me wanna gag. Wash your clothes.

A week later, another text from Cade: srsly room is disgusting.

Jay never bothered to respond to any of these, but Cade's on all the group messages for social events. And there's one to him on September 13: "Pledge party 2nite. Mandatory. Be there." I circle it and write *threatening Cade?* in the margins. More texts back and forth about the Tennessee game. They threw a huge tailgate apparently, and someone borrowed their uncle's bulldog so they could have their own Uga mascot. Concerns from one number about it being too hot for the dog. And various others, explaining said brother's place in the food chain: Kap-Os, other men, boys, the dog apparently, women, and pussies somewhere near the bottom. Plans for another tailgate, poker nights, debating what movie to show on their outdoor projector. I'm skimming now despite the ruler and my mind's wandering. A familiar sensation creeps over my skin—the feeling of watching the neighbor's kids running through sprinklers in the front yard, siblings eating Popsicles side by side on the front stoop, classmates trading lunchbox items, girls on television getting dolled up in front of mirrors and dancing around together in their underwear—I should have had that. Instead of waiting at the bus stop alone. Playing with dolls—not shopping, or Mommy, but one ginormous family: brothers and sisters and cousins who formed their own soccer teams and went camping and had cookouts in the backyard. Bringing as many dolls and stuffed animals as I could into bed—telling my father it was because I was lonely and watching his face cloud over, recognizing his expression as currency and using it whenever I could.

I look back at the page. I've moved the ruler to the bottom with little recollection of what I've read. I scan back up. It's a text exchange between Jay and Michael.

Not cool bro.

You know the rules.

This is bullshit.

No response.

He's not even here most of the time.

Not my problem. Pay up.

Whatever. Not about $$. About principle.

Two weeks later.

Fucked up to list names at meetings.

Do it every time, bro.

Whatever. Fuck you.

Srsly bro. Don't fuck with me.

My heart's pounding. This could be it. Pay up? Sounds a lot like gambling to me. And no one said anything about Michael and Jay not getting along. I think of Michael's smug face, the curl of his lip when he looked at Teddy. My spine tingles, and I pull the notes closer.

I want it to be Michael. But the desire sends off alarm bells in my head. Teddy always says there's a difference between intuition and dis-like. Still, I can't help but imagine leading Michael out of that over-large brick house in handcuffs under the shocked stares of his brothers. The reporters getting a particularly unflattering shot of him on the way to the car—his face plastered all over the news—

The heater groans, breaking my fantasy.

Not now, I think. I can relish that moment later and for real if we get him. And, I remind myself, his alibi checked out. We even got in touch with the blonde. It took us a couple of hours to identify her—apparently Michael got double points for hooking up with a girl no one knew—a soft-spoken freshman at Georgia Tech who was visiting friends for the weekend and was absolutely mortified by my phone call. But she confirmed she was with Michael all night and left the house around ten that morning.

I scan the next few pages looking for Katie's number.

Found her.

Text from Jay: Great meeting you last night.

Katie: You too! So exciting to be up for dream girl.

Jay: Don't tell anyone but I think it's you.

Katie: Really?!?! So excited!!!

A week later.

Katie: I won!!!

Jay: Congrats!! You totally deserve it.

More texts about upcoming parties. Katie telling him how many sis-ters she plans on bringing. Apparently, they all baked pies and cookies for some event, and the brothers were going to judge who was the best southern homemaker. I mime throwing up and keep reading. Nothing. Not one text that indicates they were a couple. A few flirtatious: "You looked great tonight." Coconut emojis. "Thanks," kissy face, "made the top myself." But none of the can't-wait-to-see-you, you're-my-everything-but-we-have-to-keep-this-a-secret kind of texts I was hoping for.

Then, a month ago, on October 13, a text from Jay to Tripp: Some-one's been in my room.

Tripp immediately defuses the situation: Prob drunk bro got confused. Thought it was his.

Jay, not convinced: Whoever it was went through my things.

Tripp: Woah. No one would do that.

Jay, two hours later: Prob right. Sorry. Stressing about the party.

A million more texts about the Halloween party. They turned the place into a huge haunted house with themed rooms, assigned costumes, and everything. But otherwise, nothing weird. No more references to the strange visitor. Even a handful of exchanges with Michael about the expenses. But no more texts to Katie. No more threats from Michael.

I can sense Teddy growing restless in the interview room. I need to figure out what's going on before Tripp leaves.

I'm frantically skimming ahead, looking for anything useful, when I get to the last page.

The last text.

To Tripp.

I suck in my teeth, grab the pages and my notes, and march off to the interview room.

D on't tell Mike?"

Tripp looks confused and then pales.

Teddy leans over the printed list to where my finger is pointing.

He reads off the sheet. "The last text Jay sent was"—he looks at Tripp—"'Don't tell Mike.' Not 'Talk to Mike.'"

Tripp's eyes dart across the page, but he shrugs like he doesn't see the difference.

"That didn't seem important to you?" The exasperation's clear in Teddy's voice. "Something we should know?" There's a troubled line between his brows, and I resist the urge to reach out and smooth it.

I keep telling Teddy that everyone lies. They lie about petty bullshit to save face and lie about antidepressants and past traumas, so we don't think they're crazy. They lie because lying is second nature. All day long they're telling stories about who they are and why they do what they do, where they're always the hero of their own narrative. They want to believe the world revolves around them and have to tell a million lies a day to keep it that way. We all do. If we had any grasp of our insignificance in the grand scheme of the universe but the simultaneous harm we do on a global scale—from the 660 gallons of water one hamburger wastes, to greenhouse emissions and our hand in the extinction of hundreds of other species, we'd never get out of bed in the morning. But we don't need Teddy's nice-guy act deteriorating now. So I step in.

"You told us everyone loved Jay. That everyone got along. No problems. No issues. Nothing. But that's not true, is it?" I'm standing behind the coffee table, leaning over Tripp, so he has to look up to make eye contact. "We have evidence that indicates not everyone was happy with Jay and he wasn't happy with everyone either."

Tripp glances at the message sheet again, but I snatch it back.

"Why don't you tell us more about Jay and Michael."

He snorts. "Two big personalities."

"Yeah? So they didn't get along?"

"They got on fine, but Michael's treasurer, and Jay is—" He swallows. "—was social chair."

"So?"

"So," Tripp says slowly, "it was just usual fraternity stuff. Jay planned the parties, but Michael controlled the money box. They butted heads."

"About what?"

Tripp sighs and fidgets in his chair. "Jay always wanted to throw these huge ragers. Like last spring we had this beach party."

Right, I think, remembering the text exchange "BEST PARTY EVER"—they were still reliving it months later.

"And we filled the lawn with sand, had a hot tub and umbrella drinks. One of the guys dressed up like Captain Morgan, and there were girls in bikinis everywhere. We even hired a Jimmy Buffet cover band."

"Sounds like a blast," nice-guy Teddy says, but I hear a hint of sarcasm.

"It was." Tripp's eyes glass over with the memory, but then his shoulder twitches. "But after—Mike was furious. I guess Jay hadn't approved all the expenses ahead of time, and Mike figured he did that intentionally—not an oversight, you know, but so he could do what he wanted." He shrugs. "That's just how Jay was."

"Selfish?" I ask, thinking of Samantha and Katie Coleman.

"No." Firm, no hesitation there. "He wanted everyone to have a good time. Make memories. But the band alone cost three grand—"

Teddy lets out a low whistle. "That's a lot of money."

Tripp shifts again. "Yeah, I mean, it is, but not for guys like Jay and Mike." He squirms, and I think of the scholarship and the fact that his allowance must be significantly less than the other boys'. "So Jay's all like, he'll pay for it, why is Mike making such a big deal. And Mike's trying to explain that that's not the point. That there are balance sheets and the math has to add up. And they were both kind of pissed at our last spring meeting, but then Mike was gone all summer at an internship in Atlanta, and—I don't know, they got over it."

I lean in again. "Until . . . ?"

"Until what?"

"Didn't Michael call him out at a meeting?"

"Oh, that." Tripp shakes his head. "That was nothing."

"It didn't seem like nothing—Jay sounded pretty angry in his texts."

"Do I um—do I need a lawyer, or something?" Tripp looks sheepish, but he doesn't blink under my stare.

"You can, of course," Teddy says, sitting back in his chair.

"But then," I chime in, "you'd have to wait until he gets here—and that can take forever. I mean, one time, this guy was here forty-eight hours waiting on his lawyer, because the man actually forgot about him."

This is not in the least bit true, and if Tripp did talk to a lawyer, he'd tell him we can't hold him without charging him and he can leave whenever he wants. I get that feeling again like he knows this but has been relegated the helpful role by the brothers in some larger game they're playing.

"But you're not a suspect," Teddy adds. "And we're wrapping up anyway. It sounds like we really need to speak to Michael and Katie Coleman anyway."

A quick glance at Katie's name.

"What's she have to do with this?" Tripp asks, and then turns three shades of strawberry.

I hold up the papers in my hand. "Lots of messages between them," I say meaningfully. "It seems they were really close."

I let that hang in the air between us. Tripp's eyebrows furrow, but he doesn't say anything.

"All right," Teddy says, "if there's nothing else—"

"One more thing," I interrupt him. "Jay texted you that he thought someone was in his room. Going through his things."

Teddy raises an eyebrow at me. I pointed to the line when I handed him the sheet, but he must have missed it.

"Oh, yeah." Another squirm. "Every once in a while things would go missing. You know, like, after a party, someone wouldn't be able to find a book they needed for class or their grandad's watch or—"

"A watch could be pretty valuable. Why didn't anyone file a police report?"

We've been through everything already. Not a single report filed by anyone at the frat. And only a few noise complaints, one of which must have come from Ray, filed against them.

"Mostly the brothers had just misplaced whatever it was, and it would turn up later. Or one of the pledges would have moved it while they were cleaning. That kind of thing."

"What was taken from Jay's room?" I ask.

"I don't know." Tripp thinks about it a second too long. "I don't remember."

| Eight |

At this point, the house should feel familiar—layers upon layers of beige paint and scuffed laminate floors mopped clean by a dozen pledges, scents of pine and gym clothes, fried food floating from the industrial-style kitchen. And we're marching through the house, cell phone records in hand like we're in charge. But it doesn't feel that way. Instead, the walls narrow and shift around us. A missed step, footing uncertain on the squeaky floor, and the sudden realization that it's just the two of us. And thirty or so of them.

I take a deep breath and put my hand on the door to the chapter room.

"Detective Kaplan," a voice calls behind me.

I turn.

Wherever he's come from, Michael's done so silently. He's dressed in a suit and tie, and I'm not sure if this is common for fraternity meetings or is donned for our benefit.

"Tripp said you might be stopping by."

Tripp. I knew we should have held on to him a little longer.

"My lawyer's on his way." Michael pulls out his cell phone. "Should I tell him to meet us at the station instead?"

Asshole, I think. Instead of us doing the good cop, bad cop routine, we've got Tripp and Michael playing good suspect, bad suspect, and me feeling like we're missing something huge and it's right in front of our faces.

"Right," I say. "That's really helpful. But we're actually here to see

Cade." I feel Teddy shift beside me, but he stays quiet. "Everyone's in here, right?"

I push the door open without waiting for his answer.

Instantly, the voices inside dissolve into silence. And across the rows of plastic gray chairs, over two dozen arched eyebrows turn simultaneously to me.

For a moment, I feel as if I've stepped into a nightmare. I suck in my breath and stare into a sea of identical faces. Dark curling mustaches, pale faces, and bloodred lips.

"What the fuck?" I say before I can catch myself.

Every single brother is wearing a black cape and Guy Fawkes smile.

The cloaked figure at the table in front lifts up his mask. "Detective White—and Kaplan."

It's Tripp. Of course.

"What's going on here?"

"We're conducting fraternity business."

"Wearing masks? What kind of sick—"

Michael steps behind me. "It's for anonymity." He spreads his arms wide. "This allows us to vote in real time without identifying ourselves."

Tripp's already skipped over to us, throwing confused looks at Michael in the doorway.

"Fine." I wave my hand. "We need to speak to"—I think of the guy telling the brothers what he'd do to the drunk girl but decide to leave it for now—"Cade Abernathy."

Michael's mouth twists unpleasantly, and there's a movement from the back row as Cade stands to remove his mask and cape. The two get tangled, and he elbows another Guy Fawkes in the head when he rips both off.

It would be comical if it wasn't so fucking creepy.

Back at the station, the light is completely gone from the windows, leaving only the blue-tinged fluorescent bulbs, which highlight the sad-looking bags under our eyes. I can't remember the last real meal I had. Fatigue is imminent, but my energy's sky-high.

Cade gets the same interview room as Tripp, and we leave Michael in our water-stained room so he can wait like he deserves for his lawyer.

"Thanks again for coming in," Teddy says to Cade.

He switches on the voice recorder. "Detectives White and Kaplan interviewing Cade Abernathy."

Cade's on the edge of his seat, not nervous, but in a hurry, I think, to get this over and done with.

Now that he's removed the cape, I see he's dressed quite nicely underneath—gray slacks and a gingham blue button-down. He's fidgeting and glancing at his watch every few seconds, and I wonder if we're keeping him from a date with Samantha.

"Your dad's an attorney, right?" I say.

He doesn't seem surprised we know this, and simply nods.

"So you know you have the right to remain silent." His eyes widen a little at the Miranda warning, but he nods again. *Hurry up*, I see him think. "And anything you say can and will be used against you in a court of law. You have the right to an attorney. If you can't afford an attorney, one will be provided for you. Do you want to call your father?" I'm hedging my bets here. Something about Cade's softness, the mothering tendencies we already saw from Samantha, tells me he's a mama's boy and would prefer not to involve his dad in any way.

Sure enough, he shakes his head. "I don't need an attorney." Right. *Not like Michael*, his steady gaze says. *Not guilty.*

"You and Jay Kemp have been roommates at the Kappa Phi Omicron house since last fall, correct?"

"Yes."

"How would you categorize your relationship with Jay?"

"Fine."

I raise my eyebrow. "This morning, the fourteenth of November, you told us that Jay was a messy roommate. He was, in your words," I thumb through my notes, "a slob, and his behavior was making you ill." I pause. "I wouldn't call that 'fine.'"

He shrugs.

"Care to elaborate?"

"It was fine because I stopped sleeping there and didn't have to deal with him anymore." A slight flush spreads across his cheeks.

"Because for the past two months, you've been staying with your girl-friend, Samantha Barron, at a condominium on Downing Way."

"Yes."

"And this morning, Samantha described Jay as"—I make a show of skimming my notes again—"an asshole. Is that correct?"

He nods warily, and I point to the recorder. "Out loud, please."

"Yes, she said that."

There's a tap on the door and Oliver strides in. He doesn't look at Cade but whispers something in Teddy's ear. Michael's lawyer has ar-rived.

Teddy nods. "Right, Cade, I have to step out." He stands and puts his hand on my chair. "Need anything? Water?" He smiles at me. "Coffee?"

"Coffee would be great, thanks."

"Cade?" Teddy turns to Cade, who's looking between the pair of us. I see him wonder—people in love think they see romance everywhere—and then shake his head.

"All right," Teddy says brightly. "Be back in a few."

The door shuts behind him. I stare at it a moment, wondering if he'll get anything good out of Michael with his lawyer present.

Cade clears his throat.

"Right. We were talking about your relationship with Jay Kemp. You thought he was a slob. Samantha thought he was an asshole."

"Yeah," he says, voice tired all of a sudden. I wonder what time he had plans with Samantha.

"You also confirmed Samantha's report that Jay thought brothers should have sex with each other's girlfriends."

Cade fidgets with his sleeve, folding and unfolding the left cuff.

I lean in. "How did it work?"

"What?" He looks up at me, brow wrinkling.

"I want to know how the brothers convinced their girlfriends to have sex with other men."

Cade opens his mouth.

"Because from where I'm sitting it sounds a lot like entitlement and coercion, or maybe your brothers waited until their girlfriends were good and drunk—"

"It wasn't like that."

"So," I say, "what was it like?"

"I don't—I mean, none of the guys were roofie-ing their girlfriends, if that's what you're implying. It was more like if two brothers were dating two sisters in another sorority, they would switch. They called it 'family style,' like those buffet dinners where everyone shares—"

"I get it." I wave my hand to stop him from elaborating.

"Some of the girls were into it," he says heatedly. "Guys aren't the only ones who like sex, you know." He blushes as soon as the words leave his mouth, but he stares at me evenly.

I hold up my hands. "I know how it is," I say, my voice measured. "Guys talk. What they say to each other is a bit different from what they say when their girlfriends are around." I shift in my chair, trying to find the right tone. "So, what I'm asking is, did it actually happen? I imagine most girls would feel like Sam and most guys," I look at him meaningfully, "wouldn't like the idea either."

Cade shrugs. "Brandon and Kevin said they did. But who knows. Everything's half bravado, half shit-talk."

"Sam said Jay wanted you to share her with the other brothers."

"Yeah," he says irritably, "but he changed his mind."

"Because of Katie Coleman."

"Right, because of Katie."

"She says they weren't together."

Cade's eyes widen at that, but then he sits back and folds his arms over his chest. "They were keeping it a secret."

"That's what you told us. But she said she barely knew him. They only talked about fraternity dream girl business. And," I say quickly when Cade opens his mouth again, "Jay's phone records back this up. Only messages about fraternity-related events." I don't mention the minor flirtations. Jay seems to have sent "looking good" messages to a dozen or so women every time the fraternity had a party. He must have thought they wouldn't know how they looked if he didn't tell them.

"So." I lean in. "How did you know they were together?"

He folds his arms over his chest. "I saw them."

I step into the observation gallery for interview room A, and with an unpleasant twinge find Oliver next to Teddy. I get it—in the interview, two is always better than one. Oliver saw his opportunity and took it. But inside a voice is screaming that it should've been me.

"On September seventeenth, you and Jay seemed to have an argument," Teddy says. "Can you tell us about that?"

"I don't recall."

"No?" Teddy leans in. "Did you and Jay have a lot of arguments?"

"You don't have to answer that," his lawyer says. He's neatly groomed, with stark white hair. His bright blue eyes fix a warning on Teddy.

"Right." Teddy pulls out the phone sheet. "On September seventeenth, Jay texts you to say, 'not cool bro.' To which you respond, 'you know the rules.' Jay responds that he thought it was 'bullshit.' And you tell him to 'pay up.'

"Do you remember now?"

A shift from his lawyer, but he doesn't say anything.

"Jay was a great guy," Michael says, opening his arms like Jesus giving a blessing.

I roll my eyes.

"But he lived like a pig. The pledges clean up after parties, but cleaning bedrooms is everyone's own responsibility. Some of the brothers were messier than others, so last year, we voted on an infraction and fine system."

"What's that?" Oliver asks like he's genuinely interested.

"Periodic room checks and an anonymous complaint box. You can have two infractions each semester, but the third earns you a fine. And if you don't clean your room after any infraction, it also results in a fine."

Next he'll say they came up with some kind of chore wheel. *Ask about the gambling*, I will Teddy. *Ask about Jay's car*.

"What do you do with the money?"

"It goes into our alcohol budget—for the brothers over twenty-one, of course."

"Of course." Oliver nods. "It's a win-win. Clean house and more booze."

"Exactly." Michael doesn't smile, but he looks pleased with himself, and I assume this was his idea.

"So Jay had a few infractions and didn't want to pay the fine?" Teddy asks.

"He had nine."

"And how much did he owe?"

"One hundred and eighty dollars."

"That's it?" Teddy asks. "I got the impression that wouldn't have been much for someone like Jay."

Michael raises an eyebrow. "It wasn't."

"So why wouldn't he pay?"

Michael presses his fingers into a triangle. "If I had asked him to buy a few handles of vodka, it wouldn't have been a problem. But, pay a fine for his mess?" He shrugs. "Jay only wanted to spend money on fun stuff."

"Don't we all," Oliver says with a tight laugh. Teddy shifts away from him.

"That must have been frustrating," Teddy says.

"You don't have to answer that," the lawyer murmurs.

Michael ignores him. "Just part of the job."

"So you called him out at a meeting?"

"Not just him. It's part of fraternity business. Who owes what. List-ing the names publicly keeps everyone accountable."

"But Jay didn't like it."

"No one does, but it has to get done."

"Do the other brothers tell you to fuck off?"

"They know better."

"So you must have been pretty pissed when Jay told you to."

"You don't have to answer that."

"Your response was, 'Seriously bro. Don't fuck with me.' Were you threatening Jay?"

"You don't have to—"

"Because Jay's last text was to Tripp," Teddy leans in, "and it was about you."

A flicker of something across Michael's face—anger? surprise?—but it's replaced by the smug and slightly bored expression he's worn since we brought him in. I suck in my breath. Teddy waits. Oliver looks like he's dying to say something—I can see his left foot shaking furiously against his chair leg—but he keeps his mouth shut.

After a minute of silence, Michael breaks. "What did he say?"

"You don't know?"

He leans toward Teddy. "I wouldn't be asking, if I knew."

Teddy sits back and observes him from across the table.

"He said, 'Don't tell Mike.'"

"That's it?" Michael laughs.

"Any idea what that's about?"

"God—knowing Jay, he probably booked a mansion for spring formal or a live gator for next year's Florida game."

"So you think it's about money."

"It always is."

"Right." Teddy manages not to sound disappointed, but some of the tight energy holding up his shoulders drops. "What can you tell us about Katie Coleman?"

"She's Kap-O's dream girl. She's hot. Sweet, but always down for a good time."

Oliver leans in. "You and the dream girl, huh?"

Michael's eyes skim his face. No matter how hard Oliver tries, he's not going to get on Michael's good side. Michael's looking at him like something he found on the bottom of his shoe.

"Not interested," he says. "But she came to all our parties. Made sure her friends came as well."

"How long had she and Jay been together?"

For a split second, Michael hesitates. *He knows*, I think. But then he straightens. "They weren't."

"We have a witness who says otherwise."

"Jay and Katie?" Michael pretends to ponder it. "There's no way to keep something like that a secret. If they were together, everyone would have known." He's looking at the two-way mirror. Looking through it almost—to me.

His lawyer is shuffling papers. "If that's all . . ."

I'm ducking out of the observation gallery when I almost collide with Michael in the hall. He doesn't look like he's just spent two hours in the shitty interview room, doesn't look disheveled or remotely worried. His lawyer trails behind him, snapping various clasps on his briefcase. As I shove my way past, Michael leans toward me and places his hand on my arm.

"You and your partner should be careful," he says.

A current runs from his fingers through my body. I rip my sleeve away.

His lawyer catches up with us, and Michael gestures to the glass front door and the tea-colored puddles deepening in the parking lot with his eyebrows raised.

"It's really coming down out there."

That night, I comb through Jay's social media accounts, staring at photos of him and his brothers so long I can't determine one face from the next. Cade said he saw them—Jay and Katie—twice, but always from a distance. Once during a house party. The other time in the parking lot. But, he said, from the way they were behaving, there was no doubt they were together. Unfortunately, the phone records indicate otherwise. And regardless of what happened earlier in the year, there's no evidence they had any contact since the middle of October. Nothing on Facebook or Instagram either. Maybe they were together, and they broke up. Or maybe Jay took it too far—asked Katie to sleep with someone else. Maybe every other weekend there's a massive orgy at the Kap-O house. Who knows? The question is: Does it matter? Does it have anything to do with the case? Or am I wasting my time trying to unravel the twisted love life of twenty-year-olds?

I sigh. The lover's quarrel feels like a stretch. Katie looked sad, not angry. Sam appeared more hurt than homicidal. And really, Cade doesn't seem capable of murder. All the involuntary blushes at the mention of sex. There's no way he'd be able to keep it together if he had killed someone.

I go for a walk to clear my head.

It's a still night. A slash of moonlight turns the roofs of houses indigo, and it's clear and bright enough that I don't bother with a flashlight. A car turns down the lane, and I step into the grass as the driver speeds past, oblivious to my presence a few feet away. The sound of the engine fades, and I realize the tree crickets have gone, too. It takes just one frost to end their chorus. They won't sing again until next summer. A cycle that repeats again and again. But for now there's only silence. I stop walking, feeling a prickle of cold sweat and listening for movement in the dark. I shake my head and cut over at the next street. Suddenly, I'm certain the girls have nothing to do with this. That whatever this is, it has played out before. Only the stakes have changed. And whatever's going on, it's between brothers.

When I get back, I pour myself a glass of wine and take it to the bedroom. I stare at the ceiling a long time before I fall asleep, and when I do, I dream of a brick mansion, and boys in Guy Fawkes masks stockpiling gunpowder under its foundation. Boys lighting matches and flames licking windows. I open my mouth to warn them, but the scream stays in my chest.

Something wakes me.

At first it's nothing but a whisper. Then a snap. And a flicker of light.

But I know before I open my eyes that the house is burning. The wood above my head cracks and splinters. The heat laps at my skin. Somewhere a dog is barking. But it's the smell—acrid and sulfuric—of singed hair that makes me squeeze my eyes tighter. My hair is on fire. I am on fire.

Ich brenne, I think without knowing what it means.

"*Hilfe*," I scream, and the windows shatter.

"*Hilfe*," I yell again, batting away the flames with my eyes still closed. Choking on smoke. Rolling, because somewhere a voice instructs, *stop, drop, roll, stop, drop, roll*. My body is slick. Sheets and skin indistinguishable.

I hear voices. Somewhere in the living room below are low and urgent whispers. There's a crash followed by harsh laughter. The door slams, and I split my eyes open.

White-hot flames devour the edges of the room and sear my corneas. Thick clouds of smoke deepen below the ceiling. The air tastes like leather and gunpowder, pine, and camphor oil. I swallow mouthfuls of burning clothes. The shapes of my dresser and mirror shift and slide out of place. A wineglass dances like a shadow and then explodes. Nothing is where it should be. Darkness smothers me again as I feel for the edge of the mattress.

"*Ich bin hier*," I yell, the words meaningless to my own ears. "*Hier oben. Hilfe.*" My head is filled with smoke. Mouth dry with ash.

I roll off the bed, still tangled in paisley sheets.

And then nothing.

PART II

| Nine |

Monday, November 18, 8:00 A.M.

W hen I wake, Michael's warning is ringing in my ears and my arms are restrained to the plastic sides of a narrow hospital bed.

Somewhere beyond his voice, I hear splintering wood and a dog barking. I smell smoke and burning hair.

Faint traces of a dream cling to me. A dark stage. Technicolor tubes hanging from the ceiling, and I'm jerked from side to side like a marionette.

Nothing makes any sense.

"Do you know what day it is?"

I roll my head toward the sound.

A nurse stares down at me. She's wearing a surgical mask, and I'm lying in a thin gown that out of the slit of my right eye blooms and swirls with pink polka dots. Tubes and wires stretch and twist from me to various bags and devices. As if from underwater, I hear steady beeping, heavy breathing, and a metal cart rattling down a long hallway.

"They're roses," the nurse says, adjusting the bag attached to the metal stand at my shoulder and pointing to the design flickering on my gown.

My eyes roll from the fabric to the nurse. She's wearing crisp green scrubs like an army uniform. Her hair's cropped close to her skull, and she moves with a practiced haste.

"You can call me Nurse Danae."

She runs her finger past my nose, and I take in the square room.

Everything here is dairy colored. Milk-colored walls. Butter-colored ceiling. Wrinkled popcorn curtain. White-cheddar light from a window behind my head. Maybe I'm just hungry. I don't know. My stomach's disappeared to some undefinable place. Mouth full of cotton. Lips splitting. Tongue so dry it's stuck behind my teeth.

Danae notes my heart rate, blood pressure, and temperature. Checks my blood oxygen level. Her hands avoid my skin.

"It's Monday. November eighteenth," she says. "You've been unconscious for three days."

I close my eyes. *Three days?*

I reach for them, but my memories are haze, thin as smoke swallowed by a pitiless white-hot blaze. My arms won't move, and I panic. *Paralyzed*, I think. But I kick my legs and razors shoot through my side, a beautiful constellation of nociceptors in my skin and nerve fibers radiating up my spinal cord. But aside from the pain, I have three days of nothing. Three days disconnected from the world. Three days of neurons fastened like tiny islands. Body bound to bed. Life speeding along without me.

"We had to restrain you," Danae tells me, drawing my attention to the tan padded cuffs circling my wrists and clinging to the white plastic bedframe.

I kick my legs again.

"I can restrain your ankles, too." There's no laughter in her voice.

But that was the last of my energy, and I collapse in on myself.

"The firefighters said you were speaking German. *Deutsch.* Do I need to find someone who speaks German?" She taps her clipboard, voice rising with impatience. "It says here you were born at Northside Hospital." She pauses for effect. "In Atlanta."

She puts the clipboard down and her hands move to her narrow hips. I smell scorched leather and burning lavender. See dark mustaches and bloodred lips. My skin's on fire. I can't breathe.

"Do you speak English?" she says loudly and slowly, enunciating each syllable, as the walls around me go up in flames. "Spre-ken Zee Eng-lish?"

"Of course, I speak English," I say, irritated to hear the words come out garbled and wet. "Ofufspegl" or something like that, and where moments before there was nothing, I have the sensation of drool on my chin.

"And what language is that?" She cocks a painted swoop of an eyebrow, and I suspect she's enjoying this.

Someone must have told her I'm a cop.

She lifts my gown and prods my side. "I'll be back in two hours to change your dressings," she tells me. Then she pulls a butterscotch-and-lime curtain around my bed and marches out of the room.

The light is slanting against the far wall, Danae's gone, and the curtain separating me from the cream walls has disappeared behind my head.

"Jesus," Teddy says when he sees me.

His handsome face is drawn and tired, and I can tell from the way he lingers in the doorway that I must look bad. He shuffles next to the plastic railing, thrusts a bouquet of flowers into my lap, and then picks them up awkwardly and lays them on the metal side table.

"This is the first day they allowed visitors," he says, running a hand over his mouth. A fine stubble stipples his chin and outlines the strongness of his jaw. After a brief hesitation, he sits on the cushioned plastic chair next to the bed. His brown eyes are full of concern, but he looks everywhere except my face.

I'm suddenly aware of the bad taste in my mouth, the astringent scent on my skin masking something sharp and feral underneath. I feel vulnerable and uncertain. I want him to leave and I want him to stay.

"Well," he says, picking distractedly at his pant leg. "I guess you won't be going undercover anymore." He offers a tired grin. "It's too bad, since the nurse tells me you're suddenly fluent in German."

It's a joke. I've never gone undercover. But I can't smile. I can barely speak.

When his face falls, I murmur, "I'm wrapped . . . in dead skin." And when he jumps back, I do smile—inwardly.

"Skin . . . from a cadaver," I breathe. Words are still a struggle, but I feel like they're making the right shapes on my lips. "Don't worry," I murmur. "It's only temporary . . . until they . . . harvest skin . . . from my ass." Again, I want to laugh, but the sound stays in my chest. A heavy wheezing in my throat.

Teddy smiles, but his eyes are still wide, and he's not looking at me, watching the blinking lines on the vital signs monitor instead.

He clears his throat. "Cindy was beside herself when I got the call. She'll be relieved you haven't lost your perverse sense of humor."

Cindy—right. For a moment I had almost forgotten. I shift away from his gaze. And anyway, I think it's him who's relieved.

"How's—"

"Your house? Still standing. Definitely damaged, but nothing irreparable from what I could tell. Your neighbor—what's her name, with the red hair and the two boys?"

"Donna," I say, feeling pinpricks where tears should be. The thought of my house—battered and bruised—makes it more real somehow.

"That's her. She came running out as soon as she saw me. She's the one who called it in, and wanted to know how you were doing. She also asked if she should get a guard dog, if there was an arsonist roaming the neighborhood, or if someone had a personal vendetta against you."

He raises an eyebrow.

Donna would be comforted by the idea that I have a target on my back. Random acts of violence terrify people. But tell them the fire next door is a lover's quarrel or drug related, and they're relieved. But I know that's not what Teddy's getting at.

Teddy leans toward me. "What happened?" he asks.

"I don't know," I tell him, my throat constricting again. And it's true. But I hear Michael's voice, see the look on his face as he left the station.

"What do you remember?" Teddy asks.

I close my eyes.

One moment, I was lying in bed, sipping a glass of wine, trying to fall asleep with visions of identical fraternity boys dancing in my head, and the next, I was awake and on fire.

My throat is so raw it takes enormous effort to swallow and even more to say the next words.

"I heard voices."

"Do you think—"

But we're interrupted by the appearance of a man in a white coat at the door.

Teddy sighs. He wants to touch me but can't decide where to put his hands.

He looks at his shoes. "I'll be back tomorrow."

"You better," I mumble. "Teddy," I say, and he turns. "Am I still on the case?"

He grimaces. "Later," he says with a glance at the doctor.

But I know. It's been three days. I didn't show up for work on Friday. Jay's parents arrived on Saturday. And today is Monday. I've been replaced. Oliver must be thrilled.

"Ms. Kaplan," the doctor says as Teddy disappears down the corridor.

The name tag on his coat reads JAMES FISHER, MD, SURGEON AND BURN SPECIALIST.

"How does your breathing feel today?"

"Tight," I say.

"Chest discomfort? Pressure, fullness, squeezing, pain?"

"Yes."

"Numbness?"

"I wish."

He smiles, revealing two small dimples. A lock of gray-blond hair curls around his ears.

"Your left side?"

"Sore."

"I bet." He laughs, and I warm to him a little bit.

"Everything itches," I breathe.

He nods. "Third-degree burns often cause nerve damage. I'd say those are phantom itches. But that doesn't matter if you go scratching away at your dressings." Suppressing a grin, he says, "Where does it itch?"

He puts his hand on the side of my ear, a gesture so intimate in this place where my body has been routinely lifted, shuffled, scraped, and bandaged, that something flutters in my stomach as I meet his eye, and then dies as I think of myself from his perspective. All tubes and raw skin. Bodily fluids expelling through a catheter and bedpan. Everything from my blood oxygen levels to my temperature monitored and regulated. Nothing in my control.

"I'm sorry about your hair," he says, and his fingers are light against my temple. "There were burns on the left side of your scalp."

"My hair?" I mumble, straining to touch it.

He withdraws his hand. "No one told you?" The laughter has gone out of his voice. His mouth twists and he exhales. "We had to shave it," he tells me. "Not all of it—" he says at the panicked look on my face. "Just some—the left side—pretty much the entire left side."

I try to raise my hands—what is the mark of insanity?—repeating the same action again and again. Still, I can't get used to not having control of my body.

He sighs and strides out of the room. I'm still trying to imagine what I look like when he returns with a small compact mirror, which he holds a few inches in front of my face.

It's worse than I expected.

The entire side, from the crown of my head down to my left ear, is shaved. The brown hair on the right remains but is scorched and matted, about five inches shorter than I remember. I might look like a punk rock chick if it weren't for the bandages patchworked from my left cheek to the back of my skull. There are red gashes, where flecks of skin are missing from the tip of my nose and chin.

I'm hideous.

Worse—ridiculous. Green eyes overlarge with surprise, alien-like in my face.

I'm laughing so hard, I'm crying.

Dr. Fisher studies my reaction. When the tears start, he hands me a tissue, realizes I can't do anything with it, and dabs my eyes.

I'm mortified by my vanity.

"Physical changes are hard," he says softly, reading my thoughts. "Sometimes they're more of a shock than anything else because they're visible reminders of what happened."

His kind voice grates in my ear. *Get out*, I think, wanting to lick my wounds in private.

I close my eyes and breathe so deeply I taste blood.

How long do I sleep? A minute, an hour, a day? Time's marked by unusual intervals: Danae flicking my fluid bag with her fingernail, a metal cart rattling down the hall, and irregular bursts of laughter. Who knew there'd be so much laughter in a hospital?

A door swings open. I hear voices, but they're muffled again when the door falls shut. Every inch of this place—from the lacquered floors to the concrete ceilings—reflects noise. I hear murmurs and whispers, muffled sobs, and imagine the tips of fingers wiping away tears. I think if I close my eyes, I can follow these sounds through the hall into the waiting area and out the front doors, but I always find myself trapped in my bedroom, the walls aflame, and laughter echoing throughout the house. The laughter turns to whispers. I want to scream. But my mouth won't open. It's melted shut.

There's a rhythmic tap on my door.

I squeeze one eye open and hope it's not still leaking.

The man's tall and stocky, wearing a blue button-up and a military buzz cut. If it weren't for the thick brown mustache, I'd think he was a cop.

Instead, he introduces himself as Alphonso Griffon, fire marshal.

He settles in the chair Teddy vacated some unknown hour before and crosses one long leg over the other. His boots have thick rubber soles and I wonder idly if they're heat retardant.

"You're lucky," he tells me. His voice is rich with solemnity, and I'm not sure whether he's begun this way or has been talking for a while. "With all the synthetic materials in the modern home, occupants have roughly two to three minutes to get out. A minute more—"

Fuck luck, I think. "Fluck," I say out loud, too tired to open my mouth fully. Tell that to my bedsores. To the raw, exposed flesh on my arm like hamburger meat slipped in plastic, reflecting my tenuous spot on the food chain. That my skin is thin, my body easily broken, my blood limited and susceptible to sepsis.

He gestures with his big man's hands. "Luckily, since you sleep with the door closed, the fire was limited to your room."

I snort.

Right, I think, *with me trapped inside*. The witch in the oven she prepared for Hansel and Gretel. Joan of Arc strapped to a stake. But I survived, like Shadrach, Meshach, and Abednego. A miracle.

"This enabled us to reach you more quickly. A second gained is a life saved."

I wonder if that "life saved" slogan is framed somewhere at the fire station. His watch ticks loudly, and I stare at it as he observes me. *If they had arrived two seconds sooner would I still have my eyebrows? My hair?*

"When we got to you, you were unconscious, half on the floor, half hanging from your sheets. The flames had consumed the other side of your mattress and were racing across your bed. The damage had spread to the ceiling. At that point, cyanide and carbon monoxide levels were

increasing at three thousand, four hundred parts per million. Your survival time was less than one minute."

He says all this calmly, but the way his eyes jump from me to the far
wall and back reminds me of a startled rabbit. He and his team risked
their lives for me. Saw the flames, knew the danger, and still barreled
into the hellish landscape that was my bedroom. I'm supposed to feel
grateful—I know. But I can't. I'm so tired. I close my eyes and hope he'll
get the hint.

Instead, he keeps talking. His voice is a low rumble, a perverse
bedtime story to ease me into slumber. *Once upon a time there was a
girl asleep in her bed and a fire started on her night table. No one knows for
certain, but they think she drifted off with the candles burning. One of her
neighbors, a big red fox who was making sure all her kits were tucked snug
in their blankets, saw lights leaping in the window and called 911 before the
flames turned into a blaze—otherwise the girl would be in a lot worse shape
than she is today.*

In my mind's eye, I see lavender-colored pillars, the candles Cindy
gave me for my birthday—*So you can relax*, she'd said, *treat yourself. Well,
that backfired*, I think, and then drowsily am pleased at my pun. But the
candles are decorative. I never burn them. And certainly wouldn't light
them right before bed, sitting precariously next to my pillow and under
the gray blackout curtains framing the window.

I frown.

"Another possibility is the extension cord," Fire Marshal Griffon offers.

I know the one. It's stretched from my desk to the outlet under my
bed and tethered octopus-like to my table light, standing lamp, as well as
my computer and phone charger.

"All it takes is a spark," he says, a little too enthusiastically.

I'm just nodding off, for real this time, when he says, "You'll need
the mitigation vendor to assess the full scope of the damage. They'll
test your bedroom for soot and smoke, then bring in a HEPA vacuum to
clean the air. They might need to tear down a wall or the ceiling to check

for water." He pauses to make sure I'm still listening. "Do you know when the house was built?"

I shake my head. Was it 1956, '59? I should know. I do know but can't remember.

"You might need lead and asbestos testing."

My head is throbbing. "How long?"

"Before you can return?" He's quiet a moment, and I open my eyes to look at him. His mouth twitches, and he scratches his mustache. "It depends on the damage," he says finally. "Could be anything from three weeks to"—he stares at the far wall as he calculates—"six months."

A groan forms in my chest. *Six months?*

"Check with your insurance, they might cover alternative living expenses. In my experience, friends or family nearby are best. Fire survivors often suffer from PTSD, an unfamiliar place might exacerbate—"

I close my eyes again.

"I know this is a lot of information to take in," he says mildly.

And I want to scream.

M arlitt."

My mother's hand is on my temple, nails sweeping the remaining hair on the right side out of my face. Her voice is soft, and she says my name over and over again until I open my eyes. Staring into her face, the line of her thin nose and wide mouth, I'm overwhelmed by a strange and sudden feeling of déjà vu. Another hospital. Light fingers on my forehead.

She blinks and draws into herself. The vulnerability disappears behind her black-framed glasses.

"You're awake."

"You're here," I say dryly, taking in her gray blazer and slacks, the neatness of her hair.

"I've been here every day," she says, straightening the cuff of her blouse. "You've been asleep."

To list everyone else I've seen would be petulant. But I would if there weren't cat's claws strangling my vocal cords.

Danae strides across the room, nods at my mother, and notes something on her clipboard.

"I don't know what her problem is," I say after she marches out again.

"You tried to punch her while she was sponge-bathing you. You also pulled out your ventilator and accused her of lighting matches under your bed."

My mouth drops open. "I don't remember that."

"You were semiconscious."

"Well," I begin, "she can hardly blame me—"

"None of the other nurses will work with you."

I frown.

"Where's Dad?" I ask, changing the subject.

She clears her throat. "You know your father hates hospitals. I've been sending him hourly updates. Don't think he doesn't care." She crosses her arms over her chest. "He's barely eaten or slept since we got the call—"

I roll my eyes.

My mother's defense of my father is legendary. A Rhodes scholar and world-traveling journalist, legend has it, he took one look at my book-clutching, Simone de Beauvoir–quoting mother and changed his hippie, let-the-wind-blow-him-in-any-and-all-directions ways, determined that this anti-anything-resembling-a-patriarchal-institution woman would marry him and bear his children. I was born two years later, and my mother hyphenated her last name. His friends loved to regale me with stories of my father joining peaceful revolutions in Thailand, dogging the president of Myanmar for six weeks, and tripping on ayahuasca so he could write a full-fledged report on the Achuar people. This thrill-loving, adventurous man did not match the nightmare-suffering, verging-on-agoraphobic person I grew up with, who feared everything from tornadoes to virus-carrying waiters, refused to let me participate in gymnastics, and wouldn't talk to me for weeks when I announced my plans to join the force. No one else seemed bothered by this contradiction. And the one time my teenaged self sarcastically asked, "What happened?" the laughter was sucked out of the room, my father's eyes clouded over, and my nothing-ruffles-her-feathers mother shouted at me for the first time in my life.

"I brought you some things," my mother says, the reproof of my ungratefulness hovering where it always is under her vowels. She busies herself with the canvas bag at her feet so I can't examine the look on her face.

Two slim books appear. "I can bring more," she says, confusing her ravenous reading habit for my own.

I angle my head to read the spines. True crime, I see, and recognize this as an act of generosity. I would have expected her to have grabbed something more literary from her office shelves.

I close my eyes and think I fall asleep, but when I open them, she's still there.

"Tripp Holmes," I say, remembering an unresolved question.

"He's in my intermediate class," she says. "Sweet kid."

"He read a Schiller quote"—I pause, and my mother gives me a sip of water—"at the memorial for Jay Kemp."

"Did he?" There's bemused satisfaction in her voice. "Such an impressionable fleeting thing," she says, and I'm left wondering whether she means the poem or the boy.

I jolt up from a dream with the certainty that I was speaking German. Another dark vision of tubes and wires. A strange blue light. And the sudden feeling that a void has opened up around me—a crushing, staggering emptiness. The deepest loneliness I have ever felt.

But when I open my eyes, Teddy's sitting at my side.

"*Guten morgen*," he says, confirming my suspicions.

I grimace.

"That happy to see me, huh?"

"No." I shift uncomfortably. My eyes are wet. "I just—" I go to rub my face but then stop myself. "It's unsettling—all the German bubbling out of me."

There's a tremor in my voice, and Teddy reaches for the plastic cup on the table. Offers me a sip of water.

I shake my head, and he sits back.

"It's not that strange, is it?" His eyes meet mine briefly, but then travel to the hall and the nurses' station. "I mean, your mother's German. She teaches German. It must have lodged itself in your brain without you knowing."

I shake my head, not wanting to go into the million ways my mother combated such a fate. "Learning a language is more than just stringing words together. There are rules you have to memorize. It takes time and lots of practice." *Jesus*, I think, *I sound just like her.*

But it's more than that. The dream. The hospital room—similar but so different from this one. The German. It's like the fire unleashed something buried deep within me. Like the language has always been there, and the fire set it free.

Teddy shifts toward me, a strange expression on his face. For just the briefest moment, I think he might kiss me, but then I remember. The burns, the scars, the hair, and the unspoken rule we adopted the first time this almost happened.

"I, um . . ." He chews the inside of his bottom lip. "I hope you don't mind, but I asked Cindy about the whole waking up and speaking a new language thing—I didn't say it was you," he adds quickly, "but she might have put two and two together."

I frown.

In some ways, him dating Cindy made everything easier. The tension abated because the possibility of something happening between us disappeared. But what I never told him is that it wasn't possible to begin with. Not just because we were partners, but because I wanted to go on believing I was invincible. I knew that anything even resembling roman-tic feelings would make me vulnerable. And I would never allow that. Not again.

"She said she'd heard of cases where traumatic brain injuries led to new linguistic abilities. But it's usually temporary and also impairs the patient's ability to speak their native language."

I think back to waking up here, in the hospital, the heaviness of my tongue, the nurse unable to understand me.

"There was a guy in Australia who woke up speaking Mandarin af-ter a car crash. And an Englishman who started speaking Welsh after a stroke. They both had some experience with the language they started speaking, but neither knew it fluently. She said there's this other rare condition called foreign accent syndrome that's better studied, and these cases might be related." He blinks at me expectantly. "It's possible that you suffered damage to the part of your brain that controls the speech muscles." He points to his mouth. "Lips, tongue, jaw, and larynx. I think that's what she said." He furrows his brow. "Anyway, it's less that you're speaking German accurately—you're probably making grammar mistakes—it's more that you sound fluent to non-German speakers." He looks proud and somewhat relieved that he remembered it all. "I mean, the firefighters and nurses might have recognized that you were speaking German but wouldn't have known if what you were saying made any sense."

I nod slowly, feeling unbalanced by all this information. Instead of be-ing comforted by the fact that I'm not the only one to wake up speaking a foreign language, I feel oddly shortchanged.

That was my thing, I think ridiculously.

After a stretch of silence, Teddy stirs. "What did the fire marshal say?" he asks. He leans in so close I feel his breath on my skin. "Any idea what caused the blaze?"

It's lingering there in the cautious way he's phrased this—the unan-swered question from his last visit. The possibility this wasn't an accident.

I heard voices.

It's the truth, but how does it sound? What will Truman say when word gets back to him? Marlitt's speaking in tongues and hearing things. I don't need to add mental health to his ever-growing list of patronizing bullshit.

I take a breath. "He said it was probably the candles by my bed or the extension cord," I tell him.

Teddy frowns. "Candles," he repeats.

"The electrical spark seems more likely," I say quickly, wincing at the thought of him believing I make a habit of lighting candles before bed. "Those houses built in the fifties weren't wired for all our electronic devices." I try for a smile, but he only nods distractedly, a small twist to his mouth.

I close my eyes. Michael told me to be careful. That can't be a coincidence.

But what's more likely: An extension cord sparking or a fraternity boy breaking into my house, creeping up the stairs, and setting me on fire? It sounds crazy or like I'm biased and one-track minded—all the things Oliver suspects and Truman's warned me about. And Teddy? Would he believe me after what I told him about Craig? Or would he think my hatred's spilled over, tainting everything, and ruined my ability to be objective? I can't risk him doubting my credibility, too. And so I bury my suspicions deep, waiting to reexamine the details, to see if whoever did this was smart enough to cover their tracks.

I'm in the hospital for two weeks. The doctor—who tells me to call him James—stops in twice a morning, and Danae mutters that I'm getting special treatment. She asks me so many questions about Teddy, I let it slip how great his girlfriend is, how they're in love, and it's really so sweet. And she punishes me with stories of burn patients with terrible nightmares, whose bodies reject their skin grafts, who refuse to leave their houses and wither away from loneliness. I'm also pretty sure she skipped one of my hydrocodone doses on purpose.

Teddy visits me every day but won't say a word about the Kemp case. No matter how many times I pester him, he tells me to focus on getting better and ignores the fact that I have nothing else to do but think about Jay, his brothers, the stolen car, and the broken body on the asphalt. The rest of the time, I slip between painful wakefulness and unsettling dreams, where the hospital and my house conflate into one and I can't escape either because someone's handcuffed me to the bed and the walls are in flames.

| Ten |

Thursday, November 28, 8:00 A.M.

They release me—as if I've been in a holding cell instead of a hospital room—on a bright Thursday morning. I can't say I'll miss the place, all colorless right angles and squeaky nurses' shoes, but I do swing my head around for a last glimpse of the doctor. No luck. Danae's there, though, probably hoping for a Teddy sighting. She smirks as my mother grabs my elbow and steers me toward the glass exit doors.

By the way my mother clenches her jaw I'm to know this is a great sacrifice. She must have canceled class—something she never does—and I imagine thirty or so students gleefully throwing papers into the air before speeding out to do handsprings on the brown quad or stumble back to their dorms to sleep. *You're welcome*, I think.

The books she brought me disappear into her canvas bag, and I see her lips pucker at the thumbed-down page of the first book not even halfway through.

The air outside is thin and cool, but the short walk to the car leaves me winded, and I collapse into the passenger seat of her station wagon, amazed by the strange weakness of my legs.

"You're staying with us," my mother says, as I struggle with the safety belt.

When I don't respond, she adds, "Your father's put new sheets on your bed," as if this settles anything.

I'm torn between irritation and relief. I don't like the idea of the two of them making decisions on my behalf, taking control of my where-abouts as if I'm a child, but the thought of a hotel—another nondescript space, shuffling by strangers in the morning, listening to moaning and weeping through the walls—seems too similar to the situation I just left.

I think of my parents' warm sunroom. The smell of rich coffee and floor-to-ceiling books on the shelves. The constant hum of my father's record player, NPR in the kitchen as he cooks, or his own voice as he reads the news out loud. On paper, it's cozy and comforting. But there's a reason I rarely visit. And it's more than memories of my father check-ing on me every ten minutes, his footsteps pounding up the stairs if I so much as dropped a hairbrush, the locks double- and triple-checked. It's the unsettled feeling I always have in that house. The whispers of my parents that stop whenever I enter a room. The certainty that something's been misplaced. As a child, never being able to sit still and always looking for movement just out of the corner of my eye. The unease has settled over time, but every now and then I still expect something or someone to walk out of the shadows.

I'm allowed to return to my own home first to gather some things but have been given strict instructions not to linger.

An unusual number of cars line my street. Colorful wreaths grace doorways, and smoke puffs from chimneys in houses where residents should be at work. I frown and watch a large, balding man I've never seen before drag a large pot from his back seat. The late-morning lull makes me edgy. It feels like the world's holding its breath, but for what?

I don't understand the people who are surprised that in their absence, life has gone on without them. For two weeks, I've been painfully aware that every second I was in the hospital, teenagers were pumping them-selves up to rob convenience stores, men were taking rounds on their wives' faces, pharmacists were lining customers with so much oxycodone that there'd be at least two ODs by morning, and Jay's murderer was getting further and further away.

From the outside, my little house looks almost the same. The only indication that anything happened are the thick tire marks in the dead grass and a sheet of plastic covering the upper window. But that's it. The white oak's turned copper in my absence. The ivy growing up its trunk has browned along with its leaves, and I'm left feeling shortchanged—like the worst of the fire has been seared across my skin.

My mother sighs and unclips her seat belt.

"It's not your fault," she says, misinterpreting my silence. "Things like this just happen."

I know she means the candles. Everyone seems to have assumed this was a rare moment of negligence. The shards of an empty glass and wine bottle under my nightstand didn't help.

The feeling grows that the house has betrayed me.

"I'd rather go in alone," I tell her.

Her eyes narrow as she tries to discern whether this is an insult, a product of my infinite stubbornness, or something else.

"I *need* to do this alone," I say, meeting her gaze for a fleeting moment. Playing the victim doesn't sit well with me, but my mother sneaks a look at the burned side of my face and nods.

"Fine," she murmurs. She pulls a pile of papers out of her bag. "Shout if you need anything."

I stride across the lawn, repeating the list of things I have to find: driver's license, auto registration, checkbook, passport, birth certificate, credit cards, and things to do: record damaged goods, inspect walls, ceilings. I've been instructed not to dawdle. Informed there are unseen particles waiting to do damage to my lungs. But when I open the door, I stop and take a breath.

The first thing I notice is that it doesn't smell like my house. The smoke has spread from my bedroom to the cooler areas below. It's nosed its way through the pipes, smothered my walls, and left fingerprints of its destruction throughout. Mold in the drywall, water seeping into the insulation and wood. But I'm not looking for tongues of smoke and bubbling wallpaper, I'm scanning for footprints. Wondering where the forensic examiner and the crime scene tape are. I slip my phone from my bag and take photos. I walk in a straight line, careful to disturb as little as possible.

The orange-and-red hall runner bunches at the center, and I kneel to examine its mud-caked tassels. The toe of a boot print blurs like someone was running and tripped as the rug slid across the floor. There are ruins of grass and a small pebble from the front walk. They could belong to anyone—a firefighter, my mother, Teddy, the insurance inspector—so many people have been in and out of the house after the damage was done.

I'm aware of my mother's eyes on the front windows, the urgency in her expression when I shut the car door even as she fumbled for papers to grade.

I stand. The alabaster walls seem to bow inward. The plants on the windowsill look sick. The pale sofa's askew and shuffled two feet forward. There's a vase in pieces next to my bookshelf. I search my memory. Did something wake me that night? A crash before the white-hot blaze? But instead, I see firefighters in tan suits and astronaut helmets barreling through the entryway and careening with unfamiliar objects as they head for the stairs.

I grab a duffel bag from the closet, a stack of papers and my wallet from the dining room table, and then I follow their trajectory, tracing the dark scratches on the wall and dusty boot prints on the birch steps leading to my room. A large hole's been sawed into the Sheetrock, but I wait until I'm at the door, no longer on its hinges, to peer in.

The far corner is an indistinguishable mash of wood and paper so wrong and unnatural that I can't remember how it used to look. A twisted bar of metal reminds me of the standing lamp. The mattress fans like swan's feathers atop busted wire netting. Paint swells into large blisters on the side of my dresser and the remaining shards of the mirror lie at its feet. Parts of the ceiling hang down, exposing the ribs of the attic. And suddenly I do feel as if I've gotten off lucky. A twinge of sympathy for the house.

I've been told to leave my clothes—that even if they appear undamaged, soot may live in their fibers and wearing them might threaten my already weakened lungs. I pick my way through the room over to my desk. The wood's splintered and the knobs are melted into flat faces. I wedge my fingers between the boards and poke around until I find my checkbook and the square box with my passport and birth certificate.

And then I'm stumbling through the hall and tripping down the stairs, fighting a sudden wave of panic and fire and darkness before the fall air hits me, cold and exhilarating, like jumping into a lake in early spring, and I'm waving the documents at my mother's concerned face in the car window, hoping she can't tell just how close I was to losing my shit.

As we drive beneath the sprawling tree branches on my parents' street, I'm hit with a warm wave of nostalgia. I'm seven, maybe eight. Summer tastes like honeysuckles and the promise of sugar-sweet ice pops and smells like sunscreen and mosquito-bite ointment. I'm lying on my belly at Whitney's house, two doors down, looking at old photo albums, laughing at a picture of her brother half-naked in a high chair, covered in chocolate cake. There's Whitney holding a balloon, licking an ice-cream cone, cradled in her mother's arms. With every flick of the page she gets smaller, and I'm mesmerized by this backward glance through time. The memory flickers and then we're racing, Whitney's dark braids flap as we tear across the road. We squeal whenever a car peels around the bend. Cyclists and joggers yell us on, and we run faster. My shoelaces must come untied, because the next thing I know I'm flying over the sidewalk and blood is gushing from my knee. I'm not a crier. Never have been. Whitney, on the other hand, starts screaming. My father is out the door, off the front porch, and down the seven stone steps to the walkway before I can roll off my face to examine the damage. His mouth is twisting with fury. He shakes my arm: "You have to be careful, Marlitt." He yells at Whitney, and she hightails it home. When I ask him about our family photos, he blanches and walks away. Her father will come over later that night, and then both fathers are shouting and Whitney and I aren't allowed to play together anymore.

I sigh, and my mother turns her head, eyebrows raised.

"It's only temporary," she tells me.

Then she swings a large U-turn to park in front of a vintage bungalow framed by two reddening oaks and a row of bushes at the property edge. An arched brick entrance leads to a shady front porch. My father will be sitting behind the white-framed double window at the dining room table, waiting for us. And sure enough, before my mother kills the engine, the door opens and there he is—barefoot in slacks and a striped polo, thinning once-dark hair glinting in the sun. He looks cracked and haggard, and I know my mother's telling the truth about him not sleeping. But his smile is so big in his narrow face that I almost forgive him for not visiting me in the hospital. He skips down the steps and envelops me in a hug as soon as I step out of the car. He smells like coffee and toast. His skin is papery and sallower than I remember, and I wonder if he's still having chest pains and if I'll ever get him to see a doctor.

My mother must have warned him, because he barely flinches when he takes in my face. Only the corner of his mouth tightens. I don't blame him. I imagine I look something like a maskless phantom of the opera. A one-sided hairless cat. That the scars on my face and running down my arm are reminders there are things outside his control—something as ubiquitous as a candle or an extension cord—must be killing him.

"We're so happy you're staying with us," my father says, like I'm there on vacation. Just looking to enjoy the beautiful fall in Athens when the students roll in from the Atlanta suburbs and turn our quaint summer town into a giant tailgating party.

I make a noncommittal noise in the back of my throat and wave his hands away when he grabs my duffel.

"I'm not an invalid," I tell him.

But I am tired.

I'm conscious of my body, its muscles and thin tissue, in ways I've never been before. It's all unfamiliar: the tightness in my lungs, the weakness of my legs, the thickness of my skin, grown hard and leathery.

"Nonsense," he says, but his eyes have left my face and are searching the beams of the neighbor's house. "You're our guest." And then he begins to sing under his breath—*be my guest, be my guest, put our servers to the test*—getting the words wrong like he always does on purpose. And I'm smiling in spite of myself as I follow him and my bag up the stone steps and into the light-filled entry hall with its wooden staircase and French doors that open on either side—the living room with its built-in bookshelves on the left and formal dining room with its long farmhouse table on the right—bathing us in a warm glow.

I try not to resent this place with its sepia-toned memories, the girl in pigtails I see skipping about and the imaginary brother I thought I should have. The sun-bleached floorboards and red-stitched rugs. The cracked clay coffee cups my father insists on keeping because I made them in elementary school. The turkey handprints on the wall. But it's all too much of a reminder of before. The pretty little child running somewhere just behind me. The reluctant student with flowing hair and brow furrowed over books at the kitchen table. Not at all matching the scarred, half-bald reflection glaring back at me from the glass of the microwave cabinet.

"Coffee?" my father asks as he slides a mug into my hands.

"Thanks," I say, remembering the perks of living with other addicts.

Pressed between my palms, the cup's warmth is comforting. I take a sip and watch through the kitchen window as half a dozen children spill out of a minivan across the street.

"Looks like the Harts are having a party," I murmur.

"All those grandkids," my father says, a bit wistfully. "It's Thanksgiving."

I blink, and then do the math in my head. The fire was some time in the early hours of Friday, the fifteenth. I was unconscious for three days. At some point, skin was shaved off my thigh—not my ass, like I told Teddy—and grafted onto my face and arm. Mornings began with dressing changes, then there were physical and occupational therapy sessions, and my dressings were changed again. Applications of antibiotic ointments. Visiting hours. Somehow, as the whiteness of my skin graft slowly shifted to pink, hours turned into days, days into weeks, and today into Thanksgiving. And the strange cars and odd stillness on my street and my doctor's absence this morning and Danae's grumbling about having to be at work suddenly make sense.

"I hope you don't mind." My mother eyes me over her own cup. "But Verena's coming for dinner. I know," she says at the look on my face, "that you'd prefer not to see anyone. But I invited her weeks ago. And she's still new, doesn't know many people, her boyfriend's—"

"Fine," I say, thinking that some things never change.

Ever since I can remember, my mother has taken a junior faculty member under her wing, turning our quiet dinner table into a train stop for visiting assistant professors, graduate students, lecturers, and adjuncts. All staring up to my mother with that same grateful smile, talking about unfair course loads and the job market. Looking around our house, thinking that one day, if they play their cards right, they might find some kind of stability. My mother never has the heart to tell them it doesn't work like that anymore. And the next holiday, there's a new face at the table, the last one back to Germany or their parents' house or furiously writing op-eds for whoever will publish them.

At least with Verena here, she and my mother will do the talking. I feign the need to unpack and lie down, but my mind is racing. This Thanksgiving, the Kemp family will have an empty seat at the table. His murderer is out there somewhere eating mashed potatoes and green bean casserole thinking he's gotten away with it. Teddy will be at his mother's house laughing with his sisters at the long picnic table set up in the back-yard. Truman will be stretched out on the couch watching football while the boys roughhouse on the floor, Nancy, his wife, cooks, and Alice sneaks him extra slices of pie. And I'm here, with no idea what's going on. No idea if after what's happened, Truman will feel sorry for me and let me back on the case or feel sorry for me and insist I take more time off.

I collapse on my childhood bed and check my phone for the twentieth time. But there's nothing. No updates, check-ins, or other confirmations of existence from Teddy or Truman.

Verena—a tall woman about my age with dark hair and amber-colored eyes—arrives at a quarter to five wearing a burgundy A-line skirt and a pair of no-nonsense tennis shoes. She carries a bottle of wine in one hand and two casserole dishes in the other, bringing with her the scent of melted cheese and caramelized onions.

My father materializes from the kitchen with an apron tied around his waist, brandishing a tofu dish and a turkey to Verena's complimentary applause. He beams at her and glances at me. My smile's too late or too much of a grimace. I see it in the hesitation of his step before he reaches the table.

"So, Verena," my father asks as he sits across from my mother, "how are you liking Athens?"

"Oh." A grateful smile, the hint of a German accent. "It's great. For a small American city, there's a lot to do. Restaurants and music."

"Do you miss Bamberg?"

Verena's cheeks flush. "Yes and no. I miss the cafés—on the river, you know? And being able to walk everywhere. But I don't miss the snow. And all the tourists on the weekends."

My father laughs. "Here, you just have UGA fans."

It's always the same questions. Always the same answer. I swirl a thick egg noodle with my fork.

"And how's life at the university treating you?"

"It's . . ." A pause, while she exchanges a glance with my mother.

"Go ahead," my mother tells her magnanimously. "They've heard me complain for years now."

"It's just a lot of work. Between all the department and committee meetings, lesson preparations, office hours, and student emails, I haven't had any time—"

To work on my research or for myself, I finish for her.

"For my research," she says.

I smirk. I wonder if the boyfriend's wised up yet. A relationship with an academic is no picnic.

"And, I don't know, maybe it's because of the bigger classes, but I've already had problems with students cheating."

My father nods in a way that conveys he's heard all this before.

"But not just looking at someone's paper during a test or download-ing essays from online—which is bad enough. But I had a student send in one of his friends to take a test for him." She puffs up her chest, and the German accent underscoring her vowels becomes more prominent. "And then lie about it. As if I wouldn't notice."

"They do it all the time in big lectures," my mother tells her. "It's es-pecially rampant in Greek life. They'll send a younger brother in to sign an attendance sheet—"

I put down my fork, thinking of Jay's professors, the way they de-ferred to their teaching assistants and grade books. "Wouldn't you recog-nize your own students?"

My mother clears her throat. Verena helps herself to another serving of spaetzle.

"I would," my mother says patiently, "but my classes are capped at thirty. We're talking about lecture halls with hundreds of students." She gives me a knowing smile that says, *Indulge Verena, she's new.* "On large campuses—cheating's practically an industry."

She turns back to Verena. "We're professors—there to teach, not to police." A weird nod at me.

I frown.

"Ultimately, it's on the students if they decide to cheat. We can't chase down every infraction. Just have to know that that kind of behavior will catch up with them eventually."

"But what if it doesn't?" I ask.

"What do you mean?"

"I mean . . ." I fidget in my chair. The room feels hot all of a sudden, and I wonder if my father remembered to turn off the oven and have the sudden paranoid urge to go into the kitchen and check.

"What if that behavior doesn't catch up with them? What if they cheat, get away with it, and keep doing it? What kind of lesson is that?"

A line forms between my mother's eyebrows.

"Pie?" my father, ever the peacekeeper, interjects. "Verena," he says, drawing her attention away from my mother and me, "have you ever had pumpkin pie?"

She shakes her head, looking equally grateful for the distraction.

"You're going to love it."

After two pieces of pie and a cup of coffee, my mother sends Verena off with her cleaned casserole dishes and three plastic containers of leftovers.

In the living room, I hear the subtle strings of Schubert, louder now that Verena is gone.

My father and I sit at the table surveying the scattered plates and glasses, all the proof of a good meal.

"What's your plan for tomorrow?" he asks me. "I know you'll probably want to sleep in, but I thought, if you're interested you could help me go through a few papers . . ."

He doesn't need my help but wants to give me something to do. It's a Kaplan family trait—the need to be occupied.

"I'd love to," I say, "really, but I need to get back to the station."

He's silent a moment, picks up his wine and puts it down again without drinking.

"You're not going in tomorrow? It's the day after Thanksgiving."

I lift an eyebrow. "Crime doesn't stop for holidays."

He shakes his head. "Surely there's medical leave or time off or—" He looks at my mother for help.

She shrugs. My mother is very good at pretending she's listening when she's not. Her eyebrows lift at all the right moments, and she'll make noncommittal noises of agreement or sympathy depending on your tone. And if you ask her a question, she'll hesitate only a split second before guessing the right response. I attribute it to years of listening to students while grading papers, making mental lists, or thinking of her own answer to whatever question she posed in class. Most of the time my father doesn't notice or care. But today, he's impatient.

"Helena," he says. "We're talking about Marlitt. Her physical and emotional well-being." A note of a reprimand in his voice.

"If she's ready to go back," my mother says, standing and stacking our plates, "I don't think there's anything you or I can say to change her mind."

Points to me for being stubborn all my life.

My father sighs and plucks at his napkin. I'm too old for him to forbid me to do anything. But he would. If he could.

The truth is, unstructured time makes me itchy. Some days nothing exciting at all happens at the station, and I'm left scratching my nose at Teddy, flipping through newspapers, or playing Scrabble on my computer, but there are always reports piling up, a phone ringing, and procedural meetings. The thought of puttering around the house, sipping coffee, and gazing out the front window waiting for my phone to ring makes me want to rip what's left of my hair out.

My father's still staring at me, and I slump in my chair like I must have done a million times since I was twelve.

"It's nothing strenuous," I say to my father's forehead. "Paperwork, really. Just a few loose ends to wrap up and making sure Teddy and Oliver didn't mess up everything while I was gone."

I expect him to smile. My father, despite his distaste for my job, likes Teddy. I think he took one look at his calm face and thought that at least if I was in this line of work, Teddy would be by my side. But he only grimaces. My mother runs the tap in the kitchen.

With Verena gone and the dishes cleaned, we have nothing left to say to one another. I climb the stairs to my childhood bedroom and listen to my parents argue in hushed voices in the dining room below.

Hours later, I awake in a cold sweat with the sensation I might have been yelling in my sleep. The dream is faint and clings to me like a spider's thread, an almost invisible assailant in the night. I close my eyes, but there's only blackness. And not the dark lids that shutter my pupils, but an inky, unnatural shadow consumes me. And then, a whisper, a snap, and I explode in flames.

"Marlitt." My father's voice, a question written in it, behind the bedroom door. "Everything all right?"

"I'm fine, Dad," I murmur, my voice gravelly with sleep.

The door opens a crack and he shuffles in, still dressed in his striped polo and slacks.

"You're up?" I ask.

"Just studying a little Athens history. Did you know Athens Regional started as a facility in a private home? There were only twelve beds." He shakes his head in wonder. "And Ben Epps designed an airplane four years after the Wright brothers flew theirs at Kitty Hawk."

He sits in the coral armchair angled in the corner and props his feet on my bed as he talks.

"I'm fine, Dad, really," I say distantly.

He sighs and settles a little deeper into the chair. "You know, when you were a girl, you didn't like to sleep either. You weren't afraid of the dark—nothing like that," he says with a hint of paternal pride, "but you always insisted someone be here with you. That you should have had brothers or sisters, and since we—your mother and I—were depriving you, one of us had to sit with you instead until you fell asleep." His voice is amused, but a note of sadness creeps in.

I glance at him. That's not entirely how I remember our nighttime routine. Instead, I remember waking to find the door open, him peering in to make sure I was asleep in my bed, still breathing, not blue faced, or abducted, or whatever he feared might happen in the middle of the night.

He yawns and settles deeper into the chair. "If it's okay with you, I think I'll stay just a little longer."

I mean to tell him a third time that I'm fine and to please go to bed, but somewhere between thinking and speaking, the words drift away into that unidentifiable river of sleep and I'm enveloped in its tide.

| Eleven |

Friday, December 6, 8:00 A.M.

When I wake it takes me a moment to realize where I am. A dark crack runs the width of the ceiling above my head. The amber light streams through the white curtains at the wrong angle, and the framed photographs on the dresser are eerily all of me: There I am age three or so, pedaling a tricycle, a look of grim determination on my face. Seven, gap-toothed and grinning half-submerged in a pile of fall leaves. Sixteen, hair done into an ungodly updo, and Craig by my side looking three shades of uncomfortable in his father's suit.

Truman told me not to come in the day after Thanksgiving. I've been at my parents' a full week, twiddling my thumbs, and waiting for my phone to ring.

I hear the slow exhale of a city bus and the grinding stop of a garbage truck. The dark crack in the ceiling yawns, waiting until I close my eyes again to swallow me whole.

I have only a handful of my own clothes. A pair of jeans and a couple of T-shirts my mother discovered in the dryer when she went by my house with the insurance inspector. We're roughly the same size, and she's hung a few blouses on the back of my closet door. I'm not sure whether she crept in this morning while I slept or they've been there since last night, but don't have the energy to think on it further. I opt for a pair of my own ripped jeans and a blouse long enough to cover my arms.

Across the street, men are repairing the roof of the neighbor's house.

I listen to the sounds of hammers and the humming of some unseen machinery, and watch as they clamber across the roof without ropes or cables. *Just a slip*, I think. But the men look sturdy, with their quick feet and tool belts, throwing scraps of black membrane below. *But that's just it, isn't it*, I think bitterly. The tightrope walker is careful, every fiber of her being attuned to the vibrations of the rope, the expanse of air beneath her feet. The rest of us are just racing across shingles, too sure of our own purpose to secure a lifeline before we're tumbling backward into nothingness.

I shake out the concoction of pills the doctor prescribed and avoid my reflection in the mirror. The bandages on my face were removed before I left the hospital, but the wounds are still pink and raw-looking. The biggest risk is infection, so I'm supposed to inspect each burn for redness and swelling. There's mineral oil to massage into my skin twice a day and a compression sleeve for my arm to prevent the thickening of the skin graft. I've been told not to leave the house without sunscreen and to drink plenty of fluids. That I may tire easily, and my body may have difficulties regulating its temperature. That the new layers of skin will bruise, and the redness may never fade. Essentially, that this is my new normal, so to get used to it.

Once I finish, I leave the house in a hurry. On my way out, I grab a navy ball cap from the coatrack.

I park near the station entrance. Truman's car is there, as usual taking up two spaces. But I don't see Teddy's bike or Oliver's VW.

I call Teddy before I even realize I'm doing it and hang up before it goes to voicemail. Normally, we'd go into something like this together. Strategize how best to sweet-talk Truman to get what we want—Teddy's strong suit, not mine. But it doesn't look like that will be happening today.

I straighten my shoulders as I walk through the lobby. Amy's nowhere in sight, thank god, but Truman's door is open, and I hear the pounding of keys under his heavy breathing.

When I knock on the wall, he stands and moves toward me, arms half-opened in what looks alarmingly like a hug.

"Hi, Lieutenant," I say casually, putting the chair next to his desk between us and tilting my head to give him a good look at my face under the cap.

His mouth forms a surprised O before he can cover it.

I smile, and instead of a hug, he places a warm hand on my right shoulder.

"Good to see you up and moving, Kaplan." He laughs, and for a split second I worry that he witnessed me slack-jawed and unconscious in the hospital. "Sorry I couldn't pop in for a visit, but—" He waves his arm over the slanting stack of papers on his desk.

I shake my head, relieved. "Well," I say. "I'm back now."

He sighs and settles into his chair, cracking his knuckles one by one. I wonder if at some point this had been intimidating. Now it just makes him appear arthritic.

"Look," he says, "you've been through something traumatic." He holds up his hand before I can interject. "Hell, a fire? I've been unplugging everything before bed and running back into the house like Nancy with the damn hair dryer every time I leave to check the stove's off. Then I run back to make sure none of the boys have been smoking and hiding the evidence in the closet so the whole place goes up." His eyes flicker to my face and his voice softens a fraction. "You don't have to prove yourself, Marlitt. Just take the time off. It's a paid vacation. Maybe I should let Nancy leave all her hair stuff plugged in and throw everything into the bathtub for good measure. A little juice"—he mimes getting electrocuted—"and I could take Nancy on that honeymoon she's been badgering me about for thirty years."

This new, weirdly jovial Truman catches me off guard, but perhaps it's meant to. There are so many things wrong with what he just said that if I chase any one of them we'll never get to the point.

"I've already had my paid vacation," I tell him. "What about all the budget cuts? Teddy and I have office chairs that we can feel the wheels through our asses, but I can take three weeks off?"

"Language," he says.

"I'm fine," I say patiently. "You're understaffed."

He sighs, and the phone rings.

He almost breaks.

I see the exhaustion in his eyes—the late nights, the dinners he'll miss, all the lowlifes filing past his office—and the determination starts to waver, but then he looks at me. The resolve around his mouth tightens.

"We'll manage," he says. "Now leave before I decide to make it time off without pay."

He turns back to his computer, and I know there's no use arguing. I get the feeling that my point about the budget only reinforced his idea that he's doing something chivalrous. And he's too old-school to realize how patronizing and irritating that is.

There's a knock on the door frame and a figure moves into the threshold.

"Lieutenant," Oliver says. "We've got another one. Girl showed up this morning. She's requesting—Kaplan, you're back?"

I don't like the way his voice arches into a question.

"Graves." I nod.

He pulses in the doorway, unsure.

"Marlitt's taking some much-deserved time off," Truman cuts in behind me. I feel him stand and move around his desk. And although I want to hear the rest, the thought of Truman patting me on the shoulder again sends me sliding out of the room.

"See you in a week," I say to Oliver. His eyes, like Truman's, land on my face, and he looks like he might try to hug me.

"Two," Truman growls at my back. "Oliver, in here now."

Oliver shuts the door with a weary smile that's supposed to make me feel better, but I know he would close the blinds on the window if there were any.

I glance at the whiteboard.

In the weeks I've been gone, alibis have been checked and double-checked. Tripp. Michael. Cade. Even Samantha and Katie. The look alike Jays. All eliminated. Every brother and classmate, professor and childhood friend have their names crossed off. Photos of the vehicle and license plate have been circulated from here as far as Virginia, Mississippi, and Florida. If the guy was still driving it, we'd have him by now. Looks like after the tearful interview given by the parents and the promise of a reward for information, the phone was ringing off the hook. But no credible leads. Nothing. No enemies. No illegal activities came up on him or his brothers. There's a scribbled note that Jay was on antidepressants and painkillers at his time of death, but they were doctor prescribed and legally obtained.

It doesn't take a genius to guess what happened next. They had no real suspects. Enough time had passed that the witnesses started doubting what they'd seen. Maybe the light had still been green. Maybe the driver hadn't sped up. Maybe he hadn't smiled, hadn't looked like Jay at all. Maybe no one had been driving! While I was in the hospital, Teddy told me that once information about the antidepressants got out, witnesses started changing their minds and saying Jay deliberately ran out in front of the car. The parents denied this. Said Jay was happy, had so much going for him—good grades, friends—absolutely not suicidal. And even if he was, that didn't change the fact that a hit-and-run takes two to tango. But Teddy and Oliver had no more leads. No more theories. No suspects, period. Someone—I put money on Oliver—must have floated the idea that we'd been looking at it wrong. After all, I was the one who insisted on intent. And I was out of commission, not there to defend my line of reasoning. So maybe I was wrong. Maybe the whole thing had been an accident—a mere coincidence that the suspect was driving Jay's own car. That witnesses say he was smiling—a trick of the light. That he accelerated instead of slowing—only natural as he came down the hill. You'd think people would want answers. But ultimately this solution would have appeased everyone in their own way. Because if it was

intentional, premeditated or otherwise, if someone did want to murder
Jay, then at some point, you would have to ask why. And even though the
family thought they wanted to know, when you really start pressing, all
of a sudden, the everyone-loved-him story falls to pieces. The parents
remember behavioral problems. Bullying. Petty theft. Maybe drugs—
not everything shows up on our records. Rich kids' parents can bury a
number of their children's sins. In the end, there are a lot of reasons why
someone might want you dead, and it's rarely because you're an upstand-
ing guy. But if it's an accident? Well then, it can't be Jay's fault. He's an
innocent victim and stays that way. An angel in heaven—a decal on the
back of a car window—gone too soon.

On our side, it's better, too. When there's motive, you can trace
the pieces—drugs, abuse, broken relationships, whatever they are—
backward. From head hitting windshield, to perpetrator getting into car,
to stealing keys, to roommate fistfight, scorned lover, drug deal gone
wrong, or gambling debt. It's harder to find a murderer if they've chosen
someone at random. That's one reason they say truck drivers make good
serial killers. Always on the road, moving from place to place, no time to
form connections who might rat you out but enough time to stash the
body. But no one thinks there's a serial hit-and-runner out there. They
think it's a car thief, who somehow managed to hit the owner of the
vehicle nowhere near the location it was stolen, freaked out, and drove
off. The driver ditched the car in the woods, drove it into a lake, or hid it
in a garage. Whatever he did, without the car, there are no ties. Without
motive, even fewer. No strand to follow. Nothing to go on.

I stop by my desk and feel Truman's eyes through his window. My
folder with the call sheets is still there, but it's closed and neatly put aside,
like Teddy or Oliver had been rolling back and forth between their desks
and mine, flipping through my notes, and decided they were no longer
necessary. There's also a button blinking on my office phone. I shake my
head as I dial my voicemail. Why people still call this thing instead of
my cell, I'll never know.

"Hey, Marlitt, it's Ben" —a small hesitation— "from Missing Persons."
In my mind, I see a wiry middle-aged white guy with thinning hair and a
tired smile. The kind of guy you could meet and instantly forget, except
we go back—Missing Persons has to call us in more than they would like—
and one of my first cases started with a phone call like this, with Ben's soft
voice on the other end, asking for assistance on a missing-woman case.
"Listen, I sent over a file for you, may be nothing, but just take a look and
let me know what you think. Give me a call this afternoon if you can."

Perhaps it's the lack of urgency in Ben's voice—normally a call from
Missing Persons has you feeling like you're racing against an accelerating
clock—but I forget about Ben's call and the manila envelope as soon as I
slip it into my bag. Instead, I flip open the Kemp folder and run my finger
down the call sheet. There's something here, I'm sure of it, just like I was
before.

The door to Truman's office opens, and I stuff the folder next to Ben's
envelope before Oliver turns.

I call Teddy again on my way out the door, but it goes straight to
voicemail.

I check my watch. It's 10:15. A month ago, Jay was going about his
day, planning parties, and refusing to clean his room, with no idea that he
had less than a week to live. And here I am with time to kill.

The day stretches before me like a serpent, endless and threatening
with its stillness, yawning in the sun. Going back to my parents' house is
out of the question. The thought of spending the afternoon alone with
my father and his books makes my stomach clench. He'll either want to
know why I'm not at work or why I've been yelling in my sleep at night.

I'm still sitting in the station lot with the keys in the ignition, when I
chance a look at myself in the rearview mirror. The face staring back at
me is grim: dark stubbly hair from the crown of my head down to my left
ear and brownish-pink scabs like oblong birthmarks stretching across my
cheek and chin.

Fuck this, I think. They might be willing to brush the case aside, but there's someone out there who's responsible for Jay's death, and I'm going to retrace my steps—from visiting my mother's office that Tuesday morning to running down Lumpkin—and figure out what I missed.

C offee in hand, I twist past the students sitting on the stone steps in front of the university's arches. The scarlet oak's turned silver since the last time I saw it and is drowning in a sea of burnt-orange leaves. A student dozes on the ramp to New College. He's tucked his knees up to his chin and must be freezing. The day's much colder than the morning Jay was hit. But the tingling's gone—that sense that something was wrong; I don't feel it at all.

I pass the library without reading its motto and enter Joe Brown with only a cursory glance at the staircase to nowhere.

When I slip into my mother's office, she holds up a finger and keeps typing.

In the hall, there's the sound of singing—a woman's voice, rich and warm, as she greets students. My mother smiles, and I know before I see her that it's Amina Adebe, professor of psychology and women's studies, who's known me since I was in diapers and possesses a fondness for brightly colored dresses and dashikis. The rest of the faculty shuffle back and forth from classrooms to offices in a sea of gray, brown, and black. Not Amina. Today it's a red dress with yellow butterflies.

"Be bold, child," she'd say when she found me pressed into the corner of a classroom, head down, dragged to campus on a teacher workday, pretending to do my fifth-grade homework while my mother's students filtered into their seats. "Nothing is gained by making yourself small." And then with a wink: "Pay attention. You might learn something." And I did—but not about German. Who was the Erlkönig? What did he symbolize? No idea. But I was pretty sure the student wearing the Glands T-shirt was doing his math homework and hadn't slept the night before.

And that the girl with glasses and dark eye shadow had a crush on him. Pay attention—that's the first rule of detective work.

Today, Amina doesn't miss a beat.

"Marlitt," she says, when she peeks her head into my mother's office.

Like my parents, she wasn't keen on me joining the police force, and I experience the same flash of guilt I always feel when I see her. She knows I'm not a hugger but envelops me in her fleshy arms anyway.

"Your badass points just increased exponentially," she whispers in my ear.

Pressed against her chest, I know what she's trying to tell me. That she's glad I'm safe, that I survived.

I catch a glimpse of my mother's face above her shoulder and suddenly realize how hard this must have been on her—the phone call, the fire, the hospital—on both of them, really.

Amina releases me and turns to my mother, who's finally looked up from her screen.

"Pour us some of that liquid gold," she demands, and both laugh, my mother quietly, Amina with her head thrown back, exposing the undersides of her teeth.

As I sip my own cup, I imagine them as junior faculty members, this being an ongoing private joke they've shared for years.

"And so?" Amina asks, sitting next to me and leaning forward to take in my burns.

My mother shifts in her seat. We've discussed insurance forms and claims and documentation but haven't talked about what happened. I think she's embarrassed for me.

I shrug. "They say I fell asleep with the candles burning."

Amina sips her coffee and looks at me evenly. "Ridiculous," she says firmly.

Something in my chest tightens and then releases. I've been wrestling with that very same thought. It is ridiculous. The candles. So unlike me,

it shouldn't have even been in the realm of possibility. But to acknowledge this fact means to acknowledge the voices. My suspicions about
Kap-O's involvement. And I'm not ready to grapple with either yet.

We look at each other.

Then Amina glances at her watch and turns to my mother. "We better get going if we want a good spot."

"Right." My mother frowns at her computer. "Those emails can wait.
I think I'm going to add something in my signature that any questions
concerning material stated plainly in the syllabus will be automatically
deleted."

Amina laughs. "Good luck with that."

"Marlitt, will you be okay the rest of the afternoon?"

I frown, not liking the assumptions buried within the question. One,
that I might not be okay on my own, and two, that I will ever be okay again.

"Where are you going?" I ask.

"Yoga," Amina says, adjusting her dress as she stands.

"At the Ramsey gym?"

My mother nods, and grabs the keys off her desk.

"I thought you didn't like working out in front of students."

They both laugh.

"When I was younger. True." My mother turns to Amina. "I always
said I wanted to keep a respectable distance."

"I remember. You didn't want them to see you sweat," Amina grins.
"Or in stretchy pants."

"But now . . ." My mother shrugs. "The gym's free to faculty, and
they have classes all day so I can squeeze in a little me-time."

"Me-time surrounded by all those needy students?"

She grimaces. "It's the one place where no one bothers me. In my
office, at home . . ." She sighs. "There's always questions, or something
that has to be done *right now* or your father—" She hesitates. "But at the
gym, I have time for myself."

"Why don't you join us?" Amina suggests.

I shake my head. I hate gyms. All those people and machines. Give me a pair of sneakers, headphones, and some old-fashioned asphalt and I'm good to go.

"Families get a reduced rate," my mother tells me, "but I think you might have aged out."

"Funny," I say, drumming my fingers on the arm of my chair, thinking of being seen, but not bothered, in a public place where most people keep their heads down, everyone equally as self-conscious or self-centered, eyes on the floor or on the mirrors. I think of sweaty gym clothes and that empty block of time on Jay's call log. "If I told them I wanted to join, do you think they'd give me a tour?"

"You're really interested?"

I know she's thinking this is a good sign—self-care and something to focus on other than work—but my mind's speeding ahead to the East Campus Village and the sprawling gym with its indoor pools and basketball courts, hundreds of stationary bikes and elliptical machines with everyone staring at tiny built-in screens or their biceps.

I blink at my mother, already forgetting the premise of my visit.

"Right," she says. "Didn't think so." She clicks out of her webmail and stands. "You can come if you want, but we have to hurry."

The gym is a kaleidoscope of students in crop tops with toned legs and active young bodies trying to sweat out the lingering baby fat and stave off the freshman fifteen or sophomore twenty, all self-critical and with no understanding that they'll look back at their selfies ten years from now and wish they'd realized they were young and beautiful instead of killing themselves at the gym for the sake of some fleeting image of perfection.

Amina and my mother leave me at the front desk.

"Otherwise there won't be spaces in the back," Amina yells as she and my mother rush through the tripod turnstiles.

It's not until they disappear up the stairs that I pull out my badge. Then the two students behind the desk start moving, overly helpful, while trying not to stare at my scars.

It occurs to me that even if I've solved the hour gap on Jay's call log, it doesn't matter. Unless he pissed off some dumbbell-waving psycho who stole his car and ran him over with it, Jay's presence here doesn't make any difference. But still, I want to look around, to get a feel for the space. Maybe there's an alcove where people buy well-written essays and test answers, or drugs, I think hopefully. Maybe Jay was selling drugs.

"I'd like a tour," I say.

"A tour?" Student A repeats. He's pale and pockmarked with newly formed muscles stretched under his tight shirt.

"Yep, the whole thing."

I tap my badge on the counter.

"Um, okay." He casts a glance at Student B, but she's sunk back in her phone. "You all right if I show this lady—"

"Detective," I say.

"—detective around?"

Student B rolls her eyes. "I think I can handle it," she says with an irritable gesture to the empty lobby.

He buzzes me through the gate next to the turnstiles, and I stomp past like I know where I'm going.

"This way," he says, when I turn in the wrong direction. "We usually start with the pool."

For the next ten minutes, I'm assaulted with the scent of chlorine, the sounds of squeaky sneakers on the waxed basketball court, echoes of missed shots, and the heavy breathing of students running on treadmills. Through a pair of glass windows, I witness one group practice karate moves while another gyrates in front of a wall of mirrors. No one pays us attention or goes all shifty as we stride past. Quite a number are on their phones—texting as they pedal stationary bikes. Turning up music before they take another lap on the track.

I groan, and Student A glances at me with concern. I motion for him to continue.

Of course, if Jay were here, he would have his phone. There wouldn't be an empty gap on the call log at all. If anything, we'd probably have selfies of him flexing and posing in the mirror. I shake my head. This has been a complete waste of time.

"The women's locker room is here," Student A says. He steps aside in case I want to peek in.

"Day lockers are emptied after hours. Contents left in the lockers are placed in lost and found."

I begin to move away. His spiel sounds rehearsed, and I don't need to look to know I'll find a bunch of toned muscles and scar-free skin stretched beneath red-and-black sports bras.

"Or, if you prefer, you can rent a locker. Service terms for students are for the semester. You can rent a half or full, for fall, spring, and summer."

I stop. "You can rent a locker for the entire semester?"

"It's a different rate for students, faculty and staff, alumni—"

He's not sure what box to put me in.

"I'm curious about the student rentals."

He blinks. Not the box he thought, apparently. "Are you interested in a spring rental?"

"Actually," I say, walking briskly back to the front desk, "I'd like to see a list of current rental holders. Men's rental holders." Jay probably didn't rent a locker. Why would he, when he'd have to lug all his clothes back to the fraternity to wash? But I'm not going to leave without checking.

"I, um—" Student A jogs to catch up with me. Student B doesn't even look up when we return. "I don't know. Maybe I should get the facilities manager—"

He looks so unsure it's easy. "That won't be necessary. I just need a printed list. And if my guy's on there, I'll need to see what's in his locker."

A flicker of curiosity and an obedience to authority long ingrained from whatever sports training—soccer, from the look of him—he's received has him nodding as I speak. *Yes, Coach,* I imagine him thinking as he slips under the counter and dutifully clicks buttons on the computer. *Okay, Coach.* The printer hums.

I hold my breath and scan the list. It's short—not many students rent lockers. Most have "faculty/staff" listed in the box next to their names. But at the very end of the sheet is the name I'm looking for.

Jay Kemp, locker rental checked out on October 14, two months after the semester started.

I was right. My heart is hammering, and I know I should call Teddy, but I can't. I can't wait for his reluctant voice, Truman's inevitable lecture, and risk being sent home without seeing what's inside Jay's locker. And it may be nothing more than a shampoo bottle and a pair of dirty gym shorts. But that same voice from the day of the hit-and-run is yelling: *It's mine. I found it.* The only-child selfishness rearing its ugly head.

"Perfect," I say, trying to keep the excitement out of my voice. "I need you to take me to locker fifty-four."

"In the men's—"

"In the men's locker room."

He looks more unsure now than ever.

"You can ask the guys to clear out if you want, but I don't care either way."

"Hey," he says, staring at the list. "The locker belongs to Jay Kemp. Isn't that the guy who—"

"Yep," I say, breaking him off and casting a long and obvious look at the students filtering in and out of the lobby.

"Oh, right," he whispers. "Keep it on the low."

"Exactly," I hum back, and wave him on.

The locker room smells like Jay's bedroom, only more concentrated and lined with some kind of citrus disinfectant. Next to the door is a gray bin full of wet towels. Above it, someone's graffitied SEND THE RICH MY BEST in Sharpie on the wall. I hear sounds of running water and singing and a couple of guys discussing the latest football game and some player named Swift.

"Lady in the locker room," Student A yells as we enter. My eyebrows shoot up, and he flushes right to his hairline. "I mean, woman in the locker room?"

"Vagina in the locker room? I don't care," I say. "Whatever gets the message across."

"Really?" he asks, not sure whether to grin or look away.

"No." I march past him. "Police," I yell. "Everyone out."

There's a startled pause in the conversation and then the sound of lockers slamming, and a handful of guys jog past me—one still holding a towel around his waist.

Student A looks impressed. He must not get out much. Cindy—to this day—still loves to yell "Police!" anytime Teddy and I arrive at a bar or a house party and watch everyone scramble a minute or two before they realize it's just us. I even ducked once when she did it for Oliver—that flight response long ingrained from my high school years.

"Where's fifty-four?"

"Here." He points to a top locker halfway down the row lining the back of the sinks. Other than a dent in one corner, fifty-four is non-descript, the same as all the others, just with a shiny blue padlock.

"Shit," I say, pulling on the lock. "There's not a master list of combinations or something?" I ask doubtfully.

"We have our ways," Student A says slyly. "Wait here."

He returns seconds later waving red bolt cutters and looking proud of himself. "We mainly use these on the day lockers, but since he's, you know—"

"Go for it," I say, and step back.

He obeys, and I yell, "Police business" at a couple open-mouthed jocks who burst unexpectedly into the room. They shuffle out just as

I hear the satisfying crunch of Jay's last hope of privacy. The padlock breaks and falls to the floor.

"Don't touch it," I say when Student A bends to pick it up.

He jumps away from the locker like he might incriminate himself just by breathing.

"If you don't mind," I say, pulling a pair of gloves from my bag, "hang out by the entrance and let the guys know the locker room's closed for cleaning."

He does me one better and pulls a yellow bar out of a supply closet with a chained sign and an empty mop stand to boot. He lingers by the door anyway, casting occasional glances in my direction, but like a good boy, he stays where he's told.

I prize the door open carefully in case it's stuffed to the brim and a whole wave of hidden objects come tumbling out. But there are very few things inside. A towel hangs from the top hook—clean, thank god. I can only imagine the stench if it had been molding in there for over half a month. Underneath is a pale blue folder and—I suck in my breath—a small black flip phone.

I press the side button with my finger. Dead. No surprise there. I flip it open. It's old-school. No touch display. Just buttons and a small square screen. I had one like it in high school. I feel a flicker of anticipation. No apps with disappearing messages on this thing. Just texts and phone calls. I turn to the folder. What could Jay have wanted to hide so badly that he'd stand in this foul-smelling, fluorescent-lit room any longer than absolutely necessary?

I take a breath and open it.

Inside are dozens of folded pieces of paper. *Love notes*, I think before I flick the first one open.

I blink.

In large black letters, reads one word: *Traitor.*

Then the next: *Traitor*, and the next. *Traitor. Traitor. Traitor.*

All variations of the same message, just different slanting handwriting. And one *Judas*.

Something cold grips my chest.

They were unanimous, his brothers: Jay was well-liked. The life of the party. Everyone loved him. But a month before he died, he purchased a rental locker and hid these notes and a second cell phone. Why? What changed?

"Closed for cleaning," I hear Student A say.

"No problem. I'll grab my—"

I recognize the voice before the person rounds the corner, and shove both phone and folder into my bag.

"Detective Kaplan." Hair sweaty at the temples and racquet in hand, Michael Williams stares at my scarred skin as if I owe him an explanation.

"All done here," I say to Student A, and murmur, "Not a word," as I stride past. Michael is looking between me and the now-empty locker, and I think something like panic streaks across his face.

Outside the gym, I'm weighing my options.

    I should call this in. Teddy will be pissed. Truman furious. But it's a good find. Still, I risk them patting me on my head—*Thank you very much, we'll take it from here. Go back to sleep until we can tolerate looking at your wounded flesh.*

I could call Dara. Have her run the phone as a favor. Her guys are pretty good at breaking passwords. She could have the call logs to me tonight if I pressed her. But by now, she'll have heard about the fire. She might ask questions or send the logs to the office fax machine, ripe for Teddy, or worse, Oliver to pick up.

I look at the gray-white sky, the students with their bright, determined faces as they barrel in and out the gym doors, others on benches cramming in a last-minute study session as they wait for the bus.

Or, I think, *I could buy a charger and do it myself.*

Mine.

| Twelve |

Thirty minutes later, I'm tucked into a corner booth at Walker's, coffee cup in hand, and charging the phone on a wall outlet.

I don't touch Jay's folder. I'm dying to reexamine all the bits of paper but will leave it for the document examiner. It's amazing what they can do. All the crime shows these days are about hacking someone's computer or accessing CCTV cameras to trace their movements. Zooming in, enhancing photos so even the grainiest image reveals the perpetrator—we've got him—and the ensuing police chase. But a simple handwritten note can give you lots of interesting information. Each letter (uppercase, lowercase, the ways they loop and link together), punctuation, spelling mistakes, lazy scrawls, hard indents, and impressions—it all gives you something. It's not just comparing handwriting samples to identify the author; a document examiner can look at a piece of paper and tell you the guy's mood, the kind of desk he wrote on, even if he's writing under the influence of alcohol, illness, or duress. So I leave the notes tucked away for fear of contaminating them further.

It takes less than a minute for the phone to have enough juice to light up. One unread message. Password protected. Four-number combination. Go.

Dara told me once that if a password has less than six lowercase letters, she can crack it in a few seconds by hand. If it's seven, it might take her around ten minutes. Most people use obvious numbers like birthdays—

their own, their parents', or children's. Information that's easy to find and codes that take a fraction of a second to guess. People like personal names, too—siblings, pets, nicknames. But you won't believe how many people's password is "password," she told me. Or "password1234." Or "password" plus their birth date. "Monkey," she said. That's a pretty common one. "Ninja," "sunshine," or "let me in."

Then you have to know if there are any requirements: Number. Special character. Capitalized letter. People tend to put numbers at the end, usually 1 or 2. Same goes for special characters. They almost always capitalize the first letter. Those grammar rules are hard to break.

I hold the device in my hand. There are no password requirements for these kinds of phones; if anything, there are restrictions. For starters, the password must be number based. Jay may have used the letters associated with the numbers on the keypad, but certainly not the special characters or capitalization options. On the other hand, there's no Hint button either. But if Dara could crack this in seconds, I should be able to do it in an hour.

The file from my office in front of me, I try various combinations of Jay's birthday: two-digit month, two-digit year, four-digit year, double-digit day. I do the same for his parents' birthdays. Everything I can think of related to UGA football. DAWG. SICM. KRBY. Dates of home games. The last four digits of his social. The first four. I try KEMP. JAYK. JKMP. BIRD. Because I briefly remember someone calling him Jay-bird. My eyes flicker from the phone to the sheet and back again. Looking for anything that stands out. I rub my temples.

Katie, I think.

She'd been swept away into the Unimportant folder after the messages between her and Jay turned out to be as boring and innocuous as she claimed. But what if this phone was for her? I imagine Jay on the stationary bike texting away sweet nothings. Katie lying on her bed under twinkling lights and soft blankets, texting him back. Arranging times to meet.

KATI.

KATE.

K8CO.

The screen brightens and I'm looking at an image of the aurora lights. No apps. Just three options at the bottom: Contacts, Menu, Messages. I know before I click there will be only one contact, but I press the button anyway.

Katie.

I double-check the number listed on the first call sheet. Same.

Then I check the messages. They're all there. Starting October 14. I scroll to the beginning.

Jay: Hey. New number. This is safer.

Katie: Hey you. Can't believe your brothers would steal your phone!

This is followed by twenty or so funny stories with some names I recognize, some I don't. Plans for upcoming events. The Halloween party. But then, two weeks before Jay dies, the tone changes.

Jay: Feel like I've let you down. Very sorry.

Jay: Know you're mad but please don't tell anyone.

Jay: Don't trust anyone.

Jay: Need a Xanax. Couldn't sleep last night. I don't think I can take this anymore.

Jay: Please talk to me.

Katie: I just need some time to think.

I remember the wreck of a girl at the Gamma Delta house. It was clear she was grieving. Why did she lie about their relationship?

I scan the messages again. I think of the restraint in this digital era, when everyone's looking for immediate gratification, instant access, people sharing photos of what they ate for lunch and every thought that bounces off their heads, and here's Jay allocating just one hour a day to message Katie. I imagine him tucked into a back corner machine at the gym, texting furiously while he pedals the stationary bike, in the weight room sitting on an adjustable bench, holed up in the locker room squeezing every last minute he had to see if Katie messaged him back, then coming home to find "traitor" notes shoved under his door. He wasn't some guy who stepped blissfully out into the road, a carefree social chair whose only worry was whether or not everyone had a good time at the latest party. He was scared.

I hold the phone in my hands. I'm still wearing gloves, which might normally warrant one or two glances. But everyone seems determined not to look at me. Even the student eyeing the extra space in my booth and access to the power outlet keeps walking once she gets close enough to see my face.

I check the call log.

Nothing to or from Katie. But there's another number.

Dozens of outgoing calls. Increasing in frequency from the beginning of November until 9:00 A.M. the morning Jay died. I frown.

I run down the call log from his other phone. Check it against every number. No match.

What the fuck? I mouth.

I pull out the sheet with his parents' numbers, already knowing it won't be them. I scan the dates and time stamps again. All the way to the beginning. They precede the first message to Katie by almost a year. I rearrange my picture of Jay again. This phone wasn't for Katie at all. But the Katie messages match the rental of the locker, the gap in use of the other phone. I check the messages versus the calls, making notes on a napkin.

At the beginning of the call log, the calls are going back and forth, no particular pattern, once or twice a week. But after the texts to Katie start, the calls are only one-way—Jay phoning the other number. Once or twice, and then up to the day he died, ten or so times a day. Another girlfriend? Maybe that was Jay's thing. He's desperate to keep both secret so he gets the locker, and hides the phone? Why? Because now he's two-timing with the dream girl? Because he doesn't want to share? Because of the room trespasser? My mind's spinning in circles, one thought replacing the other until they all blend together. I have the feeling if I could just get it to pause, I could see how everything connects, like slowing down a carousel at the fair to disentangle the animals. I look at the call log again, the urgency as the times get closer and closer together and they remain unanswered. Whoever Jay was calling, he was frantic or pissed or both.

I can't hold this for myself any longer. Not now that I know my instinct was right about Katie. Right about there being more to this case than a random hit-and-run. Right about something amiss at Kap-O.

I pull out my own phone and message Teddy: "Meet for a coffee? Walker's?"

A beat later, he texts me back: "Hey! Sure. When?"

"Now?"

This time he takes longer to respond. And I find myself attracted by the moving objects on the television. A survival instinct honed by my ancestors to spot saber-toothed tigers lurking in the tall grass now makes it impossible to look away from the news report of a five-year-old who shot his two-year-old sister in the head while playing with a gun. "He knew not to touch it," the closed captions under his father's face keep repeating.

My phone buzzes. Teddy: "I can be there in ten."

He walks through the door in less than eight, gives me a wave, heads straight to the counter, and returns with a cup of coffee.

"I bought you a refill," he says, swipes my cup, and fills it from the stationary pot with dancing goats.

"Thanks," I say as he slides in across from me, one hand on his coffee, the other unwrapping the cellophane on a blueberry muffin.

"How's everything going?"

A stab of anger under my ribs. *How does he think it's going?*

"How's Oliver?" I ask.

He sips his coffee.

"Fine," he says after a pause. "Getting along well with everyone."

By everyone, he means the brothers, the parents, Truman.

"Great," I say, the word bitter on my tongue.

I scratch a phantom itch behind my ear. This is not how I wanted the conversation to go. I'm feeling petulant, not getting the response I want from Teddy. Not even sure what I'm looking for. I guess a part of me was hoping he'd launch into how horrible Oliver was and how Truman's making his life miserable and everything's going to shit without me. But even if it were true, it's not like Teddy to say so. He's Mr. Positive. Won't say a bad word about anyone.

He looks everywhere except my face and his gaze falls on the folder.

"Is that—" He glances at me quickly and then away again. "That's from the Kemp case."

"I swiped it this morning."

He sighs and shakes his head.

"I told Truman he wasn't doing you any favors giving you time off. That you'd be more stressed sitting around your parents' house than at the station." He hesitates. We've worked together long enough for him to know that I hate the question, "Are you okay?" But it's there, in the way he lets the sentence linger, in the thoughtful sips of his coffee: he's worried about me.

I take a breath. This isn't about me, I remind myself, it's about Jay.

"Remember how long Jay's phone records were?"

He flicks the call sheet with his finger. "My eyes are still sore from reading them." A small smile.

"Right? So Jay's making calls all day—writing hundreds of messages—until a month before he dies."

"I don't remember there being any fewer messages—"

"A month before he dies, there's a gap between three and four."

"He was in class—"

"He wasn't. Remember? We checked his class schedule. And being in class didn't seem to stop him anyway. He had some kind of compulsion or something—unless he was asleep, every other minute he's sending messages."

"So?" Teddy sighs, deciding to play along. "Why the gap?"

"He was at the gym."

We're both seeing his room, gym clothes, Gatorade bottles. It was so obvious, we missed it.

"Okay, that's great, Mar, but—"

I'm literally on the edge of my seat, I'm so eager to wipe the concerned, patronizing expression off Teddy's face and to bring out Jay's second phone with a ta-da-style flourish—when I hear a familiar voice.

"Marlitt?"

My eyes flicker to the dark-haired guy striding toward our table.

"Oliver," I say, and glare at Teddy. So much for our private conversation. Oliver rounds the booth.

"Teddy?" he sounds surprised. "Great minds, huh?" A flash of something, and then it's gone. "I needed something better than the emergency pot today. Can I grab you guys anything?" He's walking to the bar, but the offer makes it clear he's coming back.

I grit my teeth and lean across the table. "You told Oliver we were meeting here?" I hiss.

"No." Teddy looks baffled. "I just said something about coffee."

"Jesus." I grimace. Coffee might as well be my code name, so often we're said in the same sentence—*Coffee, Marlitt? Marlitt, coffee?*

"So what was Jay doing at the gym?" Teddy asks as Oliver walks away. I see Oliver's head twist at Jay's name and resist the urge to shush him.

"Look," Teddy says when I hesitate. "Whatever you've got, you're going to have to share it with Oliver eventually."

I start to protest, but he holds up his hand. There's a muffin crumb on his thumb.

"Truman was clear. You need time to recuperate. We may not like it, but that's where we are."

I appreciate the "we," but *we're* not off the case, *I* am.

"And—" His eyes finally meet mine. I look away. The concern etched in his irises is combined with something else, and it sends a surge of panic through my chest.

"Fine," I mumble into my coffee before he can say more. *God damn Oliver,* I think, *taking the wind out of my sails.* "We might as well wait for him, so I don't have to go through it twice."

A sick feeling turns in my stomach. Even though Teddy denied it, I see him and Oliver sharing a laugh at the station, him getting my text, showing Oliver, telling him to wait ten minutes and then join us. Either because he thinks I've got something, or because he can't stand to be alone with me any longer than that. The thing in my stomach sours.

Oliver sits next to Teddy, facing me. He looks too excited, and I wonder how many cups of coffee he's had already.

"Sick hair," he says, nodding at my face. "Makes you look like a badass."

A wry grin from Teddy into his muffin.

"With all the layers peeled back you just get a better look at my soul," I tell him.

He laughs, unsure, glances at Teddy, and then back at me.

"So . . ."

I think it's finally dawned on him that neither of us invited him to sit. Unless this was their plan all along.

"Marlitt found something."

"Really?" Oliver turns to me. The smile's still there, but his eyes are scrutinizing mine.

I take a deep breath, enjoying the last moment of owning the piece that might blow the case wide open before I have to give it away.

"Jay had a secret phone," I tell them. "He kept it in a rented locker at the Ramsey student gym and used it to message Katie Coleman and to make calls to another unidentified number."

Teddy's still.

Oliver's eyes widen a fraction.

"He was scared—Jay. Told Katie not to trust anyone, that he wasn't sleeping, that he couldn't take it anymore."

"That sounds more like he was suicidal to me," Oliver offers. He's sitting back now. Whatever it is he thought I had, his interest is gone. "It makes sense. Jay's under pressure. School. Fraternity. Parental expectations. He can't deal with it anymore. Sees a car coming down Lumpkin, speeding up to catch the light, and thinks—*This is it. This is my out.* Maybe he doesn't think the collision will kill him. Maybe he just thinks it will give him an excuse to quit, but in a way that he's not a quitter. In the hospital a few weeks. Back at home to convalesce. Mom taking care of him. No classes. No parties to plan. Hell, maybe even someone to clean his room for him."

I look at Oliver. Some part of me knows he's thought this before. Not for Jay, but for himself. And I wonder what kind of pressure he's under and whether it might be undermining this case.

I shake my head. "Then why go through all the extra trouble? The secret phone? The locker? The gym? And why does he tell Katie not to trust anyone? And what about the fact that he was hit by his own goddamn car?"

"He was being hazed," Teddy says slowly. "That would explain the bruises Aisha found on his body. His fear. As for the car—"

"He was a junior. Hazing's for new recruits. Freshmen mostly." Oliver shakes his head. "If anything—and I'm not saying Kap-O hazes its pledges, but if they did—Jay was doing the hazing, not the other way around."

"So maybe the other brothers were taking it too far. Jay didn't like it. Told Katie. The other brothers found out and were pissed." It's a stretch, but at least it explains Katie's sudden refusal to answer Jay's texts and her response about needing time to think. But none of this explains why the driver was in Jay's car. It feels like the missing piece to the entirely wrong puzzle.

"What about the calls?" Teddy asks.

They're both eyeing the phone on the table, but I'm not willing to pass it over yet. I pull out my napkin and show them the times I've worked out.

"Looks like our boy was still a ladies' man," Oliver says. "Secret phone for one. When he gets tired of her, uses it for the next."

"That's what I thought, too," I say. "But it still doesn't explain the sudden secrecy."

"Whoever this was," Teddy looks at the long list of phone calls the day before Jay died, "Jay was desperate to get in touch with them."

"So either he wanted to warn them, or—"

"—something else was going on and whoever it was might have killed him—yeah, that could work."

"If it was a fraternity brother pissed about him spilling secrets, he could have grabbed Jay's keys and then chased him down. Run over by your own car seems like pretty cruel revenge."

Oliver's looking between us, his eyes widening as we speak. "Wait a second. I mean, yeah, the secret calls are worth looking into, but I mean, killing someone because of fraternity secrets?" He shakes his head. "That's ridiculous. The family's ready to move on, Truman's on us to wrap up the case—"

"This is new evidence."

"But does it really change anything? We're still looking for the car, but everyone's alibis checked out—"

"And why do you want to wrap up the case so badly?" I spit at him. "Some of your golfing buddies part of Kappa Phi Omicron? Tired of their old fraternity being in the news?"

"What?" He looks genuinely baffled and then offended. "You think I would skewer a case just because a few of my friends didn't like it? Would you blow up an assignment just because you were getting a little outside pressure?" A twitch of his eyebrow. "No," he says. "You'd want to know why they gave a damn and see if it had anything to do with the case."

"Did it?"

Had I asked, Oliver might have gone cagey. But this time, the question comes from Teddy.

Oliver shifts in his seat and then exhales slowly. "No. I think maybe the hazing—I mean ten years ago, it was par for the course, you know? Like a rite of passage or something. Stay up all night tied to a tree. Eat some nasty stuff. Play a punching bag for a week." He says it casually, like this kind of abuse is no big deal. The way people shrug and say, "Boys will be boys." As if bullying and bad behavior are written into the Y chromosome.

Oliver's still talking. "So I think they were probably just remembering some bad hazing of their own and didn't want it getting out. Nothing connected to the case."

Except the hazing part, I think. But even if a fraternity hazed its members a decade ago, that doesn't mean they're still doing it. Especially now that there's more accountability, policies in place, and fraternities getting suspended left and right for violations. They'd either tone it down or be really diligent about keeping it under wraps.

I stare out the retrofitted garage windows. Three little kids holding hands, arranged biggest to smallest, trail after their father. A woman carrying her bike helmet and a guy with a plastic bag of takeout zigzag behind them trying to get around, the father oblivious. The woman loses patience, steps out into the street—

I drop my cup.

"You okay?"

"Fine," I say, mopping up the spilled coffee with the edge of a napkin.

The woman's on the opposite side of the street now, waiting to cross at the light.

Life can be snipped out in an instant, and we're so flippant about it.

Teddy's phone rings. He stands and moves away from our table.

I chew on the side of my cheek and glare at Oliver, hoping he'll take the hint, remember he wasn't invited, and leave.

Instead, he clears his throat. "Teddy told me you had a friend in a fraternity," he says.

I stare at him.

His voice softens a fraction. "A friend named Craig."

I take a deep breath. My heart begins to hammer. And I know. I know that he knows.

"The thing is . . ." He glances behind him, but Teddy's still on the phone, pacing the length of the bar. "I kept wondering why you were so certain the fraternity was involved with Jay's death."

He glances at my face.

I look away. *Don't say it*, I will him.

"And then Teddy told me about Craig, and I thought at least that explained why you hated fraternities so much. But it still didn't explain why you were convinced they were guilty. And so I googled 'Craig' and 'Georgia State.' That's where you went to college, right?"

I stare out the garage windows, feeling pinpricks at the corners of my eyes.

"And it took some digging—but I think I understand."

I take a deep breath like they teach you in therapy. And then another one. But still, the memory comes flooding back.

A gray spring morning—the kind that turns the day upside down and leaves you squinting at the world like a fish from the bottom of an aquarium. I was hungover, foggy from the night before, when I got the call.

They said he was laughing right before it happened. They said this as if somehow it made it better—snipped out in the prime of his life while laughter filled his lungs. As if this is how he would have wanted to go— just shy of twenty, laughing, drinking with his friends. It was only later I learned that those same friends left him there, alone, dying in the backyard. *We thought he got up and rejoined the party. People fall out that window all the time.* As if this excused their negligence.

My second year on the force, I pulled his file late one night after everyone else had gone home. The coroner wrote that he fell backward out the window—there was no chance of him landing on his feet. His spine fractured near the top, his aorta transected. There was profuse internal bleeding. Before he died, he might have felt a tearing inside his chest, experienced a shortness of breath, a coldness in his legs. He, who had always been stronger and faster than me, would have experienced weakness in his limbs, which is why he wasn't able to stumble back into the party or call for help. But the coroner also noted traumatic brain injury—like Jay—and the assertion that he died within minutes, meaning that even if his friends managed to call an ambulance, get him into a car, he would have died on the way to the hospital. He didn't suffer, I remember everyone saying later, but we can't know that for certain—and it's those minutes I can't forget. Him—lying on his back, staring at a starless sky, a building ablaze with light and voices coming from all sides, but he's all alone in the dark. I feel his body go cold, the drops of rain on his forehead, and my own heart dying in my chest. When they found him, he was lying in the grass, covered in morning dew. He had been there all night.

So yeah, I hate fraternities. I hate their party, live-for-the-moment life-style as if nothing they do will ever have consequences. As if they don't die as easy as the rest of us. I hate anybody who could watch someone fall out a window and not check to make sure they were okay. I hate that Craig died alone. And I hate myself—for refusing to pick up the phone, for letting his apologies go to voicemail, and for not being there for him in the end.

By the time I arrived, his body was gone and blue lights flashed off the edges of his brothers' faces. But I was the one sobbing, while they huddled somberly out front. I was the one screaming for them to take responsibility, when they collectively refused to admit fault.

I moved back to Athens. I knew that if I stayed, I would have seen him everywhere: on the street corner where he chose his brothers over me, in the dining hall where we threw fries at each other, in my dorm room where he sometimes fell asleep. I didn't have a plan, didn't have anything except a dark pit that lurked somewhere deep in my stomach. It would be prettier to say I chose to return because I knew I would have the opportunity to work these kinds of cases. The cases with young people who should have grown old, the cases ruled accidents. The cases where peer pressure and reckless behavior and lack of impulse control create dangerous cocktails that obscure lines between guilt and responsibility. But the truth is I didn't know where I would end up. And to dismantle one institution, I joined another. And I hate myself even more for being naïve enough to think I could make any difference.

"Did you tell Truman?" I hiss. "Teddy?"

Oliver shakes his head.

"Good," I say, and sit back. "Craig has nothing to do with this."

I cross my arms and will Oliver with all his sympathetic glances to disappear.

When Teddy returns, Oliver and I aren't speaking.

"That was Truman," Teddy says.

They exchange a look, and I feel a stab of panic. I can't be left out of the loop, not now. And I can't have them chasing every lead but the right one.

"There was something else in the locker," I say.

Oliver's eyebrows lift.

"A folder. With a bunch of pieces of paper." I grab a handful of napkins and lay them across the table before I take the folder out of my bag.

I open the folder and flick through a few of the notes with the back of my pen.

"Traitor," I say slowly.

Another flick.

"Traitor."

"Judas."

"Shit," Oliver swears. "That's not good."

I give him a meaningful look. "It's clear Jay had enemies."

"And he kept the notes," Teddy says.

We take a second to process what that means. Jay didn't toss the notes or even shove them in a desk drawer. He collected them, one by one, put them in a folder, and then hid them in the locker along with his secret phone. People who feel safe don't do that. They get pissed, crumple the offending pages in their hands or tear them to pieces. These are flat, pristine. I would bet they're preserved just as he found them. I think of what the witness—Morgan something—said: that when Jay was hit, he was looking at his phone and laughing. She assumed he was laughing because that matched her image of him—good-natured, the life of the party. But what if he wasn't laughing, I wonder numbly, what if he was shaking—from fear, anxiety, tears?

I lean forward. "Remember how Jay thought someone was going through his room?"

Nods from both.

"So first, that explains the need for the locker. In fact, he sent that text to Tripp on October thirteenth and rented the locker the next day." I point to the call sheet.

Slower nods this time, not at all seeing where I'm going with this.

"But we never knew what—if anything—went missing that night. And based on the texts, I don't think Jay did either. He just had a sense that things were out of place, maybe thought someone knew about his second phone, which is why he hid it."

Oliver sips his coffee. Teddy finishes off his muffin.

"But what if that's the night someone stole his car keys?"

Oliver snorts. "You don't think he'd notice—?"

"Why would he? He didn't need to drive anywhere. His BMW wouldn't have been the pick for tailgates. He didn't need groceries, wouldn't have paid to park on campus when he could walk or take the bus. And—" I take a breath. I've missed this so much. Working a case. Examining all the pieces, seeing how they fit. I feel almost delirious with happiness. "—whoever took Jay's keys might have swiped his driver's license that night, too."

Oliver sits back and spins his paper cup between his fingers.

"Why?" he asks. "It's not like the guy could keep driving the car after he killed Jay. We've got everyone looking for it. And if he was pulled over, showing a dead man's license wouldn't get him anywhere."

"He might not have thought it through when he took it."

"Maybe." Oliver sneaks a look at his watch under his sleeve.

Teddy studies the folder and all the pieces of paper. "We're going to have to talk to the brothers again."

"And Katie," I add.

There's an uncomfortable silence. Oliver stuffs a napkin into his empty coffee cup. Teddy glances down at his hands before he turns to me.

"Thanks, Marlitt."

"Really, I don't know how you—" Oliver says, all congratulatory, thinking I'm waiting for praise or something.

Teddy breaks in before I can tell Oliver what to do with his empty compliments. "We'll check this out, but Truman—"

I grimace. My cheeks feel hot.

"Yeah," I say, shoving the folder and phone toward him. "I know."

Teddy uses the remaining napkins in lieu of gloves to slip the folder and phone into his bag. "We'll give it all we got."

The "we" feels like a slap, but Teddy stands, and Oliver is already walking away. At the door, Teddy turns like he might say something but gives a short wave instead.

| Thirteen |

Friday, December 6, 4:00 P.M.

Fifteen minutes later I slide behind the wheel of my car, avoiding the implication of what Oliver said—that what happened all those years ago to Craig might be clouding my judgment now. It doesn't matter, I tell myself. Because the evidence is there. The "traitor" notes. Jay's fear. Everything points to the brothers. What I need is to get back to the Kap-O house. To observe the way they interact in their natural habitat, not behind the glass of a two-way mirror or face-to-face in an interview room. I drum my fingers on the steering wheel. I'm almost back to my parents' when I pull over, fumble in my bag for my phone, and dial a number I've had for months but never thought I'd call.

"Marley," the cheery voice on the other end chimes before I even say hello.

"Cindy," I say, and realize how happy I am to hear her. "Day off?"

"I worked a fourteen-hour shift last night. You know if you're not married with kids, they always expect you to work longer hours."

"Jesus, I'm sorry, Cind—" I say quickly. "Did I wake you?" I'm already starting to second-guess myself. I hadn't thought it through. And asking what I called for sounds more ridiculous the longer I wait.

"Nah. I'm just flipping through home improvement shows on television."

"That explains the hammering in the background."

She laughs harder than my comment warrants, but I feel something thaw in my chest.

"Listen—do you think you could help me with something? I don't want to keep you from getting some well-earned rest—"

"Are you kidding? With a full day off and Teddy and all my hospital friends at work, I'm bored—hey, which I guess you are, too. I mean—" she hesitates. "Teddy told me Truman wants you to take it easy, and—"

"Yep. I'm bored out of my mind. So I was wondering . . . do you think—if you're not too busy—you could give me a kind of makeover?" I continue in a rush, embarrassed to hear even the words come out of my mouth. "I'm going to a party tonight and would like to look more Marilyn Monroe than Frankenstein's monster."

She snorts. "Marilyn Monroe? Sometimes I think you're in your sixties instead of—wait—how old are you again?"

"What? Who would you have said?"

"I don't know. Someone younger—still living, even. Selena Gomez. Priyanka Chopra. Emilia Clarke—"

"All right, well, make me the mother of dragons then."

"This is going to be so fun," Cindy says before I hang up.

Cindy lives on the south side of town. For the past year, she's been making subtle and not so subtle hints to Teddy that they should move in together. His place still looks like a bachelor pad—clothes thrown in a corner instead of a laundry basket, nothing but condiments in the fridge—and I think it's the knowledge that Cindy won't put up with that combined with the fact that his mother would murder him if he moved in with a woman without marrying her first that has Teddy dragging his feet and me driving past the botanical gardens.

When I arrive, Cindy's wearing an oversized sweatshirt, a spoon in one hand and pint of ice cream in the other.

"Oh," she says, taking a good look at my face. Then she grins to cover her surprise. "Did you do something to your hair? Something's different." She laughs when I don't. "It's just—I almost forgot."

I blink at myself in the entryway mirror behind her head.

"Lucky you."

"Ah, don't be like that. Want some ice cream?"

She holds out her spoon to me.

"I'm good, thanks," I say, wondering if the love of junk food is the glue that keeps a couple together.

"I baked brownies, too," she offers.

I shake my head.

"Okay, then, follow me."

She leads me through a gray-and-purple living room, down a hall, and into the biggest bathroom I've ever seen in an apartment. Double vanity and all, with a walk-in closet at the back.

"Nice," I say.

"I know, right? It's half the reason I signed the lease. So . . ." She extends her arm to a counter covered in an assortment of tubes and bottles. "Ta-da! They're somewhat old—I don't bother wearing makeup to work these days. And with the long hours—it's not like Teddy and I go on a lot of date nights." Something resembling reproof in her voice, and I'm left wondering why all the late hours if they've scaled back the Kemp case and what Teddy and Oliver have been doing without me.

"Anywho, I think I've got everything we need."

An hour later, I feel ridiculous. Cindy's smattered me with so many concoctions of skin-colored potions, my face feels heavy. I'm in a dress two sizes too small, with my phone tucked into my bra strap, and wearing enough makeup to cover a cheerleading squad.

"There," Cindy says. "I can barely see the burns. You'd have to be"— she leans in so her nose is almost touching my cheek, her eyes going crossed as she looks at me—"this close to see anything."

I chance a look in the mirror and blink. The woman staring back has my cheekbones, but they're finer, the nose slimmer, the brows fuller, and the eyes magnified by the thick lashes Cindy's glued to them.

She grins at my reflection.

She likes me better now.

It's a mean and unfair thought. Cindy's always been nice and has tried very hard this past year to befriend me. But somewhere at the back of her eyes, around her pupils reflected in the mirror, I see it. A softening as she takes in my scars, the shaved hair—something like compassion and something like relief.

I glance at my face again and have the wild urge to laugh. "What did you do to me?"

"It's called contouring."

"It's bizarre."

"Now, for the final touch." She pulls a blond wig from a drawer, and when my brows raise, she shrugs. "It's from Halloween. There." She fits it on my head. "You look like a Barbie. Party Barbie."

"I look like a sorority girl," I say grimly to the woman in the mirror.

"What's wrong with sorority girls?"

I blink at her. "Don't tell me—"

She laughs. "Yep. KD. At Auburn. You're going to hear us roar!"

"What's that?" I ask, laughing despite myself. "Your slogan?"

"We had hundreds." A grin.

"Go on," I prompt as I tug the wig around my ears.

"Okay." Her gaze turns to the ceiling as she tries to remember. "Another was 'The sorority with authority.' And 'Why walk when you can fly'—I always liked that one, you know, because of Auburn's battle cry. And 'We bring the fire'—" She stops abruptly.

I meet her eyes in the mirror. "Well, just keep it away from me." I'm trying for levity, but Cindy's upset with herself anyway.

"So," I say to fill the silence, "why did you join?"

She gives a small, wistful smile. "It was my home away from home," she says. "I showed up without a friend in the world, racing around the campus like a lost puppy, worrying I'd have to eat all my meals in the dining hall alone, but then I rushed and found a whole house full of sisters. 'Friends forever, sisters for life'—that's another slogan."

She points to a photo taped to the bottom of the mirror. A collection of women in long dresses laugh into the camera, their arms thrown around each other.

"I still keep in touch with five of the girls and have been a bridesmaid in two of their weddings. They're the first people I call if I need to talk. I'm an only child, so they're my family, you know?"

She shrugs to reconcile the difference in our opinions, but her eyes are bright.

I gaze at the photo. Greek life promises brothers and sisters to replace the family you left behind or to fill the gap that's always been there. And maybe it could have done that for me. Maybe if I had struck out on my own instead of clinging to Craig, I could have found sisters like Cindy. But I didn't, and a fraternity stole him—my best friend, the closest thing I had to a brother—from me.

She grabs a tube of mascara and opens her mouth wide as she applies it to her lashes. "Now tell me about this party."

"Oh, it's just . . ." I stall, blinking away thoughts of Craig as I run the fake hair through my fingertips. ". . . a get-together with a few friends."

"And you're going like this?" She points at the sparkly fabric on my chest. "I don't think so." She leans close to the mirror and looks at me in the reflection as she starts on the other eye. "I want in."

"What?"

"Wherever you're going. I want to go, too."

I open my mouth, but she cuts me off.

"Look. It's my first night off in ages, and Teddy already called to say he's working late"—that twist again, he's working my lead without me—"and I want to have some fun."

"It's not for fun," I say. "It's for work."

"So you're what? Going undercover or something? To a party?"

I try to backpedal, come up with excuses, but my mind's blank. I'm too distracted by the uncanny alternate vision of myself in the mirror, the thought of Teddy and Oliver interviewing the fraternity brothers, and Cindy's eager glances.

"I'm going."

"No—"

"In case you need backup."

I laugh, and Cindy folds her arms over her chest.

"Teddy would want me to go."

"Teddy would definitely not want you to go. He wouldn't want either of us to go."

She clenches her jaw. "Well, that settles it, then." She smiles. "We're going."

I try for another thirty minutes to talk her out of it, but even as I'm coming up with more and more elaborate reasons why she shouldn't go, I start to see the advantage of having her there. She's young, stunning, and has enough bubbly energy for both of us. Like a sexy magician's assistant, she'll divert the attention away from me.

"Fine," I say. "But we're only staying half an hour. I just want to look around."

"This is going to be so much fun," she says, and then spends the next hour hunting through her closet for the right dress to wear.

Based on the handful of girls shivering in bikinis, guys in board shorts, and surfboards propped up in front of the house, the theme of the party must be something like summer in December or spring break in winter.

"Hawaiian nights," Cindy beams, when a guy drapes a pink plastic lei over her neck.

"Aloha," he says to her. A cheer goes up behind him as a girl lands a glow-in-the-dark ring on top of a plastic pineapple. I roll my eyes. It seems like all the party themes are just an excuse to get everyone seminaked.

The guy turns, and I sweep the blond wig over my face and give him my good side. I recognize him—David something—from the hours I spent poring over the fraternity photographs. He wasn't at the top of our list, and Teddy must have recorded his statement because I can't remember anything about him besides the Frat Daddy shirt he was wearing when the picture was taken.

"Aloha," he says to me, but his eyes are still on Cindy. Behind him, tiki torches gleam in the dark. "Boat drinks in the house. Band starts at eleven. Oh, and here." He slips a ribbon around my arm. "Wristbands."

Inside, the house has transformed. It's no longer the bare and pristine Pine-Sol-smelling entryway. There are inflatable pool rings hanging from the ceiling. Plastic pink flamingos and paper palm trees. A pair of guys wearing neon sunglasses chase each other with Super Soakers. A girl in a green bikini pretends to ride a unicorn pool float. A couple makes out on the back of a blow-up swan. The doors to the chapter room are open and there are people everywhere. Strewn across couches, pressed into corners, writhing slow and steady to the music pulsing out of large standing speakers connected to a laptop at the far side of the room.

I'm standing open-mouthed, taking it all in.

"This is fun," Cindy yells in my ear. She almost slips in a pool of water from the Super Soakers and grabs my arm. "I feel like I'm back in high school—crashing one of my cousin's parties." She looks dramatically over her shoulder. "I hope we don't get caught!"

I force a smile. Her enthusiasm is usually contagious, but I'm on edge. Something tells me that the wig and the darkness can only hide me so far.

I had the vague idea that once we got here, I'd sneak off to Michael's room, open drawers, rummage through his closet and dirty laundry. But what was I expecting to find? The pen that wrote the "traitor" notes? Jay's missing driver's license? Surrounded by strobe lights and inflatable floats, it all seems so juvenile. The notes. The phone. Betraying the brotherhood. Like someone let his girlfriend into the boys-only tree fort and they blamed him for cooties. But Jay was murdered. The notes. The phone. Those prove there was more going on than childish secrets and a car thief with a heavy foot. There must be something else. Something I'm missing.

"I'm going to grab us drinks," Cindy shouts in my ear, and then mimes drinking just in case I missed it. "*So we blend in,*" she mouths.

I give her a thumbs-up and move to a side wall as she dances over to the pine straw–topped pseudo tiki hut in the opposite corner. There's a paper tree with brown coconut balloons next to my head and I swat one absently. I wonder whether Jay would have approved of this party. Somehow, I think it would have fallen short of his standards. It seems like a recycled version of the one everyone thought was so amazing last semester, like without Jay no one has any original ideas anymore. In the slashes of strobe lights, I see girls with their mouths open, singing to a song so loud I can't make out what it is. Long fingers hold Solo cups, people sway and bounce and stumble to the music. A girl slips, but her friends grab her before she falls. The guys prowl the sides of the room marking the most vulnerable.

It's strange, being this close to them, like sneaking into the zoo after hours and scouting the edges of the lions' den. My eyes find Michael. He's clutching a handle of rum and surrounded by four guys wearing frilly pirate shirts. Michael hooks his arm around the back of one of the guy's necks and draws him in close.

"Hey," Cindy yells, beside me again. "I couldn't find you for a second. The bartender wanted to see my ID. Can you believe it—even with the wristband!"

"What did you do?"

"I showed him. His eyes got all big, but I think he decided it must just be a good fake." She sways to the music. "All right, so what now?"

"What's in this?" I suck in my teeth. The drink is cloyingly sweet.

"He called it hunch punch, so who knows? Probably a little of every-thing."

Great, I think, examining the contents of the plastic cup. I debate how much I can splash on the floor without anyone noticing.

"Thanks for letting me come," Cindy shouts.

"Sure," I yell back.

"No, really." She puts her hand on my arm. It's sticky, and I wonder if she's already spilled her drink or if she's playing the same game as me. "I needed this. With work and Teddy—" She sighs. "I feel like I haven't had fun in ages."

That's the second time she's mentioned problems with Teddy, which means she wants me to ask, but I know better.

"Well, we're having fun now," I say. "Cheers." We clink plastic cups.

It must look like we're having a great time, because a guy suddenly slides up on the other side of Cindy.

"Hey," he yells over the music.

"Aloha," she says with a big smile. She gives me a wink.

"You having fun?"

"Yeah," Cindy says. "Cindy," she points at herself, and "Mar—"

"Mary," I finish for her.

"Like the virgin?"

"No," I say, "like Mary Tyler Moore?"

He frowns at me and turns back to Cindy. It doesn't escape my atten-tion that he hasn't told us his name.

"Where're you from?" He's shoulder to shoulder with her and leans down to yell in her ear.

"What?" she shouts back.

"I said, where—are—you—from?"

"Ohhh," Cindy says, "here, I'm from Athens. I went to Oconee."

"No," he says, gesturing with his cup in a circle. "I mean, where are you from—originally?"

It takes a moment for the question and its meaning to dawn on Cindy, and by that point another guy has joined. "Ice luge in Jack's room," he yells, pulling our new friend toward the exit.

"Sweet." He turns back to Cindy. "Want to join? It makes your mouth go all numb." He licks his lips.

Cindy blinks at him.

"I've never been with an Asian," he shouts as the other brother drags him away.

Cindy's smile falters, and she stares into her drink, hunching her shoulders like she wants to disappear.

"What the fuck?" I turn.

"Don't worry about it," Cindy slurs. "I've heard worse. Once"— she leans in, bumping my cheek, and I can taste the alcohol on her breath—"a guy told me I looked like his maid. What kind of"—she murmurs—"fudged-up shit is that? I think he was hitting on me, too. I mean . . ." But she stares at a group of guys posing for a photo on the back of a blow-up crocodile and doesn't finish her sentence.

Michael's on the move. He says something, and the brothers laugh. Then he seems to pick a guy out of the crowd at random and the others grab him by the shoulders. The adrenaline surges down my fingertips. Something's happening. And I don't know if it's the flashing lights or the hunch punch or the music pumping so loud I can feel it in my skull, elevating the feeling of recklessness, or if it's just me slowly starting to return to normal. But that invincible, I-can-do-anything, impulsive, stand-on-my-handlebars, jump-off-the-swing-set, live-without-fear kind of feeling I've been missing since the fire is coursing through my body, urging me to follow.

"Stay here," I yell to Cindy. "I'll be right back."

I walk through the house, touching armoires and trophy cases, admiring a boat in a large glass bottle on a high shelf. All the while holding Michael's back in the corner of my eye. I kick a beer can and have a vision of the pledges on their hands and knees tomorrow with rubber gloves and soapy water. The same skills you need to cover up a crime scene.

Somehow, I've ended up in the kitchen. There's a girl vomiting into a large industrial sink, her friend in a grass hula skirt rubbing her back and making cooing noises in her ear. But no Michael. I'm about to leave when I notice a small wooden door. It's slightly ajar, and there are small brass padlocks hanging open on the top and bottom that latch to the wall. I frown. This wasn't a part of our house tour. In fact, I don't think Tripp showed us the kitchen at all. I glance back at the girls, but they're not paying attention. I slip both locks into my pocket.

I slide the door open and am met with a damp smell and a dark stair-well. A pull string looms overhead, but when I yank it, nothing happens. The bulb's dead or not there at all. I fish my phone from under my bra strap and turn on the flashlight. The wooden steps are smooth and slope inward from a century's worth of wear, and I'm reminded that despite the industrial kitchen, the laminate floors, and flat screens in every room, this is an old house.

The smell hits me again—wet and musty and acrid like stale urine. It's a mixture of creeping vegetation, animal stink, and fear. My stomach twists. A flash of a cabin in the woods, the back of an unmarked van, a derelict apartment on the north side—all my worst cases have been marked by that smell. I pull the top of my dress up to cover my nose. I take one step and another.

And then there's nothing beneath my feet.

I land hard on my knees.

"Shit," I swear, and turn the flashlight back toward the staircase.

The last six steps have been sawed off, leaving a hole that gapes like an open wound. I think of the footstool leaning next to the door in the kitchen and wonder if I was supposed to bring it with me. I stand and brush off my legs, realizing with a sickening sensation that one is bleeding. I'm now a part of this, my DNA on the floor and whatever's on the concrete now under my skin, circulating through my bloodstream. I take a deep, shud-dering breath, gag, and then shine my flashlight around the room.

There are dirty blankets in the center. A pair of buckets in the corner seem to be the most likely source of the foul odor. I bite back the revulsion. Unnerving black stains draw sharp contrasts against the grayish stone floor. The edges of the room are covered with a thick layer of dust, but at the far end, it's been disturbed, like something large and heavy has been dragged across it. Somewhere to my left comes a steady dripping. I turn the light toward the sound, and it lands on a set of handcuffs nailed to the wall. I swallow. Next to the handcuffs is a riding whip and a pair of rusty pliers.

What the fuck?

But I know. Hazing. Here's the proof. It's like they took their cues from a bad horror movie.

I turn off the light and try to imagine what it would be like to be locked down here. Something scurries in the darkness. And I shiver. It's involuntary, but now that it's started, I feel my whole body shaking. The light from the slits around the kitchen door casts sharp shadows across the damp walls. My whole body is screaming at me to get out, run, but there's nowhere to go.

I think of Jay's secret. Of Tripp's sycophantic smile. Of Michael's smug arrogance. All future leaders. Corporate executives. Senators. Congressmen. The best and the brightest. And this is what they do to one another.

Above my head, the bass is pumping, people are dancing and shouting, clutching plastic cups with paper umbrellas, with this—this nightmare— the whole time festering beneath their feet. Would they have locked pledges up during a party? So they could shiver in the dark and listen longingly to everyone celebrating above like browbeaten prisoners on Alcatraz staring across the bay at the blazing city?

I am suddenly so angry I can't breathe.

Fury is a wild beast caught in a trap biting its own limbs to get free. I can't afford to give in to that instinct now, so instead I settle for rage.

I will take every one of these fuckers down, I think, as I flip the flashlight back on. *I will leak this to every journalist I know so the world sees what they've done, and the school has no choice but to expel them all. They'll never get hired to Dad's law firm or whatever cushy job they have lined up for their future. There will be no house with the three-car garage, pretty spouse, and kids in private school.* I'm standing in the shadow of the jagged steps, snapping photos, even though they won't turn out in this light.

I'm still fuming at the tattered blankets when my phone rings.

"Marley?"

It takes me a few seconds to match the discrepancy between Cindy's voice and the horror scene I've dropped into, and even longer to remember I've left her alone in a house full of the animals who did this.

"Marley, I fell."

"It's okay, Cindy." I glance at my own knee, the trickle of blood running down my shin, and glare angrily at the room. "Don't move. I'll be right there."

"I'm outside." Laughter and cheers swell somewhere behind her.

"Okay." I stare at the sawed-off staircase and realize suddenly I don't know how the hell I'm going to get out of here. "I'll find you," I tell her.

There are footsteps in the kitchen. Dark shadows break the slit of light under the door. I hang up and hold my breath. The door opens a fraction, a tall figure backlit, but then slams. I squeeze the padlocks in my hand. *At least,* I think, *they can't lock me down here.* But then I hear it, the sound of something being pushed across the floor. The light behind the door vanishes.

Shit, I think. *Shit. Shit. Shit.*

I let my flashlight trace the outline of the room again, moving from the walls inward. I don't discover anything new, and my flashlight circles back to the buckets in the corner.

This time the girls turn when I emerge from the basement.

"What's that smell?" the standing one asks. Never mind the footstool that my kick sent flying across the kitchen. Her hula skirt's fallen around her ankles, so she's in only her swimsuit. The one leaning over the sink vomits.

"Don't go down there," I tell them.

The footstool was so light, it couldn't have been intended to block me in. And, I tell myself, nobody could have seen me standing in the dark. Someone must have noticed the locks missing and dragged it there to keep wandering guests from falling down the sawed-off steps. As if that's all the basement was—a safety hazard.

I walk through the house in a daze. Someone hands me a drink and I swallow it. The blow-up floats have started to deflate and sink in on themselves. The yells have turned lazy, perfunctory. I see violence everywhere. Mouths open, gleaming white teeth. Cheers melting into screams. The whole scene—pale, half-naked bodies churning out of dark shadows, red cushions, and carnivalesque animals—reminds me of that Delacroix painting—*The Death of Sarda*-something.

Outside, a couple of guys are sitting in a blow-up pool. One would think they'd be freezing, but they look content and hot-blooded, and I wonder if they took part in what happened downstairs. I gaze at my feet and consider sticking them in the pool.

Instead, I walk to the green hose pulsing water onto the lawn and shoot cold blasts down my legs, around my ankles, and between my toes.

"At least spray it on your tits," a voice yells.

I drop the hose and walk away.

Cindy's sitting on the sidewalk. Light glints off her black hair, and I'm flooded with relief. *I just need to take her home and call this in*, I think, *get her a cab, and—*

"Shit," I say when I get close enough to see her face.

"I fell," she says, holding up her hands so I can see the scraped skin of her palms.

She must have bitten her lip, too. There's blood running down her chin.

I glance back at the house. All around us silhouettes dance to disjointed rhythms under string lights strung across the cast-iron sky.

"I'm fine," she murmurs when I lift her by the elbow. She grins and there's blood caked between her teeth.

"Jesus," I swear.

"What happened to your leg?" she asks in a drunken slur. "And your shoes?"

"Long story," I tell her. But the short of it is, I couldn't get a handle on the bucket in heels, so I had to leave them and stand on its edges in bare feet. I'm pulling out my phone, feeling guilty about not accompanying her home, when she squirms out of my grasp.

"Teddy," she breathes.

"Shit," I swear. She must have called him while she was waiting for me.

"Cindy, what—?" Teddy grabs her by the arm when she stumbles, and examines her face, the blood on her lips and chin. "Are you okay?"

"Me? I'm great! We went to a par . . . ty!" She draws out the last word and smiles, showing the blood between her teeth.

"What the fuck, Marlitt?" Teddy turns to me. He's clenching his jaw so hard the bone juts under his skin.

"What are you doing here? And why"—he moves to get a better hold on Cindy, who has one hand on his shoulder and is spinning around him lazily—"did you bring Cindy?"

"Later," I say. "There's something you need to see."

"No." He shakes his head. "Now. And I'm not leaving Cindy like this."

"Fine," I say, hearing the drunken petulance in my voice but unable to alter it. "Then I'm calling Oliver. See how you like it."

I take out my phone clumsily and search through my contacts.

"Jesus, Marlitt," Teddy says. I hold the phone to my ear. It's ringing. "How selfish can you be?"

"Me?" My mouth drops open. "I'm the one who got set on fire," I hiss. "And then dropped from my case."

"Yeah, right." He sighs. "And instead of trying to heal or realizing that the guy who did that to you might be in this building"—he gestures to the brick house, every window ablaze with light—"you march in there—without backup—and not only that, you take Cindy with you."

"The candles . . ." I murmur.

"What?" He rakes his fingers through his hair. "I don't believe that. Do you? And . . . wait—" He holds up his hand when I try to speak. "Oliver and I have been trying to figure out who did this to you—pulling in extra hours on top of the Kemp case, sacrificing . . ." A slight angry wave in Cindy's direction and then a sigh. "The least you could do is take care of yourself."

"Marlitt?" Oliver's voice, low and hoarse from somewhere far away. "It's two in the morning."

"Yeah." I cup the phone with my hands, eyes still on Teddy. "I've got something you need to see."

"Where—" I can hear him fumbling around for something. "Where are you?"

"I'm at the Kap-O house. It's a Hawaiian nights party, and I'm calling with an anonymous tip."

There's a pause, and I hear him swallow before he clears his throat.

"Teddy's here, too, but he has to leave." I stare daggers at him in the dark.

"Teddy's there?" Oliver repeats, sounding a little more awake.

"Yeah, but he's gots to go." The roundness of letters escapes me and I'm losing the shape of my sentences. My mind flickers to the warning label on my pain meds about not mixing with alcohol.

Teddy waits with me wordlessly until Oliver arrives, holding back Cindy's hair while she vomits onto the concrete. I almost prefer the sound of her getting sick to the silence that stretches beneath the thuds and yells of the ongoing party. I feel something irreparable shattering, threatening to break entirely between us, but have no idea what it is or how to hold it together.

Twenty minutes later, I see Oliver's VW Golf pull down a side street.

He turns off his headlights immediately, and Teddy flashes his phone so he can find us in the dark.

"Hey," Oliver says, frowning at my blond wig and too-short dress. He's wearing street clothes, but not a pirate shirt or board shorts. He looks like a detective, which means he believes me. Means he's not dressed to blend in, take a look around, and leave. He's prepared to flash his badge and bring a team in.

"What've we got?" He's looking at Teddy.

"This is all Marlitt," Teddy says, and waves his free hand in my direction. His voice sounds tired. "I have to take Cindy home." And as if on cue, Cindy vomits, nearly missing Oliver's shoes.

Under the fluorescent kitchen lights, Oliver's green, with his shirt clutched to his mouth when he opens the basement door.

I've been standing guard, in a manner of speaking, replacing the vomiting bikini girl, making ungodly heaving sounds, and yelling "I might be contagious!" whenever someone wanders into the kitchen.

On his way down, I handed him the footstool and warned him about the bucket—I kicked it when I made the leap for the stairs and sent its contents flying everywhere.

Oliver's gulping in the kitchen air and shaking his head, wide-eyed, at me. "That was . . . worse," he says between breaths, "than I thought it would be."

He pulls out his phone.

"Leave before anyone sees you," he tells me.

I stare at him. For a brief moment he meets my gaze, and I see him bristle at the distrust he finds there. Then the person on the other end picks up and he walks away, leaving me standing alone in the kitchen.

Only the two of us know about this. Oliver could bury the whole thing before anyone else finds out, and the fraternity could have the basement empty and clean by morning. But as I watch him weave through people dancing in the hall, I realize there's nothing else I can do. I'm too tired and maybe a little too drunk to protest. And it's very likely that I just destroyed any of my remaining credibility.

The guy driving my Uber wrinkles his nose when I open the door but doesn't make me get out of the car. I stare at my reflection and streaked makeup in the window and wonder if Teddy will ever speak to me again.

Selfish, I think, *was I really being selfish?*

That night I allow myself to remember the fire. I pull out all the details one by one and flip them over, examining their edges, like a kid picking up seashells, wondering what kind of strange creature left them behind. Start at the beginning, that's what we tell witnesses. What did you do that morning? That afternoon? Right before it happened?

Stretched out on top of the quilted bedspread in my childhood room, I blink at the ceiling and picture myself as I got dressed—she's already a different person, the woman I see in my mind's eye, with long brown hair, naïvely preparing for her day. That day started with Cade and Samantha barely able to keep their hands off each other and learning that Jay didn't want to keep his hands to himself either. Katie—a mess, tearful, with a headache, but with enough energy to send her house mom in a tizzy and on an angry phone call to Truman, which he relayed in his own furious way to us. Then the phone logs, bringing in Tripp, then Cade again, and Michael. Feeling that they were hiding something. That it was right in front of our faces, but we weren't able to see it. Michael, telling me to be careful. It felt like a threat.

I took the photographs of the brothers home with me, thought if I stared at them long enough, one of them might tell me their secrets. Then I pored over Facebook. Jay's page already had hundreds of messages. But all were somber—*gone too soon, he'll be missed*—and expressions of disbelief. *I just heard—I can't believe it—I saw him last weekend.* As if somehow seeing someone one day promises they will be there the next.

There was nothing from Katie. And no: *he got what he deserved*. Or: *good riddance*. But who would be so obvious? I remember needing air and to stretch my legs. I took my usual route—up Pineneedle Road, down Sylvan and Talmadge, an ellipse of sorts. The night was quiet, all the kiddos in bed, lights out or blue glows from televisions behind curtains, but there had been something . . . off. I thought it was just Michael's voice echoing in my head. He didn't seem like the kind of person who'd make threats without following through. But his threats were the rich-kid kind—*Be careful, or I'll talk to my dad's friend the mayor; be careful, or you'll be out of a job*. Those kinds of threats. But the skin on my arm prickled. I remember distinctly now, that strange sensation of looking over my shoulder. I close my eyes and try to focus. What was it? Something or someone just past my vision—a vibration in the air, the sensation of being watched. I had felt an uneasiness and brushed it off. But I remember I cut my walk short, turning back at Willow Run instead of continuing down to Westover.

I open my eyes. I've been squeezing them so tight, my cheekbones are sore, and I imagine them black rimmed, my face racoon-like, yellow eyes blinking in the dark.

Well that's something, I think. Even if it was just a feeling, it was an unusual blip during an otherwise usual day. I exhale.

And then what? And then I poured wine into a glass and took the bottle up to my room. I don't think I finished it. I undressed, pulled a crumpled pair of shorts and a tank top from my dresser, and fell asleep. The next thing I remember is waking up on fire and screaming in German.

| Fourteen |

I've slept less than four hours and wake with the hazy sensation that something's wrong. I had horrible dreams—locked in a dark cage like a gladiator, hearing cheers and lions pacing the arena above. Visions of a panicked gazelle. Flash of teeth. *Stop*, I tell myself. My head is pounding, my breath foul. The house is quiet, and I imagine my parents whispering over coffee, fearful to wake me, perhaps suspecting my nasty hangover. But when I stumble downstairs, the kitchen's empty. There's a note on the counter: *Went to Mama's Boy for breakfast, call if you want anything.* The thought of food makes my stomach roil, so I settle for the cold coffee at the bottom of the pot.

I check my phone.

Out of a sense of loyalty or guilt or perhaps a better understanding than me that this might be my last case, Oliver has invited me to the station to watch the interviews.

All the way there, I'm running through scenarios of how to avoid Truman and what I'll say to Teddy when I see him. I figure my best bet is to take the front entrance and try to duck into the observation room without Truman noticing. But I'm not sure how to handle Teddy. My mind's wrecked, still rattled by whatever concoction was in the hunch punch last night and hazy with lack of sleep.

Turning into the station lot, I catch a glance of myself in the rearview mirror. I look awful. The bristly hair and bags under my eyes give a strange, slightly unhinged impression.

Truman and Oliver are already here. No sign of Teddy yet, but there are a surprisingly large number of vehicles I don't recognize out front.

I dodge a guy unloading a camera from a van and another on his cell phone and enter through the lobby with my head down, so focused on blending into the background that I don't see the man barreling toward me until he's breathing into my face.

"We've been waiting three hours," he growls. He's medium height, wearing an ill-fitting dark suit, and somehow—in spite of my civilian clothes—has pegged me as a detective.

I look up to find the station crawling with young men in various states of soberness. One's on the floor, with his back against a bench, feet splayed, mouth agape, and snoring loudly. Another's wrapped into a ball with an arm tucked under his head. There's a faint smell of stale beer mixed with vomit, and Amy rounds the corner with her lips curling in disgust.

The man blocks my path.

"You know," he leans toward me, "a journalist wanted to talk to me on my way in here." He gestures to the handful of people outside the glass entrance. "I think I might tell him how my son's being treated, when it's clear he's done nothing wrong."

I look at the crumpled boy on the bench behind him. He's gray faced with a bruise-colored shadow under his right eye. A pale reflection of his father, still in flip-flops and board shorts, but with a hoodie pulled up tight around his ears. And I know immediately what his role in all this was.

I sigh. "What's your son's name?"

He puffs out his chest. "Ryan Bennett."

His son flinches. I turn to study him, but he refuses to meet my gaze. He pulls his hoodie sleeves over his fingers so that the fabric swallows any visible flesh, and rocks back and forth on his toes. I feel sorry for him, but his father will find out eventually, and I think if I've judged him right, telling him now will get him out of my face and keep him away from the press.

"Mr. Bennett," I say as Oliver appears behind him. "Are you aware of what was found in the basement of Kappa Phi Omicron?"

"My son had nothing to do with that."

For a split second, I think Ryan's lips have moved, but when I look at him, he's staring at the floor.

"Your son," I say, and take a breath, knowing by the hollows of Ryan's cheeks and the way he folds in on himself that I'm right, but that being right won't make this any easier, "was locked in that basement."

I wait. Confusion colors the father's face. He opens his mouth and shuts it again. All the pieces are reorganizing in his mind, and I can tell he never, not even once, not with all the fraternity suspensions in the news and everything we know about hazing, considered that his son might be the victim of such violence, instead of its perpetrator.

If he hasn't seen the photos, I'm sure he's heard the rumors—whips, pliers, buckets of waste. He shakes his head and turns, looking at his son as if he's seeing him for the first time.

Ryan crumples like the weight of the world's on his shoulders, and his father takes two steps toward him, hands raised, before he deflates.

I leave him standing helplessly in the middle of the waiting room surrounded by his son's tormentors.

Oliver's lips tighten when I approach. He's wearing the same clothes as last night and smells of burnt coffee.

"There was a better way to go about that," he murmurs.

I shrug. "He wanted to talk to the press. I thought he should at least know what he was telling them. Maybe decide, you know, with his son, if it was information he wanted to share."

I glance at the news crews moving behind the windows. "Someone should talk to them though. People need to know what goes on in those houses."

I look at Oliver sideways, but his face has closed. He was in the basement a lot longer than I was. The impression's left a mark in the lines around his mouth.

He shakes his head, and I think he's already regretting allowing me to be a part of this.

Truman's door is shut, but I hear raised voices—none of which belong to the man himself.

When Teddy arrives, he puts his helmet on his desk and walks into the interview room like I'm not there at all. And this hurts worse than all the unkind accusations and harsh truths I was expecting and all the arguments I already hashed out with him in my head.

Red-faced, I slip into the observation room just as Oliver flips on the tape recorder.

"Detectives White and Graves interviewing Ryan Bennett."

Ryan has disappeared turtle-like into his hoodie. His arms are crossed against his chest as if he's trying to physically hold himself together. He's shaking so badly it looks like he might break apart.

Oliver must consider it a kindness to interview him first.

"Ryan, are you a member of Kappa Phi Omicron?"

Head nod.

"Out loud for the tape recorder."

"New member," he says in a voice so small I doubt the recorder picked it up.

"Okay, good. That's great." Oliver's tone takes on an encouraging note. "Now I'm going to ask you a few questions about your experiences at the Kappa Phi Omicron house."

"Okay," Ryan says softly, his eyes on his hands in his lap.

"Great," Oliver says. "This will be a big help. So, Ryan, can you tell us about what life was like at the house?"

Ryan blinks. "It was fun, I guess."

"Okay, good. And what kind of fun things did you do there?"

He squirms. "There were movie nights and, I don't know, parties and stuff."

This is going nowhere fast. It's clear he's scared of something, and I wonder if he's afraid his father is watching or worried about incriminating himself for some minor infraction like underage drinking.

Get on with it, I will Oliver.

"Okay, great. And were you ever forced to go into the basement of the Kap-O house?"

Ryan rocks back and forth on the legs of the metal chair. He shakes his head.

Oliver and Teddy exchange glances. This is the problem with nonverbal responses—they could mean anything. Does this mean he didn't go in the basement, he wasn't forced to, or that he doesn't want to answer the question?

"Ryan, were you ever in the basement of the Kappa Phi Omicron house?"

He makes throaty noises that might be humming.

"Were you ever forced to do anything against your will?"

Something like a strangled cry. A glance at the two-way mirror. Then more humming, eyes fixed on the table.

"Were you ever in the basement for an extended period of time?"

Hands on his ears. Humming as if he can drown out Oliver's words.

"Tell us what happened in the basement."

Humming as if he can drown out his own thoughts.

"What's that?" Oliver leans across the table.

Ryan's hands drop from his ears and disappear beneath his thighs.

"Are those cigarette burns?"

I've been watching Ryan's face so only catch a glimpse of skin—dark circles around his wrist, and a larger red sore on his forearm. He gives a frantic shake of his head.

"Did one of the brothers do that to you?"

Head shake.

"Then what happened?"

Ryan blinks furiously at the floor.

"You're not in any trouble. We just want to understand—"

The humming reaches a high, strangled note.

After another five minutes of this, they finally let the poor kid sign a statement and return to the lobby.

The next student looks less aggrieved and more in awe of what's happening. Brown curly hair and a slight pudge around his middle; he's wearing a gray pullover on top of board shorts and boat shoes.

"Holy shit," he says when he sits down. "This is like *CSI* or something." He shakes his hair out of his eyes to get a better look at the room and smirks at the water stain like he recognizes it from television.

"Without the good-looking cast." Oliver grins.

It's clear they've decided to interview the younger brothers first. The reason, although neither felt inclined to share it with me, is twofold: so they can get the victims' side of the story before they pull in the older brothers and likely perpetrators, and so the older brothers can watch the younger brothers disappear into the interview room one by one, wonder what they've told us, and start shitting themselves.

"Right, Detectives Graves and White interviewing Garrett Ross."

"Cool," Garrett says.

"And Garrett, can you confirm that you're a member of Kappa Phi Omicron?"

He nods. "Joined last fall."

"Great." Oliver makes a note. "Okay, Garrett, so by now you know that we've seen the basement."

He's nodding and beaming like this is the best thing that's ever happened to him.

"And we're hoping you can give us a better idea of what goes on down there."

"Oh, man." Garrett runs his hands through his hair. "I would love to help, you know, the investigation and all, but it's a brotherhood secret. All the rituals and stuff, we can't talk about them."

"I get it," Oliver says. Another cool-guy grin and his voice lilts. I know he never joined a fraternity. But something in his mannerism makes me think he did. Garrett cocks his head and examines him. "But here's the thing." Oliver leans forward. "One of your brothers was murdered—"

Garrett makes a noise like he's about to object, and Oliver holds up his hand.

"We've found new evidence that the hit-and-run wasn't random. That someone, or maybe a few people, wanted Jay Kemp dead."

I would have saved this gem for later, but something in Garrett's face shifts.

"Whoa," he says, and stretches his arms behind his head. "I thought all the guys liked Jay."

"That's what everyone kept telling us, but no. He had enemies."

Oliver lets that sit. Lets Garrett wonder what else he doesn't know about his brothers.

Teddy hasn't said a word. He doesn't need to. Oliver's doing fine. It's strange though, and I angle to get a good look at him, but he's positioned himself so his back is squarely facing the two-way mirror, and I can't help but think it's because of me.

"How about this: for now, we'll tell you what we already know. That way you won't be betraying any brotherhood secrets. You can just confirm what we've got and if you think of anything you can share without getting into trouble, then you say so."

Garrett sits back in his chair. Something like relief washes over his face, and I wonder if the chill guy who walked in a minute ago was a bit of an act.

He nods.

"Great." Oliver opens the folder on the table casually. "This is what we found in the basement."

The photographs are blown up to the size of textbooks and look like they're screenshots straight out of *Saw*. Stone floor splattered with dark reddish stains. Bucket turned over on its side spilling unmentionable contents thanks to me. Pliers nailed to the wall. Threadbare blankets lying in a heap.

Garrett closes his eyes once and presses his lips together. Maybe, I think, he's blocked it out. Told himself it wasn't that bad. And anyway, it's over. He's had a year to forget. Now he has beach parties, girls in bikinis, and all the hunch punch in the world to wash those memories away.

"Must have been cold down there."

"Yeah," Garrett breathes.

"There were two blankets. How many pledges slept there at a time?"

It's a guess—that they had to sleep in the basement—but a good one. Oliver says it like he already knows.

"We all had to stay there twenty-four hours."

And just like that, he's told us.

I sit back, impressed. Garrett doesn't seem to know what he's said. I guess the ritual is more detailed, but this alone—physical discomfort, emotional distress—constitutes hazing. And maybe even a motive. Often students think that hazing is only when someone forces you to do something against your will. But the fact is, for some people, the desire to belong, to fit in, whatever, will have them killing themselves trying to please. And anything that endangers the safety or mental or physical well-being of a student is considered hazing.

"How many guys were there?"

Garrett rubs his face. "Sixteen, I think."

"What was in the buckets?"

His nose twitches like he can still smell them. He hesitates, but again seems to decide that since we already know about the buckets, there's no harm in talking about them.

"They, um, leave them like that," he murmurs, "never clean the blood or the vomit or . . ."

"Urine?" Oliver says helpfully. "Shit?"

"Yeah."

"It makes it seem like something out of a horror movie."

"Yeah." Garrett fidgets. "That's what I thought, too, but they said it was so we understood—that it was our history, our shared tradition, you know?" He looks at Teddy, but Teddy's unmoved. He turns back to Oliver. "So we understood that someone did it to them, they'd do it to us, and we'd do it to next year's pledges. They kept reminding us of that. That it would make us closer. We'd know things about ourselves and our brothers no one else knew."

And that would keep them quiet. Fear that if they told, their own humiliations would be exposed to the world. I think of damp walls and dark corners, the foul smell. Some of the boys would close in on themselves, biding their time until morning, thinking about nothing except getting out of that place. Others, though, others would look at the rusty pliers on the wall, the handcuffs, and imagine themselves on the other side, how once they got through it, they would make it ten times worse for the next group.

I grit my teeth.

Strip away all the slogans and flags and famous graduates, look beneath the preppy clothes, straight teeth, and swoop haircuts, all the markers of class and conformity, and you have the way humans have been organizing themselves for centuries: power and dominance hierarchies. Leaders need followers and followers need leaders, and here it's all fast-tracked. In one night they're shifted out one way or the other.

"They said it was like those trust falls at camp. You know, where you all stand in a line, cross your arms, and fall backward? You have to trust that the guy behind you will catch you. That's what they said when we were in the basement. We had to trust that our brothers would let us back out."

I want Oliver to ask about the footstool. I picture Michael at the top of the steps, his eyes bright with his hand outstretched, saying, "It's about trust," as the pledges look at one another. No one wanting to hand their escape route back to him. Any one of them could have done the same as me; the buckets were tall enough. But I imagine that was part of it—the additional way out even after the footstool disappeared. But if you take it, climb onto those buckets of filth, you forfeit your opportunity to be part of the group. I resist the urge to bang on the glass. *Why would you want to be friends with people who do that to you?* I want to scream. *How could you just hand away your autonomy?*

Oliver withdraws a photo of the handcuffs. Garrett flinches.

"Were you forced to wear these?"

Garrett squirms.

"We weren't forced to do anything."

"You see that?" Oliver leans in, tapping a murky splatter on the pliers next to the handcuffs. "That's blood."

There's no way he could know this already. It's just as likely a darker spot of rust. But Garrett won't have any idea how long it takes to get lab reports back. His eyes are wide and haven't moved from the place above Oliver's finger.

He shakes his head. "No one used the pliers."

I see Teddy shift. Oliver senses it, too.

"And this," he moves his finger back to the photo of the handcuffs, "was covered in prints and skin particles. Someone," he says, his voice a hushed whisper, "snapped it down tight. See here," he points to the inside of the cuff, "that's where it dug into the flesh so hard it drew blood."

There's nothing there, but it doesn't matter. Garrett's shivering, eyes transfixed by the photo, and my heart starts to hammer.

"Who wore the handcuffs?"

Garrett's silent. He's trembling so hard now, you'd think we'd cranked up the AC, but I know he's remembering. The cold from the basement, it's buried somewhere deep inside him, and Oliver's questions, the photos, they've shaken it free.

"I told them not to." It almost explodes from him. And he's looking back and forth from Oliver to Teddy, pleading with them to believe him.

"I told them we had to stick together, but twenty-four hours—it seemed so long—and then, I don't know what time." He rubs his face. "But it was late and the door opened, and someone called down that there was a whip on the wall. As if we hadn't noticed. He said if we didn't come up with bruises they'd know we'd been jerking each other off all night. And they didn't let faggots into Kap-O." An ugly flush creeps up his neck. "He said we should take turns."

He touches a place on his shoulder, and I wonder what kind of bruises were left on his skin.

There's a rap on the door, and Garrett's head jerks toward it.

"Take turns doing what?" Oliver leans forward, ignoring the knocking until it dies.

I hear his footsteps before the door to the observation room opens. Truman's backlit, but the outline of his shoulders tells me all I need to know. He steps into the room, folds his arms over his chest, and stares at the boy in the window. All the swagger has gone out of Garrett. His face slumps, and he blinks at the grimy table. I look at Truman's reflection in the two-way glass. His eyes have hardened and he's grinding his jaw.

"Take turns doing what?" Oliver repeats.

The boy in the chair is silent.

"Garrett," Oliver says softly. "This will all be over soon. We've talked to six of your brothers," he lies. "There are twelve more after you. At this point, we know a good deal about what happens in the basement."

Garrett shifts but says nothing.

"What we're trying to do now is confirm whether the stories match. I know it's hard to talk about—"

"We crawled on the floor on our hands and knees," Garrett says, his voice barely more than a whisper.

Next to me, Truman is completely still.

"We all took turns with the whip." Garrett sounds bewildered as he hears it said out loud. He rubs his shoulder again. "It was so dark. You couldn't really tell if you were hitting the guy or the floor." A sharp inhale. "Except for the sound."

His hands are shaking now—like Ryan's—and he balls them into fists. I taste something like bile in my throat. I think back to last night at the party, stalking Michael with Cindy by my side. I'd been so focused on looking for predators baring their teeth and sharpening their claws that

I hadn't noticed how many of them were already bruised and bloodied and dancing toward oblivion.

"Who wore the handcuffs?"

"There wasn't a key. So only one person could go in the handcuffs."

"Who?" Oliver's edged in so close, their faces are almost touching.

I'm leaning in, too, wanting so badly to hear it was Jay—that this would explain his fear and paranoia, that I don't see the obvious flaw in my wish, that Jay wasn't a pledge, that he was a junior, the social chair, and that, if anything, he was on the other side, holding the key.

"We called him 'Chains,'" Garrett says.

Oliver's eyebrows lift at this obviously cruel sobriquet.

"But his name was Colton something, I think." He shrugs. "I don't remember his last name."

I inhale. Colton. The name means nothing to me.

Oliver shuffles through his notes. Teddy is still stone-faced, his eyes on Garrett. I don't think he's moved at all in the last five minutes. And I'm not sure if that's for Garrett's benefit or for mine.

"There's no Colton listed as a member of Kappa Phi Omicron."

"Yeah, well." Garrett rubs his hand over his face. His eyes are bloodshot. "He wouldn't be, would he? Didn't make it." There's a mixed note of disgust and pride in his voice.

"He didn't make it," Oliver repeats, and I know we're both wondering if we need to be looking for another body.

"Through hell week," Garrett says quickly, suddenly understanding how it sounds.

"So what happened to him?"

Garrett shrugs. "I don't know. That night—in the basement—he freaked out—completely lost his shit. Called all the brothers 'assholes.' We didn't see him after that."

And just like that—this other boy who'd been in the horrorscape with them was erased from Kappa Phi Omicron. No one to catch him during his trust fall. No bonds tight enough to hold these would-be brothers together.

And there's something else, too—there in the way Garrett says "we." Victory, maybe even defiance. *We earned it,* his look says, *he didn't.* We're not victims, despite what you found in the basement, he is. Colton. The loser who didn't make it.

It takes another five interviews to get the full story on hell week.

Essentially, it went something like this: The first day, the pledges are locked in a room and not let out until they finish several cases of warm beer. They get black-out drunk, and the active brothers wake them at four the next morning. Somehow they've managed to strip the pledges down to their boxers and move them outside, so they are thoroughly confused when they get their bearings. It's still dark, so the members of the fraternity's executive board are holding torches. "Ladies," they say, "welcome to hell." Then they explain the rules of hell week. Rule number one is that pledges must hand in their cell phones. There will be no video or photographic evidence that any of this happened. No contact with friends or parents, anyone who might talk sense into the pledges or complain to the university. Rule number two is that pledges speak only when spoken to and must talk about themselves in the third person. Basically, they lose their right to speak and to the word "I." Rule number three is that they will wear a coat and tie to class all week, which—combined with rule number four (no showers)—I assume is meant to humiliate them. Rule number five is that pledges eat one meal a day: canned tuna the first, canned Spam the next, and so on. And rule number six is that the pledges must sleep when they're told and where they're told. They're given no explanation what this means, but they know it's not going to be good. After listening to the rules, the pledges follow the active brothers back into the house and watch them eat a full breakfast of waffles and eggs. All while being told they won't get their canned tuna until noon, but the thought of canned tuna itself is so repulsive to the hungover brothers that by the time noon rolls around, half don't eat it. Days three to five comprise hours of cleaning, getting ketchup and hot sauce smeared on their bodies, sober driving, drunken push-ups, eating onions and Alka-Seltzer tablets, throwing up on each other, and getting beer cans pelted at their heads—and remember, no showers. Each night they receive sleeping assignments based on how well they answered questions about the fraternity's history and founding principles: the best get to sleep in the study, the worst in the first-floor bathroom. At the end of day five, they think they've made it. The active brothers take them out for a nice dinner. They eat like they've never tasted bread before. They get drunk.

And then they wake up in the basement.

This is where the stories diverge, and I get the feeling none of them are telling the whole truth.

I don't see Truman leave, but suddenly the door to the investigation room opens, and he's there, eyes boring into Teddy and Oliver.

"Both of you. My office. Now." He looks at the two-way mirror. "You, too."

The observation gallery has a funny way of disrupting time. Back in the task room, I blink under the fluorescent lights. Our desks and computers are all hard right angles, casting blue shadows. We're silent as we follow Truman to his office. His head is down, shoulders a hard line. *The bull*, I think, *ready to charge.*

"I have never," he says, gazing out his window, his back to us, "in my thirty years on the force, seen anything like this."

I think of the photos. The tattered blankets and handcuffs.

He turns, his jaw set. "Students curled up in the lobby. Parents raging in my office." He gestures angrily toward the door. "The president of the university is on his way here now."

Michael's father. I blink, and then try to catch Teddy's or Oliver's eyes. Neither will look at me.

"Well," I say when no one speaks. "He should be. This happened under his watch."

Truman's mouth tightens, but he ignores me.

"We do not investigate fraternity business." He slams his hand on his desk and the computer screen rattles. "We investigate murders. Jay Kemp was not a pledge. His death was not related to fraternity misconduct but a driver with a lead foot."

I open my mouth.

"Do you hear me?" Truman's voice has gone low. "His death had nothing to do with Kappa Phi Omicron. These young men come from good families. They have bright futures in front of them. We are not going to ruin their lives for some misguided, probably alcohol-fueled, ritual with a senseless investigation."

And just like that. Justice takes off her blindfold and gives a wink. Free from investigation, free from judgment, free from consequence. A lesson learned for life.

Truman sighs, taking our silence to mean that we accept his point.

"All of the members have alibis for the morning of November twelfth, which you double- and triple-checked, correct?"

Oliver nods.

"Then I want you to inform the young men waiting in the lobby that they may go and caution them against speaking to the press." He rubs his hand over his jaw. "This is bad enough already."

Oliver and Teddy turn on their heels. I plant my feet.

"Marlitt, you stay," he says without looking at me.

I nod. I wasn't planning on leaving.

There's a moment of silence, both of us expecting explanations from the other.

I stare at the back of the silver-framed photograph on his desk.

He breaks first.

"What were you thinking?"

His voice is low, and I know that doesn't bode well, but I feel the heat rise to my face.

"What are you thinking?" I yell back. "Those guys—young men"—I jab my finger toward the hall—"are monsters."

I sense, more than see, Oliver move into the open door behind me. Truman shakes his head and his shadow disappears.

"You weren't there"—my skin goes hot and then cold—"you didn't see—they locked them in for twenty-four hours. Made them hand back their only means of escape—causing physical and emotional distress." I'm clawing for the right words. "It was cold and damp. Did you see Ryan Bennett? He was shaking so hard his teeth were chattering."

"We investigate murder," Truman repeats like he's explaining something obvious to a child. "Not the misdeeds of Greek life."

"Misdeeds?" I growl. "There were whips and handcuffs on the wall."

"They took it too far, but—" He shrugs. "Look, you didn't have siblings, right?"

A flash of anger at the change of topic, and then a sharp, familiar pain twists in my chest.

"No," I mutter.

"I had brothers. Three of them. And I was the smallest."

I look at him appraisingly.

"My brothers tormented me for years. Until"—he grins, and I can almost see the little brother in there, a boy with light hair and sharp eyes—"I hit a growth spurt. Then," he cracks his knuckles, "it was my turn."

"So, what? You're saying this is just roughhousing? Boys will be boys?" *And retribution*, I think.

"No. I'm saying that when people live together, there's a constant shuffling. Everyone's trying to figure out where they fit, devising strategies to sort out the weak link."

Teddy said something similar what feels like forever ago, but that was before we knew the extent of the abuse.

I stare at him, feeling like we're talking about two totally different things.

He leans forward, all his body language telling me he's conceding something, but his eyes are watchful.

"It's clear things got out of hand." He raises his voice when I open my mouth. "And there will be consequences. But we—aside from bringing this to the university's attention"—a nod at me—"will have nothing more to do with it. And you are suspended until further notice."

He says it so softly that at first I think I must have misheard.

"Suspended?"

"You were on leave, entered a private residence with no search warrant filed. You put yourself in danger and Teddy and Oliver in an impossible position. None of this would hold up in court, so you're lucky, in fact, it didn't turn up anything related to the Kemp death."

He doesn't say a word about Cindy, which means Teddy didn't tell him. I glance out the door. Somehow, this makes me feel worse than everything else.

He says some more that sounds a lot like noble cause corruption and self-licensing, but I'm not listening anymore. He hasn't told me to hand in my badge or clean out my desk. He also doesn't send me to Internal Affairs. But I register the words "no police powers."

He touches the photo on his desk.

The way he's framed this, I know I should feel like I've gotten off lightly. But I don't. I feel like the rug's been ripped out from beneath me, that everything I believed in is a lie, and I'm free-falling toward a truth I don't want to see.

"And Marlitt—I mean it." He glares at a spot to the right of my ear. "Stay away from the Kappa Phi Omicron house, the brothers, and the university. Anything that looks even remotely like it has to do with Kappa Phi Omicron, I want you to turn and run in the opposite direction. Is that clear?"

I nod.

He gives me a long look. Wishing, I think, that he could believe me.

| Fifteen |

Outside the station, the pale sun slips in and out of the jagged pines without giving any warmth. Somehow, December's begun without me noticing. The news crews have vanished, but a man emerges from a black car. He's heavy around the middle with silver hair and an air of dispassionate confidence that is so similar to Michael, it's clear this is Ed Williams, his father, the university president. But he doesn't look like a man who's just found out his son has been torturing freshmen, an administrator who's discovered scandalous fraternity misconduct has been happening at his university. His face is impassive and hard, and despite myself, I feel a fleeting shiver of sympathy for Michael.

I glance back at the gray building with the feeling they're all watching—my departure or the president's arrival, I'm not sure. Just in case, I stride deliberately to my car, back straight, head high, hands clenched into fists.

The fatigue hits as soon as I pull out of the station lot. The wide, treeless highway has me feeling exposed, and I turn onto a side street, letting the narrow lanes hold me close.

I don't mean to drive by the house. The beautiful one with the slender black columns and pristine white paint. But I find myself parked outside.

Katie sits on the brown lawn, tucked beneath an oak tree. I watch as other girls filter up and down the double front staircase, casting her occasional concerned glances. One runs across the grass and gives her a fleeting hug, but Katie doesn't react, and the rest treat her like a piece of yard furniture or a resident ghost. This new version of Katie is antithetical to their buoyancy. Their lightness and laughter are no match for her grief.

I shut the car door and walk toward her cautiously. Dead leaves crunch under my feet, but she doesn't look up.

"Mind if I join you?" My tone is practiced, soft, and it rings false to my ears. But she shrugs, resigned, as if she's been here, waiting for me this whole time.

"Do you remember me?" I ask. "I came to see you a few weeks ago. To talk about Jay."

She doesn't flinch like I was expecting. Simply stares out across the lawn at the fountain like she's not really seeing it.

We sit in silence, watching girls race across the grass with yoga mats, shopping bags, books, and laptops. Everyone moving, singing, smiling. Everyone, except Katie.

"Is that why you're here?" I try again, gesturing from the tree to one of her sisters video chatting on her cell phone. "It's okay to need space to grieve."

She pulls a blade of grass from the lawn. Scrunches it between her fingers.

I take a breath through my nose, decide honesty is the only option I have left. "I know what it's like to lose someone you love," I tell her, and her eyes flicker loosely to the edge of my face, drawn—in spite of herself—to the vulnerability she sees there. "And Jay—he seemed like a good guy."

The interest I won with my confession dissolves, and she glares as if she registers the lie.

"You don't know anything," she hisses. Then she grabs her bookbag and stumbles to her feet. And as I watch her walk away, I think that might be the truest thing anyone's ever said to me.

My parents' house is bathed in golden light, that fall sun that turns everything green and yellow, illuminating patches of pine straw.

I take the stone steps two at a time and unlock the front door with a quick glance over my shoulder.

It's quiet inside.

"Hello?" I call.

But no one answers.

I expect a flood of relief at having the place to myself, but it doesn't come.

What I need more than anything is sleep. But I keep hearing the hard edge in Teddy's voice when he called me selfish, seeing Cindy with her scraped palms and bloody lip, the rusted handcuffs on the wall, the boy reduced to wordless tremors.

I make myself a pot of coffee and sit at the kitchen table. My eyes close, and I draw up Lumpkin Street. Walking through North Campus, clutching a coffee cup in my hand, taking the cut-through path by the Founders Garden—the smell of cedar, dead leaves, and late-autumn flowers wafting over the garden wall. Sliding through the side entrance of Joe Brown. A glance at the staircase to nowhere. My mother's appraising gaze. The echoes of a scream and then sprinting down Lumpkin—I must have run right past the driver, but everything around me—pale sidewalk beneath my feet, the student I sidestepped, colliding with the brick wall, my fingers skimming rough mortar, a bike waiting to turn at the light—is a blur. There's a car speeding past, I'm sure of it, but when I try to bring it into focus, it refuses to take shape. I'm looking down the street, not across, so determined to get to the center of the action, to be in the middle of it all, that the car's only in my peripheral. And then there's a metal railing, trees blocking a clear view until I close in on the intersection and see the students gathered, and Jay Kemp is lying in the road, already dead.

I'm awoken by a hammering outside. The roofers, I think, blotting a smudge of drool on the table with my fingers, but the sound is much closer.

I stand and roll my neck, thinking longingly of the bed upstairs, but the hammering has turned into knocking, and I realize there's no one to make it stop but me.

Through the windows that frame the entryway, I see a swoop of brown hair and the last person I would expect after everything that happened in the past twenty-four hours.

"Oliver?" I open the door.

He looks small and disheveled standing there between the brick arches, and I wonder what Truman said to him after I left.

"You need to come back to the station."

"Yeah." I rub a knot in my shoulder. "I don't think that's a good idea." I glance behind me at the kitchen, the coffee that's spilled on the floor, and wonder if there's a crease of the table's edge running across my forehead. "Truman was pretty clear—"

"This has nothing to do with the Kemp case," Oliver interrupts me. "Or at least, not directly, anyway. Just, um—" I assume he's about to tell me to clean myself up. Maybe splash some water on my face. But then we think the same thing: it won't make any difference. I lift an eyebrow and almost smile.

"Let me grab my bag."

I've never been in Oliver's VW Golf. It's cleaner than my car. No candy wrappers on the floorboards or clothes littering the back seat. No greasy slashes from Teddy's bike. We drive in silence, and I stare at his hands on the steering wheel. His nails are bitten down to the skin.

"How did you know," he says after a while, "that Kap-O was hazing its pledges?"

"I didn't."

He takes his eyes off the road to look at me. "Then why did you go there last night?"

I shrug. "I knew they were having a party and I wanted to get inside and look around."

He shakes his head, and I have the feeling he's waiting for me to say more. That if I confirmed his earlier suspicions, my actions last night might be forgiven—not condoned or dismissed without punishment—but that if I said Craig's name, split open my chest to reveal my bleeding heart, Oliver would at least understand my desperation.

A t the station, Truman's Charger is gone. I assume he's at the university doing damage control. Teddy's bike is in its usual place. And I realize that whatever's going on, he wanted nothing to do with it. Or more specifically, nothing to do with me. I try not to look at the handlebars twisting against the metal railing when I follow Oliver up the stairs to the back entrance.

He stops before he opens the door. "Nothing that happens today will bring back your friend," he says slowly, "but maybe it will give you some peace."

I think of the skin around Craig's eyes crinkling when he looked at me. The way his hand held mine. How it felt to love someone and then lose them.

I shake my head wordlessly.

I'm not looking for peace.

A my shuffles into the task room with an armful of folders and frowns like I'm missing my hall pass. I glance at Teddy's desk, but Oliver ushers me into interview room B.

There, huddled in a corner of the couch, sits Ryan Bennett.

He moans when he sees me and draws his knees into his chest.

And then I know. I know why he wouldn't look at me earlier. Know why he hid behind his father, why he was scared. Just like I know why he's here now, why Oliver brought me in, and why Ryan has a large red welt covering his forearm.

Oliver stands in the doorway.

"I kept thinking about those burns," he says quietly, "and how scared he was. Something didn't add up." He crosses his arms and frowns at Ryan. "After the interviews, Teddy and I followed him to the Kap-O house. His dad dropped him off on the street without so much as a wave, and Ryan went straight to the parking lot and pulled a gas can out of his car trunk."

I shake my head.

"The candles," I murmur.

"Yeah, the can was full. Brand new. But—"

Ryan's crying now. Head in his hands, rocking back and forth.

"I guess we spooked him. He confessed right away. To lighting the candles and holding them to your curtains, your bedsheets— He didn't need the gasoline."

Ryan's whole body is shaking.

"I didn't mean to—" he sputters, gestures to my face, and, meeting my eye, looks away.

Maybe it's the look of horror—or disgust—at what he's done and how he's disfigured me that erases my pity. I feel my mouth harden.

"And Jay?" I spit, latching on to something other than my burns, the absurd notion that this sniveling boy is the cause of my suffering. "Is Ryan our driver? Is that why—?"

Oliver shakes his head.

"He has an alibi. He gave a, um—memorable—presentation in his history class that morning. Opposite side of campus. The professor, several of his classmates confirmed."

Memorable for Ryan probably means his teeth chattering through it, staring wide-eyed at his peers, forgetting what he had on his notecards.

"Then why?" I repeat.

Ryan takes short, shallow breaths as he tries to compose himself. He clenches and unclenches his hands, looking at them like he's never seen them before. "It was just to scare you," he whispers.

"Scare me? Why? Because of Jay? Because we were getting close, and one of you killed him?"

Oliver glances sideways at me but doesn't say anything.

Ryan shakes his head furiously and wraps his arms around his chest.

"Then why?" I lean in. I can't touch him, but I want him to look at my face, to see my scars, the wounds his candles inflicted on my skin. "Did someone tell you to do it? Did Michael—?"

Ryan shakes his head again. "No," he whimpers, the word catching in a sob. "He didn't know. No one knew. It was me. Only me . . ."

"So what? You were just showing off? Trying to impress your brothers? To prove you could keep the big bad detective away?"

Spit clings to both sides of his mouth when he opens it, but then he shuts it again.

"Tell me." My shout ends in a plea, and I hear the desperation, feel Oliver behind me, Teddy a few doors down. I lower my voice. "There has to be something more." I just can't believe it. It's too extreme, too devastating. There must be a reason.

We wait in silence. Ryan wraps his arms around his entire body, squeezing his legs to his chest so he's in the fetal position. He's humming softly, the same as when we asked him about the basement this morning, but that feels like forever ago.

Oliver seems to think Ryan's done talking. He walks around the table.

Ryan's jaw moves, just a fraction.

"Wait," I say.

His humming picks up but then slowly, very slowly, turns into words.

"It happened so fast," Ryan whispers into his chest. "Everything went up," he snaps his fingers weakly, a quick upward glance at me, "like that."

I close my eyes and there are flames at the edges.

"And you started moving under the sheets, and I knew I had to get out of there. You were awake." He gives me a pleading look. "I thought you were right behind me. I swear—I heard you on the stairs."

I shake my head, smoke clouding my vision.

"I waited," he tells me, "until I saw the firefighters. I knew you'd be okay."

I fix him with a stare, and he melts back into the couch. Swallowing proves difficult. The light shifts, and the walls go shapeless.

"Who told you to do it?" I ask again, my voice as sharp and brittle as broken glass.

"No one," he whispers. "No one told me to. It was my idea, me . . ."

And there it is, the flicker of something he's been hiding with his tears. *It was my idea—look what I did for my brothers—me.*

"I just didn't think—" His voice breaks and there's that distressed look, the tears again, the humming.

And still, the question remains: Why? Even if no one told him to do it, why did he want to scare me? What are they hiding at Kap-O that's so damaging, so bad that Ryan thought he had to keep me away? I grit my teeth. Oliver already thinks I'm biased. And despite him presenting Ryan to me as a gift—*Look what I got you, the fire starter*, pleased as a cat that's left a tangled mess of a bird at your doorstep—I know Oliver will call Truman once I'm gone and tell him everything that was said here. So I bite back my questions and chew on them in silence.

Oliver waits. A part of me wonders if this is what he wants, for me to prove I've lost my objectivity, to lay it all out like I've got nothing to lose, but when I remain silent, he nods.

"Let's go." He puts a hand on Ryan's arm. I see the faded burns, but they don't move me the way they did when we brought him in this morning.

Ryan sits for a moment. His eyes are still wet, but he stares at both of us now as if fully recognizing where he is and what's about to happen. His lips part, but just hang open. Oliver ushers him out of the room.

I lean back against the wall and breathe deeply, smelling lavender, and running my fingers over the taut, burned skin on my cheek. Whatever Ryan says, I don't believe he acted alone. He may have lit the match and burned his own hands in the process, but he was doing someone's bidding. I think of Michael's warning, the sense that he knew something I didn't. And I'm certain it wasn't just Ryan, it was Kap-O. One way or another, they have to be involved.

In the office, the mood is jovial. Even Amy gives me a begrudging nod, and Oliver offers to buy me a drink later. But Teddy is gone, and their congratulations aren't meant for me, not really. They're for Oliver, for picking up on signs the rest of us missed. And they're out of relief, that there's not some maniacal fire starter on the loose. Just a scared kid who wanted to fit in and now will spend anywhere from one to twenty years in prison.

Despite the fatigue and flames chasing me, enclosing the walls of my car, and racing across my skin, I make it to my parents' house. But by the time I reach the porch, my legs are shaking so violently that I have to steady myself against the railing.

I open the front door and hope I can make it up the next flight of stairs to my room without them realizing I'm home.

"Marlitt, is that you?" My father's voice from the kitchen. I take two steps toward the banister, but he peeks his head around the corner.

"How was your day? We brought back some biscuits—" He drops the book in his hands. "Helena," he yells as he closes the gap between us. "Come quick!"

My teeth are chattering. *Hilfe*, I think. I'm holding Craig dying on the sidewalk, yelling for help, clawing at my skin, ripping off my jacket like it's on fire, scratching at my throat as if I could open my airways by force. *"Ich atme nicht,"* I say, and then everything goes black.

When I open my eyes, I'm in the living room, my head propped up on a yellow pillow, blinking at the Japanese maple semiobscured by curtains.

"Helena," my father whispers. "She's awake."

"What happened?" I ask. My mouth's dry and tastes of ash.

"You, um . . ." My father clasps his hands together. And suddenly I'm mortified.

"You stumbled into the house," my mother says behind him. "And then you passed out."

"I fainted?" I scoot my shoulders against the couch corner, trying to sit up straight. "Like some nineteenth-century heroine?" I'm furious at myself and my body for betraying me.

"Well, first . . . ," my mother begins.

My father shakes his head knowingly. *See what you've started*, his look says.

"Most of those heroines were written by men glamorizing the *femme fragile* in a thinly veiled guise to promote male dominance. And"—my head is pounding; I wish I hadn't asked—"real women had plenty of reasons to faint, suffering dozens of pregnancies, undiagnosed tuberculosis, and anorexia. And you—" She peers at me from above her glasses. "When was the last time you slept? Ate something? Why weren't you able to breathe?" She moves to see my face. "The doctor said your lungs need time to heal. And you need to rest."

"I can breathe fine," I mutter irritably.

"You said you couldn't breathe," my mother says, "right before you passed out."

"No—" I begin.

"You said, '*Ich atme nicht.*' I'm not breathing."

"I said it in German?"

My mother purses her lips. She's so used to translating from German to English she hasn't realized she's done it. She looks at my father. Something passes between them that I don't quite understand. He gives a tiny shake of his head. And I think of the whispered conversations that defined my childhood, the voices that stopped when I walked into the room, the feeling of something left unsaid.

"What's happening to me?"

"You know," my father says, shifting his body away from both of us before standing and walking toward the record player, "when you were little you used to follow me around and bang your head on the floor."

"What?" I say, more confused now than ever.

"I'd be sitting at my desk," he runs his fingertips along the records, "and you'd come into my office and start hammering your head against the rug by the door. So, of course, I would rush over, pick you up, and then not get any work done the rest of the afternoon."

I open my mouth and close it again.

"One day, your mother came home and saw you do it."

My mother nods.

"I told him to leave the room."

"I didn't want to," my father says reassuringly, "there's concrete underneath the floors, you know. But the moment I did, you stopped."

"You just wanted attention," my mother says.

I have no idea why they're telling me this. Do they think I passed out from a need for attention?

"Debussy?" he asks my mother.

"I . . . ," I begin, not sure how to defend myself.

"Did something happen at work?" my father asks, putting the record on.

"They, um . . . ," I mumble, feeling completely unmoored. "They found the person responsible for the fire at my house."

They both stare at me. Until now, I'd been hiding my suspicions and letting them believe it was an accident—a frivolous indulgence gone wrong. I'm not sure that my mother ever believed it, but she hasn't asked.

"Well, that's good news, isn't it?" my father says.

I know he wants to ask more. But he's studying my face uncertainly, assessing whether I can handle any more questions.

"I don't know," I say.

And it's true. I should feel relieved, vindicated even—it wasn't a momentary lapse in judgment or a silly extravagance; it wasn't my fault at all—but instead I feel nothing. I'm met only with the certainty that the fraternity was involved and the crushing knowledge that there's nothing I can do about it. And without that sense of purpose, of justice, I feel completely lost.

We sit in silence until the record ends, and I make my way upstairs.

It's not until later, after I've inspected my burns, applied my salves, and slipped into bed, that I realize neither addressed the fact that I was speaking in German.

| Sixteen |

Morning comes too soon, and I'm pulling a jacket over a pair of my mother's navy slacks with only half an idea of what I'm doing.

The dreams are getting worse—mechanical bells, a confined space, the sense that some integral piece of myself has been ripped away, and then an infinite, indescribable loneliness. And German. Always German. A German that I don't understand in the morning. That I didn't know before I fell asleep. And the feeling that the fire uncovered something buried. Not just what happened with Craig, but something deeper. A reverse funeral pyre—stirring living shapes from the ashes and making them whole.

Forbidden from going to the station and with nothing better to do, I unload the contents of my satchel onto the kitchen table like I used to unpack my backpack in high school. The folder with the call sheets. My notes from the interviews. And something else. After everything that happened in the past forty-eight hours, I forgot Ben's voicemail and the envelope I slipped into my bag when I left the station Friday morning.

I've got something for you. Nothing else. We do that sometimes—say as little as possible. It might be to pique someone's curiosity, but most of the time, it's because we don't want a biased response. After all, if you give someone a Rorschach test and tell them they're looking at a giant moth, they're likely to see a giant moth. But if you wait and let them see for themselves, they may come up with something entirely different.

But the top document tells me what I need to know: missing student report.

Colin Haines. Nineteen years old. White male.

I shrug. Now I know why Ben wasn't super urgent in his message. A child, everyone drops what they're doing. The first hours are the most critical—gathering evidence, interviewing parents, alerting the public. If it's a stranger kidnapping, children might be murdered within a few hours, and if not, then within the first two days. It's a sick feeling, knowing that one false lead could mean the difference between life and death. If it's a young woman, she has a little longer, but not much. A nineteen-year-old male, though? He'll turn up in a couple of days.

I thumb through the file. The parents reported him missing a week ago. He was supposed to return home to—I flip back to the front sheet—Marietta for the Thanksgiving holiday and didn't show. But he has a history of blowing off visits. There's a report from earlier this year—June—when his parents expected him back for the summer, heard nothing, and called the police. According to the notes, an officer found Colin safe and sound—just living at a different location than the one his parents provided, some derelict apartment on the north side. There's a short observation scrawled in the margins: says he has a summer internship, doesn't want his parents to know where he lives, skittish, no drugs or other paraphernalia.

Financial problems, I think, leaning over the kitchen table to snag an apple. Probably embarrassed for his parents to see where he lives. Or maybe they're controlling. Or emotionally abusive. One note says that when the parents couldn't get in touch with him, the mother drove around Athens for two days and stalked the university admissions office demanding his class attendance records, which of course, they wouldn't give. I suspect Colin's an only child. Another note that the mother was "hysterical."

I snort and take a bite out of the apple.

I flip the page. More notes. She's insistent this behavior was unlike her son, despite all the recent incidents. Wants her call put on record.

I dial Ben's number.

His voice is soft and calm, but not in a way that makes you impatient. He's simply a man who wants all the details, who won't miss something in the middle of an emergency.

Talking to him, I have the strange feeling that he'll take care of everything with Truman and at the fraternity, before I remember that he called me, not the other way around.

I'm just opening my mouth to tell him I've been suspended, that he should reach out to Teddy or Oliver, when he says: "Colin's been missing over a month. Didn't show up for Thanksgiving break—that's when his mother sounded the alarm. But when I started talking to his professors, most couldn't remember him at all. The only one who kept an attendance sheet had taken his last date of attendance on Friday, November eighth."

This makes my ears perk up. It's only a few days before Jay was hit.

"And . . ." He pauses. "His parents say he's a member of Kappa Phi Omicron."

"He's not," I tell him, focusing my attention back on the apple. I've pored over that list of names, those doughy faces and preppy haircuts, so many times I would have recognized him immediately.

"I know."

I sigh and flip to the end of the documents. Paper-clipped to the last page is a photo. The edges are folded and lined—taken out of a frame. A happy family smiles back at me. The father's arm is thrown haphazardly around the son. The mother ducks under the son's shoulder, her hands lightly on his waist. I cringe at their blue jeans and matching white shirts, at the premeditation of what's supposed to look like a spontaneous moment. But aside from the sheepish, somewhat self-conscious grin, the boy's dressed as he was told. He looks nice. Shy.

I shake my head.

I know why Ben thinks I might be interested. Physically, perhaps, he resembles Jay. White male, late teens to early twenties, with dirty blond to brown hair. Medium build, and I'd say five ten or eleven based on the height relationship between him and his parents—but so are half the other male students on campus. The date he went missing is suspicious. So is the parents thinking he was a member of Kappa Phi Omicron. But they're mistaken.

"I don't know," I say.

Ben cups the phone in his hand, and there's a murmur of voices from the other end. "Look," he says, "I've got to run, but the parents are coming in today. I thought you might want to hear what they have to say."

I stare at the scattered sheets across the kitchen table, the call logs, the fraternity head shots, and then the small family photograph.

I should tell him I'm suspended. I almost do. But then I think of Truman saying things had just gotten out of hand. That there was nothing wrong with a little reshuffling. Roughhousing. Retribution. I think of Jay's lifeless eyes, the driver with his face, and boys in suits and ties, mothers with handkerchiefs waving sons off to war, bunkers and trenches, the type of men who choose their fate with purpose and write their own creeds, and the kind who follow the footsteps of others blindly, unable to see past the hundred backs that marched before them. I was just following tradition, following orders, following my brother, never recognizing that following was also a choice—a weak man's choice, it's true, but still a choice after all.

"What time?" I ask.

The sky is sunless, a brilliant white, casting everything else into pale shades of gray. I drive slowly to the nondescript concrete building on the west side that houses the Missing Persons Unit. It still doesn't seem real to me that someone crept into my bedroom while I was sleeping and set it on fire. It feels like it happened to someone else. But one look at the rearview mirror is enough to remind me—I can't pretend it didn't happen.

Florence Haines doesn't resemble the woman in the family photograph. She's lost the sun-kissed skin and the laughter in her eyes from the beach. When Ben introduces me—a colleague; he says nothing about me working Homicide—I can't look away from her face. It's clear she's tried to pull herself together for this meeting—A-line skirt, silk blouse, smattering of lipstick—but I'm transfixed by the smudge of mascara on her cheek, the twitching blue vein under her eye, and the twisting of her hands. This is a woman who knows something is wrong.

She, on the other hand, pays little attention to me. Her gaze flicks from Ben, to the file on his desk, and back again as if he's holding a lifeline and she's treading water, as if she's been treading water for hours, for days, for months maybe, and Ben's her last hope. Her husband sits next to her, receding blond-gray hair, dressed in khakis and a wrinkled golf shirt, his hands folded neatly in his lap. He hasn't said a word since I arrived and stares at a place on the wall behind Ben's desk. Since he didn't bother to introduce himself, I don't know his first name.

"I made a few phone calls," Ben says to Florence. "And the last date of attendance I could find on record was Friday, November eighth."

"That was a month ago." Florence's voice rises. She looks helplessly from Ben to her husband. "Why didn't any of his professors alert the university?" She glares at me.

"From what I could gather," Ben says softly, "Colin frequently missed class."

She shakes her head. "He's a good student—he graduated high school with a three-point-nine GPA. Has a HOPE Scholarship—" Another glance at her husband. "And even if," she taps her finger against Ben's desk, "even if he missed class—to stop going entirely?" Another shake of her head. "There must be some kind of alert system, or notice, or—" Again that helpless look that turns angry at its edges. She's twisting her wedding band around her finger, and every spin casts furious reflections across the wall.

"You would think so," Ben says diplomatically. "If someone doesn't show up for work, it's likely their employer would call their house—"

"Exactly." Florence throws up her hands. Her husband flinches.

Ben shifts in his chair. "—but these days, students only list cell phones on their contact sheets. They leave for week-long vacations with their families and don't tell their professors. They drop out without filing paperwork. It happens so often that few professors think to sound the alarm. FERPA prohibits the university from sharing student information with parents. And few administrators would consider an absence before a holiday reason for concern."

I'm nodding without realizing it—I've heard stories like this over dinner, my mother's frustration that there's nothing she can do, and anyway she's so busy, and it's not as if she can hunt X or Y student down herself—that I'm surprised to meet Florence's angry stare.

"Well, they should," she says bitterly. "Once we find him"—another unreturned look at her husband—"we should sue."

"Let's focus on locating Colin first."

His name sends something sharp across her face. Another glance at the file.

"What—" She clears her throat. "—what have you found?"

"As I said on the phone, Colin did not appear to have a stable residence. The last two known addresses we have for him were on the north side. One at Water Oaks and one on Marlin Drive."

"No," Colin's father says, addressing Ben for the first time. "He was a member of Kappa Phi Omicron. He lived at the house."

Pride, I think. It's out of place but unmistakable. There's pride in his voice as he says this.

"I spoke to the fraternity president earlier this afternoon," Ben says in that delicate way of his. "Colin is not a member, has never been a member, or lived at the house."

Mr. Haines's mouth hangs open and then twists unpleasantly as he closes it.

"He pledged last fall. He sent us photos of the house and everything." Florence Haines's voice has softened. She puts a hand on her husband's arm. His shoulders stiffen, but he doesn't move away. "There must be some kind of misunderstanding."

Ben and I drive to Colin's last known address. He's been sharing a small two-bedroom house with a quick-tempered ex-marine, who spends a suspicious amount of time in Florida and hasn't seen Colin in over a month. From what he told Ben, the pair were rarely in the house at the same time, and if they were, Colin kept to his room. The guy couldn't even remember what Colin looked like. He's out of state again and wasn't pleased about us entering the residence until Ben started hinting at investigating the numerous Florida trips.

It's a short drive. We're both quiet. And I wonder if Ben's remembering the first case we worked together—the one with the missing woman. In the end, we found her in a motel room two miles outside Athens. She had a television cable wrapped around her neck and had been dead for three days. Her death was ruled a suicide despite the defensive wounds on her hands. And although the front desk attendant initially identified the man who accompanied her to the motel as a married local district commissioner, he later claimed that she had arrived alone, that she appeared distraught, and that he wasn't surprised that she hung herself. No charges were made, and for a long time after, I couldn't look anyone from Missing Persons in the eye.

The road dips and narrows, and I watch the couple behind us in the rearview mirror. Mr. Haines's mouth moves in short erratic bursts. Florence's face is marbled with reflections of the sky on the glass, but her shoulders are set in a rigid line, steeling herself for whatever we find.

We turn down a straight, barely paved street with houses close together on either side. Ben takes the bumps in the road slow, and we pass a man sitting in a rusty pickup. His arm hangs out the window, skinny like a tree branch in winter, so pale and corpse-like I have to do a double take. But the engine's running, and I see white puffs emanating from the tailpipe. I eye Ben, and he shrugs.

Despite the uneasy sensation creeping up my spine, it's turned into a beautiful day. The sun has emerged and draws patterns of light across the cracked pavement. Birds flutter in between the leafless branches.

Still, as we pull up in front of the address listed on Ben's notes, I shiver with anticipation. The overgrown bushes that hide the windows, the NO TRESPASSING sign on the front door, the broken glass beneath the security light—all speak of residents who prefer to be left alone, and maybe something more troubling.

I slip out of the car and stand, taking in the street with my hands on my hips. I smell fire, but no smoke comes from the chimney. One or two slats of the roof are missing, and the corroded gutter slopes under the weight of leaves and branches.

Behind me, I hear Florence Haines arguing with her husband. The car doors open.

"Please, if you don't mind—" Ben's voice mixes with the crisp autumn air. "Stay in the car until we give the all-clear."

Free papers decay on the front steps, and a stale scent emanates from the door. There's nothing to indicate anyone's inside, but the sense of unease increases as I follow Ben up the weed-strewn walkway.

Ben knocks. "Police."

I sense curtains shifting in the other houses.

He knocks again. Looks at me.

I step forward to try the handle.

It's unlocked.

That prickly feeling crawls over my skin again.

I push the door open with my fingertips. It swings forward easily.

The smell of disuse is even stronger from inside. A plaid sofa sighs in the middle of the floor next to a wooden chair. A folding card table leans against the opposite wall.

"Police," Ben yells a second time. We advance, and a floorboard creaks. I spin around, but there's nothing besides an unframed mirror and my own perverse reflection in the tarnished glass.

There are two bedrooms. Both empty. The primary one, if you can call it that, with the bed neatly made. Yellow Gadsden "Don't Tread on Me" flag hanging next to a black poster with the words "Marines Don't Die, We Regroup in Hell."

I shake my head. It's clear this is our landlord and he's missed the irony of his decorations.

The second bedroom consists of nothing but a sheetless twin mattress on the floor, a handful of wire hangers in the closet, and a cardboard box that seems to have been used as a dresser drawer.

I bend to examine its contents and frown. Underneath a dirty T-shirt is a stack of textbooks and a lined yellow notepad. Pens and pencils roll at the bottom. Not a dresser, I think, but a desk, and the only indication that this room was occupied by a student.

Behind me comes another creak of the floorboards and a gasp. Florence stands at the bedroom entrance with a hand over her mouth.

"He's not here," I tell her.

She shakes her head, eyes on the cardboard box.

"No," she whispers.

Her husband's followed her into the house. Through the bedroom door, I see him standing in the middle of the living room, swinging his head from side to side.

"We gave him an allowance," he blurts. "Money. Every month."

Behind him, a cockroach scurries across the kitchen counter. Ben goes through the drawers and cabinets, his face unreadable. There's nothing but a few cans of beer in the fridge and a bottle of vodka in the freezer.

"He told us about parties, about fishing trips to the lake, girls—" Mr. Haines chokes on the last word.

"There must be some kind of mistake." Florence's voice is pleading. Anger gone. "He wouldn't live like this." She hasn't moved from the bedroom threshold, but she raises her hand to the wall, and I sense more than see her legs give way.

I step to her side and grab her arm.

She glances at her husband, still blinking, staring open-mouthed at the empty fridge.

"He's had a hard time at work," she murmurs to me. "More than hard—he lost his job." She swallows. "The fraternity—it was his proudest accomplishment—the best time of his life. It was supposed to guarantee Colin's future. His success."

We both gaze at the stripped mattress.

"It doesn't look like Colin's been here in some time," Ben calls from the kitchen. "We'll talk to the neighbors. You should go home in case Colin tries to reach you there."

Florence's shoulders slump; the weight of her body presses heavily against my own.

"He hasn't been back in months," she says.

"But he could return," Ben reminds her. "He may need food, money, shelter. Your home will be the first place he thinks of."

Florence shakes her head.

I imagine a boy cut adrift, navigating choppy seas. Where is *home* in your early twenties? A distant blip on the horizon, the place you left, perceived as a failure to return. Instead, you've set sail into infinite possibility, eager to make your own way, only to find yourself lost, clutching at a broken compass, with the realization that there never was any real destination to begin with.

"We should search the Kap-O house." Mr. Haines grits his teeth. "He might be hiding there."

Ben sighs sadly.

I stare through the grimy bedroom window. Across the street, a gray squirrel scours the dead grass for something to sustain him through winter. I think of the Kap-O kitchen stocked with food, the halls full of people. Boys passed out in supply closets. Cade stuffing a pillow in a cabinet and sleeping on a couch in the rec room. But Cade was a member. The whole point is exclusivity. It seems unlikely the brothers would let some guy crash at the house for weeks unless he was a good friend. And Ben said none of the brothers knew Colin.

I see the basement with the tattered blankets. The buckets in the corner. The locks hanging from the door but unclasped. Would anyone sleep there willingly? I don't think so.

"If that's the case, it would mean Colin doesn't want to be found." Ben again, his voice soft but firm. "Colin's an adult. We can't search the Kappa Phi Omicron house without permission or a warrant." I grimace, but Ben doesn't look at me—and if he knew about my suspension, I wouldn't be here. "There's no indication of foul play. Or anything to suggest he's in immediate danger."

Mr. Haines's jaw tightens. "He hasn't accessed his social media accounts or credit card."

"Which again indicates that Colin may not want to be found," Ben tells him. He takes a short breath, glances between Mr. and Mrs. Haines. "I know this is hard. It may be that Colin just needs some time to himself. It may be that he wants to start again someplace new." He pauses.

"Detective Kaplan and I will talk to the neighbors to determine the last time Colin was here. We'll see if they noticed any suspicious activity. In the meantime, I suggest you go home. Use your own social media accounts to gather information. Continue to contact hospitals and homeless shelters. Be available if he returns. And please get in touch with my office if he contacts you."

Florence slumps against me as I walk her to the door. I feel a strange protective urge to hug her. Outside, her husband helps her the rest of the way to the car, his jaw clenched and his eyes fixed on some distant point on the horizon.

The neighbors are not a garrulous bunch, but a few remember Colin. One saw him the night of the eleventh, moving up our last date of sight through the weekend. But none report seeing him since.

Ben doesn't say it, but the case is closed.

There was no evidence of violence. No indication that Colin was forced to leave the house against his will. And although he left his books, we didn't find his wallet or cell phone. Everything points to him skipping town. It's a shitty thing to do—to disappear, start somewhere new, and leave your friends and family wondering what happened. But this isn't a job for the police. If the parents really want to know what happened, they can hire a private investigator.

As we pull away, my skin prickles. It's that same unsettled feeling as when we arrived, and I turn for a second glance, trying to place what it is.

The houses along the street are all seven shades of derelict. Brittle grass that has never seen a mower. Plastic toy trucks and doll heads scatter like dead leaves. But still, every single one is decorated for the holidays. String lights, wreaths, a blow-up snowman. Decaying pumpkins from Halloween. But the front stoop and windows of Colin's house are empty. Nothing hangs from the door or blinks on display in the yard. *Soulless*, I think. It's a house without a soul.

But there were books.

I swallow a sharp intake of breath, and Ben takes his eyes off the road a second to look at me. His expression falters, and I assume he's forgotten for a moment about my scars.

"So what do you think?" he asks as we turn back onto MLK.

I exhale the breath I forgot I was holding. I think of Colin's smile in the photograph on the beach. The way Florence clutched his shirt. The proud lines of his father's shoulders. Parents who would do anything for their son. Parents who built a safe nest in the suburbs, charted a map for his life—the right college, fraternity, job—and then ran behind him with outstretched arms to protect him from falling, from failing. But when it was time for him to fly away, his wings were clipped and stunted from never having to test them. I think of Cicero: "A room without books is like a body without a soul." Colin left his books, does that mean he left his soul behind? I drum my fingers on the windowsill. I think: *But it's not just that. It's the books themselves.* They feel familiar in a way that they shouldn't: Plato's *Republic* and *Trial and Death of Socrates*, Aristotle's *Politics*, Nietzsche's *On the Genealogy of Morals*, Machiavelli's *Prince*, *Ethics in Practice*, *Criminal Law*, and *Universe: Stars and Galaxies*. I think of parties, lake houses, and girls. I think of Katie Coleman, Jay's sudden good grades, and Michael and Jay's last fishing trip when Jay was supposedly writing a stellar philosophy essay. I think of students signing false names on attendance sheets. And I think of the second phone. The other number. The one Jay called so many times in the hours before he died. I think of the lies Colin told his father, stories of life at Kap-O, parties, girls, and the lake. The lake where Jay spent his last weekend with Michael. The one place we haven't looked.

I think, *If I'm right, I can't tell Ben. Not yet.*

I say: "I don't know."

The fraternity's broad brick face lurks at the edge of my vision, shimmers black and red, mirror images reflected on a body of water.

I don't look at him when I ask: "Do you have Colin's cell phone number?"

| Seventeen |

Sunday, December 8, noon

It's 11:15. The doors of Athens First Baptist fly open and a pair of boys run out, tearing at their shirt collars as they circle the fluted columns and trip down the stone stairs. With them comes the scent of varnished wood and old hymnals. Somewhere behind the heavy mahogany doors, an old woman flips pale sheet music with her thumb and "Nothing but the Blood" thunders through the hall. I lean against the far railing and watch as families spill across the portico. Children bundled in peacoats clutch monogrammed Bibles and paper programs. A gust of wind sends a girl no more than five scrambling after a cut-out lamb. Traffic slows on Pulaski Street and someone lays on their horn.

I swallow the feeling I shouldn't be here.

Teddy's dressed for Sunday service—gray slacks and pressed white shirt. He's even forgone his usual colorful sneakers for brown suede boots. His sisters chatter behind him—Josie must be visiting for the holidays—wind whips their scarves and hair as they lean close together, laughing.

Before I can change my mind, I slide from my post. I hardly realize his sisters have stopped talking. But when they do, Teddy turns, immediately alert, and sees me.

"Marlitt?" His voice catches between disbelief and uncertainty.

Josie, tall and athletic like her brother, gives Cassandra, a little shorter and softer around the edges, a sidelong glance.

"You weren't answering your phone."

His look makes it clear we both know why, but he's unwilling to say anything in front of his sisters. I would be lying if I claimed I hadn't counted on this.

"It's important," I say.

"Go on." Josie nudges him. "We'll see you at Mom's." She grins slyly at me.

Teddy gives an exasperated shrug. "Fine." He forces a smile at Cassandra. "Just save me some, all right?"

We watch them, arms linked and heads bent together, as they disappear around the corner of Hancock Street.

"Cassandra must be happy to have Josie home," I say.

He sighs. "What are you doing here, Marlitt?"

"Have the phone records come back?" As soon as the words leave my lips, I know it's the wrong thing to ask. My stomach tightens as the smile pasted on Teddy's face falters and then vanishes. But the fact that he's here, at church, and not at the station means he doesn't have anything yet.

I take a breath.

"I know who killed Jay," I tell him.

I meant to save it, to give him the whole story first—the missing-student report, textbooks, matching phone number—but I have the feeling that if I don't tell him the punchline now he'll walk away.

He folds his arms and leans back as if to scrutinize the sky. His jaw works under his skin. Then he gives in. "How do you know?"

The congregation has thinned. The pastor—silver hair, blue suit—emerges with an older couple, and his eyes scan those of us left on the portico.

"Let's take a walk," I suggest.

I trudge down Pulaski to Clayton. Teddy trails at my heels. The street is strung with twinkling lights, and I'm struck by a sudden longing at the thought of Christmas. We pass a brick storefront hung with vintage dresses and thick red sweaters. Curls of laughter echo out the door.

I tell Teddy about the call from Ben and watch him frown with the knowledge that I didn't report it. I lob my theory about the student missing since the day before Jay was hit. The rented house and the room with textbooks for all the same classes as Jay. I tell him about the fraternities that send in pledges to sign attendance sheets. The number that matches our mystery caller.

The hill inclines steadily. A car swings into the parking space to my right, brakes squealing, and I flinch.

Teddy bends his head to hear me as we walk. And despite his efforts, the chill between us warms, if only slightly.

"Where is he?"

I dig my hands into my pockets. We've stopped in front of a bright blue painted sky; overlarge onions and exposed roots cover the side of the building.

"I want to bring him in," I say, trying hard to look Teddy in the eyes.

"No." Teddy shakes his head and shifts toward me to let a man and his large golden retriever pass. "You're off the case. Suspended."

I take a breath, my gaze on the retreating dog instead of Teddy. "Then I can't tell you."

For a moment, he's too stunned to be angry.

"Marlitt," he says, his voice calm but with a warning edge.

I jut out my chin.

He sighs. "If you do this, we're done. Even if—and right now that's a big if—but even if you're right, and even if Truman doesn't fire you for insubordination, we won't be partners anymore."

"So you would let this guy just walk away?" I have the sudden urge to slam my fists against his chest. "He'll think he can get away with it? The parents with no answers?"

I see him pause, thinking perhaps that if I'm right, this isn't the answer the parents will want to hear. Not Jay's. And certainly not Colin's.

"No." He shakes his head slowly. "You would tell me what you know. And Oliver and I would apprehend the suspect." He's watching my face. "But you won't, will you?"

"Not if I'm not going with you."

"Look," he says, and I catch it, the way his voice has shifted, no longer surprised, or pleading for me to do the right thing; his tone is impersonal and distant. "You were right about something amiss at Kap-O and the empty time on Jay's call log. You found the second phone and folder when our other leads had dried up. But you entered a residence without permission—twice, if we consider the fact that you never should have gone with Ben. You're currently suspended without police powers. I don't know if the fire messed with your memory, and you've forgotten the rules, or you just don't care. But we don't all get second chances, and I can't trust your judgment anymore."

"Trust," I repeat bitterly.

I know he's right. I've seen the statistics, know that every time I drag him into something, he takes a greater disciplinary risk. But something ugly and angry bubbles inside of me.

"What about you leaving me for Oliver?" I demand, the hurt so raw and real, it must be visible on my face. "I'm in the hospital, and suddenly Oliver's on the case? You knew how important this was. You knew"—I take a breath—"about Craig. But you let Truman replace me. And *I'm* the one you can't trust? Oliver wants to wrap up this thing so badly, it's clear something else is going on." I fold my arms over my chest. "All I did was crash a party."

Teddy shakes his head. "It's not about that." He takes a breath. "Forget that you went into the house without a warrant. That if you found anything, it couldn't be used in the investigation. How do you explain what you did to Cindy? You thought the Kap-O guys were violent and you brought her to their house. Worse"—he lifts his hand when I open

my mouth—"you left her there, drunk and alone with potential murder-
ers, arsonists, or both, while you poked around the basement."

I look at myself reflected in his eyes and I don't like what I see. The
anger that had been buoying me cracks, and I feel my shoulders deflate.

"She trusted you," he says. "She still defends you, by the way. Said she
begged to go, wouldn't take no for an answer. But, of course, she didn't
know what you were really doing, and you didn't bother to tell her."

He stares at me, and I squirm under his scrutiny.

"How could you leave her like that?"

I bite my lip. He's right, of course. So right it hurts. He's seen me all
along. That selfish, self-destructive little girl, banging her head against
the concrete just to watch everyone run. And for a moment, I wish we
could start over. I wish I could rewrite that entire morning, so I was
nowhere near campus when Jay was hit. Anywhere but at that house
the night of the party. Suddenly I'm so tired that I have trouble keeping
my spine straight. My feet feel heavy, like I've been dragging my body
around in someone else's shoes.

The restaurant door swings open, and I smell coffee and roasted carrots.

"I'll resign," I say. "When this is all over, I'll hand in my badge."

He reaches his palm out, as if to take back the words, but then he
drops it.

"That's not what I want," he says.

No, he wants me to sit in the stands. To obey orders and risk justice
looking away again. I can't do that. As much as I want to—for him, for us,
whatever we are. I can't let another fraternity skip freely away from their
responsibility. And so this is what I have to offer: the job that brought us
together but is tearing us apart.

"You said it yourself." I smile sadly. "I'm a good investigator, but a
terrible cop." I take a breath. "And I'm sorry," I say. Sorry for being a shit
partner. Sorry for Cindy. Sorry for what this might mean for my career.
For our friendship. But I'm not sorry for solving the case. Not sorry for
chasing leads he didn't. Not sorry for not giving up.

Teddy, I think, sees all of this, too, as if it's seared plainly onto my flesh. He nods and turns away from me, his voice stiff.

"All right," he says. "Let's go."

air Play, South Carolina, is two exits north of the Georgia–South Carolina line. The lake house—the one from the infamous fishing trip, the one Colin told his father he visited—belongs to Michael Williams. Not his parents. Not an uncle or grandfather. Him.

Despite what I told Teddy, I don't know for certain Colin's there. It's a hunch, but a good one. Michael said he and Jay went fishing at the lake the same weekend Dr. Watanabe told us Jay was writing his class essay. Mr. Haines said Colin spent his time partying at the house and at the lake, but the brothers claim not to know him. We now have two conflicting stories regarding Jay, Colin, and the lake, and no one has been up there yet to check it out.

After I make my case, Teddy texts Tripp asking for the address. Tripp replies immediately. Apparently, in addition to warm and fuzzy fishing trips, the fraternity used the house on multiple occasions for parties. Getting an individual invite was considered quite the honor even though other brothers had nicer vacation properties at their disposal. The point was it belonged to Michael, and they could do whatever they wanted there. Tripp also confirms that no one's been there since Jay's death, and tells Teddy that if anyone asks, we didn't get the location from him.

By the time we arrive, it's almost dusk. I switch off the headlights and roll down my window before making a wide turn onto the gravel drive. We couldn't have found the place without Tripp's instructions. The address is unlisted. There's no road sign. No mailbox. That prickle I've felt since the fire is back. My breath shallows and buries itself somewhere deep inside my chest. Teddy senses it, shifts toward me, but then stops himself. Outside the window, I hear the faint rumble of cars from the main road and the wind in the trees. Branches crunch under the tires. I kill the engine.

"Let's walk from here."

Teddy nods but says nothing as he opens the passenger door and shuts it with a faint click. Something scurries in the underbrush, and I slip the car keys in my pocket with the sinking realization that if we have to call for backup, I've blocked the only entrance.

We walk fifty feet or so before the lane opens into a clearing. In the light from the moon glints a brown house with wooden slat siding and a front porch that swoops over the sides. The windows are curtained, but a hazy glow slips through. Chips of paint flake off the boards, and a tangle of woody kudzu vines noses its way through the steps.

It's colder here than in Athens, and I tug my jacket close to my skin. My father's voice brushes my ear: *You have to be careful, Marlitt.* There's a sudden gust of wind, and with it I hear Michael: *You and your partner should be careful.*

Pine trees shiver in the dark. Their silhouettes draw skeletal shadows across the dead grass. Somewhere in the distance a dog barks, and I can't help but wonder how long it would take someone to go crazy alone out here.

We circle the house, crouching near the ground and careful to make as little sound as possible. When Jay was last here, the woods might still have been humming with life. Mosquitoes, bullfrogs, and cicadas buzzing and chirping. Now the woods are still, watchful.

There's a sudden intake of breath from Teddy. And then I see it, too.

Parked under a sycamore tree is our black BMW.

He's removed the license plates but that's his only attempt to disguise it. There is surprisingly very little damage on the hood, but the front windshield is cracked. The broken glass spiderwebs out from the center, catching slivers of moonlight and something else. Something that looks a lot like blood.

"Don't," I whisper, but Teddy's already moving toward it. I follow him, crouched low with one eye on the house, the other on the broken headlight.

The dog barks again, closer this time. And inside the house, a floorboard creaks.

An edge of a curtain flutters and slants to the side. A white oval flashes and then is gone. I flatten against the passenger door.

"He's here."

Teddy signals for me to follow him, and—for a split second—I see Craig's face.

After he died, I still thought I was invincible. What changed is that I became acutely aware the people I loved were not. And so I cut them out—friends, classmates, even my parents. I put distance between us before their loss could cause me pain. Even though I thought I was indestructible, I knew I couldn't survive another heartbreak.

Seeing Teddy crouched next to the car, eyes on the window that's dark again, I have the sudden urge to call it off. The realization that his is a friendship I'm not willing to risk slams me against the chest. But it's too late.

"Back door," he hisses, and then runs low around the sycamore, skirting a row of dead hydrangea bushes as he takes the long, semicovered route toward the rear of the house.

I trace his path and feel the ground slope and soften beneath my feet. It's only a few yards, but when I reach Teddy, my breath is shallow and ragged.

Wordlessly, we stare out toward the dock and listen as the water laps the shore. There's no movement inside. I squeeze my hands together, trying to bring warmth back into my fingers. The smell of wet earth and decaying wood's heavy in the air. The lake is almost completely black, just a slash of yellow moon ripples along its surface.

Teddy knocks twice. The sound reverberates across the water. An owl hoots as if in answer. And then nothing.

I hold my breath. A high-pitched vibration in my ears makes me think of music.

There's no response. But we didn't expect there to be.

"Ready?" Teddy whispers. He's looking at me now, and there's something soft and almost tender in his voice.

I resist the urge to meet his eyes. I can't let myself be distracted by all that's left unsaid in those two syllables. *Ready?* All I know is that this is the beginning of the end.

Teddy nods. That's it, then.

I try the handle. This time it's locked.

We work in tandem. Silent. Our movements swift and practiced. Teddy checks the hinges, takes a step back, and drives his heel into the door. Something scurries in the leaves, and the owl takes flight.

I move first, Teddy close behind me.

Inside, low wooden ceilings trap in the damp, musky scent—it's more potent now, and heavy, too, like an animal's den. We're standing with our backs against the wall in the kitchen. The counter's littered with dirty dishes, empty aluminum cans, and half-eaten frozen dinners—nonperishable things found in cupboards and freezers. No fast food. Nothing to indicate he's left the house in weeks.

Yellow-colored paper runs the length of the wall to the right and continues into the dining area. The left side is obscured by a cupboard and pale green shelves with tiny hearts etched into the corners.

That buzzing again, so light I can barely hear it above the rhythm of our breaths.

I risk a glance at Teddy.

Television, he mouths, and gestures with his elbow to the faint colors flickering on the far wall.

And now I do hear them, the waves transmitting invisible patterns of images and sounds. The faint hum of voices.

Teddy motions for me to follow.

I catch a glimmer of something in the corner of my eye, and turn. To the right of the shelves, matted against a green felt board, are framed pins from the '96 Atlanta Olympic games, dozens of colorful torches, and, below them, a fist-sized hole.

We move slowly and silently. The living area is a collection of mismatched furniture oriented around an old box television. At the center is a cloth loveseat, shapeless from decades of abuse, and a red-and-black quilt thrown haphazardly across its frame.

In the middle of the sofa, head and shoulders backlit from the fuzzy light of the television, sits Colin.

A floorboard creaks beneath Teddy's feet, and I grip my gun tighter, but Colin doesn't move or make any indication he's heard. I take another step. His shoulders are still, and I realize the other thing that's bothering me, the strange sensation I've felt since we barreled through the door—the house is no warmer than the woods outside. It's so cold, I can see tiny puffs of breath around Teddy's mouth. The numbness has returned to my fingers and taken hold of my toes.

We step to either side of the sofa. And I'm prepared for Colin to turn a gun on me, prepared for him to be gray faced, dead from an overdose, or to find black stains covering his shirt from a shot to the chest. What I'm not prepared for is for him to turn, with just the slightest inclination of his head, and say, "Hello."

Teddy pivots in front of the sofa.

"Colin Haines," I say, my voice oddly hollow.

Colin considers this, looking past me to the framed photographs on the wall.

"No," he says, smiling a little sadly. "There's no Colin here." He moves to stand, but Teddy takes a step toward him, and he sits back, folding his hands in his lap.

"I'm Jay," he says after a confused pause. "Jay Kemp."

| Eighteen |

Monday, December 9, 1:00 A.M.

We drive the long stretch of dark highway in silence. I keep glancing at the boy in the rearview mirror. He's quiet, staring at his own reflection against the black of the car window, and my mind's flipping through images like one of those memory games. Each time I grasp the features of one boy, it vanishes and becomes the other. Jay with floppy brown hair and a sheepish grin on his student ID. Colin on the beach with one arm draped over his mother's shoulder. Jay on the asphalt with blood leaking from his lips. Colin on the couch with white puffs emanating from his mouth. It's not possible, I keep reminding myself. Jay's body was identified by his parents. His photo was on display at the fraternity memorial service, his face circulated in the news. But another voice whispers that Jay's professors saw those photos and thought it was the boy in their classrooms. None of his brothers came forward to tell us we had the wrong name. Katie was distraught; and certainly, she above anyone else would know the difference between Jay and Colin.

We set him up in interview room A. When I caution him, he blinks and then flinches. He looks alternatively confused and nervous, ghostly under the fluorescent lights with greenish circles under his eyes.

"Coffee?" Teddy offers.

It's the first word he's said since we put the boy in the back of the car, and it's directed at him rather than me. I can see why: Colin-Jay— whoever he is—is cowering in his chair and he's shivering. The sugges- tion of coffee's an attempt to warm him up.

It's not cold though. In fact, after the lake house, it feels almost balmy at the station. All that trembling is the adrenaline coursing through his body, increasing his heart rate, sending blood racing toward his muscles, and causing his limbs to shake. He's scared, or nervous, or both. And it's time we find out why.

But coffee gives Teddy the pretext for leaving the room. I sit there for a minute like an idiot, blinking at Colin-Jay and the empty seat next to me, and then follow him.

When I march back to the bullpen, Teddy's on the phone with Oliver. In the car, I rang Truman with fingers crossed he wouldn't answer—at this hour, it would be like waking a sleeping bear—but the call went to voicemail.

I begin pulling photos off the whiteboard. Jay's face, ashen and bruised. His bitten fingernails. The autopsy report. For a moment, I won- der if it might be possible that Jay faked his own death—that this is some grand scheme with false death certificates and new identities and Jay off on some remote island sipping umbrella drinks. I laugh.

Still on the phone, Teddy raises an eyebrow.

But I'm giddy and agitated all at once. My hands are shaking as I pick up Jay's transcripts and thumb through the call logs.

Is it crazy, though? The umbrella drinks, maybe. But Jay was scared. There was something going on with his brothers. The "traitor" notes. The two phones. Money might have been involved. Maybe Jay needed to disappear. Maybe he ran over Colin, not the other way around. Maybe his parents were in on it. They identified the body, could have signed a false statement. Maybe Michael was involved, too, hiding Jay at his cabin until he figured out what to do next. I shake my head. It's too convoluted, too complex. If anything, Jay would be hiding from Michael. And where would Colin fit in?

By the time Oliver arrives, I've worked my way back into a circle, where Jay becomes Colin, Colin becomes Jay, and then it all starts over again. One must cancel out the other, but which one remains?

I bring Oliver up to speed, casting occasional glances in Teddy's direction.

As I go over the missing student report, the visit to the house on Marlin, and the events at the lake, Oliver's eyes widen. He's still too groggy to mask his surprise that I convinced Teddy to apprehend the suspect without him and annoyance that he wasn't called sooner. But when I finish, he looks alert and excited.

He turns to Teddy. "We going in?"

It stings a little, this assumption that it will be the two of them interviewing Colin, but he's right. I'm suspended. Technically, I shouldn't be here at all.

Teddy shakes his head. "This one's yours and Marlitt's."

Oliver opens his mouth to point out the obvious—me being there could compromise the investigation; if we get anything good, Truman's going to have to lose the suspension paperwork—but Teddy reaches up a hand to stop him.

"I'm filling out the report now. And then I'm going home. To sleep."

Something passes between them—an understanding, no doubt built during the weeks they've been working the case without me—and Oliver nods.

"Okay then." He turns in my direction a little warily. "Shall we?"

I want to laugh again—the fatigue is really getting to me—but I pull it together and follow Oliver into the interview room.

He stops halfway to the table. I didn't tell him the last part about the lake, about the boy we thought was Colin telling us his name was Jay. And I know what he's seeing. Looking at the boy in the chair is like looking at a person in one of those distorted carnival mirrors: it is and yet isn't Jay's reflection. His hair's grown out. Face gaunt from lack of sun and fresh food. A patchwork beard stretches from his chin to his cheekbones. But still, if you blur your eyes a little, it could be Jay.

I decide to go with my initial impulse.

"Colin—" I begin.

"Colin," the boy repeats. His voice strangely empty. "Such a stupid name."

I pause just a fraction. "Is that how it started?"

"What?"

"You pretending to be Jay."

We stare at each other. His sweater's overlarge, thick with grime, and fraying at the sleeves. He's fiddling with a string that's come loose. Under one cuff, I glimpse a nice watch, the type that has to be wound and ticks loudly. It bothers me, for some reason.

Oliver opens the folder on the table. Inside are Jay's transcripts from his freshman year, fall of his second, and this past spring.

The boy leans over. Smirks to see the line of Ds on the first column. I tap the one with As and Bs.

"Seems like Jay underwent quite the transformation sophomore year," I say. "If he kept that up, he might have made the dean's list."

He gives an ugly, twisted smile, but something sad ebbs at the edges.

"We know you were sitting in for Jay. Signing his name on attendance sheets. Writing his papers. Taking his tests. All we have to do is show the professors your picture next to Jay's and we'll have confirmation it was you in class." I close the folder. "But we're not attendance police. We don't care about any of that. We just want to understand Jay better. And why someone might want to kill him."

He stares at me.

I lean back in my chair and match his gaze.

"When did you meet Jay?" I ask.

He blinks in confusion and then smiles. "I guess you could say I've known him my entire life."

Cute, I think. *So this is how it's going to be.*

"And is this how you remember him?"

I pull the worst of the morgue shots—grayish skin, lips receding, eyes pinched—and put them faceup on the table.

He blanches, and for a brief moment I think he might be sick. Then he touches the spot on his cheek where there's an ugly bruise on the photo, the busted lip. The resemblance is there, certainly. But side by side, it's clear the dead boy and the living one are not identical. They're close enough that if you were friends with one and passed the other on the street, you might do a double take, maybe even raise your hand in greeting, but if he turned, you would realize your mistake. The boy we're looking at, the living one, is Colin.

He shakes his head but says nothing.

I pull out the picture on the beach—the happy son and parents.

He holds his breath, looking between Jay's photo and the family. Something flickers across his brow. Does he realize how good he had it? Everything he gave up?

I make a show of comparing the two photos, holding each on either side of his cheeks.

"I don't know." I turn to Oliver. "It would suck to be this guy." I shake the photo of Jay. "But then again, I wouldn't be caught dead dressed in all matching clothes with my parents, so . . ."

An angry flush creeps up his neck.

"Too soon?" I say.

Oliver checks his watch. I glance at the small video camera in the corner, calculating how long we have before Truman hears my message and is barreling down the hallway.

"No comment?" I arch an eyebrow. "All right then, let's start at the beginning." I smile at him. "How about the day you were accepted to UGA?"

A flicker of something on his face.

"How did you feel?"

He winds the string from his sweater around his finger.

"Come on," I say. "This is an easy one. They're only going to get harder."

He takes a deep breath. "I don't know," he says finally. "Excited, I guess." He stares at the table. Maybe he sees his hands shaking as he opened the envelope, himself reading the fateful sentence, maybe even his feet leaving the floor as he gave a tiny leap of joy.

"What about your parents?"

He shrugs.

"Were they excited?" I make my voice cheerier than I feel. "I bet they were so proud. Your dad—"

A sputtered, coughing noise. "Yeah," he murmurs, "he was thrilled."

"Because he went to UGA." I lean forward. This is something I can relate to. "And wanted you to follow in his footsteps."

He blinks, and I realize I've tapped into something that runs deeper than Jay.

In all the various molds and models he's cast himself into over the years—teachers, coaches, fraternity brothers—his father's the first. The one underneath it all. The person he's striving to be, trying to impress. For Colin, the beginning isn't Jay. The beginning is his father.

"He wanted you to join Kappa Phi Omicron," I say, latching on to this break—Colin thinking of his own experiences, prior to his life as Jay.

A strangled noise at the back of his throat. He closes his eyes and for a moment I think I've lost him. These Greek letters we've been dancing around the past few weeks. I should have saved them for the right moment. Instead, I blew it.

Colin lets out a breath. "He said they'd make a man of me."

Oliver shifts in his seat. I give a small shake of my head. *Not yet*, I will him. *Don't push yet.*

"That fraternity men are leaders. They're honorable men. They understand loyalty and respect." A bewildered twitch of the mouth.

"Did they?"

"I guess it depends on what your definition of honor is."

I pause for Oliver's benefit, to let that sink in.

"So your father was a Kap-O," Oliver says. "You were a legacy."

Colin grimaces, and I think of the weight of that word: "legacy." Like "birthright" or "inheritance," it's a way for the past to insert its will over the present. And with that special status comes high stakes. If Colin hadn't gotten a bid, his father would have seen it as a personal rejection. And after his job loss, he would have taken it particularly hard. No wonder Colin lied to him.

"You were a pledge last fall," I say.

"Yeah."

Both Jay and Colin were pledges. But Jay would have pledged the year before. This is another confirmation we're talking to Colin and not some alter-Jay persona.

"What was it like," I ask, my voice brimming with curiosity, "at the house?"

"Fun." He shrugs. "Lots of parties. Girls. Alcohol." He raises an eyebrow, testing to see if we'll react—lecture him about underage drinking—but he should know we're well past that.

"Did you go through hell week?"

"Everyone did."

"We talked to some of the brothers who went through it this year." I lean in, feeling we're getting closer, my heart hammering, seeing Truman buckling his seat belt. "And they told us about the basement."

Colin pales. "They shouldn't have done that."

"Done what?" I ask, giving him a puzzled expression. Although I know. Loyalty. Brotherhood. Thoughtless allegiance.

"And we know Jay told Katie," I add. "About what happened there."

I'm only guessing, but it doesn't matter.

His eyes shoot up. I half expect him to insist he's Jay again and steel myself for another round of detangling identities.

But he simply shakes his head.

I frown. "The other brothers thought he was a traitor."

"Well he was—wasn't he? They were just wrong about why."

And there it is—the clear delineation between Colin and Jay: referring to Jay in the third person.

But my mind is reeling. "Then why was Jay a traitor?" I ask, the pieces shifting and twisting as I try to pull the plot back together.

Colin drums his fingers on his knee and stares at the ceiling.

"You aren't a member," Oliver says, when Colin remains silent, "which means you don't have to keep their secrets." He leans forward. "It also means you don't have to attend their classes. Which brings us back to our original question: Why were you pretending to be Jay?"

I stare at the bags under Colin's eyes, the chapped skin on his lips, and then at the boy in the photograph. The easy, shy smile. I think of his father—the pride in his face when he said his son was a Kap-O.

"Isn't it obvious?" I say, eyes on Colin, but addressing Oliver. "He wanted to be part of his father's fraternity. To make him proud." I nod as if in approval. "But then . . ." I sit back in my chair, watch Colin's body language. "It's not what his father said it would be. It's not all cookouts and parties, but getting shoved into corners and called by a number and tested to see if you are worthy by some perverse set of rules everyone knows but you." I shrug. "Maybe he made it until the very end. Maybe he made it to the basement. But then he cracked."

A cruel snort from Colin, but also a look that says, *You've got to try harder than that.*

"I bet he pleaded with Jay to give him a second chance. He had to be a Kap-O. His father left him with no other option. And Jay saw an opportunity. His grades were suffering—that's clear from his transcripts. School's not the point of college anyway—just look at the brochures. It's all about the experience, football games and whitewater rafting and thousands of your peers dressed in red and black. His classes are big. Who's to know the difference?" Oliver raises an eyebrow, but I keep going, seeing the heat in Colin's face rise with every word. "A few tweaks to Colin's clothes, his hair, and now he's Jay, trying to hold down two sets of classes so Jay can party and do whatever he wants." I drum my fingers on the table. "No one notices the switch. And why would they? If this started at the beginning of spring semester, Colin would simply introduce himself as Jay the first day and his professors wouldn't know the difference. It works so well, Jay figures they might as well continue their arrangement in the fall, all while promising he'll make sure Colin gets a bid this year." I take a breath. "But then he met Katie."

Oliver nods. "Jay and the dream girl."

"No," I say calmly.

I think of Katie under her covers insisting she barely knew Jay, the absence of flirtatious texts on Jay's phone, the way even the fraternity-related messages stopped late in October.

"Not Jay. Colin."

Colin folds his arms over his chest but can't help the faint smile that plays on his lips.

Oliver swivels toward me. "Colin and Katie?"

"Cade thought Jay and Katie were together but had only seen them twice, and that was from a distance—after Colin started dressing like Jay."

I study Colin's face, wipe away the purplish shadows under his eyes, breathe color back into his sallow skin. Like Jay, he's handsome in that bland, all-American kind of way. Who would Katie, sweet, beautiful Katie, wind up with? Jay, who viewed girls as fraternity property? Or Colin, the shy and sensitive boy who wanted to make his father proud and got in over his head? I think of the panic attack—real or faked—when I asked Katie if she thought someone might have wanted to hurt Jay. The tears, her refusal to answer our questions—it wasn't because she was devasted at Jay's loss. But because Jay was dead, and that could mean only one thing.

"Jay and Katie weren't keeping their relationship secret," I say. "Colin and Katie were. And that's why the other brothers thought Jay was a traitor." I stare at Colin's face, impressed by his audacity. "Because Colin told Katie about the basement. And she asked someone about it." I tap Jay's transcripts, thinking. "Tripp," I say, slamming my hand against the table. "Of course." Colin flinches. "But Tripp assumed her source was Jay. And then he went and blabbed to everyone that Jay was sharing fraternity secrets."

I think of Jay's phone password: K8CO. Him apologizing, trying to get Katie to respond to his messages.

"Because Jay, like everyone else, was a little in love with Katie Coleman." I gaze at Colin, the satisfied curve of his lips. "It must have felt good to sweep away the dream girl from Kap-O," I muse. "Did you tell her about your and Jay's agreement? Or just about the basement?"

His smile falters.

"It doesn't matter," I say. "Because Jay knew it was you, and there's no way he'd uphold your arrangement after that. He wanted out. After all, you failed hell week, the other brothers knew, they would never let you join—"

"Join?" The word explodes out of Colin. "Join? I wanted nothing to do with those assholes. You think Jay wanted out? *I* wanted out." He hammers a fist against his chest. Then he screws up his face and slams back in his chair. It grates hard against the linoleum.

"You wanted out?" I repeat. "Then why didn't you just stop pretending to be Jay? Stop going to his classes? Let him fail—?"

Relief washes over Colin's face, and I stop talking.

We're missing something—something bigger than Jay, bigger than Katie Coleman.

I look at Oliver. He caught it, too.

Outside the station window the sky's turning lavender at the edges. In the early-morning light two pines cast shadows on the asphalt that look like gallows, and all I can think is that we are the weary executioners clutching at tattered ropes.

I fill the water for another pot of coffee. We've been going at Colin for hours. He declined a lawyer and a phone call, so I make one for him. Around four in the morning, I ring Ben. Not his cell, but his office line. I owe him that much and more, but we need as much time as possible before Colin's parents arrive.

I sneak a glance at Teddy. He's hunched over his desk, dutifully typing away. When I fill his coffee cup, he nods, but doesn't ask how it's going. Each stab of his finger feels like an accusation. I turn back to the window to watch the leaves blow across the nearly empty parking lot and try to drown the panicky feeling that everything's spiraling out of control.

Earlier, while we were observing Colin through the two-way mirror, Oliver told me that for weeks the station has been receiving anonymous tips about a suspicious-looking Black man hanging around the Kappa Phi Omicron parking lot the week before Jay was killed. Different numbers, different voices, but all the witnesses gave the same description and suggested that this was the man who stole Jay's car. The description matched Teddy—right down to the bright running shoes. He said that the day after I woke up in the hospital, Teddy received a noose in a package with a note saying he'd be next. That he hasn't been sleeping. That he's had patrols checking on his mother's house. On Cindy's apartment. His sisters. Even my parents. But mostly, he's been driving around himself, making sure everyone's safe.

Now, standing in front of the window, I watch Teddy's reflection against the glass, too ashamed to face him directly. I think of Michael's upturned lip, the whispered words at the memorial service, the legacy of racism, chants, slurs, and microaggressions that mark so many fraternities. I knew Kap-O would be no different but chose to ignore it because I wanted Teddy working this one with me. He rolls his shoulders, writes something on a sheet of paper, and then begins typing again. The heat's on full blast, but he's still wearing his jacket—like he can't get rid of the chill of the lake house and can't put enough distance between us.

I will make this right, I promise myself.

I open the door to interview room A with one hand, two cups of coffee clutched in the other.

I tilt my wrist to check my watch and the coffee laps over the edge. I figure we have less than an hour before Ben gets my voicemail. Less than two before Colin's parents are here with a lawyer in tow.

"Sure you don't want anything?" I ask, setting one mug in front of Oliver and bringing the other to my lips. "It's been a long night."

This warrants a small ironic smile from Colin, bottom lip clasped between his teeth, and I think that for him, every day since Jay's death must seem like one long night.

"All right then. Let's start at the beginning."

We've started at the beginning three times now. Why did he introduce himself as Jay? How did the BMW end up at the lake house? What happened to the windshield? We circle close and swoop away, but Colin hasn't given us anything to hold on to yet.

Instead of sitting, I lean against the two-way mirror. I want Teddy to be behind me, watching Colin over my shoulder. But he's still at his desk, logging our movements. And I know that when he's done, he's going to walk out of the station without a word.

Colin gives me a blank stare, and Oliver shifts impatiently. I let the silence grow thick. Colin looks away.

I push myself off the wall and sit down heavily across from him. Then I pull out the phone records.

"These are calls from Jay's secret phone. He only used it to contact two numbers. Katie Coleman. And you."

A small shrug.

I lean in closer. "Do you see this?"

I draw a line with my pen down the list.

"Jay called you almost thirty times in the hours before he was hit and then"—I make two slashes at the bottom of the page—"nothing. Why was he so desperate to get in touch with you?"

My phone rings.

Ben, it has to be.

A tense shift ripples between us.

I silence it.

"Here's what I think," I say. "I think you enjoyed pretending to be Jay a little too much. Jay was popular, rich, had about a million friends. And I think for a moment, you forgot it was all pretend. You started to believe you were Jay."

He folds his arms over his chest, as if offended. As if he didn't spend the first twenty minutes here pretending the very same thing.

"You started to feel entitled to his life. His possessions." He opens his mouth, but I keep going. "It was just little things at first. Things Jay would never have noticed—a pen, a pack of gum—but you'd been pretending to be him for almost a year. You wanted something more personal: his grandfather's watch." I gesture to the timepiece under his sweater—the other things I'm only guessing, but this I know for certain.

I turn to Oliver. "Tripp told us things had gone missing from the house, but there was never a police report."

"Did he know?" I ask Colin. "Did Jay know you were sneaking into his room? Taking his things?"

There's a moment when I think he'll concede, or maybe even make something up—he won the watch in a bet, it was payment for cheating—but he sits on his hands.

"Let's see it," I say, and he withdraws his palms. I don't know anything about watches, but it looks old—and expensive.

"Right," I say, "we'll be bagging that as evidence."

"So," I pick up the thread. "You had gotten quite comfortable taking Jay's possessions." My lip curls. "I guess it's not a surprise really, that you wanted something bigger, an even nicer token of your," I pause, "unique relationship." I lean in. "How many times did you steal Jay's car before that morning? How often did you drive it before you saw Jay in the crosswalk? How did you know he'd be there?"

His eyes dart around the room, looking everywhere but at my face.

"Do you know what the witnesses said?" I don't wait for him to answer. "They said that Jay waited at the intersection with everyone else.
He saw the car, but the light was changing. He must not have recognized
it. Must have thought it would stop, because he stepped off the sidewalk,
looked down at his phone, and—bam—" I slam my fists on the table.
Colin jerks. "Dead"—a snap of my fingers—"just like that. And you
know what all the witnesses agreed on?" I lean in. "That the driver was
smiling."

"I—"

The door to the interview room flies open with such force it rattles
the wall. I don't think Truman even bothered with the handle. Florence
Haines is behind him—eyes wide and body still, yet there's something
about the curve of her shoulders and the tightening of her jaw that
makes me think that beneath the smooth hair and down jacket thrown
on in a hurry is a wild cat that would bite, scratch, and claw her way
through all of us to get to her son. Her husband's half-hidden in the corridor, pale and drifting, a shadow of the man I met a day ago.

Truman is red-faced with fury, trying to keep it together in front of
the parents, but even Oliver flinches when he steps into the room, his
voice so low it's almost a whisper.

"Out," he says.

I stall, but there's no use.

Colin's mouth is still open. He's staring at us and blinking hard like a
rabbit surrounded by a pack of dogs who've just been called back by their
owner. One more minute, I think, and he would have confessed it all.
The cheating. The stolen car. Slamming his foot against the accelerator
instead of the brake.

Truman stops me at the door. Florence rushes past, and I watch her
embrace her son as I hand over my badge.

I resign, just like I promised.

Mr. Haines doesn't move. He's still wavering in the doorway when I
follow Truman out of the room.

I cast one last glance behind me and realize almost as an afterthought that the ill-fitting sweater Colin's wearing must also be Jay's, and he must have worn it, still fresh with Jay's scent, since the day he died.

As I look around for Teddy, I wonder absently what that means—Colin wearing Jay's sweater. But Teddy's nowhere in sight. His desk is tidy, jacket and helmet gone.

All the adrenaline abandons me then. The high wire I've been tripping across for days seems to vanish beneath my feet. My stomach rises to my chest and leaves me feeling weightless, the ground rushing toward me at an undefinable speed, too empty to know whether its impact will damage me any more than I've already destroyed myself.

It will be Oliver's job now to fill in the details. Check video footage along 85 for signs of Colin driving the BMW. See if he stopped for gas. Anything that can link him directly to the car that day. Florence will fight tooth and nail to protect her son, but Colin's instinct for self-preservation has already been worn down by the year he spent as Jay, the weeks alone at the cabin, and the long night in the interview room staring at gray ceiling tiles and waiting for the hybrid beast he and Jay created to finally swallow him whole. Oliver will try to grind him down hard enough so that he breaks. When really, he's already broken. They all are. Suddenly it all seems so meaningless.

| Nineteen |

I keep my head down while I gather my things. Oliver's still in Truman's office with the door closed.

I feel a shift in the air and look up to find Amy, arms crossed, watching from the doorway as I shuffle pens and candy bars into a cardboard box.

The clock on the wall reads 7:10. She arrived just in time to see the end of my not so illustrious career. The idea that she's been sent to escort me out is so ludicrous and I'm so delirious with fatigue that I let out a high-pitched and strangled laugh that might be mistaken for a sob.

"What?" I ask when she clicks her tongue.

She arches an eyebrow like I owe her an explanation, but she'll find out soon enough.

"I'm not your personal mail courier," she says.

"Mail courier?" I repeat, with no idea what she's talking about. The laughter's turned my voice whiny and breathless.

"Some young man demanded I give this to you or Detective White, whomever I saw first." She waves something small in the air. "Said not to follow him." She shakes her head, wire glasses shuttling across her nose. "Like I'd bother."

"When was this?"

"Not two minutes after I arrived."

I dart past her down the long hallway to the front entrance.

The cold air slaps me awake, and I'm blinking in the sun across the parking lot. But there's no one.

Beyond the pines, cars speed along the highway. Amy's young man could be driving any of them. He could be parked on the opposite side of the street in front of a warehouse building watching me now. I squint and see the fall of a sparrow from a power line, its descent lost somewhere in dead limbs and black wires.

Inside, Amy's already back at the front desk. She brought my box out with her.

I purse my lips.

"What did he look like?" I demand.

"Who?"

"The young man," I say impatiently.

Amy makes a show of turning on her computer. "He was wearing a ball cap, so I couldn't see his face." She types in her password, screwing up her lips trying to remember, as if she doesn't enter it every day.

"Short? Tall? Fat? Thin?"

"Tall." She nods thoughtfully. "And skinny. His head bobbed like a praying mantis." She scrunches her nose. "Had blond hair, too, I think."

Blond. Tall. Skinny. Not a lot to go on, but who else could it be besides our helpful giraffe?

I narrow my eyes at her. "Where is it?"

"I think it should go to Detective White, seeing as how . . ." She gestures to the box.

"I'll take it now." I hold out my hand.

She sighs and makes a show of pulling open her desk drawer. "Suit yourself," she says, and drops a small black flash drive into my palm.

It takes less than a minute to race back to the task room and two for the file to load. I drum my fingers impatiently, casting furtive glances over my shoulder. Truman's office door is shut. But I know I don't have much time before it opens again.

I hold my breath and press Play.

The image is dark with only a flicker of light at the top corner. The beam moves in small, hesitant increments and then drops to the bottom.

I sink into my chair.

On the screen, I see the blurred outline of a figure and various objects illuminated by a hazy glow. A handful of tattered blankets. Buckets in the corner. Then the light disappears.

I feel like someone's thrown cold water over me.

I'm watching myself in the dark. Thinking the same thought now as I did then. Those fucking assholes. The light switches back on, circles the room, illuminates the handcuffs on the wall, and then returns to the buckets. I see my leap to the steps and the bucket's contents sloshing across the floor. My stomach clenches. The video goes dark. And then there's Oliver.

The transition's too quick. There should have been at least half an hour of dead footage before he arrived. But there he is, tracing the same path as me a few moments earlier, only he's got the footstool.

There are other files. All dark, but with figures who move across the room, take the whip off the wall, sleep on the floor. It could be anywhere, any windowless, subterranean space, but I know exactly what I'm looking at.

Hands shaking, I yank the flash drive out of the computer.

"Detective Kaplan?" Amy calls as I march out the door.

Somehow, I manage to unlock my car and maneuver it onto Broad Street. My mind's speeding faster than the cars in front of me—an oversized pickup and a child-emptied SUV puttering along the highway.

There's video footage of me and Oliver. Me—near falling into the basement. Trespassing. Poking around private property without permission or warrant. Me—even after my resignation, still managing to undermine the case. But then there's Oliver, who trusted me enough to roll out of bed that night. Oliver, who'd also be in trouble if the footage gets out. And Tripp, who loaded the video on a flash drive and dropped it into our hands.

The day's clouds are turning the street a heavy shade of gray and evergreen. A few raindrops splash the window, and finally the oversized pickup opts for a midmorning Varsity stop, freeing me to speed around the mom in the SUV and turn onto Milledge.

In my mind, the street has transformed over the past month—all those beautiful mansions. From the outside, they're manicured lawns, sweeping front porches, and rocking chairs, but inside, the old floors are splintering and cracking beneath the shiny laminate, sinking into a pit of their own making. What are these houses if not idols, where firstborn sons are sacrificed to gods of conformity, offered with a prayer for good fortune, their cries drowned out by the beat of trap music, football chants, and drunken recitations of the fraternity's creed?

I stop in front of the overlarge redbrick building and stare at its Doric columns, wondering how many secrets they've supported over the years. Rain splatters the windshield. There's no way I can go inside. Not now.

Someone behind me honks, and I realize I'm holding up traffic and drawing attention to myself. When I start driving again, I catch a glimpse of movement in the parking lot beside the house. *Oh fates*, I think, *is it possible the tides have turned?* That for once in the past miserable few weeks, something could work in my favor? I turn into the parking lot with my head low, a watchful eye on the windows, and roll up right next to him.

"Get in," I hiss.

Tripp flinches. By the way he ducks his head, it's clear he's startled but not entirely surprised to see me. And if I had any doubt that he was Amy's blond praying mantis, it's erased by the resigned slump of his shoulders and his own paranoid glances back at the house.

I speed off before his door closes, and he sits low in his seat, legs folded ridiculously underneath him, so his ass is almost touching the floorboard and his chin's tucked between his knees. I smirk, but I get it. Neither of us wants to be seen together.

I tear down Milledge and in another small miracle actually make the Five Points light. I swing left onto East Campus, worried that if we drive as far as the botanical gardens he might think I'm abducting him. It's raining harder now, so I can't hear what he's muttering under the sound of the windshield wipers. The brown fenced-in grass of the intramural fields flashes above his head and reminds me of hot summer days spent by a lakeside beach, flag football, and drunken nights tempting death on the train tracks. It seems like a safe enough choice for a rainy day.

But the empty fields feel open and exposed, so I drive deeper into the park until the leafless trees close around us and the tennis courts come into view. A pair of women run with rackets over their heads, laughing. A man lounges in his car, a cell phone at his ear, but when I pull up next to him, he glares at me and drives off. On the courts, a guy in rain-streaked glasses dutifully throws up balls and hammers them at the green tarp that lines the side of the court, completely oblivious to us.

"Coast is clear," I tell Tripp.

He emerges from his floorboard cocoon with a groan and blinks out the window.

"Where are we?"

"What is this?" I ask, and wave the flash drive in his face.

His shoulders creep up around his ears.

"I just"—he gives a self-conscious shrug—"I thought you should know."

"Why? Is this supposed to keep me quiet? Blackmail?"

"No, I—" Tripp's gone white. "It was so you knew there was footage—of the basement." He gestures helplessly to the car roof. "The camera's linked to a motion detector. So there's video whenever someone goes down there."

He stares at me expectantly.

"Anytime?"

He nods.

"And no one ever turns it off?"

"No one knows about it. Except me and Michael. And before . . . Jay."

I take a deep breath, mind racing with hazy images—me dropping to the concrete floor, Oliver dragging the footstool, boys with whips in their hands, bruises on their shoulders. I've been looking at this all wrong. The point isn't that Oliver and I are on the video. The point is that there's video of the basement. And everything that happens down there.

"Why?"

"Why what?"

"Why did someone put a camera in the basement?"

Tripp chews his bottom lip.

"Look," I say impatiently, "you hand-delivered this flash drive. You got in my car. You're here now." *You made your decision already*, I want to tell him, *this morning, yesterday, maybe the day we showed up on Kap-O's doorstep.* Some people are like that. They can't live with the guilt. And whatever Tripp's hiding, he's dying to come clean. "It's too late for reticence now."

He stares out the window.

I will count to ten, I think.

"It started with probation," he says softly.

"You're on probation?" I repeat, twisting so I can see him fully.

A fraternity on probation means no social events—no recruitment, no tailgating or intramural sports. No parties at the house and no alcohol. Certainly no beach-themed ragers the week after Thanksgiving. It means a fraternity at risk of a revocation of their registration, one that would either be on their best behavior, dotting their i's and crossing their t's, or one that would go to great lengths to hide any infraction. This should have come up in our interviews, in Truman's meeting with the university president. It should have been starred and highlighted, at the top of all our notes.

"We *were*." Tripp emphasizes the past tense. "Social probation. Two years ago. The usual stuff," he says when I open my mouth, "distribution of alcohol to minors, alcohol-related misconduct, violation of university policy. But Michael had a word with his father. He assured him that he'd keep us under control." He shrugs. "Anyway, he managed to persuade him to lift all the social restrictions. It was a bad look anyway, you know, the president's son at a fraternity in trouble with the university." He takes a breath. "So that fall—our sophomore year, right before rush—Michael called a meeting. He wasn't treasurer yet or in any leadership position, but since he got us out of probation—we all deferred to him."

I snort. "So Michael gets probation lifted and holds a meeting to tell you how much you owe him," I say.

"Not exactly." Tripp's fingers tap a furious rhythm on his knees. "He called us into the chapter room, told us we'd be able to have recruitment that year, but that we needed to be on our best behavior, and"—he hesitates—"that he installed cameras throughout the house—"

"Michael installed the cameras?" I repeat incredulously. "And there were more? Not just the one in the basement?"

"He didn't say anything about the basement. That was, you know, top secret. We didn't talk about it—ever. No one even considered that he would—" He takes a breath but doesn't continue. His eyes skitter across the rain-streaked glass, and I think maybe I've lost him, that the full force of what he's just told me will have him clamming up any second.

"So," I push. "Michael tells you he's put up spy cameras, and everyone was like, what? Yeah, okay, that's cool?"

"No." Tripp waves his hand. "People were pissed. But Michael said that's what he had to do to get probation lifted early. It was bullshit. I mean, what, his dad hired some team to do twenty-four-hour surveillance on the cameras?" He shakes his head. "Of course not. Michael wouldn't tell us where the cameras were, either. A couple brothers practically ripped the house apart trying to find them. They dismantled the wall clocks and fire alarms, unscrewed all the light switches. But no one

knew what they were looking for. And ultimately, they didn't find anything, so we assumed Michael was lying—just trying to get us on our best
behavior, you know? And after a while, we forgot about them." He gives
a strained smile, as if in another life this might be amusing.

"You said only you, Michael, and Jay knew about the video. You
mean, you and Jay knew the cameras were real? Not just a threat to en-
sure good behavior?"

Tripp takes off his hat and runs his hands through his hair. "Michael
told me when I became president. I don't know when—or how—Jay
found out."

"But Jay had footage of Colin Haines."

It's a guess, but what else could it be? I think of Colin's look of relief,
the feeling we were missing something. His "Well, Jay was a traitor—they
were just wrong about why." What was this, if not the ultimate betrayal?
Not telling brotherhood secrets but recording them. Maybe even using
them against you.

Tripp looks like he might be sick, but he nods.

"So," I say slowly, "Jay was blackmailing Colin. Not using him as an
unofficial pledge, forcing him to attend his classes, so you'd let him join
after a probationary period?"

His brows crumple in confusion, but then he shakes his head. "It
doesn't work like that."

Now it's my turn to blink at him.

"What do you mean?"

"I mean once you're out, you're out. No one can unilaterally decide
who gets initiated. And there's no way we would have given Colin a bid."

I bite the inside of my cheek. "Why didn't Colin get accepted last
year?" I ask.

Tripp shrugs. "He quit. As soon as we let him out of the basement.
Said we were all assholes, that we didn't share a brain between us, that
our talk of brotherhood was bullshit—"

I think of Colin's clenched fists, his fury—it was real. And then I remember another pledge calling the brothers "assholes"—the boy from the story with the handcuffs.

"Chains," I say suddenly. Not Colton—Garrett couldn't even remember his name right. But Colin Haines. C. Haines—a moniker derived from his real name.

Tripp nods. "That's what we called him."

I shake my head thinking he was there all along, buried somewhere in our notes. Colin Haines was the pledge who "freaked out" in the basement, but not—as I assumed—from fear, but from anger.

"So Colin quits, and then Jay blackmails him to attend his classes?"

Tripp shrugs. "Jay was pissed. He said we should have never given Colin a bid, that he was a liability, and needed to be kept under control." He clears his throat. "He was getting Colin to do stuff. His laundry. Give him money. He said"—pink slashes bloom on his cheekbones—"he wanted to make Colin his bitch. I guess the class attendance was part of it."

I exhale. So Jay's reason for blackmail is twofold: to keep Colin quiet and to punish him. All those menial tasks, all that pretending was designed to strip Colin of his individuality and turn him into the very thing he hated: Jay himself. But Jay's not a complete idiot. Blackmail's a criminal offense. So he gets a prepaid phone, the burner kind, not linked to his name. And it worked: had I not found it, we'd never have connected him to Colin. How long can something like that go on? Months? Years? I purse my lips. Maybe it would have continued even after they left the university. But then, Colin met Katie. And something shifted. He changed the rules of Jay's game. Jay was worried enough to rent the locker, hide the cell phone he used to call Colin, to message Katie begging her not to tell anyone about Colin or the basement. But Jay made a fatal mistake. Most blackmailers stay anonymous. These days almost everything is online— they send encrypted messages and use untraceable email accounts that hide their IP addresses. But Colin knew exactly who the blackmailer was, and at some point, he must have realized that the threats end when you eliminate the one making them. So it was Jay and Colin together all along. The pair of them working in tandem to destroy each other, and in doing so destroying themselves.

Outside there's a crack of thunder.

"And Michael—"

"He didn't know."

"Don't tell Mike," I say.

"Yeah," Tripp exhales. "His last text. Jay didn't want Mike to know about Colin."

"But Michael put up the cameras," I remind him. "He must have given Jay the video."

"No—I mean, look, Michael was just as pissed at Colin as Jay, but he would never have shared the video of the basement. Our rituals are secret. That's a huge violation."

"But he recorded them—"

"Yeah," Tripp concedes. "But it was just to . . ."

"Control you? Manipulate you into doing what he wanted?"

He exhales impatiently. "That's what I'm trying to tell you. At least if we were in Kap-O, we were brothers. Mike would never have released the footage." He stares out the window. "He and Jay were the same, really," he says after a pause. "Only children. Asshole fathers. We were a family." He sighs. "They'd do anything to protect Kap-O. We all would. Michael and Jay just went about it in different ways."

We all would—this is why no one came forward. Not about the suspected cameras or the basement. Not about things going missing or boys being beaten up in parking lots. It's the same narrative you get when you hear about corrupt officers and find out the entire department was involved. It's war. Us against them. Never mind those drugs were planted, never mind the weapons were recovered through illegal means. I will fight and die for my brother without ever stopping to examine who I'm fighting for and why I'm so eager to die to begin with.

I shake my head. "But Colin told you to fuck off."

"Yeah. After the basement, he was furious."

"So why didn't Colin go to the university? I mean, if he was that pissed about what happened . . ."

Tripp stares at me.

"Right," I say, feeling like an idiot. "Because of Michael's father." I drum my knuckles on the steering wheel. Colin would have known that Ed Williams was the university president—a fact I'm sure Michael lorded over the pledges at every opportunity. What would President Williams have done? I remember his face when he came to the station—blank, emotionless. He wasn't furious at the flagrant misdeeds of his son's fraternity or concerned about the welfare of the boys scattered across the floor. He was doing damage control. Just like Jay when Katie found out. I thought his love for her made him come clean, but really, he was trying to keep her quiet. And then he hid his phone where he knew his brothers and Colin couldn't find it.

"Then why didn't Colin come to us?" I ask. "To the *Athens Banner Herald*? Or the *AJC*?" I can think of any number of news organizations that would have loved to rehash all the sordid details.

"Because of what was on the video," Tripp says.

I think of the boys crawling on their hands and knees. The buckets of waste.

"Colin was forced to wear the handcuffs," I say.

Tripp looks up, surprised I know this. "Yeah," he says gruffly. "He was. But do you know why?"

"Torture? Humiliation?" I offer.

Tripp shakes his head. "He snapped—in the basement. Started flailing. Broke another kid's nose. Kept punching. The other pledges pulled him off, put him in the cuffs. We had to take the kid he hit to the emergency care unit. Say he fell down the stairs . . ." His voice trails off. "Jay edited the video, blurred out everyone's face but Colin's. They'd all been drinking, but Colin—he looked deranged. Dangerous."

I blow out my breath. So only Colin was implicated in the footage—a lone boy in a dark room, throwing punches into a sea of unidentifiable faces. How is that for trust falls and brotherhood? It was never about building a bond based on honor and respect—for that they could have gone camping, taken a ropes course, a cooking class. They could have organized meals for a homeless community, hosted an athletic event, or simply had a normal fucking conversation. Instead, the brothers forced the pledges to participate in demeaning activities, designed to strip them of their humanity and bring out the worst in each other. I think of the pride in Colin's father's voice when he said his son was a Kap-O. The edge those Greek letters should give you in the hiring process. What would his father have thought if he'd seen Jay's homemade horror film? What would have happened if the video had been circulated online? Would Colin have been able to stay at the university? Get a job when he graduated? To destroy Kap-O, Colin would have had to destroy himself. His father. His future. Jay knew that.

I think of boys in basements and boys racing through mansions with matches. I think of Michael's warning to be careful that night at the station. Why?

I smack the steering wheel.

Tripp stares at me wide-eyed.

Because of Ryan, I think.

And I'm back to the question I asked two days ago: Why would Ryan break into my house? Why would he set fire to my curtains? My sheets? What did Ryan have against me? Nothing.

"Did Michael blackmail Ryan Bennett?" I ask Tripp.

His hands are strangling his seat belt. "He didn't have to."

"What do you mean?"

He shifts in his seat. "Michael never blackmailed anyone. All he had to do was imply there might be footage of what happened in the basement, that if the police kept poking around, they might find it. Someone—any number of people—would get the hint that something needed to be done to keep you away. No one would want that footage getting out." He sucks in his bottom lip. "But especially not Ryan . . ."

I raise my eyebrow.

"His father's Todd Bennett," he says.

The name is familiar, but I shake my head.

"He's in the run-off elections for Athens-Oconee district attorney."

I sigh. Of course he is. What did Teddy's security guard say? *They're all well connected.* In a dehumanizing system that turns victims into perpetrators, there are so many things Ryan might have done that could have hurt his father's chances at the election. I think of the video, the boy writhing on the floor, shame and the desire to belong forcing him to protect their shared secrets, and my anger flickers, verging toward pity, so instead I remember that night. The flash and heat and searing pain. The voices. The certainty there was more than one person.

"Were there others?"

"I don't know." Tripp slumps against his seat.

I give him a hard look, but he doesn't blink.

So it was all of them. The manipulated and the manipulators. Doing whatever they wanted without care or consequence.

Jay took what Michael started one step further. He turned Michael's threats into action and directed them at someone who refused to buy into their bullshit, who pointed out the contradictions between their behavior and their creed. But Colin didn't want the footage getting out either—wasn't willing to risk destroying his own image to unmask the fraternity. And ultimately, all the pretending to be Jay slowly chipped away at his identity. He thought the brothers were assholes but still made up stories for his father about Kap-O parties and the lake. He hated Jay as much as he wanted to be him—a cycle that could only end with Jay's death.

Tripp's watching me, a defensive flinch in his eyes.

"What else?" I ask, zeroing in on the guilt in his face.

He runs his hands over his hair. "I don't know," he says miserably. "The thing with Colin—it was getting out of control. That's how I found out—Jay told me Colin had been sneaking into his room. Messing with his things. He said Colin told Katie about our initiation rituals, about the basement—" A bewildered shake of the head. "Said it was the only explanation, but I—" He squeezes his eyes shut. "I didn't believe him. I thought Jay told her about the basement to impress her or something. But then it backfired." A sharp exhale through his nose. "She was disgusted, you know. Katie. With Jay. With all of us. She came to see me— said she didn't want to be the dream girl anymore. That people should know we were hazing our new recruits."

"She said that?"

Tripp nods, his face ashen. And I think of Jay's texts that someone had been going through his room. What if Colin was looking for the unaltered footage? What if Katie encouraged him to expose what happened at the frat and he was searching for proof? How could he balance the boy who wanted to be brave, to get revenge, and impress the girl with the boy who wanted to be important, belong to a group, and impress his father? The boy who was Colin and the boy who wanted to be Jay?

Tripp runs his hands through his hair. "Jay told me about the footage and how he'd been blackmailing Colin—and I mean, what could I do?" He clenches his jaw. "I called a meeting of the executive board. Not about the video—god, can you imagine if everyone found out?" His eyes dart to the window. "But about Jay telling fraternity secrets. I mean, even if Colin told her, it was still Jay's fault. The video was much worse, so at the time, I thought Jay was getting off easy. And"—he swallows—"I was glad the other brothers were angry. Everyone wrote what they thought of him on a piece of paper. Dropped it in a hat. They were unanimous—he was a traitor. Didn't belong in Kap-O."

"When was this?"

Tripp takes a breath. "The weekend before he died."

"At Michael's lake house?"

He nods. "Mike thought it would be best to keep it away from the younger brothers." Tripp blinks and looks away. "In case we had to dole out punishment."

I shake my head, remembering the bruises Aisha found on Jay's body.

His texts to Katie that he couldn't sleep. Not to trust anyone. That he couldn't take it anymore.

"Jay called Colin almost thirty times before he died," I say.

Tripp rubs his face. "He was going to end it—the thing with Colin. He said it wasn't worth it anymore."

"Shit," I say.

"Yeah," Tripp breathes.

We stare out at the tennis courts. The lone guy remains, hitting balls at the tarp, even as the rain turns into heavy sheets.

I still don't entirely understand why Jay blackmailed Colin. Was it anger that a pledge stood up to him? Fear that he'd tell what he knew? Laziness to avoid attending his own classes?

I sigh. Perhaps it was less complicated than that. Maybe it was simply that he could. In a world where boys make up bizarre rules like deranged emperors of tiny kingdoms, all Jay needed was to know about the video and then decide to use it.

I think of Colin rummaging around Jay's room, the stolen car keys, and the whispered word to Katie revealing fraternity secrets. Colin was fighting back. In his own way. And it was working. The brothers thought Jay was a traitor. He was losing his position in the fraternity. The dream girl was threatening to quit, to expose them. Soon, it would have been over. But Colin didn't know that, and then he saw Jay at that intersection. This time, there was no basement, no intimidation, and no one telling him what to do. Just the firm grip of his hand on the steering wheel and the feel of the pedal under his foot.

I drop Tripp off at a university bus stop.

He hesitates before he opens the door.

"I used to jog out there," he says, nodding in the direction of the fields we just left, "out past the lake."

I nod. I know the spot; there's a long boardwalk over the water, and if you run fast enough it feels like you're flying.

"One day, I got lost. It was winter, and the sun dropped quicker than I expected. I had to sprint to get back to the entrance but knew if I picked the wrong path, I'd just run deeper into the woods." He looks past the brick buildings, the thick trees for miles behind them. "That's what the past few weeks have felt like. Running in the dark, not sure of the way out."

"You did the right thing," I tell him.

"Could you . . ." He ducks his head as he climbs out of the car. "Could you not mention my name? I mean"—a glance around the empty street— "you could just say an unnamed source or something? Otherwise—"

Otherwise he'll be considered just as much of a traitor as Jay.

"I won't say anything," I tell him.

And it's true. No one would listen to me anyway.

Instead, I slip the flash drive in the mail for Teddy.

I still don't trust Oliver. Regardless of what he said at Walker's, I think someone was pressuring him to wrap up the case, to point in any direction but at the fraternity itself. It would explain his urgency to dismiss the hit-and-run as an accident, the sense that he was under stress, the way he imagined Jay looking for an excuse to quit, and my feeling that he was talking about himself. Truman wouldn't have needed outside pressure. He was already willing to look the other way because that's how it works: boys with fathers like Michael's, like Jay's, don't go to prison. They get second chances. Until, of course, like Colin and Ryan, they don't.

But I'll let Teddy put the pieces together. Decide if it changes anything. My guess is it won't. After all, Oliver didn't sabotage the case. Neither did Truman. Jay will be remembered as a victim. Nothing will be said of the blackmail. And Michael isn't the culprit. Ryan lit the match. Colin pressed the gas. The videos of me and Oliver and the others don't prove anything other than the fact that we were in the basement. That the boys got a little out of control. So what if they were prompted to take the whips off the wall? So what if Michael's the man behind the curtain pulling the strings, blowing the dog whistle? All he has to do is deny it. I haven't seen those cameras before. I've never met Colin. Don't remember Ryan.

Because it's old news, really. The day after we bring Colin in, a man sets fire to his ex-girlfriend's apartment, killing the elderly couple who live next door. There's a manhunt near an elementary school for a guy who attacked a woman with a machete. An eleven-year-old dies from a gunshot wound to the head while playing Russian roulette. And before the students disperse for the winter holidays, five other men at five different universities will have died in fraternity-related incidents—one ruled an alcohol overdose, another an accident, the other investigations still ongoing. Three of the fraternities will be suspended, two pending review, and the universities continue to maintain that hazing was not a factor in any of the deaths.

| Epilogue |

Friday, December 13

The December sky's full of low white clouds that turn dark too early. I park on a side street off Baxter and follow a sea of backpacks and cell-phone-lit faces down to the Lumpkin intersection. I watch as the students pulse, step off the curb—and perhaps thinking of Jay, perhaps not, step back on again. It's that unsettled feeling—the LA jogger attacked by a mountain lion, the tornado that takes out one house and leaves the rest, the randomness of a hit-and-run—it could have been anyone, it could have been us. But it wasn't anyone, and it wasn't random. I think of the car accelerating instead of slamming on the brakes, the white chalk outline, and the dark sticky blood pooling on the asphalt as I get close to the other side. But there's nothing beneath the scatter of boots and sneakers. The ground has been washed clean—by the rain or by the thousands of other cars and feet that have crossed since, each taking a tiny piece of Jay with them.

I think of the university's slogan and its secrets. People always remember Athena as the goddess of wisdom, but they forget her prowess in battle—that when she sprang from Zeus's head she was also dressed in armor. A fierce warrior with a strong sense of justice, Athena punished those who disobeyed her with madness.

Athens could accommodate many sins. But this doubling of Jay and the simultaneous erasure of Colin was wrong. It threatened the fine fabric holding the city together. Colin felt it—that trembling, stretching, breaking—as he put his foot to the pedal. Did Jay?

I blink at the crosswalk.

Something tells me he did. In the end.

The students are in the middle of final exams. Wrapped in brightly colored scarves and bent over notebooks, they cluster together on the front steps of buildings and whisper their fears of failure in the same breath as their plans for the winter holidays.

My mother's office door is closed, but the light's on. I tap twice before I open it.

"Students normally wait until I tell them to come in," she says dryly. Her feet are up on her desk, a stack of papers in her lap and a pen to her mouth. "You know, no matter how many times I tell them that unnecessary modifiers are a personal pet peeve, I still have papers full of 'really's, 'very's, and 'extremely's. How is what the character *really* means any different from what he means?"

I shrug. No matter what she says, she loves this part. *Really* loves it, I think.

"Mom," I say.

It must be something in my voice, because there's a sudden caution in her gray eyes as they focus on my face.

How can I explain it to her? The dreams? The voices? The feeling she knows and has just been waiting for me to ask?

"How do I know German?"

She sighs and pulls her feet off her desk, straightening in her chair as she opens the top drawer and withdraws a photograph.

It's worn around the edges and smudged with fingerprints. She doesn't look it at, just hands it, wordlessly, to me.

I stare at it for a long time, not understanding.

I recognize my mother instantly. She's young. Her hair is auburn even though the photo has yellowed with age. She stands in the center with a broad smile, but her face is drawn and tired. My father must be behind the camera. But the rest doesn't make sense. I look up.

"This," she says, placing a finger on the photo, "is you."

I blink and stare hard at the picture. I've seen a similar photo. Just once. My mother holding me on the sofa. Smiling in that weary way of hers. But here, my mother isn't holding just me. She's holding two babies in polka-dotted gowns.

"Twins have higher chances of congenital heart defects," my mother says. "Did you know that?" She touches the edge of the photograph and sighs. "It's more common in mothers with advanced maternal age. And since I waited until I had tenure . . ." Her voice trails off. She clears her throat and stares at her hands for a long time. "They knew something was wrong—as soon as you were born, they whisked you both away. They brought you back hours later, but Henry," she touches the face of the other baby in the photograph, "he was diagnosed with truncus arteriosus, a rare heart disease. Only two hundred or so cases a year in the US." She swallows. "He was only two weeks old when he had his first open-heart surgery." She gazes at the corner of the ceiling. "But there were complications. Another surgery. We brought him home, but then he started to cry all the time and had difficulty breathing. He couldn't catch his breath while breastfeeding. He wasn't gaining weight or sitting up—"

She turns to the window so I can't see her face.

"The doctors didn't know what to do so we flew to Germany—there was a pediatric cardiologist in Berlin who was an expert in truncal valve defects." She fiddles with the handle of her desk drawer. "The university was incredibly supportive—organized a fellowship for me at the Freie so I could teach, nurse you, and see Henry every day."

I swallow. "How long were we there?"

"Two years."

I blink. *Two years?*

"Your father stayed the first six months, but there were bills and work and he couldn't stay any longer. He visited as often as he could but," her voice breaks, "I don't think he's ever forgiven himself for not being there, when—" Tears trace lines down her cheeks. She takes a breath. "Henry died early in October. You and I were there when it happened."

I touch my sternum, but there's no scar, no flutter or murmur, no sign of the loss I've always felt but never understood.

"I used to wonder if you remembered," she says softly. "Your father and I—we couldn't talk about it. It was just—too painful." She smiles sadly. "But you were the bright star in the darkness."

I try to swallow again but my throat's dry. I can't think. Can't wrap my head around anything. I keep looking at the desk, the scratches from years of my mother's chair bumping against it. I blink at the handful of student papers lined with red ink.

My mother gazes at me apprehensively. Waiting for me to say something. But there are no words. Nothing. Not in German. Not in English. Just a void where language should be.

Instead, I think of our house, always full of noise—the television in the living room, NPR in the kitchen, a record playing upstairs, as if it were full of people. And yet, oddly quiet. The constant rotation of young faculty at our dining room table. The silences of my parents, sitting side by side on the sofa. Holding hands but rarely talking, rarely looking at each other. My father's sudden change from free-wheeling journalist to agoraphobic researcher. His overprotectiveness and disapproval of my job. Me never feeling good enough. Of needing to be like a son, but that was wrong, too.

"Your father just wanted to protect you," my mother says, reading my thoughts. "After what happened with Henry—if anything happened to you," she blinks at the ceiling, "I think he'd be completely lost."

Her computer pings. A meeting reminder flashes on her screen.

A memory of spraining my ankle at basketball practice. My father white-faced, shaking with anger. Screaming that I was off the team. His fury when I joined the force. *Why don't you do marketing? Public relations?*

"Helena?"

Amina stands in the doorway, concern written across her face as she looks from my mother to me and back again.

"Let me get you some water," she says, and disappears. I listen to the sound of her footsteps fading down the hall. But I can't look away from my mother's face. It's as if I'm seeing her—truly seeing her as the woman she is and not the person I imagined her to be—for the first time.

"I don't understand," I say finally. "Why do I know German?"

My mother rubs the bridge of her nose, her fingers drawing small circles outward until they reach her temples.

"I don't know." She sighs. "It's possible you heard the nurses in the hospital. They talked to you every day. Held you while I was with Henry. I spoke to you in German, too. Somehow . . . it made everything easier."

I'm staring at the student artwork on the wall. "Heimat" is painted in the colors of the German flag, and I know it's German but don't know what it means.

"It could be associated with trauma," my mother's saying. "The high stress of the fire sent those memories, those words, flowing back. Or perhaps you just pieced everything together from so many hours spent in my office." She gives a small smile. It's meant to be a joke, but there's no laughter left in me.

I close my eyes. The shades are drawn, the light is dim, and I see a menagerie of tubes and wires. Hear an orchestra of beeps, voices, and alarms.

It's a scene from a movie, I'm sure, because I know I do not remember. But the pain feels real. The loss. The deep, indescribable longing I feel at the thought of a brother. Filling in his seat at the dinner table, his presence next to me on the school bus. I think of the German fairy tale where the girl cuts off her finger to save her brothers who were turned into ravens. What wouldn't I sacrifice to have him here with me now?

Colin sacrificed a part of himself to have brothers, I think, but that's not quite right. He sacrificed his entire self for the idea of brothers, for grandiose slogans, and lofty principles that not one of the men at Kappa Phi Omicron met. And me? Didn't I do the same thing? Believe I was part of something bigger, trained to serve and protect, when really, I was meant to serve a broken system and protect the people who broke it? I was wrong when I thought Truman's letting the fraternity brothers go after what we found in the basement was justice giving a wink. Justice is blind because we blinded her. So we could choose whom to punish and whom to set free.

We're quiet a long time.

Amina joins us. She sits next to me and wraps one arm around my shoulder.

After a while, she squeezes my hand. "I miss him, too," she whispers.

I look into those familiar brown eyes, the way they crinkle at the edges, and begin to cry.

After the death of a loved one, some people wrap themselves in their old clothes. They close the door to their house to keep the ghost of their memory in. They surround themselves with photographs, cook their favorite meals, and continue to talk about the dead in the present tense. I did the opposite. After Craig died, I stripped every reminder of him from my life. I couldn't take it—the guilt, the feeling that I should have been there, done more, not let the fraternity, my jealousy over his new brothers, separate us. I moved out of the dorm room where we shared Doritos and laughed until late in the evening, I left the university he convinced me to attend, and I avoided his mother, whose every gesture and full-throated laughter reminded me of him, but whose presence now is the only thing keeping me together.

Suddenly, I understand the closeness between my mother and Amina, and the way their friendship has evolved over the years. In a span of a few decades, both women lost sons. My mother in a hospital in Berlin and Amina at a fraternity house in Atlanta. And I realize that all my life I've been searching for this lost brother, only to lose him twice now, first in Craig and then in Teddy. I couldn't save Craig. Even in my dreams, I always show up just before it happens, my hand outstretched as he falls. But Teddy needed me to be a good partner, and I failed him.

I leave my mother's office with less clarity than when I entered it. On a hallway chair I see two familiar faces, near twins but never brothers: Colin and Jay. For once, they are side by side and beam up at me from the student newspaper. The headline is simple: HIT-AND-RUN DRIVER ARRESTED.

I find my way to the staircase to nowhere, press myself into the top step under the strange painting like I used to as a child, and skim the front page. There's a statement from the university president expressing the university's loss, offering Jay's family his personal condolences, and reminding students of the counseling services available at the health center, the importance of crosswalk safety, and driving with caution around campus. The student writer did some digging. Found out that Kappa Phi Omicron members had been taken in for questioning. She even reached out to the fraternity headquarters, which issued a statement not unlike the president's.

The words are so empty, I have to read them twice to derive any meaning: "Jay Kemp's death has saddened the entire Kappa Phi Omicron community. We mourn the loss of this Honorable Gentleman deeply, and the future has lost a great leader. His death is the result of the actions taken by a troubled young man who is not affiliated with Kappa Phi Omicron." When pressed about the hazing accusations, the fraternity issued another rote statement: "Kappa Phi Omicron promotes brotherhood and respect for humanity, two tenets that stand in stark contrast to any allegations of hazing."

I crumple the paper and then smooth it out again and leave it at the top of the stairs. I think of the young man who stayed behind over the Thanksgiving holiday, his hallmates complaining of the smell, young men dying all alone in rooms full of people, young men who desperately want to belong and find themselves in prisons and in morgues and in boardrooms as CEOs of Fortune 500 companies and in police stations as lieutenants willing to look the other way. I wonder what the point of it all is. If we ever learn anything, if we can change systems so ingrained in money and power, and if there's such a thing as justice, or if justice is just one of those lofty ideas that sounds nice in theory but is completely without substance in practice.

I'm not asked to testify at the trial. Too risky considering there's a video of me snooping around the basement of Kappa Phi Omicron, uninvited and without a warrant. But I know that the techs found a strand of Colin's hair on the driver's seat of the BMW. Aisha told me that Colin tried to clean the car with Windex but did a shit job, like he started and then lost the will to keep going. But the real evidence came when they canvassed the area. They found a neighbor with a backyard wildlife camera. It's meant to spot deer and coyotes, and sure enough, on the afternoon of November 12, there was grainy footage of Colin driving past the property in Jay's BMW.

Michael continued to deny any knowledge of Colin. When pressed about taking Jay's laptop, he admitted to deleting photos but insisted this was to protect Jay's family from further emotional pain. He's never associated with Colin. The fact that Colin was hiding at his lake house was dismissed by his lawyers. They said Jay kept handwritten directions to the house in the BMW. Maintaining the line about the car robbery gone wrong, they argued that Colin stole the car, ran over Jay, and then discovered the address in the glove box. Michael's name never appears in the paper. The fraternity is given a warning, but no one's suspended, and President Williams manages to keep everything we found in the basement out of the news.

I've seen Teddy only once since my resignation. It was outside Walker's, and he didn't stop to speak with me, but he did offer a silent wave. After that night at the station, I left him a voice message to apologize.

But I know it's not enough. One day, I hope to earn back his friendship and find the courage to explain why I quit. Until then, I'm helping my father with his new book. We work in the living room until the light slips beneath the Japanese maple and my mother comes home and turns on the lamps.

Colin is awaiting trial. His parents hired their own private investigator and attorneys. Katie visits him every day.

| Acknowledgments |

E ven in the best of times, there would be so many people to thank for transforming my debut manuscript from a hope and a dream into the book you're now holding. But the brilliant and generous souls at ICM, Flatiron Books, and Pan Macmillan Australia have been with me for what has been the best and worst year of my life—one in which I experienced the joy of selling my novel, moved back to Georgia to be closer to family, married my best friend and partner of over a decade, and then lost him suddenly and unexpectedly four months later. The level of support, compassion, and understanding offered by the publishing community was more than I could ask for, and I am so grateful for not only your unfailing professionalism and unerring guidance, but also your kindness, your thoughtful messages, and your patience.

I owe immense gratitude to my agent, Hillary Jacobson, for her early advocacy and excitement for this novel and for reading draft after draft of these pages. Thank you for your enthusiasm, your unflagging hard work, your wisdom, critical insights, and all those brainstorming sessions. You've been with me through everything, and your support means more than words can convey. This would not be the same book without you. And many thanks to Josie Freedman at ICM and Sophie Baker at Curtis Brown UK, I'm so grateful for all that you do.

To my editor Zack Wagman at Flatiron, who loved Marlitt from the start and took a risk on a professor turned novelist. Working with you has been a privilege. Thank you for your indispensable guidance on how to make this book better. And to everyone at Flatiron Books, to Bob Miller and Megan Lynch, and with special thanks to Molly Bloom, Maxine

Charles, Erin Kibby, Christina MacDonald, Claire McLaughlin, and Sue Walsh: Thank you for working so tirelessly to bring this book into the world. And to Julianna Lee: Thank you for capturing the novel's dark tones with this striking cover.

To Alex Lloyd at Pan Macmillan AU, who understood my vision and helped me fine-tune it, thank you for your keen insights and enthusiasm for this project. Thank you to everyone at Pan Macmillan AU and Curtis Brown AU, and a warmhearted thanks to Tara Wynne for believing Marlitt could have a home in Australia.

To the bookstagram community, for all the book recommendations, shared enthusiasm of the written word, and constant affection showered on Bowie. Thank you for the outpouring of love and support you've shown me this year.

To my parents: Thank you for instilling a passion for reading in me early, for that adolescent year spent in Germany (even though I sulked for most of it), and for supporting my decision to spend a decade in pursuit of higher education. In hindsight it's clear that all those experiences shaped this book, and your constant belief in my capabilities gave me courage long before I found it in myself.

To my sister, my confidante, my longest friend, and the strongest woman I know: What would I do without you? Thank you for everything.

To Gray's family: Thank you for raising such an incredible human and for sharing him with me. None of this would have been possible without him.

It is a rare group of people who come into your life and stay forever. To my friends (you know who you are): Thank you for showing up and caring for me when I didn't know how to ask. Thank you for the home-cooked meals, opening up your living rooms, stopping by with food and paper products, all those Monday messages, and showing me that laughter was still possible even when everything hurt.

To the friends who shared with me their experiences in Greek life and the brave souls who've written articles exposing the shameful secrets of some of these institutions: Thank you. To those mothers, fathers, brothers, sisters, families, and friends who've lost loved ones in hazing-related incidents, I'm sorry for the ways in which this book fails to articulate the pain. I'm sorry for every life that should have continued and was cut irrevocably short. It shouldn't be this way. And it's time for change.

To my students, colleagues, and all the college towns I've ever lived in: You inspired the best parts of this book; the worst were (mostly) a product of my imagination. And to Athens in particular: You're where I met my soul mate, the city where I spent so many years as a student, taught my first classes, and wrote my first book. I hold a special place in my heart for you and have looked for you everywhere I've lived since.

Gray, this book was always going to be dedicated to you. It was your encouragement that made me believe I could write my own novels after so many years spent teaching students to analyze them. Your stories of growing up in Athens inspired a wealth of these pages. You named characters and were my first reader and eternal champion. Thank you for being my partner, my best friend, and the short but wonderful months as my husband. Thank you for making lunch so I could keep writing, for all those conversations about craft, for showing me that a life of creativity was possible, because you lived it. But most of all, thank you for teaching me what love is. I still can't fathom that you won't hold this book in your hands. But this is for you. Forever and always.

| About the Author |

LAUREN NOSSETT is a former professor turned novelist with a PhD in German literature. She currently lives in Atlanta, Georgia. *The Resemblance* is her fiction debut.